THE STARLIGHT DRAGON

LIZ DELTON

Cover design by JV Arts
Map by Angeline Trevena

TOURMALINE
& QUARTZ
PUBLISHING LLC

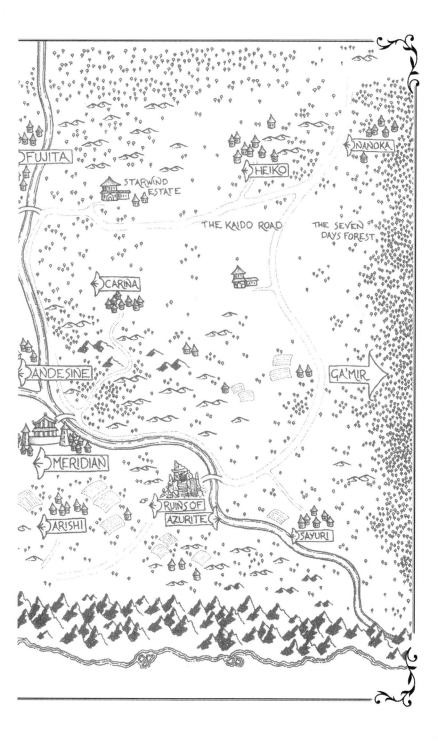

CHAPTER 1

THE ADVANCEMENT

K ira Savage was not going down without a fight.

She flung herself to the ground as a storm of arrows hurtled down from the sky. Crouching, she summoned a perfect shield above her with Light magic. She breathed a sigh of relief when it didn't splinter apart as the barrage of arrows struck it, each one sending a jolt down her arm. She peered out from under the edge of the shield to mark where her assailant stood on the cold moonlit mountaintop.

Outlined in the light of the full moon, and glowing with Light magic, the woman stood fifty paces away, already lifting her hands in their long tapered sleeves to dismiss the magic arrows. The woman shifted her feet slightly, the movement masked by her wide-legged trousers, but Kira saw the barest hint of her attacker's intentions.

With a sound of grinding rock, a barricade of spears sprung out of the ground, winking into existence with

1

the briefest flash of bright white. Kira flung her hands down, simultaneously dismissing her shield, and letting out a blast of Shadow wind below her to thrust her out of harm's way. She hovered several feet in the air before realizing her arc of wind had propelled her forward—where she would come crashing down on top of the deadly spears sticking out of the ground.

Summoning another shield-like barrier of Light under her feet, she slammed down on the spears, riding the shield down and safely forward.

She had gained more ground.

Taking advantage of her attacker's momentary surprise, she turned her movement into a roll, coming even closer. She just had to get to the edge of the mountaintop. She had to get past Mistress Nari, one of the most skilled Light knights in the entire Realm of Camellia.

That was all they had told her when she arrived at the top of the mountain at dusk. She had trained as vigorously as possible in both Light and Shadow magic this past year. It all came down to this moment. And she would not fail.

Because a lot more rested on her skills than just passing this test.

Only twenty more paces to go. Nari still stood her ground close to the edge of the mountaintop, just as she had from the moment Kira began her test. Kira had won plenty of ground already, but she was tiring. She wiped cold sweat from her forehead with a sleeve. The trial had not been easy. She was just glad she was allowed to use her Shadow magic, too.

As she sent a powerful wind toward Nari, laced with Light knives, a wave of exhaustion swept over her. Almost forgetting the goal of her tactic, she sprinted forward on the back of the wind. When she came to a halt, her eyelids fluttered, and she took a steadying breath, her hands still thrown forward with her magic. She needed to pace herself. Drawing this much magic from her surroundings had a price.

Nari deflected Kira's knives with a quickly summoned shield on one arm. With her other hand, she summoned a large scythe. The sight of the enormous blade made Kira gasp a little. Kira was not even five paces away from her goal now. She crafted a massive polearm, fairly confident that the bladed staff would be a match for Nari's scythe. She *had* to complete this test. If she failed, she would never become a Gray Knight like her father had been. And more importantly, she would never get her chance to exact revenge on the disdainful Lord of Between, Tigran Tashjian, who had split her family apart, and nearly killed Kira herself.

She took a deep breath to calm her rabbiting heartbeat, feeling the buzz of the magic stored inside her core. She was almost there; almost done.

Somewhere behind her in the amphitheater-style seating sat her grandfather Ichiro Starwind. Kira couldn't see any of the spectators, and she suspected that was part of the test, too. She hated people watching her from behind. It made the whole exposition even worse. And knowing her grandfather was watching was both reassuring and nerve-wracking. She knew he wanted her to succeed, but as one of her instructors, he was also there to judge her abilities.

With a quick thought, she darted to the right, jabbing with her polearm at the silhouetted form of Nari. Nari swept her scythe forward, just as Kira ducked and banished her polearm, trying to slip under the blade.

Nari was too quick. Kira jerked herself backward, narrowly avoiding the sharp steel. Her heart pounded as she tried to figure out her next move. If only there was a way to distract Nari somehow. And then a slight grin overcame her. How could she have forgotten her secret weapon? With a swift intake of breath, she drew from her memory something she had spent countless hours teaching herself back at the Spire.

As she breathed out, a burst of magic flew from her fingertips—literally flew toward Nari. The wings of her creation spread out, and the crowd behind her collectively gasped at the sight of the *sentinel*—a magical construct of sorts that Kira had only just perfected before returning to Gekkō-ji. Formed as a crow, but glowing with the Light magic that made it solid, the sentinel soared right at Nari's face, flapping violently. Nari jerked back a step, hesitating for a moment. And that was all Kira needed. She lunged to the right, still weaponless and agile. She only needed to gain a few more feet.

But she had miscalculated. Nari wasn't the Mistress of the Light temple for nothing. Nari recovered from her surprise and brought her scythe down with forceful precision; it sliced through the air by her cheek, and she felt the bite of the blade just before she dropped to the ground. She rolled in the dirt, her heart pounding. She was inches from Nari's feet, and she needed to move before the sweep of the scythe found her again.

The pain in her cheek went unnoticed as she forced herself up, nearly stumbling as she gained her footing. She whirled around, eyes wide as she faced Nari, who was spinning around with the momentum of the scythe. The sentinel crow flapped off into the distance without further direction, a bright spot in the moonlit night.

Nari stopped when the scythe completed its arc. Kira's chin trembled, her mind blank. A vague pain emanated from her cheek. She poured the Light magic from her core into her hands, ready to summon something, anything, when Mistress Nari dissolved her scythe. The Light magic dissipated, winking out of existence into the night air around them, returning to the world.

Kira's jaw dropped when she realized. She had made it.

Suddenly the sound of clapping filled the silent mountaintop—polite, quiet clapping, but the sound was almost deafening in the cool early spring air. Kira sighed, somewhat afraid to turn her back on Nari to survey the crowd. Instead, she sent a thought out to the sentinel—reaching out with Shadow magic to summon the creature back to her. It banked on the wind, turning in a slow half circle before soaring back to her, its flapping wings silent.

Had she really done it? Was it really over? Not just the trial, but her time training at Gekkō-ji?

Numb with shock, Kira watched the sentinel instead of facing the audience. Her sentinel was different from the ones used by Light masters—Kira was quite familiar with Mistress Nari's fox messengers that roved all over the realm. They had been spotted coming in and out of Gekkō-ji more and more frequently lately, what with the rebellious chaos brewing in the temples. Those messengers were one of the few ways they could trust that messages leaving Gekkō-ji made it to their intended recipients—because Tigran Tashjian, the Lord of Between, had ways of intercepting every other method they might use. Nari's fox messengers could only communicate with Nari and whomever she thought of while creating the sentinel. It was high Light magic, and Kira didn't know if she had the ability to do something that complicated. Instead, while she had spent months training at the Spire in Shadow magic—mainly doing meditation, it seemed—she had figured out how to make her own version of a sentinel. Maybe she couldn't send messages with it, but it worked.

On rainy days, she would sit in the training room in the Gray Wing and attempt to create her own creature. Whether she used Light magic or Shadow, she didn't know or care. Sure, she could create anything solid with Light magic—weapons and tools mostly—but a creature that actually *moved*, well that was something she had wondered about since first landing in the Realm of Camellia two and a half years ago.

The crow landed on her outstretched arm with a comforting weight, and she grinned at it. It opened its beak in what Kira imagined was a silent *caw*. Still avoiding turning around to see the crowd's reaction to her trial, Kira stood still and waited. The cut on her cheek stung something fierce, and she felt blood seeping from it, but she refrained from touching it, not wanting to acknowledge the mistake of getting too close to Nari.

Mistress Nari faced her and gave her a straight-backed bow, her long braid sliding over her shoulder as she swept low. Kira fought to keep her face neutral, though the shock at seeing Nari bow so low to her made warmth rush to her face. Kira returned the bow, shaking hands placed flat on her thighs.

Chills ran up her spine as Kira heard Nari speak the words she had never hoped for in all her life until now: "Lady Starwind."

Her heart began thudding painfully in her chest. She *had* done it. Really done it. The hours of training—years, really. It had been the focus of her entire life since landing here in Camellia.

The crowd behind her murmured the words in response to Nari, and the words "Lady Starwind" echoed across the cool mountaintop.

But the ceremony wasn't over yet. There was one final part Kira had been looking forward to for a long time.

Nari held up an arm, her bell-sleeve hanging, as she pointed to a different path than the one Kira took up the mountain right before her trial of combat. Alone, Kira trudged forward, still not looking back at the crowd. She wasn't ready to see the faces there—not until she was truly done. Not until she had finished the ceremony completely.

The simple dirt path led into the woods, and Kira carefully picked her way down it, able to see just fine in the midnight-darkness, with help from her Light magic. Everything around her gave off a subtle glow, showing her the Light essence in the world. It was this essence that she "borrowed" from the world to make objects with Light magic, and when she was finished with it, she was always sure to disperse it, returning it to the balance of the world.

A sudden noise to her right made her halt in her tracks, and she wondered if this was part of the test. And then she saw the source of the noise. A small creature flitting from tree to tree parallel to her path.

"I can see you," she said quietly.

A musical chortling echoed through the trees. She didn't have time for Thistle's games.

"I'm kind of in the middle of something here," Kira hissed, not wanting to raise her voice in case Mistress Nari or anyone else was following her.

"Then I'll be brief, Starless Girl," the voice of an old man said.

Kira gasped, feeling her cheeks flame with embarrassment. Another figure materialized in the woods, the silhouette of an old man, hunched over a cane. The spirit of the mountain, Gekkō. His flying squirrel, Thistle, leaped down from the branch above him to rest on his shoulder. Kira bowed to the spirit as low as she could. When she straightened, he gave her a nod. She suddenly wished she had cleaned up her cheek; blood now trailed down her jaw.

"There are two things I need to tell you," he said, and Kira glanced down the path she was supposed to be following to finish her trial. He seemed to know her predicament. "As I said, I will be brief. There is a disturbance in the balance of the realm again—much like the time you entered the Realm of Camellia, except far worse. The spirits do not yet know the source of the problem, but it's starting to erode the very fabric of the realm, and will likely have equally toxic consequences."

Kira's stomach twisted at his words. That didn't sound good at all. Normally, she would have said that it wasn't her problem, but it *was*. She was about to become a knight—if she ever completed this ceremony, anyway. It was literally going to be her *job* to protect the realm and those in it. The prospect was quite daunting, but it was a legacy her father had left her. And perhaps even more importantly, it was something she felt she had the right to do—the power was within her, after all.

She knew without him saying that the person behind this unbalance was Tigran. She swallowed. "And the second thing?" she asked in a quiet voice.

"There is someone who wants to meet with you."

"Oh?"

"She will reveal herself to you soon."

Kira opened her mouth to ask more, her brows furrowed, but Gekkō disappeared, leaving only his chortling companion behind. She turned back to the trail to finish the ceremony, an uneasy dread now tainting her victory. She sighed, trying not to think about whatever unbalance was about to erode the realm now.

If only they could *do* something about Tigran. But it had been months since the Gray Knights were arrested, when Kira had found out *Tigran* was the one behind all the realm's troubles these past years. Months spent attempting to convince the Empress to free the Gray Knights—without naming her trusted advisor Tigran as the culprit—and trying to gather any evidence to indict him. They were lucky the Empress had agreed to push back the Gray Knights' trial so far—thanks, in part, to Kira's pleas.

Thistle leaped from branch to branch like a tiny ghost flitting through the trees.

"Well?" Kira demanded when he remained silent. "Are you going to tell me who Gekkō wants me to meet?" She bit off the rest of her irritable tirade in case Gekkō could still hear her somehow. He was the spirit of the entire mountain, for goodness' sake. But she didn't know why he picked now of all times to ambush her, fresh from her fight with Nari, and not even finished with her ceremony.

She glanced over her shoulder. Was anyone following her? What was the point of this trail, anyway?

"Oh, it's nothing to worry about," Thistle said. "She's just shy is all. And I think she can help you."

"Help me? With what in particular?"

But before Thistle replied, Kira spotted an opening in the trees that signified the end of her brief journey. This was it. The end of the ceremony. The end of her training at Gekkō-ji. After this, she would be a Light knight—and once she finished her training at the Spire, she would join the ranks of the fully fledged Gray Knights, the only other six people in the realm to have both Light and Shadow magic, besides her friend Jun anyway.

She took a deep lungful of the clean night air. It tingled sharply in her lungs, the bite of the winter chill only just starting to release. She left Thistle in the trees and passed through a stone archway, which looked similar to openings in the wall around the temple square. As she walked out onto the familiar pavers, she realized that was exactly where the path lead her.

"But there's no opening there—there's never been a path here," she said quietly to herself, turning around.

From the trees, she heard light chuckling. And then she turned back to the path and saw the entrance was gone. Like it had never been there. The stone wall that surrounded the courtyard of Gekkō-ji was intact. Kira stumbled away from it, finding herself near the front entrance to the square. Apparently, she hadn't learned all of Gekkō-ji's secrets. The large three-columned gate loomed black and gold at the front of the square, the stairs beyond leading down the mountain. On her right and left stood the two dorm houses, L-shaped wooden buildings that framed the main gate. Straight ahead loomed the large stone castle-like building called the Moonstone, its enormous clock glinting in the light of the full moon, showing her it was one minute to midnight.

Directly in the center of the square, a crowd had gathered to witness the ceremony around the ever-blossoming cherry tree.

Her mentor Nesma was beaming at her, along with their roommates, Hana and Michi. Kira's eyes roved over the crowd of trainees, knights, and masters until she spotted two of her favorite people—Zowan and Anzu. The lady knight had dressed her part, her usual full body leather armor with the bright white sash at her waist. Kira beamed at her, still in disbelief that she was joining the same ranks as Anzu, the bravest and most courageous woman she knew. And then her gaze slid to Zowan, who stood so close to Anzu their arms rubbed together, almost as if they wished they were holding hands. His black shoulder-length hair rustled in the slight breeze that wove through the limbs of the cherry tree behind them, but his tight black mage robes remained still.

Kira scanned the crowd again and was glad she didn't see the equally tall figure of Zowan's uncle, Lord Raiden. They had all agreed—one night in the underground library where they usually met to discuss matters of the realm they didn't want overheard—that the Storm King shouldn't make himself a target by leaving the Spire to attend the ceremony, no matter how much he wanted to see Kira and Jun's rite of ascension. Raiden would get to see her Shadow mage ceremony, whenever that would be. He didn't need to put himself in harm's way in case Tigran had anything up his sleeve.

Much to Kira's joy, she didn't spot Tigran, either, even though they had notified the palace of the ceremony to take place this full moon.

Jun stood at the front of the crowd, the only other knight to be tested. He had gone before her, and she hadn't been able to see his exhibition. She supposed the ascending and descending from the peak were all part of the ceremony.

The sight of him made her start walking again toward the group of people, who were all crowded around the glowing cherry tree. It stood like a beacon in the night, even to those who couldn't see Light in the darkness. The blossoms on the tree all glowed bright white, illuminating the courtyard. Each one had been made by a knight who had trained here, upon completion of their training.

And now it was her turn.

As Kira reached them, Jun grabbed her hand and drew her forward, the excitement unmistakable on his face. She spotted her grandfather Ichiro close to the tree, alongside Mistress Nari, and her stomach gave a pleasant flip.

Nari gave her a somewhat suspicious look, her eyes briefly darting to the hidden mountain path behind her, and Kira's shoulders stiffened. It wasn't her fault that the spirit of the mountain had taken a liking to her and often made a point to speak to her.

She and Jun reached the opening in the crowd around the tree. Ichiro smiled as they approached. Saying nothing, he held out a hand and gestured at the tree.

Kira looked up at it in wonder. How many times had she passed this tree in the square during her days here? How many times had she thought about what it would be like to create her own flower to place upon it? Her gaze fell upon a few blossoms on the nearest branch. Could she really forge her own?

Sure, she had practiced, and could make most anything with Light magic. But would it last?

She realized she had stepped forward and left Jun at the edge of the crowd. Looking back at him, he gestured for her to go ahead. She was already there, inches from the nearest branch. *Well, here goes nothing...*

With a focused breath, she pulled a small amount of Light magic from the world around her. She wouldn't need much. It came from the very air, from the stones at her feet. In her core, she focused her intent on the exact shape she would form it into. As she breathed out, tiny tendrils of Light flew from her fingertips to the branch, forming the outline of a delicate five-petaled flower.

But that was where it stopped. The outline grew shaky, and refused to solidify.

Kira's face flamed. She couldn't create the blossom. She heard whispers behind her like leaves on the wind. She suddenly felt like she was going to throw up. Was there something wrong with her magic again?

Jun shifted on his feet just behind her. *Wait, what if this is part of the ceremony? Like another test or trick?* she thought desperately. She forced herself to keep channeling Light magic into the blossom. She was going to create this flower. She would. Her father's flower was on this tree, and all the Light knights now and before. She would join them. She deserved it. She wasn't still broken!

Doubt assailed her as she tried to pull more magic from her surroundings, feeling as if there wasn't enough. It was impossible. Was there some way the tree knew she wasn't worthy to become a knight? Wasn't worthy of her father's name? Sure, she had grown up in the Starless Realm—she didn't call it the *real world* anymore—and had never expected to find out she had magic or travel to a place where spirits walked among people. But she had proven her worth, proven her commitment, hadn't she?

As even the outline of the flower faded, Kira noticed the crowd around her shifting uneasily. She had failed.

With hot tears prickling at the corners of her eyes, she turned to Ichiro to admit her defeat when she noticed lights coming up from the main gate. The crowd turned too, to see a man pass through the gate with two rows of people behind him, all equipped with swords at their waists.

But that wasn't the only thing they carried at their waists. The soldiers—the Commonality, she knew without a doubt—each carried a curious glass bottle hanging from a cord at their belts. Strange luminescent liquid sloshed inside the bottles, drawing Kira's eye. For a second, she forgot about her burning humiliation as a boiling hatred consumed her.

The man at the front of the Commonality was none other than Tigran Tashjian, and he, too, carried a luminescent bottle that Kira knew could be nothing good.

CHAPTER 2

ABOMINATION

Tigran advanced, the Commonality soldiers coming up behind him in a practiced march and forming a wall between the crowd and the gate. Kira stiffened and bile rose in her throat. She thought of tearing through the small crowd and advancing upon him, throwing as much Gray magic as she could at him.

But no. She couldn't do that. She took a deep breath and reminded herself how important Tigran was to the Empress, the slimy knave. He was still the grand steward. For now.

She simmered in anger but marshaled a polite expression onto her face as he came forward. The cut on her cheek stung as she attempted a smile that was more like a grimace.

"Greetings," he said and bowed slightly, a glint in his eye that made Kira want to smack him right in his false face. She knew for certain he could shapeshift using some abomination of Shadow and soul magic, and last year, she had seen his true face. This one was merely a mask.

He went on, "It appears we are interrupting your ceremony; I do apologize. However, the Commonality is here to transport some prisoners back to our new fortifications in Meridian."

Forgetting all about her failed ceremony, Kira's brows knit together. *Prisoners? He can't mean...*

Before she could speak, though, Mistress Nari drew forward and gave Tigran a small bow.

"Surely the palace knew of the knighting ceremony," Nari said, her smile even more of a grimace than Kira's. "I personally sent a messenger to invite Her Highness."

Tigran looked politely puzzled, though Kira suspected it was an act—it was always an act.

"It appears the message was not received. I know Empress Mei would have been greatly offended not to be invited to the knighting ceremony for her two favorite Gray Knights." He nodded at Kira and Jun.

Jun huffed, and Kira could hear his teeth grinding together.

"Easy," she hissed at him, holding an arm out inconspicuously to keep Jun from advancing. She didn't blame him, though; Tigran had arrested his father and scapegoated Jovan for every vile deed he himself had done.

Ichiro spoke sharply from where he stood, not bothering to move forward to address Tigran. "Then it is a good thing we also sent another invitation to the Empress, by courier. We wouldn't want her to be offended because of a simple miscommunication."

Miscommunication my eye, Kira thought, glaring at Tigran.

"Ah, well, in any case, we will let you go about your—er—ceremony. Mistress Nari, you will take Commander Hagane to retrieve the prisoners." A slim man with short-cropped gray hair in Tigran's shadow lifted his chin.

"Prisoners?" Nari echoed in a hollow voice. "The only prisoners we have are—"

A gasp came from somewhere behind Kira. Without turning, she knew it was Nesma. Nesma, whose sisters Nia Mari and Nikoletta had been imprisoned deep beneath Gekkō-ji for some time. Their mind-manipulating magic had been no match for Mistress Nari's safeguards. And where there had once been three prisoners, there were now only two—the woman known as the Darkener, whose powers could suppress magic, had died in her cell, and no one knew the cause.

Tigran had urged the Empress to push back the sisters' trial every time Kira had gotten the Gray Knight's trial moved. Every move they made, Tigran made another on this infuriating chess match of dark and light.

But they had all felt safe knowing the sisters were imprisoned underneath Nari's magical wards.

"No," Nari commanded. "They cannot be moved. As soon as they leave the cells, they will have access to their magic. There is nowhere safer in all of Camellia that can hold them."

The disgust in Nari's voice did not go unnoticed by Tigran. With an unpleasant smirk, he put his fingers on the bottle dangling from his belt, the luminescent liquid glittering and swirling just like...

"Wait... that's *Light*," Kira gasped.

All eyes focused on Tigran as he lifted the bottle out of its ties. "A marvelous invention by—er—someone in the Commonality. They pull magic from their surroundings, consequently making it impossible for the prisoners to use any magic. And with the added benefit that Light and Shadow can be stored."

He went on, his once attractive voice now sending rage through Kira's veins. "At last, us commoners have access to the Light and Shadow magic that surrounds us all—a balance in Camellia at last. What we've been working toward all these decades." He closed his fingers over the bottle into a fist. "At any rate, these decanters can now ensure that the prisoners can be taken off your hands and safely removed to Meridian. That is where the Empress' other prisoners are held, at any rate."

Kira took an angry breath. *They'll just rejoin you*, she seethed inside, but kept silent.

"But—" Mistress Nari began, still staring at Tigran's fist where he held the decanter. "That's Light magic, you can't—"

He held up a hand to stop her. "I understand of course that Gekkō-ji has enjoyed a monopoly on Light magic for quite a few decades. After the tragedy at Azurite, you became the last Light temple in the realm. But Empress Mei charged the Commonality with keeping the realm's commoners safe, and logic only follows that to be on equal footing with our magic-wielding brethren, magic must be available for all."

"And those decanters...?" Nari's nostrils flared in affront even as she clenched her fists, as if wishing to summon a weapon.

"They are a curious invention," Tigran told them. "They are able to passively siphon magic from the environment, which will keep our prisoners from drawing any magic into themselves."

Kira stared down at her hands in horror. Was that the reason she hadn't been able to make a blossom for the tree?

Now that she looked around the courtyard, she realized there was hardly any residual Light magic around them. She hadn't noticed with the bright glow of the full moon. And as she glanced at the other decanters of the soldiers, she wondered if they were brighter than when they had first arrived. Her mouth dropped open, and she locked eyes with Jun, a chill running up her spine.

Tigran had magic; they already knew that, even if he pretended he didn't. But now his soldiers had some too. And they were stealing it from the world. They had taken all the Light magic from the area already.

"That's—That's—" Mistress Nari stuttered, taking an aggressive step toward Tigran. "That's blasphemy! You can't just *hold* Light essence like that. It must be returned to the fabric of the Realm!"

The spirit of the mountain's warning now made sense. Kira felt a wave of apprehension roll through her. She wanted to speak out, to come to Nari's side...

Jun jabbed a sharp elbow into her ribs.

"Ouch!" she hissed.

"Don't," he said through gritted teeth. "We're neutral. Remember?"

She let out an angry breath that she was shocked to notice wasn't actual flames of anger.

"There is no evidence that the magic cannot be held," Tigran was now saying.

Somehow Nari had gotten closer to Tigran, and now stood a mere foot away from him, her towering height apparently not cowing him in the least. He stood tall, unafraid.

"I will not allow it," she said in a low command that could be heard across the entire courtyard.

The deadly scythe flashed back into existence in Nari's hands, and she whirled it in half an arc, easily bringing the curved blade up to Tigran's chin.

He didn't even flinch.

Kira's breath hitched; she couldn't tear her gaze from Tigran and Nari. They had lain low this entire year, to Kira's great annoyance, so that they could gather evidence to take Tigran down. Nari herself had forced them to remain neutral. And now this?

"Will you join the other prisoners then?" Tigran said so quietly Kira almost didn't hear him.

"No," Kira muttered under her breath, glancing at Jun in panic. *We can't lose Nari! Not with all the Gray Knights imprisoned!*

She took a step forward, ready to fight off Jun if necessary, but two other hands on her shoulders made her halt. One was the strong and callused hand of her friend Anzu, and the other, the large sun-warmed hand of Zowan. The fire inside Kira surged and guttered, as if wind had scoured her flaming heart. Zowan shook his head.

Kira's eyes fluttered closed, and she nodded, acquiescing. Zowan had always been there for her, and she had spent the last year apprenticing under him, learning all he had to teach her about Shadow magic.

She would have to trust him.

"I will not allow it," Nari said again, even louder. She maintained her hold on the scythe, and seemed to know she had gone to a place she couldn't return from when she pressed the blade to Tigran's throat. He blinked.

"You *cannot* hold Light essence captive. It is an abomination. And—" she paused a moment as though steeling herself, though Kira thought she already looked quite steely, "—I won't stand by any longer as you desecrate the realm with your hideous actions, including framing Sir Jovan for your deeds as the Lord of Between."

The silence that rang across the courtyard was as cold as ice. Tigran narrowed his eyes at Nari.

The contingent of soldiers behind him didn't react, and finally, Tigran gave a short bark-like laugh.

"As I expected, unfortunately," he said to his soldiers, tilting his head slightly away from the scythe's blade, still no fear in his eyes at Nari's weapon. "I knew there would be some who would blame anyone else but Sir Jovan and his knights for their misdeeds, but really, Mistress Nari, I am surprised at you. You have always been an intelligent leader. Why, in all the years of feuding, you were the sharpest—"

Nari readjusted her scythe, forcing Tigran to inch up onto his toes to avoid having his throat cut.

"I think you'll find my blade quite sharp, if you don't agree to let that magic go," she said to him. "I cannot pretend any longer. This is the most abominable thing you've done yet *Kage*," she spat, and only the flinch of his eyelid told Kira he disliked being addressed by his real name, a name he hadn't used since getting kicked out of the Spire for practicing vile soul magic.

Tigran's face still remained calm, but a vein was pulsing at his temple. "And I cannot put up with your treason any longer, Mistress Nari. If you do not lower your weapon and allow me to collect my prisoners—"

Nari lowered the scythe, but immediately swept it back as she stepped away, sinking into a defensive stance.

"No. I will not allow you to retrieve the prisoners only to release them to further harm Camellia," Nari said, in reality addressing the Commonality soldiers. "I know your darkest deeds, *Kage*, but this is too far." She jerked her head at the bottled magic.

Kira bit her lip in panic, but Zowan's hand still squeezing her shoulder kept her from interfering. *You can do nothing to fix this from inside a prison cell*, the words she had spoken to Jun last year came back to her.

"I grow tired of your ranting," Tigran went on. "You are embarrassing yourself, and Gekkō-ji... that is, unless you speak for all of Gekkō-ji?" he said with a sneer, his chest rising.

Nari shook her head, and Ichiro stepped forward. "She does not," he said clearly, and an unreadable look passed between him and Nari. "Gekkō-ji complies with all the Empress's wishes, including those of her Commonality."

Nari set her shoulders, her chin jutting out high. She understood. She had chosen.

Tigran gestured to the soldiers closest to him. They marched forward, putting themselves between Nari's blade and Tigran, but they hadn't drawn any weapons.

For a moment, all was still. A slight breeze rustled through the cherry blossoms, and Kira thought perhaps Nari could still back down. After all, they had put up with Tigran and the Commonality all year, pretending to be docile until they could find some evidence and make a move against him. He had been peaceable; the soldiers had kept to mundane matters. But apparently, he had been secretly working on this new atrocity of magic.

The breeze rustled Nari's long bell sleeves, and she slid one foot to the side, sinking into a fighting stance.

The soldiers eyed her warily, and then reached for the decanters at their belts. Kira watched in fascinated horror as one man uncorked his bottle, appeared to pour the contents out, forming a rough sword.

Kira's gasp wasn't the only one. They were not only bottling up Light magic, but could use it too? How was this possible?

The Light bunched up oddly around the soldier's hands as he held the sword. It wasn't as perfect as one forged by someone trained in Light magic, but it was jagged—quite dangerous enough.

Nari swung her scythe in a circle several times, weighing her options before advancing. Quicker than Kira could see, she lunged to the right, the scythe as much a part of her body as her limbs.

The soldier quailed under the force of her strike, but he held his ground. Locked together, they began to turn in a slow circle. The soldier tried to push off from Nari, but she bore down on him even harder.

"This is wrong!" Nari grunted. "And you know it. Magic is the very essence of our realm; it cannot be held captive in large quantities. It's an abomination."

LIZ DELTON

Nari's face contorted with indignant anger, and the soldier's with confusion and fear. The two looked as if they would be locked together forever.

The second soldier Tigran had beckoned forward seemed to think so too. He uncorked his decanter, but he couldn't pour the glowing essence into his hands. The contents of the bottle didn't seem to want to cooperate, so he flung the jar at Nari when she next revolved in his direction.

Shards of Light flew from the bottle like deadly flying icicles. Kira had never seen anything like it.

The shards went forward, stretching somehow, sharpening, like real icicles as they soared toward Nari. The Light magic was *wrong*, twisted.

Nari's back was turned to the advancing shards, and she barely had time to register the danger. She disengaged from the soldier she had locked blades with and only just had time to spin and use her scythe to shield herself from a fraction of the shards.

As if in slow motion, the shards pierced Nari's side, her long flowing garments still whirling as she turned, the scythe blade raised before her like a narrow shield. But it wasn't enough for the twisted daggers of Light.

Kira's legs went numb. Surely they had, because she was rooted to the spot, watching in horror as the shards of

Light pierced Nari's side, at least half a dozen of them. Even with the lack of ambient Light magic, Kira could see the blood that bloomed from each puncture.

Nari dropped to her knees on the hard stones, one hand reaching for her middle.

The scythe fell to the stones with a clatter. Nari curled her whole body around her middle, hunched on the stones in the moonlit square.

Tigran cleared his throat, as if readying to begin a pretentious monologue.

Nari lifted a bloody hand. Something tiny and bright appeared there, and flew toward Tigran.

Fearing deadly retaliation, the two soldiers stepped hastily back toward their comrades, some of whom were armed with traditional weapons. Tigran—the coward—had somehow gotten behind two rows of his soldiers, Kira noted with ire.

But the projectile from Nari wasn't a dagger like Kira had assumed it would be. It was a tiny bird.

The bright white sentinel sailed toward Tigran. The soldiers and the whole temple congregation stood agog in silence. A flicker of memory from Kira's combat trial ghosted through her, but this bird was more like a sparrow. As it turned, its wings stretched out flat as it pivoted in the air, and more birds appeared behind it. Sailing in the wake of the first sentinel, now a whole flock of sharp-looking glowing birds descended on the soldiers, going straight for their heads.

A riot of complaint rose up as the birds pecked and scratched. The cloud of sharp-looking birds dove at the soldiers, who tried to cover their faces to varying degrees of success. Wings fluttered, beaks and claws scratched, and the Commonality quickly became a scattered mess.

Kira looked down to where Nari had crouched to see only a couple splotches of blood dark on the stones. The Mistress of Gekkō-ji had disappeared.

CHAPTER 3

SQUIRE

I t took some time for the sentinels to abate their attack. Kira watched as a few of the soldiers tried to use their stored Light magic to defend themselves, all the while their cursed decanters sucked in more magic. Mistress Nari was right, it *was* an abomination.

And as much as Kira knew it was wrong to hold too much, she siphoned just a little more Light magic into her core, for fear of there being none left after the soldiers had taken it all. It tingled at her fingertips as she pulled it in, and sat warmly in her center, radiating power throughout her body.

Then, as quickly as the bird sentinels had arrived, they burst into glowing flares and disappeared, popping out of existence over the soldiers' heads one by one. Kira glanced around the square, wondering where Nari was now, and whether she had dismissed the sentinels, or whether perhaps they had only gone because they fulfilled the purpose

LIZ DELTON

the Mistress had given them. It only took a moment for the soldiers to compose themselves.

The slim man behind Tigran gave a sharp whistle, and the soldiers regained their perfect formation. He eyed the few with rumpled clothing and gashes on their faces with disdain, but said nothing.

"Commander Hagane," Tigran said, gesturing him forward. The man stepped out of Tigran's shadow and approached Ichiro. Kira stiffened, watching the commander stop inches away from her grandfather.

The two men were about the same height, but the commander was wiry and somehow full of an aggressive energy, whereas Ichiro had politely clasped his hands inside his sleeves, and inclined his head in a respectful nod.

"The prisoners," Tigran said, barely able to hide the gloating look on his face. Kira wished he would drop the pleasant act; didn't everyone here know he was steeped in the evil deeds that had wracked Camellia for decades?

A wave of tight fire rose up her chest, and she tried to calm herself. Deep down she knew they had to let him do it. For now. Otherwise, the soldiers would arrest everyone—or worse, once in custody, Tigran would steal the magic from their souls to use for his foul experiments. She tried to focus on her grandfather, who was whispering something to Master Tenchi before leading the still-silent commander toward the Moonstone, where deep underneath, two of their most powerful enemies lay.

Master Tenchi didn't bother glancing at the soldiers and Tigran before announcing to the Light knights and trainees, "Tonight's full moon ceremony is ended."

Kira let out a small gasp and looked at Jun. They hadn't gotten to place their blossoms on the tree. Were they technically knights? She knew she should be worried about the present situation with Tigran, but couldn't help the disappointment that welled up.

"The hour is past for completion," Master Tenchi went on, "And we will resume the ceremony at a later date," he added vaguely. Kira wondered if he was purposefully keeping the information from Tigran, who had clasped his hands in front of him and was staring at the place where Ichiro had disappeared with Commander Hagane.

"You may all go now," Tenchi snapped.

Kira stood stock still as everyone who came to watch dispersed, taking a wide path around the soldiers to get back to their dorm houses, or in the case of the knights and masters, the cabins on the mountainside.

Tenchi glared at Kira and Jun, who still hadn't moved.

Kira glared right back at her combat teacher, a man who normally struck fear into her heart with his rigid training techniques, harsh criticisms, and fighting prowess. But she was saved any confrontation by Anzu, who placed a hand on her shoulder and said tersely, "Come, I'll walk you to your dorm house."

With a heavy sigh, Kira acquiesced, and Jun and Zowan came along behind them. The soldiers they circled around stood in a disciplined silence as they waited for their commander to emerge from the underground cells.

Before they parted for their separate dorm houses, Kira gave Jun a significant look. He nodded almost imperceptibly before going off with Zowan toward the boy's dorm houses.

Anzu all but steered Kira toward the open gallery that ran along the front of the girl's dorm house. They went up the steps together, and the knight—her *fellow* knight, she realized—accompanied her down the labyrinthine corridors until they came to Kira's room. Of course, it wouldn't be her room much longer, this small room she shared with three other girls. Hana and Michi were already in bed, perhaps having fled the ceremony when the fighting started. Nesma sat fully clothed on her blankets, gazing anxiously at the door.

"Kira," Nesma said with relief.

Kira opened her mouth, but couldn't say the words she wanted to—*It's okay*—because it wasn't. Tigran would soon have his Shadow mages returned to him, with their insidious mind manipulation proficiencies. The two girls who had tortured Nesma all throughout childhood.

"We'll make it right," Kira said in a strangled voice.

Nesma gave her a terse nod, her lips pressed in a thin line, her long hair falling over her face.

"Everyone stay here," Anzu ordered. "I know you might want to—do something about all this," she said mostly looking at Kira. "And with Mistress Nari gone, I know it's—it's confusing." She looked like she wanted to say more, but perhaps for the sake of Hana and Michi refrained. "Just stay here. There's nothing that can be done tonight."

The other girls muttered their agreement, but Kira gazed at Anzu, silent. She was a knight now, even if it wasn't official, even if she hadn't put a blossom on the tree. She had the authority to make her own decisions.

But she wouldn't argue with Anzu, not right now, anyway.

It was likely true that they couldn't do anything tonight, what with the contingent of soldiers Tigran had brought, but that didn't mean Kira was going to sit on her bed, wondering how Ichiro fared down in the dungeons, or how the "prisoners" would walk out of Gekkō-ji in chains only to be freed a mile down the road.

Anzu slid the wooden door shut with a soft *whoosh*, and Hana raised her hand to extinguish the four lamps in the room. Each metal lantern socket in front of their respective beds went dark at the flick of her hand, and Hana fell back onto her pillow with a sigh. Of course, they could all still see the faint outline of Light in everything, and Kira was relieved that it appeared as strong as it usually did this time of night. So, the Commonality hadn't stolen *all* the Light magic from the temple, at least.

"Well, that wasn't how I pictured the end of the ceremony," Michi said in the darkness. "I know I'd never seen one before but really—" she gave a half-hearted snort.

Kira answered with an equally weak chuckle. "I wonder when I'll get to finish the ceremony."

Sitting on her bed with her back turned to the others, Kira opened her hand in her lap. With a shaky breath, she released her hold on some of the Light magic bundled up in her core, and focused on forming the shape in her hand.

A delicate and pristine cherry blossom sat in her palm. Her heart swelled. She closed her eyes briefly, pushing away the moisture of unformed tears. Pushing away the imaginary tingling feeling at the back of her neck—remnants of the time Tigran tried to steal her soul's magic. She was fine now. Really.

"You might have to wait until the next full moon," Hana said.

Kira jerked upright, and she closed her fingers over the flower. "I hope not," her voice came out fiercer than she meant it to.

The other girls were quiet for several minutes, long enough that the sound of slow breathing signified one or more of them had fallen asleep. Kira lay down on her side, still cradling the flower.

Finally, Nesma rolled over to face Kira and whispered, "We have to stop them."

"We will."

With a single thought, she released the magic back into the world.

***

An hour later, Kira crept from her bed and over to the door. Carefully, she slid it open and stepped out into the corridor. Before she could close it all the way, however, a small hand stopped it.

Nesma didn't say anything, only gave Kira a fierce look as she followed her out into the corridor. Kira resumed shutting the door and glanced at Nesma's tiny frame, then shrugged. She was in no mood to tell the girl to go to sleep, not when her maniacal sisters were on the loose.

When they emerged onto the gallery, they saw the temple square was empty. The soldiers, Tigran, and his prisoners were long gone.

Kira glanced at the knights guarding the main gate, hoping they weren't looking this way. She and Nesma stole across the courtyard, not bothering to stick to the shadows cast by the still bright moon—the guards and anyone else with Light magic would see them regardless, if they looked in this direction. So, they favored speed over stealth, and quickly arrived at Kira's destination, panting slightly. But they didn't stop at the top of the stairs beside the Moonstone; they descended at once, sinking out of sight.

At the bottom of the steps, Kira pulled open one side of a set of double doors, which glinted with gold filigree. Nesma came in behind her and they both put their hands on the door to help it close without its usual characteristic *boom*.

In hushed silence they strode down the aisles of the underground library, surrounded by towering shelves of books. Kira inhaled the familiar scent of aged tomes, their pages stiff, their spines bound in string and leather, some with crumbling pages, some with freshly copied ink. Peeking through the aisles on both sides were the glass cases that lined the walls, filled with all manner of scrolls and parchment.

At the end of the main aisle sat a cozy fireplace, with a low table and a few chairs, one of which was already occupied by Jun.

He turned to look at them with a mixed expression of grim acceptance tempered with a ghost of his usual mischief. Kira lifted one corner of her mouth in not-quite a smile as she settled into the chair next to him. He had made a pot of tea, and when they joined him, he poured the steaming brew into the cups from the tea tray. Kira ignored hers, gazing into the fireplace, watching the weak flames dance across the coals there.

"We should be following them," she said in a low voice, finally leaning forward to pick up her cup. "I can't believe we didn't think he would free them before this." She shook her head.

"He probably needed those decanters as the public excuse for being able to control them. He must have been working on that for a while now. Things have been too quiet since he arrested my father. Delaying the trials only gave him more time to come up with this."

Kira grimaced. "You're right. And those decanters…" She couldn't even form the words.

"It's just wrong," Nesma said.

Jun shook his head, speechless too.

After a minute, Kira said, "But you know what? I'm glad Mistress Nari stood up to him—in front of his soldiers and everything."

"Yeah, but now she's gone," Jun said.

It was hard to imagine Gekkō-ji without Mistress Nari. Especially with everything going on with Tigran. Where would she go? Kira knew nothing personal about the woman who ran the temple alongside her grandfather. Did she have land or an estate somewhere in Camellia? Family or friends who would harbor her?

"I just hope wherever she's gone, she can do something to help take down Tigran."

Nesma nodded fervently, her big eyes wide.

"Well?" Kira said. "Who knows how long of a head start Tigran has—should we go up to the stables? We're knights now," she said to Jun. "Those prisoners can't go free. They're far too dangerous. We can disguise ourselves or something, pretend we're raiders and follow them."

He opened his mouth to say something, but before he could respond, a strange shift in the air of the library occurred, and they all turned to look at the door.

There stood Ichiro, his hand on one of the double doors, having closed it quietly. And on either side of him stood Anzu and Zowan. Anzu still wore her armor—Kira could count on one hand the number of times she had seen her without it—brown leather covered her from her upturned shoulder pauldrons to her boots. Her knight's sash glowed white at her waist, and a black tunic poked out through the armor. Zowan looked as elegant as ever in his mage's garb, the fitted black robe with silver stitching that went down to his knees and the matching trousers, broken up only by his sword belt and the two katanas it carried. Ichiro, however, had changed out of the ornate coat he had worn at the knighting ceremony, and now wore a long charcoal coat and matching trousers.

Kira stuck out her chin as she watched them approach, one of her hands straying toward the crescent moon buckle at her belt sash.

Zowan looked almost amused, but the clenching and unclenching of his fist told her differently. "Well, I'm glad we didn't find you in the stables," he said by way of greeting, his voice echoing up to the glittering stone ceiling. "I told Anzu we should check there first."

Kira's face grew warm. She had a retort ready, but held her tongue—Ichiro was still Master Starwind, still leader of the temple. Though he was indeed a kind grandfather, she wasn't quite ready to banter about possibly breaking the rules in front of him just yet.

"I—well, we needed to talk," was all she said. She refused to apologize for leaving the dorm house. She *was* a knight after all. Well, sort of.

"Don't we all," Zowan said sardonically.

As soon as the three of them reached the sitting area, Anzu strode around the book stack beside them without a word. Kira could hear her walking slowly around the perimeter of the room, and guessed she was checking to make sure they were alone.

Kira, Jun, and Nesma all stood and gave a bow to Ichiro, who returned it with grace. Zowan offered Ichiro the remaining chair, but he declined, so Zowan sank into it instead.

"Well," Ichiro said, standing with his hands clasped before him, "have you decided anything?"

Not used to being addressed as if she had any kind of authority, Kira gaped at him. Then she shook herself and glanced at Jun. He seemed reluctant to speak, so Kira took a deep breath, and said, "No. We were discussing going after Tigran and the prisoners, but..."

"It would be like offering yourself to be arrested and experimented on," Zowan said, glaring at them. "I knew it—I just suppose I'm glad you were smart enough to come here and talk about it first before going after him straight away."

Kira's face flushed, and she sat up straighter. "We need to do *something*. He's just going to free them the moment he gets to Meridian. Or maybe the Commonality are all evil and will just let him get away with freeing them whenever."

"I don't think the Commonality are all *evil*," Ichiro interjected. "Merely misled."

She raised one shoulder in half a shrug. "Yeah, I suppose. Do *you* think we should go after them?" she asked.

Zowan made an angry noise in his throat, but Ichiro was the one to respond. "I think they'll be moving slowly and therefore easy to follow, given their direct route to Meridian. I do regret that Mistress Nari had to flee, for a multitude of reasons, but I believe she would have recommended following them, were she still here."

Kira bit the inside of her cheek. "Do you think she's okay?"

"I imagine if she had the strength and stealth needed to disappear from the square, then she is fine. It is us and our plans for stopping Tigran we now need to recalculate, however."

"Do you think she could just come back? How would they know?" Nesma asked in a small voice.

At this, Ichiro grit his teeth in an unusual show of anger. "They would find out," he said darkly. "They have now posted soldiers outside our gates."

Kira's eyes widened. "What for? I mean, what are they *claiming* it's for? Since he framed Sir Jovan as the Lord of Between, what do we need protecting from now in his twisted narrative?"

Ichiro unclasped and reclasped his hands. "He claimed the Empress wished to protect our realm's most valuable magic. Since we had proved in need of protection by being 'fooled' by Sir Jovan."

She couldn't resist rolling her eyes at that.

"Indeed," her grandfather muttered.

"I still say we need to follow them," Jun said. "We can find out where they're taking them."

Nesma glanced at Kira, but didn't meet her eyes for very long.

Kira spoke up, "I think it would be wise to know where Nia Mari and Nikoletta are. Their skills are way too powerful." She gasped. "They could even be used to manipulate the Empress."

Zowan waved the idea aside with a hand. "Tigran already has her ear, and the ear of all her advisors. It wouldn't make much of a difference. I don't think the Empress is in any further danger. But you three are not to go running after the Commonality right now."

"What? Why not?" Jun demanded, jumping to his feet. "We're knights now, we've completed our Light training; we're not little kids anymore, Zowan!"

Kira twisted her mouth, silently agreeing. She was seventeen now—even in the Starless Realm, she would nearly be considered an adult.

But more importantly, she was a knight now. Not yet a full Gray Knight—she still had to complete her Shadow training—but she was fully trained in Light. She sat in silence as that thought sunk in for a moment. The knight ceremony already seemed ages ago, even though it had only been a few hours since her mountaintop fight with Nari.

"Well, we can't just go tearing off after them," Zowan said. "Those guards are here now, watching us; I'm sure this is exactly what Tigran expects."

Ichiro nodded. "Certainly, he expects it. Which is why we must do it carefully."

Kira and Jun shared a sly look as Zowan harrumphed and stormed a few feet away. Anzu was still making her rounds throughout the library, perhaps too agitated to join in the conversation. Zowan joined her and they meandered toward the door, murmuring to each other.

"Now," Ichiro said, "Since Mistress Nari is gone, sending the knights on quests does fall to me."

A thrill ran through Kira. She had been hurtling toward knighthood ever since she came to Gekkō-ji, and now it was here. Jun's chest puffed out, and he looked like he was suppressing a grin.

"But I am not going to send our newest knights after the most dangerous man in Camellia, just because you two are to be Gray Knights some day." Jun visibly deflated. "That day is not today, and we have other more skilled knights in residence. I will send a small group to find out where they take the prisoners, nothing more."

Zowan strode back over, Anzu at his side. She positioned herself so she could still see the door, but relaxed enough to lean against one of the bookcases next to Zowan.

"Well, what are *we* to do?" Jun asked. His tone was respectful, but Kira could tell he was agitated.

"Something far more important," Ichiro answered.

Kira leaned forward. "The magic—the decanters?" she said quietly.

"Yes," Ichiro said. "Mistress Nari was right—it is unthinkable, and surely a danger to the entire realm to store magic this way. Knowing the foul deeds of Tigran, who knows how much magic he could be storing, and what he might do with it? It spells certain danger for the realm."

Anzu shook her head. "I've nothing against commoners wanting to use magic—but this isn't right."

"No, it's not," Kira said. "The spirit of the mountain warned me of something as I descended from the knight trial. I guess he could already feel something was wrong."

"Indeed," Ichiro said, looking at Kira with new interest. "That is why I need you to go to the palace," he said to her. "The Empress favors you, and even if Tigran is there for every audience you have with Her Highness, it is possible you can get her to see reason. No doubt he has enchanted her with his silver tongue, but I'd like you to try to get her to revoke the Commonality's use of these decanters. She does favor you."

Kira gave him a swift nod. "You're right. I can try to convince her, maybe even get her alone. When should I leave? I could get there for morning tea if I leave now." It was well past midnight, but riding in the dark was no trouble when everything glowed subtly with Light magic.

"No," Ichiro said, shaking his head. "Wait until morning to depart. No need to alarm the soldiers. I'm sure they'll be alert for any sign of us sending anyone after the prisoners." He turned to Zowan. "What they won't see is a letter."

49

Zowan responded by muttering something unintelligible.

Ichiro seemed to understand the gist though. "Your uncle needs to be alerted right away. I don't know what else Tigran is planning for these decanters, but there could be another contingent on its way to the Spire now for all we know. He needs to be warned."

"I could send it," Jun offered.

Kira allowed a small smile at Jun, whose skills with the wind were getting nearly as good as Zowan's.

"I'll do it," Zowan growled. "He's down in the Stone Mountains with Lady Madora again—though he should be back at the Spire before you get there, Kira."

Kira balked for a second. "Oh, that's right." Her face grew warm. "I almost forgot."

Ichiro nodded, eyeing Kira for a moment. "Indeed, it almost slipped my mind as well. Now that the knight ceremony is complete, you were due to return to the Spire."

During Kira's apprenticeship under Zowan this past year, she had gone back and forth with him from Gekkō-ji to the Spire, and it just so happened that she was able to finish her Light training in order to be knighted alongside Jun.

"I guess I'll go to the Spire right after the palace then," she said with a nod.

Ichiro nodded too. "Zowan, I'd like you to go with Kira. As Raiden's official advisor, you know—"

"I'd like to come too."

Kira turned to see Nesma standing there, her hands bunched into tight little fists, facing Ichiro. Kira bit her lip. Nesma still ranked a squire, even though she had started training in Light magic a little before Kira had.

Ichiro paused for the shortest of moments before responding, bowing his head slightly, "I'm afraid with your training Nesma, such a quest—if you were apprenticing under a knight, perhaps—"

"That's what I—I was going to ask Kira if I could be her squire."

CHAPTER 4

THE WISP

"Me?" Kira whispered to herself a little while later, alone in the bathhouse.

Ichiro had politely told Nesma that Kira would want to consider such a proposal at length, and dismissed them all from the underground library to go to bed.

But Kira couldn't go to sleep. Instead, she bid the others goodnight and went to the bathhouse under the guise of wanting to calm her nerves after such an eventful night.

She stood at the edge of the enormous communal bath in her towel and didn't get in. Instead, she dropped down to sit on the edge of the bath pool and dipped a toe. Steam rose off the water in wisps and whorls, more distinct at the far end of the pool where the large bath stretched outside into a walled enclosure. The thought of floating in the water and looking up at the blanket of stars above was tempting, but she shook her head. She withdrew her foot and sat cross-legged, clutching her towel.

Nesma wanted to be her squire. Nesma. *Her* squire.

Kira had only just finished her own squireship. Why would Nesma want Kira as her superior?

She rolled her eyes at herself. Of course, anyone should be honored to be asked, and Kira would likely be pelted with requests, having Gray magic and all.

Nesma had been there for Kira ever since she arrived at Gekkō-ji—teaching her all the ropes about living at the temple, and what she knew about the different subjects they had taken together, from Light to calligraphy. But if Kira was honest with herself, she wasn't sure if Nesma was even ready for an excursion like the one she had to take tomorrow, let alone a year of squireship. It could be dangerous. Tigran could very well be there waiting to abduct her.

She sighed loudly, blowing the nearest steam clouds further into the pool. The steam parted with her breath, and the whorls kept spinning.

As Kira watched, something curious happened toward the end of the pool. The curls of steam thickened, and a half-translucent shape began floating toward her.

Kira scrambled to her feet as the shape approached, and with a swift movement, she summoned a short dagger as she exhaled. Clutching her towel with one hand, and the dagger with the other, she stood at the edge of the water, eyeing the shape. It slowed, and now hovered a few feet in front of her, the shape of a cloaked woman. Kira couldn't make out many details as she stared. The woman seemed to be made of smoke, her features blurry and wispy. But it was clearly a woman, with her delicate chin and high cheekbones, and petite frame. Kira took a step back as a familiar scent wafted over her, but she couldn't quite place it.

"Who are you?" Kira demanded warily.

The wispy woman appeared to smile.

Kira cocked her head to the side. "Who—what do you want?" she whispered. A shiver ran down her spine. This must be a spirit. She had met a few before, but the question was—what did this one want?

Because Kira knew from her experiences with Gekkō and the others: they all wanted something.

The wisp raised her hand, palm facing Kira's heart; the organ in question began to race, but then the strange wisp dissipated, dissolving back into the steam that curled thick over the pool. Kira gasped, stepping up to the very edge, still clutching her towel and her Light dagger.

"Hello?" she called, her voice echoing around the room. She glanced up at the serpentine dragon mural on the large wall to her right, caught its painted eye, and shivered. Backing away from the pool, she sped toward the changing rooms, and didn't look away from the water until the door had closed.

Thoroughly haunted, Kira washed her face and finally cleaned her cut in a basin in the dressing room, since she hadn't even gone so far as to slosh a bucket of water on herself in the main bath room. The slice of red across her cheek stung a little, and she would have to put some healing salve on it when she got back to her dorm room. She didn't think she would have time to visit the apothecary and ask the new Shadow mage to heal it for her before leaving tomorrow. Master Akasuki had arrived six months ago, having just finished his training at the Spire. He was eager to become Gekkō-ji's new healer, and Kira had enjoyed his uniquely enthusiastic lessons, even if the other trainees thought him too young. But everyone, Kira especially, would always miss the kind and patient Mistress Tori.

She slid her legs into her black wide-legged pants, and pulled on the matching vest-like shirt. They were comforting after being confronted by the spirit in only a towel. She kept the Light dagger, and slid it firmly into her belt sash. With a jolt, she realized that her sash needed replacing. She was supposed to receive her white sash at the knight ceremony. She looked down in disappointment. She had been so excited to become a knight, but the ceremony hadn't gone at all how she had imagined. And she still didn't have a blossom on the tree.

But no, she *was* a knight now. Ichiro had said so. It was only the trappings of the ceremony she had missed out on. Sashes and flowers didn't make her a knight. Her training and skills did.

She glanced around to make sure she had everything, thinking that perhaps she could ask Ichiro for her white sash in the morning—she thought it might lend credibility to her visit to the palace—when she noticed something on the bench where she had originally piled her clothes.

It was a small white flower. Not like the cherry blossom she had been dreaming of creating, but a tiny bell-shaped blossom. Kira picked it up without thinking. It looked like a lily of the valley, a plant she had seen here in Camellia, but she also remembered from the Starless Realm.

She tucked the tiny flower in her vest pocket and left the bathhouse, wanting to distance herself from the somewhat spooky feeling in the bath house.

It wasn't until she reached her dorm room that she remembered the spirit of the mountain's message earlier that night. Perhaps the person who wanted to speak with Kira might have come to her after all. Now Kira just had to figure out what the spirit wanted.

With a sigh she rolled over in bed, her muscles beginning to ache from the trial on the mountaintop. It could wait until tomorrow.

***

Four hours of sleep is not enough, Kira thought as she hauled herself up the steps to the stables in the morning. After grabbing a freshly baked bun and an apple from the kitchen house, she had taken a moment to sip some tea under the leafless wisteria branches in the corner of the temple square. Miss Mayu in the kitchen house had loaded her up with buns stuffed with sweet bean paste to take with her, even though she was just going to the palace.

Kira adjusted the small satchel of buns now, their delicious scent wafting out of the tied-up cloth that served as a makeshift bag. Her mouth watered, and she silently thanked Miss Mayu as she planned on snacking on another one on her way to the palace. Though she was sure the Empress would likely serve her an exquisite tea as she usually did, Kira had grown quite fond of the food here at Gekkō-ji. She would miss it when she got back to the Spire, where she had to cook her own food.

She found her beautiful dapple-gray horse Naga and led her out of the box stall to gear her up. Zowan's horse Briar wasn't in his stall when she led Naga past, so she wandered the aisles until she found them.

The stable was made up of two long aisles, perpendicular to one another, each housing box stalls on both sides. She found Zowan and his mount halfway down the secondary aisle, with Nesma.

Kira's stomach gave an unpleasant swoop. She had completely forgotten about Nesma's proposal last night, what with everything after the ceremony, and the wispy spirit at the bathhouse. Nesma was helping get Briar's saddle on, and she smiled shyly at Kira when she approached.

Zowan turned, sniffing. "I hope you have enough of whatever that is to share," he said, grinning and eyeing her satchel. His eyes flicked to the long cut on her cheek, which had scabbed cleanly after she had put salve on it last night.

"I do," Kira said, smiling back at him and feeling the scab pull at her skin. "As long as you're nice on the way there."

He put a hand to his heart in mock offense. "Me? I'm always nice."

"I don't know," Kira teased. "You can be pretty not-nice when we're training." She still had some bumps and bruises to show for it, though they were technically no fault of Zowan's. He had helped her hone her skills all the months leading up to her advancement, and she knew she owed him for all the time he had set aside for her. Still acting as palace liaison for his uncle Raiden, he was constantly traveling across the realm and navigating the increasingly toxic political waters. She didn't envy him, especially since she was about to wade into those waters again too.

He shrugged, still smiling. "Right back at you Starless Girl. You nearly got me yesterday." He pointed to his right shoulder, and Kira flushed. Even though she had been practicing with a dull blade yesterday morning, she had still managed to bruise him with a throwing knife.

"I—"

"It's fine," he chuckled. "That's what training's for. And you did it. You passed."

She grinned, feeling some of the belated excitement she should have felt last night. But that—like many a great thing in her life—had been taken by Tigran. The grin slid off her face.

Clearing her throat, she led Naga over to the next post, and slid Naga's lead rope into the ring there. Trusting Naga enough to leave the rope loose, she snuck a look at Nesma and headed to the tack room to get her saddle and bridle.

When she came back, Naga was nosing the bundle of food she had left hanging from a hook on the wall. "Hey," Kira said, gently pushing away Naga's nose. "Those aren't for you."

Naga snuffled and Kira patted her cheek. "Where's Jun?" Kira asked.

"I think he left for his estate," she answered with a slight shrug.

"Oh, that's right. I forgot he was planning to go back after the ceremony."

Zowan said, "I think he forgot too. I'm pretty sure he wanted to try to follow Anzu and the other knights, but the Kosumoso lands are still in quite a state what with—" He gestured vaguely with his hand, indicating the sore topic of Sir Jovan being imprisoned.

Kira sniffed. It was probably a good thing Jun had responsibilities to take care of back home. Even though she wanted to find out where the prisoners were going too, she certainly didn't want Jun sneaking off without her.

"Well, I should see him at the Spire soon, anyway. He doesn't usually spend too long at the estate. I think he's trying to find the right steward to hire to take care of it all for him. His mother can't do it all herself, either."

Zowan grunted in agreement as he combed out Briar's tail. "I'm just glad you two didn't run off last night to follow them."

Kira scoffed dramatically. "Oh, ye of little faith."

His forehead furrowed in confusion. He shook his head, likely brushing off the unfamiliar phrase as another of Kira's Starless Realm quirks.

She snorted and turned to look over Naga's coat.

"Here, I'll help," Nesma said, slinking over with a bucket of stiff brushes. Kira smiled tentatively as Nesma began brushing down Naga's beautiful dappled coat. Kira took a second brush and went to the other side.

Her heart raced as she stole glances at Nesma over Naga's back. She cursed herself for not thinking more about her squire request. But after that strange spirit came to her in the bathhouse, all thoughts of Nesma had flown from her mind, and then she had fallen into bed after what felt like an endless day, asleep before her head hit the pillow.

Did she even want a squire? She thought back to the past year training under Zowan, which had been a strange time indeed. With weeks spent at the Spire mostly meditating by the lake, or in the Gray Wing's practice room, she and Zowan had grown closer than ever. When he had time-consuming duties to perform for his uncle or the palace, she would ride back to Gekkō-ji—with backup of course—to work on her Light training. Jun had spent most of his time at Gekkō-ji, since he had squired under Anzu. But Kira had a lot of catch-up to do with her Shadow training after the soul damage.

It had been somewhat lonely staying in the Gray Wing alone for weeks at a time, but she had plenty of friends to visit when she wasn't busy with meditation or lessons. Ryn had stuck around the Spire at Raiden's request, and now taught lessons on aura magic—even going by "Master Kimura" to his students, though Kira knew he enjoyed it. Her friend Yuki was in most of her lessons, and Kira could always pop down to the Apothecarium to see Spectra and Micah. Micah had taken Kira out to the city of Heliodor on quite a few occasions, and had spent many an afternoon with her strolling the grounds of the Spire.

The Storm King—with the help of the Spirekeeper Kusari, who could tell where people were within the building—had reinforced the rules about only Gray trainees going into the Gray Wing. Kira smiled ruefully at the memory of one afternoon she and Micah had planned to have tea, only to be interrupted by the sudden appearance of a very cross Kusari. Kira, trying her best to look innocent—which she was, mostly, they had only been kissing—came out of the small kitchen. When the Spirekeeper beckoned Micah out of the kitchen too, she knew her days of having guests in the wing were over. Not even Zowan was allowed in the wing anymore.

Which left her and Micah to stroll the gardens of the temple—to stop and admire the flowers and plants, or have picnics on the lush grass and moss, or venture into the city, usually accompanied by some of the other acolytes, when Kira's schedule allowed.

That was one thing she was especially looking forward to when she returned to the Spire after her palace visit—seeing Micah again. She smiled, warmth rising up from her chest into her throat. Then she touched the leather bracelet she always wore, which had been her father's. Micah had an identical one, which Kira had made from Light magic. And though this one had been her father's, it reminded her of Micah, too.

She had received a letter from Micah just the other day, bidding her luck on her ceremony, and wishing he could be there to see it. But the Apothecarium where he worked was beset with a spate of early spring illnesses, and he had to change his plans to come see her at Gekkō-ji.

Kira blinked heavily, staring at Naga's coat, now brushed to a pristine shine. She lowered the heavy brush and dropped it in the bucket with a loud clunk. Nesma had already picked Naga's hooves and was moving over to Zowan's horse to do the same. Kira watched her go.

She let out a reluctant breath. "Nesma, wait," she called, and immediately regretted the words as Nesma walked back over. Kira's gut clenched as she struggled to find the words to start. She wished she hadn't put the brush down;

now she didn't know what to do with her hands. She settled for running her fingers through Naga's mane, which had already been combed.

Zowan tactfully walked around the other side of his horse and murmured something to Briar.

Nesma seemed to read the unsaid words on Kira's face. Her own expression fell.

"I understand," Nesma said quietly. Her eyes were shining, and Kira could tell she was trying hard not to cry.

"Oh, Nesma," Kira breathed, and lunged to hug her. Nesma's long hair spilled over Kira's shoulder, and Nesma let out a quiet sob. "I'm sorry," Kira said into her hair. "I'm just not ready to have a squire yet. But if I were—it would be you."

Nesma swallowed hard. She took a few fast breaths, but when she spoke, her voice did not waver. "It's not that," she admitted in a whisper. "Not really. It's—it's—Nia Mari and Nikoletta—" Her words choked off with a restrained sob.

Kira tightened her hug, eyes squeezing shut as her heart constricted. "I know. And I'm so sorry," she repeated. "I think we *all* slept better knowing they were safe in Nari's cells where they couldn't hurt anyone. But knowing they're out there again—I can't even imagine what that must be like for you."

They stood there for a long time. The soft noises of the stables were like a cocoon of sound around them, the chewing of hay, the shifting of hooves in the stalls. Naga whickered. Kira inhaled the familiar scents, rubbing Nesma's back.

She couldn't think of anything else to say. She couldn't do anything to change what her sisters had done.

"We are going to get them back," she said finally, and Nesma pulled away. Kira looked her in the eyes. "All of them. The prisoners, the Gray Knights, Nari. I'm going to do my duty to Camellia, even if it takes storming the palace and—and taking down Tigran myself."

CHAPTER 5

LIES AND LANTERNS

N aga and Briar were saddled and ready to go when a short figure appeared in the doorway of the stables, silhouetted against the early morning sunlight.

"Ah, good, you're still here," Ichiro said, coming forward, his face lighting up in a stray sunbeam full of dust motes. Kira finished tucking her bag of buns into her saddlebag, and quickly buckled the flap.

They all bowed to Ichiro, who returned the gesture. Nesma sank back to the edge of the aisle. Kira had seen the disappointment in her eyes, and her gut clenched in guilt.

"Under normal circumstances," Ichiro began, "I am sure Mistress Nari would have accompanied you to the palace." He eyed Zowan, and his gaze lingered on Kira. "It is with great regret that I cannot attend in her stead, but I will no longer leave the temple under the circumstances Tigran has left us in."

A slight chill ran up Kira's spine as she recalled the events of last night.

Ichiro shook his head in thought. "We knew he had been quiet too long this past year. But the time has come for action," he said, standing straighter and clasping his hands together. "But *intelligent* action. We must do our best to remain on the good side of the Empress. Their army has grown, and with these decanters, could be a formidable enemy if it turned to a physical confrontation. And not that any of us need reminding, but the Gray Knights and Nari are no longer able to come to our defense.

"So, remember: You cannot help the Realm if you're in a jail cell."

The words echoed across time as Kira thought back to the night at the crossroads after she and the others had ridden to the palace, only to have the Gray Knights arrested.

"Or dead," she couldn't help but add.

Ichiro nodded gravely. "Indeed. Now, it may be only a formality, but Gekkō-ji does need to object to this use of Light magic. If Tigran and the Commonality continue on this path, who knows what consequences will beset the Realm?"

"Gekkō already warned me something was upsetting the balance," Kira said.

"That's right," Ichiro said, nodding. "Be sure to tell the Empress about your encounter with the spirit of the mountain. Her father was a wise emperor, and she is wise too; she was always level-headed during the feud and tried to act in the best interest of the Realm. But the poisonous words Tigran has been pouring into her ear have affected her judgment. We must make her see reason."

Zowan grunted. "I doubt the advisors will see reason. Even if they're not all in Tigran's palm, they are prejudiced. It goes without saying that they still do not trust Shadow magic. Considering only one of them even possesses Light magic, I assume they are all in favor of the 'equality' Tigran is enforcing."

"But what if she doesn't listen?" Kira said, a knot forming in her stomach.

"We'll decide from there. We must do our best," Ichiro acknowledged with a bow of his head. "Oh, and one more thing."

He withdrew a small package wrapped in pretty gold and mauve paper from his deep bell-sleeve.

Kira tilted her head as she took it. A seal made from Light magic secured the paper closed, and she ran her finger under the crease, breaking the seal. Inside was a strip of fabric, blindingly white.

She lost her breath for a moment.

Then, Zowan clapped her on the shoulder. "Congratulations, Lady Starwind."

Kira tried not to blink through the tears that had materialized in her eyes, so they wouldn't spill over. Ichiro smiled warmly, and reached out with both hands to cover her own. "You deserved the full ceremony last night, but if we could not do that, this will have to do. I am so very proud of your accomplishments. Your father would have been prouder beyond measure." He gave her hands a squeeze and stepped back.

Her throat swelled, and the tears finally spilled over. She dashed the white sash away from the falling tears.

"I—Thank you."

Ichiro drew further back and angled himself so they could pass through the door. "I know you will do your best."

"We will," Kira said, her heart in her throat. Of all the stupid tea ceremonies and luncheons she had attended at the Imperial Palace over the years, none were so important as this one. She caressed the sash and tucked it in her nearest saddlebag, not wanting to fumble with putting it on in front of everyone right now.

"You better get on the road," Ichiro said, and Kira's stomach lurched.

She and Zowan led their horses out into the morning sunlight, the scents of manure and hay replaced with the crisp scent of dead leaves and thawing earth. She shrugged into her coat and mounted, with one last glance at Nesma still standing inside the stables. Then, she and Zowan made their way down the mountain.

***

Thistle joined them outside the temple walls, silently flitting out of the barren trees and landing on Kira's shoulder. He complained the whole way down the mountain about the bumpy ride. By the time they got to Meridian, she was smirking at the flying squirrel's odd complaints.

"You're lucky my mother taught me how to balance, you great hulking beast," he muttered down at Naga from atop her head. "Or I'd have cracked my skull like an acorn two villages back."

Kira snorted, eyeing the Commonality soldiers posted at the city gates uneasily. "You have a mother, then?" she asked Thistle.

He bristled, rising up on his hind legs as he clutched one of Naga's ears. "Of course I have a mother!" he squeaked indignantly. "What sort of a question is that?"

Heat rushed to her cheeks. "Oh—I mean—I just—"

"I didn't just spring from existence to serve Lord Gekkō, you know. I had a whole life before I became his companion."

"Oh," was all she could think to say. She exchanged a glance with Zowan, who looked just as surprised as she felt.

Before she could climb her way out of the conversational hole she had dug, they reached the main entrance to the palace and had to dismount. Thistle hopped onto Kira's shoulder. With apprehension, Kira watched a stablehand take Naga away, unable to stop herself from wondering what would happen if they needed to make a fast escape, and she couldn't get to Naga. She shook her head. *No, no, it's going to be fine. Even if the Empress won't listen to us. We're just going to talk.*

Thistle gently squeezed her ear, and she craned her neck to look at him. She saw nothing, even though she could feel his weight. A quiet, musical chuckle came from somewhere an inch beside her ear. Spirit magic, then.

The sight of Zowan striding up the palace steps gave her courage, and she followed in his wake, doing her best to ignore the soldiers posted everywhere. The subtle glow of Light magic in the decanters at their belts made her stomach clench.

Twenty minutes later, they found themselves alone in one of the many receiving rooms. Solid wood furniture dominated the space, many elaborately carved with chrysanthemums, a symbol of the royal family. Kira sat perched on a fabric pouf, ignoring the tea and snacks a servant had brought. Thistle had left her shoulder when they entered the palace, and she had no idea where he had gone too. He was probably trying to spy on whoever he could so he could report back to Gekkō.

She wiped her sweaty hands on her trousers and glanced at the sliding paper-paneled doors she knew led out to the garden. The last time she had been in this room, she had been navigating the political waters of a luncheon, with all of the advisors in attendance, all clamoring for her attention, for her stories of the Starless Realm.

This morning, it seemed, none of the advisors were available to receive them, and the servant who greeted them at the entrance to the palace had seemed annoyed at their unannounced visit.

Zowan hadn't been discouraged, however. He often made unannounced visits to exchange news or work on trade agreements between the regions. He sipped his green tea and stretched his long black-clad legs before him, the dark red fabric of his mage's robe stretching right across his knees.

"New robes?" Kira whispered, though the large room was quite empty, save for tinkling of water in one corner where a small fountain played.

He looked down and seemed to take in his clothing with some surprise. "Oh, yes. A gift from Anzu." The lightest of flushes lit across his face, and he straightened his back.

A genuine smile graced Kira's lips. "The color looks good on you, especially with the black." She waved to indicate his whole ensemble. "I think I need some new mage's robes," she said thoughtfully. "Now that I'm going back to the Spire for good."

It felt as if a cold rock fell into her gut. "Now that I'm done training at Gekkō-ji," she added in almost a whisper.

Zowan studied her carefully. "Then we shall get you some robes when we go back," he said with a smile. "I know the finest weaver in Heliodor." He flicked his fingers, indicating the weaver had some kind of Shadow proficiency, making Kira curious.

She returned his smile, her mood lightening again. "I *am* excited to get back to the Spire, even with—everything going on. I don't know what I'll *do* when I'm done training," she added thoughtfully. "My whole life since I came to Camellia has been spent training."

A chuckle rolled out of him. "You think you're ever done training, Starless Girl? Why do you think I took you on as a squire in the first place—you know, besides the notoriety," he added with a wink.

"Huh?" she said, finally picking up her tea and sniffing it. It had gone cold, but she took a sip and still found it delicious.

"Knights and mages and even the masters that teach at the temples are constantly training—constantly improving. Even Anzu. I've seen that *Light Lexicon* you study at Gekkō-ji—do you think that book contains everything you can make out of Light magic? Every possibility?"

Kira frowned, thinking. "Huh," she said again, thinking of the book she had studied all these years at the temple, as she and the other trainees tried to create more and more complex bits of magic. "Of course not; you're right. The possibilities are infinite—just like Shadow magic."

"Indeed, and—"

The great double doors burst open, and two soldiers came into the room, followed by Her Imperial Highness, Empress Mei. Kira and Zowan immediately stood and sunk into low bows, their backs straight, palms pressed to their thighs. They remained bowed until the Empress' sapphire slippers stood before them, and they straightened.

Kira's first thought was that the Empress looked tired. Her dark hair was piled atop her head in her usual style, with a tiara of glimmering sapphires which matched the color of her satin slippers. She wore a black and white kimono and some kind of white fur shawl draped across her shoulders.

"Greetings," the Empress said. "I am delighted by your presence." She gave them a subtle bow of her head.

Two servants brought forth an ornate chair behind the Empress, and when they backed away, Kira's insides froze. Tigran had slunk into the room, resplendent in a teal coat with tiny glass beads sewn into a floral design. He bowed at Kira and Zowan, and Kira had to grit her teeth as she returned the gesture, bending only the barest minimum required for respect.

The Empress indicated Kira and Zowan should resume their seats. "I understand you wish to speak with me about a matter of great importance?" she inquired with a regal tilt of her head.

Kira took a deep breath in through her nose. "Yes," she said, having devised a strategy with Zowan on their ride here. "It is about a visit I received from the spirit of the mountain—Lord Gekkō."

The Empress listened with what seemed serious intent as Kira regaled her with the finer points of Gekkō's warning. She steepled her fingers together in front of her face as she listened, nodding.

"I see," she remarked when Kira had finished. "And what is your interpretation of this warning?"

Kira fought to keep her eyes from flicking toward Tigran, whom she had avoided looking at since her first glance at him. But she could see the decanters on the soldiers' belts who stood at the door, and rage bubbled just under her skin.

"Well, Gekkō has warned me about the balance of the Realm before," Kira said. "And on that occasion, the spirits were being driven to chaos, going mad and becoming creatures of darkness. That was caused by the appearance of those doors to the Starless Realm—like the one that brought me here."

She cleared her throat, still avoiding Tigran's eye. She and Zowan had thought it best to avoid mention of the 'Lord of Between,' and so far, she had succeeded. "I couldn't help but notice," Kira said, "that Gekkō warned me this time just before the appearance of—" she paused, steeling herself— "the soldiers with their curious decanters."

Empress Mei's face remained neutral, and she inclined her head, inviting Kira to go on. Regretfully, Kira did just that.

"I believe it's possible—though they are a marvelous invention indeed—that storing Light essence in such a way that does not allow it to return to the fabric of the realm, could be the unbalance of which Gekkō spoke."

The fountain in the corner tinkled merrily as the words sat like an unwelcome smell between them. Kira finally allowed herself to peer at Tigran, but he had a disgustingly polite look on his face.

"The decanters?" the Empress said. "Oh, yes. They are the only way we can remain properly safe from those who wish to deceive us, and use magic to harm the realm."

Tigran still said nothing, forcing Kira to soldier on.

"I understand, yes, however I know from Gekkō-ji that there are magical ways of imprisoning—uh—prisoners," she ended lamely.

Zowan lifted his chin. "Your Highness, we understand the Commonality's wish to be on even footing with those who wield magic, but we believe that this is not the way—"

"And what way would you have it?" Tigran finally said, polite but with a hint of annoyance. "Where the realm's commoners can be abused and tricked by mages and knights over and over? Where they might suffer feuds between the temples for decades at a time, with only brief respite between the next?"

Neither Kira nor Zowan, it seemed, could think of a response to that.

"Your Highness," Tigran continued, "I am sure Lady Starwind and Lord Zowan have the realm's best interests at heart, but I tested the decanters myself, after vast amounts of research. They do indeed siphon magic from their surroundings much like a knight or mage can, but there is no proof of adverse effects on the—fabric of the realm, as it were. And if there is, it hasn't been noted. The benefits far outweigh the non-existent risks."

Empress Mei stared blankly at her fingertips, which were still steepled in her lap. Then she stood, the silk of her kimono whispering as the fabric moved. "Come with me," she said.

Kira looked at Zowan, and they both followed her across the room. Kira could feel Tigran come up behind them, and she had to suppress the creeping sensation that inched up her spine.

Two servants opened the sliding paneled doors on the side wall. They revealed the winter-dead garden, the leaves scoured from the trees, yet the white gravel paths were groomed of any fallen debris. How soon it would all begin to bloom and bud again was anyone's guess.

The Empress clutched her fur shawl tighter about her shoulders and stepped onto the small wooden deck, which stood about a foot off the garden path. Kira, Zowan, and Tigran obediently followed her out. Once outside,

Kira turned to face the Empress, who stood near her own height, though her bejeweled up-do made her seem taller.

The Empress waved a regal hand at a small lantern mounted on a post a few feet away. It looked like a new installation, the wooden post freshly cut, the lantern hewn from stone and still bright white. A subtle glow came from inside the lantern, and Kira's stomach twisted unpleasantly when she realized that it wasn't flame as she had first supposed. It was a small glass container, much like the decanters. And it pulsed with Light. Kira suppressed a gasp.

"As you can see," the Empress said, "The Commonality has installed these lanterns throughout the Palace. There will be no more magic allowed inside the grounds—it is too dangerous and unpredictable."

Kira pressed her lips tight, beginning to feel sick to her stomach. They had waited too long, left Tigran to his own devices *too long*. How could they have let this happen?

"Surely that is for the best," Zowan agreed, shocking Kira. "Your new prisoners, for example, are extremely dangerous. They were in the securest of cells Gekkō-ji possesses. Tell me, did they arrive safely?"

"They are not being held in the palace," the Empress said. "We agreed that was too dangerous as well." She shared a look with Tigran, who nodded respectfully.

"It was as Her Highness wished," he said. "They were taken to the Commonality's new barracks in Meridian, and yes, under the constant safety of the decanters and lanterns."

Empress Mei glided toward the lantern, beckoning Kira forward. She came closer, close enough to inhale the sweet floral scent that came from the Empress, tickling Kira's nose.

"They are an incredible advancement," Empress Mei said, speaking only to Kira. "But I do not take warnings from spirits lightly. You say Lord Gekkō indicated there is an imbalance already at work. Tell me, as someone with Gray magic, perhaps you can get a sense of what the lantern does—can you feel it working? Can you feel its effect on the realm?"

Kira froze, her breath halting at the Empress' request. *Me?* she thought wildly. Then she swallowed and focused her attention on the lantern, after muttering, "Of course, Your Highness."

She did her best to ignore Tigran, but his mere presence made her blood boil. She closed her eyes, knowing that Zowan was there to protect her, though the logical part of her brain told her that there was no way Tigran would try to attack her right in front of the Empress. Yet she couldn't help the chill that rattled her spine at the mere sight of that cold smile.

On an inhale, she tried pulling Light magic from the area surrounding the lantern. It was scarce. She had to pull quite hard, but realized the magic she gathered came from an area further away from the lantern. Next, she tried the same with Shadow magic, and wasn't surprised to see it had pulled all of the magic within a ten-foot radius as well. "Well, it's pulled all the magic from this area, Your Highness," she muttered, opening her eyes to address the Empress, and indicating the area with her hand.

She closed her eyes again and focused her attention on the lantern itself. She could feel the magic ensconced in the glass container, could feel its energy zinging around, confused, perhaps. But she couldn't touch it. She took breath after breath, attempting to pull the magic from the container, but couldn't. "And it's tra—uh—held in there securely," she changed gears hastily.

"Then it's doing its job," Tigran said, as if that were the end of it.

"Indeed," Empress Mei agreed. "But I wanted to know if you could feel its effect on the realm—if the spirit's warning could have been referring to these."

Kira gave a small nod, her stomach still in turmoil. She opened her mouth to say *I'll try*, but closed it, not wanting

Tigran to see her hesitate. Eyes closed, she reached out again, but this time with no idea what she was searching for. It was as before, no magic surrounded the lantern, and the magic inside was trapped and untouchable. She tapped her toes inside her shoe. Couldn't she find something? Do something? She couldn't lie to the Empress, could she? What would she even say?

She bit the inside of her lip. No, that wasn't the way. She wouldn't lie. That could get her in even more trouble, and Tigran would no doubt have a lie of his own as a rebuttal. No... she needed proof.

And as always, Tigran hid his secrets well.

Perhaps if she tried to move the air inside the magic-less area, something might happen. She reached out a tendril of Shadow magic, pushing the air there.

Her stomach dropped when she remembered the Empress stating that magic was no longer allowed in the palace, but the magic in question completely dissipated from the air as if it had gone straight from Kira's core to the glass container. No one noticed her failed attempt at magic.

She shifted from foot to foot, trying to look like she was doing something profound, but the truth was, she wasn't going to find any proof of wrongdoing here, and especially not with Tigran standing there. He would have made sure these containers were made in a way that didn't incriminate him as the despicable person he was. She would have to find proof elsewhere. She was tired of waiting for proof against Tigran, something they had been chasing for so long.

Finally, after a few more minutes pretending to study the lantern, she turned to the Empress with a slight bow of her head. *Facts*, she told herself. *Stick to the facts. We can't accuse Tigran of anything, or risk our own heads.*

"It is strong. I believe they will protect the surrounding area from magic. I cannot yet determine if they are affecting the realm, but I am certainly interested in learning more about them."

"Of course," the Empress said with a nod. "As one of our realm's next Gray Knights, you are welcome to learn as much as you can about them. Tigran—"

Tigran nodded. "Yes, Your Highness. Shall I bring the two of you to the barracks so you might inspect the workshop?"

Fear seared through Kira's insides. Her heart thumped madly at the thought of Tigran taking them to the lair of the Commonality.

It was Zowan who spoke, coming to Kira's rescue. "I think not—not today, anyway, though we thank you for the invitation, Grand Steward. Kira and I must travel to the Spire in order to complete the next phase of her training," he directed this last part at the Empress, whose face lit up.

She clapped her hands together, and even her eyes looked a little less tired than before at this news. "That's right, Tigran told me you had completed your advancement ceremony, though I am saddened that I was not there to witness it."

Kira bowed. "Our deepest apologies, Your Highness, I would have been greatly honored by your presence."

"Yes, Your Highness," Zowan chimed in, "on behalf of Gekkō-ji and myself, we were just as disappointed in the news that you had not received our invitation to the ceremony."

The Empress waved a hand. "It is all right. After all, the deed was accomplished, whether I was there to witness it or not. It is enough that our realm has a new protector, and one I am honored to know so well."

Kira allowed a smile, hiding her gritted teeth. Though they had dodged Tigran's invitation to the barracks, they still hadn't accomplished anything with their visit. Perhaps if she could get the Empress alone...

"Your Highness, would you do me the honor of going on a short walk through the gardens?" Kira said. "I can tell you all the details of my knighting ceremony while we walk." Kira felt genuine joy at the look on Empress Mei's face, and the two of them stepped onto the gravel path and began a slow stroll away from Tigran and Zowan. Kira didn't dare turn back; she didn't think she could repress a smug look at Tigran. She was sure Zowan would find a way to keep him occupied. *At least that lantern is there—neither of them can do magic.*

Kira gathered her thoughts. The air was brisk; the sun was still trapped behind the overcast clouds. The Empress had her fur shawl, but her arms were bare. Kira couldn't expect their walk to be long. As fast as she could, she relived her battle with Mistress Nari on the moonlit mountaintop. The Empress was a good audience, gasping in all the right places as Kira recounted her fight. By the time she was done—and about to tell the Empress why she couldn't put a cherry blossom on the tree, they had rounded a bend and were already on their way back. Kira knew she hadn't much time.

"Your Highness, I must say something," Kira said, her heart hammering. "I'm—I am afraid the decanters and the lanterns are going to upset the balance in the realm. I'm not sure magic is meant to be held, so much, or so long. From all that I've learned in my training, I know that magic is supposed to be returned to the realm."

The Empress remained quiet, studying her feet as they continued to stroll.

Kira went on, "I remember one of my earliest lessons at Gekkō-ji; it's like if you take a bucket of water out of a pond and put it back after an hour of use, it won't have an effect on the pond. But if you take thousands of buckets out, and don't put them back, then the pond will suffer." She held her breath, hoping she didn't sound impudent, hoping the Empress' favor was as strong as she thought it was.

Empress Mei stopped strolling and took Kira by the hand. "Have you ever heard of the *Dragon in the Camellias*?"

"What? Oh, yes, I read it in my history lessons back at Gekkō-ji."

"That reminds me of your metaphor. The great dragon who formed the Realm of Camellia. It was only because the common people were greedy and took all his flowers for themselves. I always wonder what would have happened if those people had been able to see the dragon. Would they have taken so many flowers? Ruining his precious camellia plants? Or would they have desisted?"

Kira smiled reluctantly. She had been fascinated by the story of how the realm had been formed, though she wasn't sure how much of it to believe.

"We have the original version of the story here in the palace archives," Empress Mei was saying. "The oldest copy, that is." She paused. "I do not take your explanation lightly, nor the spirit's warning. But I cannot pretend that the realm didn't suffer a heavy blow when the Gray Knights were accused of so many nefarious deeds, right under our noses. And the recent feud between Light and Shadow was not the first to ravage the realm. Commoners and magic users alike have suffered because the temples have governed themselves in affairs of magic.

"I understand what you are saying Kira, but this is the only solution I can see. If only we had this innovation during the feud. Perhaps not so many lives would have been lost. The lanterns will also help us keep the realm safe against our magic-using enemies now—even the Ga'Mir raiders grow bolder and bolder each year. These are monumental steps we are taking. But if you cannot find fault in the decanters, then I see no reason not to use them."

The Empress let go of Kira's hand and shivered. "Now, let us go back inside and find a nice warm cup of tea to take off this chill."

Kira stood still for a second, a chill that had nothing to do with the cold seeping into her core.

CHAPTER 6

SWIFT VIOLENCE

Kira tugged at the burgundy sleeves of her new robes as she wandered down the Hall of Spirits, studying each statue she passed. Zowan had taken her to a shop the other night on their way through Heliodor. Shopping with Zowan had cleared Kira's head, at the very least. Her blood wasn't boiling at the mere thought of Tigran anymore. Certainly, watching the mage who ran the shop use her Shadow magic on the weaving loom had distracted Kira for quite a while.

She sniffed, peering into another alcove. The Hall of Spirits contained statues dedicated to the various spirits of the realm, ones local to particular regions, as well as spirits that served the entire realm. She was on her second pass through it today, though, and she had yet to spot the wispy woman she had encountered in the bath house. Did she have another form? Was Kira just missing her? Or was it a spirit that Lord Raiden didn't know about?

The form of a large dog leered at her from the next alcove, and she quickly walked past, averting her eyes. She didn't need to study that one. She had gotten quite close and personal with the real thing, when it had been driven to chaos, and attacked her back in the Starless Realm.

Who was the mysterious wisp? Perhaps she would need to wait until she was back at Gekkō-ji, when she could ask Thistle. He had rejoined her as they collected their horses from the palace stables, but left her side when they passed by Mount Gekkō. She was a little disappointed that Gekkō bade him to return to the mountain. Thistle knew a lot about spirits and would probably be able to help Kira figure it out. She shook her head and continued on. *I should just ask Lord Raiden,* she thought.

With a jolt to her stomach, she picked up her pace, remembering that she was supposed to be meeting Raiden at noon. What with her training, and his duties leading the Spire, it was the first time she would get to speak with him since returning a few days ago. She had no idea what time it was, but her stomach was rumbling enough to indicate it might be nearing lunchtime. She hadn't had anything to eat all day since a quick apple before morning meditation. She scanned the alcoves as she passed, but the familiar statues didn't offer her any answers.

Since returning, she had flung herself back into Shadow training with determined abandon. Now that she had finished at Gekkō-ji, she couldn't wait to become a Shadow mage, too, and finally get her title of Gray Knight. Maybe then she would have the courage to speak freely to Empress Mei. Maybe then she could finally do something about Tigran.

Perhaps by then, they would have some proof.

Kira entered the Jade Foyer with a sigh. Part of her wanted to keep training here forever, learning all the new possibilities of Shadow magic, living in the Gray Wing where her father had lived during his time here. And if it weren't for Tigran, she might not feel as if she had to rush.

Rush and you'll ruin it, her mother used to say to her, and Kira snorted as the words floated through her brain. There were plenty of times Kira tried to rush through a school project or some baking they did together. One particular memory of the time her mother was teaching her how to make bread brought warmth to her cheeks as she recalled the hard lump of bread Kira had produced after rushing through the rising process. The twinge in her heart at the thought of her mother was a small pain, but the remembered words of advice triggered a sense of calm over her. She shook her head, clearing it. *No, I shouldn't rush. I'll train as long as I have to.*

And it's not like the Empress will automatically do what any Gray Knight says. It hadn't saved Sir Jovan and the others from being locked up.

Finishing my training will only be the beginning.

It was with this mix of dread and excitement that she gazed around the Jade Foyer. The enormous jade fountain in the center sent waves of calm over Kira as water trickled over the large sphere at the center of the small pool. Above her loomed the interior of the Spire's tower, impossibly tall, with each level smaller than the one before it. Sound seemed to press down on her from above, making the foyer feel less vast. A golden-armed clock on the far wall of the foyer indicated she still had half an hour until she needed to meet Raiden, so she trooped over to the double doors that led to the Gray Wing.

Before disappearing down the small dark hallway, she glanced over her shoulder toward another corridor that led to the Apothecarium. She still hadn't seen Micah yet, but she knew he was busy. There was some illness or other they were dealing with, and as usual, they were understaffed. Healing wasn't a very common proficiency with Shadow mages, so there were only a handful of mages who could use the highly sought-after magic to cure a disease or heal a wound. And such magic took multiple treatments, Kira knew, so the potions and salves they crafted in the Apothe-carium were in high demand too.

Maybe I'll send another note to Micah tomorrow, Kira thought. She always let him know when she had returned by floating a message through the corridors of the Spire to Micah's quarters. *Maybe my first note got lost.*

The two Commonality soldiers posted outside the Gray Wing ignored her as she stalked inside. The doors boomed shut behind her. She made for the wing's cozy kitchen, shaking off the agitation at seeing Tigran's soldiers. They had been here since last year, and she could mostly ignore them—until now.

The common room was tidy; she and Jun were sure to keep it in good order or risk the wrath of the Spirekeep-er. She entered the kitchen and began grazing on some fruit and a couple meat-filled steamed buns left over from what she and Zowan had bought in Heliodor last night. Whenever Zowan was in residence at the Spire, he always made a point to make sure Kira had enough food in the Wing's tiny kitchen, or treated her to a meal in the city every so often. And of course, whenever Jun was here, they would all eat together, sometimes in Zowan's permanent lodgings in the castle—now that no one else was allowed in the Gray Wing.

She hoped Jun would return sooner rather than later. Even though he had grown up knowing he would run the Kosumoso estate, he despised the responsibility now. Kira thought she understood. Having to run his family's estate because his father was wrongly imprisoned would certainly be an aggravating task. *With any luck, he will have found a factor to take care of the estate for him*, she thought as she washed her small meal down with some water from the pump. She grinned at the water basin, admiring whatever mix of engineering and Shadow magic that made the water flow so quickly and easily after only one pull on the pump. It was almost like being back in the Starless Realm.

Back out in the castle, she was halfway to Raiden's study when a folded piece of paper zoomed right up to her, almost hitting her in the face. She snatched it out of the air and opened it.

Meet me at the top.

-R

She groaned. She was glad she had eaten a light lunch and skipped doing a training session this morning. The top of the Spire was likely fifty stories high, and quite enough sets of stairs.

Turning around, she headed back to the Jade Foyer, where she found the grand stone staircase that would lead her up. On the second floor, the stairs turned to wood, lining the interior of each level and giving her a view of the foyer as she looked over the railing. She knew from experience that around the twentieth floor she would need to stop looking over the railing.

Lessons were taught mostly on the lower fifteen levels, and the higher up they went, the smaller and less populated the levels became. She passed offices and workrooms that the masters inhabited, and soon she began to walk past the occasional shrine to one of the various local spirits or another.

Finally, breath heaving and thighs wobbling like jelly, she drew back a heavy curtain on the final interior level, revealing the last set of stairs which led up and out.

She soon found herself at the top of the Spire, at the top of all Heliodor, the city spreading out in a circle to the south. On the north side of the temple lay some verdant mountains, with the city's wall in between.

There were no railings, no guardrail, only an open platform with a roof and the supports at the corners. The sight would terrify her more if she didn't know there was a protective magical barrier surrounding them.

In the center of the platform stood a silver statue of a dragon. It held a large spherical crystal, which was used to determine trainees' abilities by detecting the magical possibilities of the soul.

The Storm King had his back to her, seemingly admiring the view of the mountains. He turned when he heard her footsteps on the platform, and gave her a bow.

Raiden looked the same as ever, his wavy black hair bouncing lightly off his black-clad shoulders, and his mage's robes embroidered with a veritable sea of raindrops done in silver thread at the bottom. He froze when he noticed her white sash, then shook his head and bowed a little. "Congratulations, Lady Starwind."

She gave him a timid smile. "Thank you."

"I hear you met the new Commonality commander the evening of your ceremony," he said.

Kira flinched, recalling the slim man who stood by while the soldiers attacked Nari with unharnessed Light magic. "I did. He hasn't been here yet, has he?"

"He came to the Spire a few days ago—the day after he visited Gekkō-ji I believe. I'm thankful my nephew dispatched a note."

"Oh, yes," Kira said. "He wanted to warn you."

"Something has changed now that they have their decanters. *Everything* has changed. That is why we will meet up here from now on. They left even more soldiers this time; the place will soon be overrun with them."

Kira was glad her training at Gekkō-ji had kept her in such good shape. Fifty sets of stairs every time Raiden wanted to talk to her? She shook her head.

He correctly interpreted her silence. "You know first-hand there are mages who can listen at a distance," he chastised.

"You're right," she muttered. It was something she herself had been training in here at the Spire, among her other abilities. But long-distance listening was rarer than manipulating wind or water, so it required more effort to perfect.

Raiden continued. "And we can't assume Tigran hasn't recruited any other mages to his side."

Kira nodded. "At least Ryn can read the auras of the soldiers for us, see if they have mag—oh, I guess that doesn't matter anymore," she said darkly. "They can all use magic now."

To her surprise, Raiden let out a deep guffaw. "Hardly. I'd like to see these soldiers try to wield captive Shadow magic—in fact, I can't wait," he added with relish.

Kira silently agreed. Shadow magic was notoriously difficult to manage without proper preparation and training. "I don't know whether it will be a failure, when they try to use Shadow, or just complete chaos."

"Hmm," Raiden said. "Indeed. Though I'm sure we don't need to fear them accessing such intricate magic as eavesdropping or mind manipulation with simply *Shadow from a glass bottle*," he said, voice dripping in disgust, "but we do still need to be wary of spies."

"They've got these lanterns, too. I saw one at the palace," she said, and went on to explain her fruitless visit the other day.

Raiden listened in silence, studying the view as she spoke. Finally, he said, "This is it."

Kira felt a wave of something mysterious roll over her, as if Raiden had uttered a spell—one that made her experience both dread and excitement in regard to the future.

"I think so too," she said quietly. "Nari is on the run; Tigran is taking magic..." She didn't need to go on.

A part inside of her was almost excited. She *wanted* something to happen, for the scales to tip and for them to finally act against Tigran. Though she hated to disagree with her grandfather, she was tired of waiting. This whole year, the frustration of inaction had dogged her every move. It was hard to meditate when your enemies roamed free. Though, it did make weapons training easier when she imagined smashing in Tigran's smirking face with every blow to a training dummy.

Her longing to act against Tigran was tempered by the memory of just how quickly the Empress had imprisoned the Gray Knights. All it had taken was Tigran's word. And though the Empress seemed to favor Kira, Tigran had been at her side for decades.

The frustration at the situation bubbled up again, and she sighed, forcibly turning her gaze out over the city.

Raiden said, "Lady Madora thinks we should attack the Commonality and draw out Tigran; put an end to it with swift violence."

"Really?"

He nodded. "I was visiting her when I received Zowan's message—a good thing he sent it, or I wouldn't have been here to receive him. I left Lady Madora's manor immediately.

"That woman is spirited when it comes to power and those who wield it—or wish to. Perhaps with the help of the Stone Mountains we could..." He shook his head. "Madora would never help us without an obscene amount of collateral. Tigran isn't meddling with her affairs, so she has no reason to step in."

"What does she want?"

"Everything and anything. To force all the mages back to the Stone Mountains who originated there, I know for sure. She'd likely rule the Spire if offered the opportunity. And anything else that would make her more powerful."

"Hmm," Kira said, knowing she herself was something Madora wanted. As soon as Madora had discovered Kira's heritage using her past-seeing Shadow magic, Kira's value as a political ally had more than doubled, and Lady Madora had wanted to be the first to make a bid for her.

"Well, what's our next move with the Stone Mountains?" she asked, unsure.

"That I don't know. Aita is still trying to annoy Madora into helping us, or at least not harming the situation any further."

Kira repressed a snort. The diminutive former commander of the Commonality had been irritating in her determination to serve the Empress, until she realized what Tigran's real purpose for the Commonality was. The Stone Mountains had seemed a safe place for the woman after she defected. Not many people there had magic, so they didn't rely on it much, and valued other skills more. Aita fit in well, having been a skilled fighter in Tigran's army.

"I'm not afraid of Madora," Kira said.

"I have no doubt," Raiden replied. "But even if you were to ally yourself with her, you have the whole realm to serve, not just one region."

"You're right." She stuffed her hands into her pockets, thinking. "Well, I'm not against attacking the soldiers to flush out Tigran and his cronies. I can't tell if he's using magic on the Empress to control her, or if he's simply convinced her too well. Those lanterns shouldn't allow magic in the Palace, so you would think she would be safe from Nia Mari and Nikoletta. Tigran said they brought the prisoners to some Commonality barracks, but I don't know if that's true. Anzu and some other knights were supposed to be tracking them."

Raiden made an annoyed noise in his throat. "And with Nari on the run we no longer have a safe way to communicate between the temples to find out what they saw."

Kira allowed herself to grin as she thought of her own sentinel. "Actually, I'm work—"

Movement out of the corner of her eye made her turn toward the front entrance of the city. A dark mass was moving toward the city's gates, and with swaths of green uniforms on horseback, Kira only had one guess as to who they were.

"Well, that can't be good," she whispered.

CHAPTER 7

KEPT MAGIC

S he darted toward the stairs, ready to start the long descent, but Raiden's lack of movement made her pause.

"Shouldn't we—" she began.

His back was turned to her, and tiny flicks of lightning crackled around his wrists. She took a deep breath, and a tentative step forward as if approaching a rearing horse. "We should get to the foyer. We'll be down by the time they reach the Spire. And we can see what they want. I'm sure it's just more red tape they want to tangle us in."

"Tape?" Raiden said, turning his head, momentarily distracted by the unfamiliar term. "Why is red—Never mind." He shook his head and she flushed; she tried not to use odd phrases from her previous life around Raiden.

"No," he said, "we won't meet them in the foyer. I have a better idea."

He held out a hand, palm up. Drawing it in a straight horizontal line across his midsection, he let out a barely audible breath.

Kira felt a massive disturbance in the air around her, and straightened her shoulders. The new pauldrons and chest-piece she had begun wearing gave her some semblance of security. "What—"

Before she could continue, she saw the air shimmer around the four edges of the platform, revealing the invisible magical barrier that acted as walls. It continued to shimmer, wavering in the mid-day light, until finally it stopped. A brisk wind ripped through the platform, and Kira gripped Raiden's arm, her heart hammering.

"My apologies," he rumbled, nodding at the lack of barrier, which also kept out the wind at this immense height.

Kira opened her mouth but was having trouble deciding just what to say, as the realization hit her that they were now standing atop the Spire with no safety barrier between them and a fifty-story drop.

Then she realized she was still gripping the Storm King's arm like a vice. She looked up at him, but far from appearing as if he wanted her to let go, he was gesturing for her other arm.

A thrill of terror and excitement went through her as she finally realized what he intended. She nodded. She had flown with him on the wind once before, after all. "All right. Let's go," she said, and she stepped closer to grasp his shoulder. He steadied his arms around her and the wind that played atop the Spire began to condense around them. Kira's breath froze in her lungs as she felt her feet lift off the ground.

She glued her gaze to the Spire as Raiden lifted them out and into the open air. She felt another shimmer of Shadow magic, and Raiden's fingers twitching somewhere around her shoulder. The barrier around the top level shimmered back into existence as they flew away from it.

Wind whipped around them, and Kira's mind reeled.

She had never seen the tower this close from the outside. Why would she? Raiden faced forward as he lifted them on the wind toward the gates of Heliodor, so she stared at the Spire as they flew further and further from the magically balanced structure. The elaborately-tiled roof on the top level extended into the sky like a needle, and the four corners each boasted a tile with a somewhat-demonic face. The Spire's librarian had once told Kira that these tiles were meant to ward off evil—Kira had never expected to see them in person after perusing a scroll on Camellian architecture.

She had a minute to marvel at the gables and various decorative tiles on each level before they were halfway across the city. The wind whipped at their robes and she spared a second thought for what her hair might look like when they landed.

Glancing over her shoulder at their destination, she couldn't quite see the army anymore, but Raiden's path on the wind had started to descend, bringing them closer to Heliodor's gate. A thrill of worry threaded through her as she wondered whether they should have just stayed at the Spire and received the Commonality there.

But she didn't think Raiden would have gone down to the foyer with her, and it was probably best that he didn't confront them alone.

No, that was her job now, to help keep the balance and protect the realm. She shuddered from more than just the sudden drop in height as they reached the gate.

In a flurry of wind, she and Raiden landed right in front of the gatehouse, with its gabled roof similar to the Spire, but with an elaborate motif carved above the open doorway, featuring koi fish and flowing water. A rush of adrenaline surged through Kira's veins as she stood at attention, straightening her neck and throwing her shoulders back, her new armor creaking satisfyingly like leather, though she had crafted it from Light magic this morning after meditation.

At the head of the army stood the new commander, tall and wiry, his gray hair cropped close to his skull. This man, Commander Hagane, was nothing like the former commander. He exuded a strange, angry energy that made Kira uneasy. She adjusted her white sash with a crisp swat of her hand, and angled her body slightly toward Raiden, who had much recovered from their flight, his wavy hair not even looking out of place. Kira resisted the urge to check her hair, sure it would make her look self-conscious. If it was windblown, so be it.

At least Tigran wasn't here, too.

For an achingly awkward moment, Kira wondered who would speak first. Both men stood there with their lips pressed tight, staring the other down.

Should *she* say something? Her gaze flicked over the soldiers, but they all stood at polite attention, each equipped with one of those foul decanters. And then Kira noticed that the sky above them had begun to darken. What had started as a sunny afternoon was quickly becoming overcast, and one glance at Raiden told Kira just how that came to be.

She cleared her throat, unsure what to say but knowing she should say *something* to derail Raiden from losing his temper. But that was enough to spur Raiden to speak.

"Commander," he acknowledged, not bowing his head in the slightest. Kira couldn't ignore the rumble of thunder that echoed in the clouds above them, though it sounded far off.

The commander narrowed his eyes, perhaps sensing the unnaturalness of the thunder as he gave a cordial nod to Raiden. His blank expression gave off no particular offense, but somehow the nod looked like a challenge to Kira.

"Commander," she said. "Welcome to Heliodor. Is there something—uh—Can we help you with something?" Deciding to feign politeness over Raiden's obvious preference for intimidation, she added, "Is there something the Empress requires?"

As the commander smiled, Kira thought he almost looked as demonic as one of the roof tiles atop the Spire. His nose twitched in a sneer as the corners of his mouth turned up. It didn't reach his cold eyes.

"Indeed, Lady Starwind," he answered. "The Empress has ordered the Commonality to traverse the realm in order to ensure we restore balance to Camellia, in light of recent concerns."

Confused, Kira smiled back at him, but sensed something sinister beneath his words. Her hopes that the Empress had taken Kira's words to heart were short-lived—obviously the soldiers were still using the decanters.

"And how may we assist in your quest?" Raiden said. The clouds above were still overcast, but at least they weren't crackling with electricity anymore.

"It is kind of you to meet us outside the gates," the commander said in a monotone. "But your... swiftness... in doing so was not required. I apologize if our presence caused any alarm."

Raiden nodded. "It is nothing. We were merely concerned that there... could have been an emergency that required an army in this region."

Hagane finally gave a small bow to the two of them. "That is valorous of you. However, such exhibitions... Such uses of magic are not necessary." He snapped his fingers and the entire contingent parted, forming a wide channel directly behind Hagane. A train of wagons trundled forward.

Kira's jaw dropped. Not because of the wagons themselves—or whatever mysterious contents they might hold—but because they were moving without the help of horses or donkeys. They were moving by themselves. Which could only mean...

"Her Highness has decreed, in an effort to restore a balance across the realm, that magic should serve everyone."

Kira and Raiden were silent as the wagons came forward in a cacophony of creaking wood and turning wheels. "And in order to serve everyone, it must be *available* to everyone, and not be allowed to be used in excess for frivolous purposes.

"These lanterns," he said, gesturing with an arm at the wagons, "will help with that. They will regulate the amount of ambient magic available to born magic users, making an equal amount available to those of us who can now use kept magic, therefore restoring balance."

CHAPTER 8

TORN

"*Kept magic?*" Kira muttered later, pacing across her study that evening. It wasn't a large room, and her angry footsteps didn't lead her far. She needed to go somewhere else.

She slammed the door to her quarters on her way out, which made her feel a little better. Still, she strode to the right, passing the other chambers, which were all unoccupied. At the end of the hallway, she stiff-armed one of the double doors open into the training room. The scent of the polished wood floors and a hint of dust sent a small wave of peace over her.

As she breathed out, she released the magic in her armor, letting the Light magic sink back into the world around her. She didn't need it right now. When it was all dispersed, she flicked her hand at the empty lamps hanging from the ceiling, sparking flames in all of them. Though the dim glow of Light magic allowed her to see everything, sometimes it wasn't enough. She sank down to sit on the floor, not trying to meditate, but hoping to regain a sense of calm.

She *wanted* to use her Shadow magic to blast rageful winds and spiteful storms all across the training room. But she would at least need a clear mind to do it right.

The thought of Hagane and the soldiers actually using kept magic troubled her so much that her stomach had been hurting since walking back from the gates with Raiden. Though she had wanted to pick his brain about how the Commonality could have possibly figured out how to move the wagons, one look at the dark expression on his face made her keep her musings to herself.

She had nothing against commoners wanting to use magic, but storing it indefinitely couldn't possibly be okay.

A loud noise just outside the training room made her eyelids snap open, and she drew to a stand, gathering Light magic into her core. With a practiced motion, she reformed her armor, the shoulder pieces, chest, and thigh guards she favored. If it was those soldiers trespassing in the Gray Wing...

She pulled more Light and Shadow into her core like gathering a deep lungful of air as she headed for the doors. Part of her was irate that they might be here to install one of those lanterns, and take away her full access to magic.

The other part of her was chastising herself for releasing her armor—not only would it protect her, but she might need the very magic stored there. She opened the training room doors with both hands, and the breath exploded out of her as she almost ran right into Jun, who was moving a small trunk into his quarters just outside.

"Oh, it's you!" she exclaimed, letting out a heady breath, and most of the magic she had gathered, save for a small portion she kept, just in case.

Jun glanced around, sensing the amount of magic returned to the space. "That bad, huh? What happened?"

Kira shook her head morosely and quickly explained about Tigran's lanterns. "When I heard you, I thought they were bringing one in here. I have no idea how many they have or where they'll be putting them, I just know Tigran is interfering with using magic for 'frivolous' purposes, and somehow he convinced the Empress this is how to return balance to the realm. Maybe me and Zowan visiting the palace pushed him into it... I don't know."

He shook his head, putting a foot on his trunk and leaning into his knee in a subconscious stretch. "So this will be a boring stay at the Spire then; got it."

She scowled at him. "*Ha ha*. Whatcha got there?" She nodded at the ornate wooden trunk.

His face lit up, and he glanced down at it. "Oh, just some stuff from home. I don't think I'll have to return there so frequently anymore."

"Oh, did you find someone to manage the estate?"

He nodded, a sly grin coming over his face. "Yep. All set. I won't have to answer any of the tenant's rent questions or even help with the barley anymore. Honestly, I don't know how my father did it all."

Kira studied him. "Wow, they must be someone you really trust. They're handling rents, too?"

His grin had become more and more like the Cheshire Cat's, and finally he said, "Oh, I trust them all right."

She rolled her eyes and let out a dramatic sigh. "Are you going to tell me who?"

"It's Ari."

"*Ari?*"

He nodded, beaming. "Master Starwind is allowing it. Ari can leave Gekkō-ji on occasion because technically he's squiring for me, and this will count for his year of squireship."

"What—what," Kira paused, shaking her head explosively at the idea. "What!" she repeated, then laughed.

Jun joined her, and Kira felt a pleasant jolt in her stomach to see Jun looking so happy for the first time in a while.

When they had finished, their fits of laughter egging each other on, she said, "So, wow, Ari's your squire?"

"Yeah," he said, his eyes shining. "What did you say to Nesma, did she go to the palace with you?"

Kira's face fell quite suddenly, and Jun froze at her expression.

"Oh," he said. "You said no?"

She grimaced, shrugging slightly. "Yeah; I mean, I wasn't ready for a squire, someone to depend on me for—I don't know, wisdom or protection and training."

He took his foot off his trunk and leaned up against the door jamb to his quarters, arms crossed. "I don't know if all that's required," he mused. "When we were told to pick a mage or knight to follow, it just said we needed someone who would set a good example—whether it be in skill or deeds."

The echo of what was likely Ichiro's words on that letter she and Jun had been given when they became squires made her smile a bit. "Yeah, I guess you're right. Maybe just after all my time with Zowan, I didn't feel like I could be that for Nesma. Not yet anyway."

Jun scoffed. "I think your skills and deeds are example-worthy. In fact, I think they're probably worth writing poems about—"

She punched him in the shoulder, somewhat hard. "Will you ever drop that?"

He grinned back at her, massaging his shoulder. "Never. Not until you get your own poet like that other Starless visitor."

She snorted, shaking her head. "Which I'd never allow. I guess I'll have to put up with your corny jokes forever. Well, do you want a hand with that?" She gestured at the trunk, eager to change the subject from squireships and poets.

"Sure," he said. "I think my shoulder might be broken now, I'll need the help."

She glanced at him in concern but his face was alight with mischief. "I'm sorry," she said earnestly.

"It's fine, Starless Girl," he said, lifting up one side of the trunk as she got the other; it was quite heavy for its size. "It was a light tap compared to what I had to go through during the knighting ceremony, or my entire training with Anzu, come to think of it."

Kira gasped, "We never got to talk about our trials!"

His mouth hung open for a second, then he said, "Oh yeah!"

After they placed the trunk inside his study, they went out into the common room and poked up the fire in the hearth, recanting each other with the tales of their combat trials with Nari. Jun absently pulled out a journal and began idly drawing while they talked. When Kira got to the part about her walk down the mountain, she let out a small gasp.

"What?" Jun demanded, lounging on one of the cushions and putting a ribbon in his journal.

"Gekkō told me there was someone who wanted to talk to me, and that night this spirit visited me in the bath house—he said she would help somehow with the balance."

He closed his journal hard, an eyebrow raised. "A spirit in the bath house? I've never seen one in there; you'd think the temple would ward it against such things, wouldn't they?"

She let out an involuntary chuckle. "Yeah… that is odd. I'd have to ask Ichiro. It wasn't weird or anything. But I can't seem to figure out who she is…" She told him every detail she could remember, and of her futile search of the Hall of Spirits.

He leaned back on his floor cushion, arms laced behind his head. "Ah, well you know where you could check—"

"The library," they said together, and she chuckled, shaking her head. "I don't really think I have time to search for a spirit on top of the research I was just assigned for illusionwork yesterday, and the practicing I'm supposed to be doing for my sound proficiency."

"Oh yeah, how's that going?"

"Good, Master Koichi wants me to experiment with other ways of using Shadow magic for sound, other than listening from far away. Like projecting a sound, or making something else quieter or louder." She shrugged, secretly pleased. It was one of those uncommon niches, but that meant she had to figure it all out on her own. "I'm just going to ask Thistle about the wisp next time I'm back at Gekkō-ji. Oh, I meant to ask Raiden, but—"

A knock at the door jerked them both to attention, and Jun's journal slipped to the floor. Kira stood as he gathered the papers that had come loose, and she said, "I'll get it."

She ran a few fingers through her hair as she sauntered over to the door, then pulled the heavy iron handle.

"Oh, hi Zowan," she said, wondering whether he came to invite them for dinner.

"You two, come with me," Zowan said, jerking his head at the dark corridor behind him.

Kira nodded, a cold coil of fear sliding into her stomach at his words. All thoughts of a nice dinner with the three of them slipped from her head.

Jun came to the door, his diamond-patterned chain mantle glittering into existence across his chest as he walked to the door. He lowered his chin in silent question at Zowan, who shook his head. *Not here*, his narrowed eyes clearly said.

As soon as they reached the end of the narrow corridor that led to the Jade Foyer and spotted one of the Commonality lanterns posted at the corner, Kira's pace faltered. But this was not what Zowan had come to show them, apparently, because he kept walking.

Kira glanced at Jun, but he just shrugged, the chain mantle he wore looking good on him. She frowned at Jun's tribute to his father's signature armor. She couldn't even imagine what Jun felt about his father being imprisoned for so long.

Zowan led them down the hallway toward the Apothecarium, but that wasn't their destination either. Instead, he turned left to open a tiny side door that Kira had never noticed before.

"Where does this go?" she whispered. They were alone in the corridor, but she couldn't help but worry about eavesdropping, after Raiden's warning earlier.

"Catacombs," Zowan replied tersely.

Kira didn't ask anything more, just stood back as Zowan summoned a small orb of flame in his palm to light the way. Kira and Jun followed suit. Even with the dim glow of Light she could see, it was still dark down there. She quickly brushed aside the idea that the Light essence was dimmer than usual—surely the lanterns couldn't work that quickly, or pull from the entire castle... could they?

The three flames hovered safely above them in the twisting narrow stairwell, the high ceiling almost dripping in cold condensation. Kira sniffed, inhaling the scent of dusty air and stone that is never completely dry. At least the closeness of the stairwell and the warm light of their fiery orbs drove the sense of unease from her shoulders, the sense that they were being watched or listened to. It was just the three of them, and the far-off sound of dripping water.

Zowan apparently thought they were safe from eavesdroppers as well, for he said, "There's something you two need to see, I—"

They all heard the soft sound of a footstep on the stairs. Kira's heart thundered in her chest as she summoned a dagger in her hand, the space being too cramped for her throwing knives or polearm. She watched eerie shadows bounce off the walls as first a small orb of fire came into view, then the immensely tall, cloaked figure of Raiden.

Kira exhaled, not dispersing her dagger, but lowering it.

"I got your note," Raiden said shortly, holding up a scrap of paper, his gaze on his nephew.

Zowan grunted, and turned back down the stairs as Raiden caught up to the group. At the bottom of the stairs, they came out into an open space, completely empty save for a small shrine in the center.

"Zowan..." Raiden began, but Zowan had started walking again. Kira followed, catching up to Zowan as he strode down the left side of the large square room, their flaming orbs floating above them. All along the wall were small squares of stone jutting out, each carved with names and symbols. She had never been down here before, but had heard of the place that was supposed to mirror the multi-tiered Spire above, going just as low as the Spire went high.

Though she was intensely curious, she didn't say anything to Zowan, knowing that oftentimes he just needed company and not someone constantly asking him questions or telling him things. With a start she realized that was likely why he and Anzu got along so well; the stalwart knight was not very free with her words either.

Kira bit her lip as she wondered when they would hear from Anzu. Shouldn't she be back by now? After all, Kira and Zowan had gone to the palace the next day after the prisoners had been taken from Gekkō-ji. Kira already missed Nari's fox messengers. They would have known whether Anzu had returned safely from spying on Tigran and the prisoners.

She would just have to teach herself how to make her own sentinels carry messages. Her skill at sending notes on the wind was really only good enough to cover the temple grounds, not long distances. The sentinels, if her will was strong enough when creating them, could traverse the realm.

When they got to the corner, Zowan led them down another staircase, to another floor, then another. On the third level down, Zowan finally spoke as he continued walking.

"I came down here earlier and found something," he told them, turning the corner to yet another staircase, each level becoming smaller than the last. "I can't help but wonder if it happened because of those new lanterns."

"What is it?" Jun asked.

"You'll see," Zowan said darkly. "I can't rightly explain."

Kira pressed her lips tight. She had a feeling she knew why Zowan had been down here, but she wasn't going to ask, and she was glad Jun hadn't either. Surely his wife and child had a stone marker down here somewhere.

Her eyes flicked back to where Raiden strode quietly behind her, and Kira wasn't surprised to see the normally forthright and boisterous man walking reverently along the unmarked path beside the wall, eyes downcast in respect.

At the next floor Zowan halted, and stepped aside so they could see.

They were five stories down, and this level was still fairly large, but the thing that Zowan had found was obvious from the far corner in which they stood.

Kira hadn't known what to expect, but the jagged tear in the very air in the center of the room was not it. It was an electric blue color, but with sickly bright edges, and there was a sort of manic energy in the air around it. There was no audible sound, but all of Kira's senses could feel it. It was wrong, like sticking your tongue on a battery, but also like being in a wind tunnel with no wind—her very ears and skin were assaulted by some unseen force.

Raiden drew himself up. "Ah," he said, and went right over to it.

Kira eyed the back of his retreating cloak in a mixture of fear and respect. "Is it—is it a portal to the Starless Realm?" she asked in a small voice, though it carried across the wide open space. Thoughts whirled in her head as she thought of New York and buses, tall buildings, and fast food. Her entire vision swam for a second while her stomach experienced something similar at the memories she hadn't touched in a long time. She swallowed, amazed her mouth was watering at the mere thought of salty French fries.

"I'm certainly no expert," Raiden said, turning back to look at her for a second. "But I don't think so. This looks far worse than a portal to another world."

Kira, Jun, and Zowan came closer, but stopped perhaps eight feet from it. She had no desire to get any closer; the horrible feeling or vibration coming from it made her head ache and her teeth hurt. But what was worse was the ache in her gut at the thought of what this tear might mean. "Gekkō said the balance was broken," she said in a whisper, "He said something about the very fabric of the realm eroding."

They all stared at it in silence, with Raiden getting a closer look and circling around it. "I think you're right, Zowan," Raiden finally said, drawing away and rejoining them. "This can't have been here before, and those *lanterns*—" he nearly spat the word "—are pulling in as much magic as they can across the castle, and who knows where else."

Zowan nodded, not looking at his uncle, but instead gazing at a set of stone markers inlaid in the wall to their right.

"Then there could be more, couldn't there?" Jun said.

"We'll search the castle," Raiden said. "And send messengers across the realm, but avoid speaking with the Commonality, for now." He brought a hand to his chin in thought.

"Before the whole realm is torn apart."

CHAPTER 9

PROOF

Kira yawned as she shifted to get a twig out from under her leg. She sat on the bank of the brook in the corner of the Spire's grounds. Taking another deep breath to re-center herself, she was glad to see that her concentration hadn't faltered; her sphere of water still hovered a foot off the brook.

Carefully, she reached out with more Shadow magic and added more water to the sphere. It grew larger without bursting, and she waited another moment before continuing on. Her trousers were already a bit damp from earlier. Her nature proficiency lesson hadn't gone very well, and she needed to squeeze in some extra practice.

She would have to head back to the castle soon. She was supposed to be meeting Micah for a late dinner out in the courtyard by the lake, finally. He had apologetically responded to her note this morning and found time in his schedule. She still needed to stop by the Gray Wing to grab the picnic she had prepared.

The mage who taught nature proficiencies, Etaro, hadn't laughed when she got soaked earlier by a rogue waterspout. In fact, he had gone on to explain the same rhetoric she had been taught about Shadow magic from the beginning: if you don't approach Shadow magic with your thoughts and emotions in control, then you can't expect to control Shadow magic.

She had merely nodded and let Jun apply some warm air to her clothes before carrying on. It was clear that Kira had stronger proficiencies for water—even if it was still erratic—whereas Jun excelled with air. After she had moved an entire waterfall at Azurite, she wasn't surprised, but she was coming to learn not to expect such impressive results every time she worked with Shadow magic—it was only ever as good as her focus was.

And right now, it was all she could do to tamp down the fear and anxiety the sight of that tear last night had instilled in her.

Kira and Jun had stayed up late last night deep in conversation in the common room, the hearth radiating a pleasant warmth against the early spring chill as they discussed what Zowan found in the catacombs. No one had seen anything like it before. Even when Tigran had sum-

moned a primitive portal to escape from Gekkō-ji's cells
way back when they thought they had captured him as the
Lord of Between. His escape portal had looked nothing
like this tear beneath the Spire. Kira always thought he had
gone to the Starless Realm and come back elsewhere, the
possibility of which was somewhat terrifying and thrilling.

She had often entertained the thought of somehow returning to the Starless Realm ever since she had come here,
but with the passing of years the thoughts had grown less
and less frequent. It was usually only when she thought of
her mother, and their life together. But with her mother
gone, there was really no point. Her life was here, where
she had learned about the rest of her family, and the magic
she was capable of. And, even more importantly, she had
friends here, and people that were just as close as family,
and of course her last living relative, Ichiro.

But the idea that Tigran might go there sickened her.
What would he be doing there? Was he just using it to pass
through? Could he use his magic there?

Surely he could, she answered herself as she gazed unseeing at her water orb. Even before Kira had come to
Camellia, she had started seeing Light magic before she
knew what it was. She remembered all too well those few
days where she thought she was going crazy.

She tried to focus her eyes again, to concentrate on her water sphere. The swirling water bobbed a bit, and she tightened her focus.

Yet she couldn't help her thoughts from returning to her fears. Tigran. The decanters. Anzu still missing from her quest. And the tear.

What scared her most was the look on Raiden's face last night. Even he looked afraid.

Did Tigran even know what horrible consequences his decanters and lanterns had unleashed? And if he *was* aware of them, then his intentions were even more sinister than they had imagined. When he had summoned those doors around the realm, driving the spirits to chaos, surely he knew the consequences, since he kept repeating the experiment. But this time... Kira wasn't so sure. The tear, if that's what it was, seemed much more dangerous.

But if Tigran could escape to the Starless Realm, then, well, perhaps he didn't need this one after all.

A spray of water hit her in the face, and it was the only warning she got before the entire sphere burst, sending water all over her and the mossy bank. She opened her mouth in surprise; water dripped down her face and she closed her lips. She shook her head and arms, flicking cold water off herself.

"I really need to stop doing that," she muttered to herself, cursing for letting her mind wander so freely.

Laughter erupted behind her, and she whipped around to see Ryn Kimura striding long-legged down the path through the small woods toward her, his dark robes with silver fasteners down the front a rival to the extravagance of Lord Raiden's. She grimaced good-naturedly at her obvious predicament, happy to set aside thoughts of Tigran and the realm for the moment.

"With your aura as angry as all that," he said, smirking, "I'm surprised you didn't get water on *me*."

Kira felt her cheeks warm but shrugged it off. "Yes, well I think I have good reason."

"I don't doubt it," he said, coming to join her on the bank and standing over her.

"Sit down, why don't you," she said, "I'll break my neck looking up with you hovering over me like that."

Ryn brought a hand to his chest as though wounded. "Well. I should have known better than to stand over an angry Gray mage."

Kira covered her face with a hand. "I'm sorry," she said. "It's not your fault, Ryn. I'm just soaked—again—and there's just—a lot happening."

"Well of course there is," he said, lowering down and testing the moss for wetness. Apparently, he found a dry spot and sat cross-legged beside her. "It wouldn't be life if nothing were happening."

A wry smile brought up one corner of her mouth. "Well, aren't you clever."

He returned the smile with a genuine one, his narrow face lighting up. "Why, thank you. You're pretty clever yourself, Miss Knight. Or should I say Lady Starwind?" he said with a little bow.

She looked down for a second at her white sash then smiled back up at him. "I think 'Kira' is fine still," she said loftily, flicking some imaginary dust off her sash. Ryn nodded seriously, and she burst into a fit of giggles, dropping the sash.

When Ryn's chuckles subsided, he said, "Oh, I wish I could have come see your test, but Lord Raiden wouldn't let me."

"Really? I didn't know that."

"Well, when I'm not teaching, he has me randomly scanning auras throughout the castle. Since I can recognize the shapeshifter."

A shiver ran up her spine at that. "Wow, I had no idea you were doing that. He thinks Tigran would try to come here disguised?"

"Apparently," he said, shrugging.

Suppressing a growl, she said, "Well, we know where Tigran was the night of the ceremony anyway, right there at Gekkō-ji."

A bird flitted through the trees and landed on the opposite bank to dip its beak in the water. Kira glanced at the path that led out of the woods and back toward the castle, the towering Spire always visible no matter where in the grounds she was.

"Mmm," Ryn agreed, and Kira filled him in on the finer details of the Commonality's visit during her ceremony. When she got done telling him about Mistress Nari's sentinels, she shivered, a cold breeze turning the water on her skin and clothes to ice.

"Do you want to head inside? I'm freezing. I wish spring would hurry up," she added under her breath. "Oh, and I'm meeting Micah for dinner in a little while; I should probably change." She took a second to focus and pulled in some Light magic to form a wool-like wrap around her shoulders. Knitting the Light into fibers with her mind always gave her a strange pleasure. Something she had spent hours upon hours learning, condensed into the space of a breath. Then she stood, pleased with the warm result as she pulled it tight around her.

Ryn grinned as he unfolded his long legs and joined her. "You're pretty good at that."

She snorted. "Knight, remember?"

"And soon to be Gray Knight," he said, touching the silver inverted-V pin on his chest, the symbol for the Spire.

"Probably not anytime *soon*. Not if I still can't hold a bucket's worth of water longer than a minute without getting soaked." She picked up her leather satchel that contained her notebooks and brush pen and ink, and the two of them headed down the path.

"I'm confident you'll get it," he said. "I seem to remember you moving the entire Falls at Azurite and holding onto all *that* water."

Heat flooded to her face. If only she could repeat such control. She quickly changed the subject. "Were you just going for a stroll out here or what?"

They followed the gravel path up a gentle incline from the wooded area, heading for the castle. The surrounding lawns were a muted green, still dull from winter. Suddenly, everything around her began twinkling with Light magic. She turned to the west and realized the sun had set.

"I was looking for you," Ryn said.

"Why?" Adrenaline rushed through her chest. "Is something wrong?"

He shook his head. "No, no, obviously not. I would have said so in the first place, not passed the time of day with you about knit shawls and knighthood." He gestured vaguely at her with a mischievous smile. At her questioning look though, he said, "Well, I finished giving my afternoon lecture, but I couldn't *stand* being in my study; those roaches from the Commonality installed one of those *things* right outside my quarters. I heard what they do, but I can feel it too, you know? Like a constant ebbing in the magic around me. So I went to Lord Raiden to see if he could do anything about it—but when I did, he told me about the... the tear that Lord Zowan found?"

"Ah," Kira said. "Yes. What do you think? What did Raiden tell you?"

"Well, I haven't seen it yet. You tell me. What do *you* think, Lady Knight?"

Despite his good-natured ribbing, Kira bit the inside of her lip. As they neared the castle, they slowed, so she could explain in detail everything she had seen last night in the catacombs. Though Kira desperately wanted to get out of her chilly clothes and, if she had time, take a quick bath to warm up her extremities, she wanted to speak freely with Ryn.

"...And Gekkō warned me. At first, I didn't really know what he meant; he's given me warnings before and he is never really very clear about them. And of course, when I told the Empress, she said his warning was important, but didn't want to listen to us about the decanters or the lanterns. All because we didn't have any proof that storing magic like this would be harmful." She gasped. "But now we *have* proof! She can't pretend this tear isn't a problem—one that appeared right after they put in all those lanterns here."

They were nearing the base of the castle, the stone foundation towering over their heads, more than three times as tall as Ryn. Some of the stones were as big as a chair, while a handful were even bigger than cars. Just like the Spire tower, the castle at the bottom had been shaped by Shadow magic.

They reached the entrance, and she glanced at Ryn. They nodded in unspoken agreement, knowing they could be overheard by anyone as they entered the castle. Kira lit a small flame that she held in front of her. Since the sun was down now, she could see by the dim Light essence around her, but the warmth of the flame was heavenly.

Ambient Light essence was noticeably dimmer by the time they reached the Hall of Spirits, where a lantern stood at the entrance. Kira glared at it as they walked past and banished the flame she had summoned. She pictured the lantern sucking up some of the essence she let go of and huffed.

"Well, that's one good thing about them," Ryn said. "That you can use it as proof."

Kira nodded slowly as they walked by a statue of an un-remarkable boy who was apparently the spirit of mischief in the Seven Days Forest, according to the plaque. "You're right. I bet I can go to the palace again. I can ask Lord Raiden tomorrow. But what will I even tell the Empress?" she asked, not expecting an answer. "We don't even know what it is."

Clucking his tongue, Ryn said, "I don't know, I haven't even seen the thing."

They had reached the wide Jade Foyer, where four lanterns stood, one in each corner, soaking up ambient magic essence. How much magic were they storing? And where would they bring it?

To Tigran, surely. And what he would do with all the stockpiled magic of the realm was anyone's guess. Obviously, the Commonality was already using captive Shadow magic for transporting more lanterns, but the possibilities were endless now that someone had figured out how to use the kept magic.

Anger burned through her at the idea. She reached up to her knit wrap and released the magic there, dispersing it into the air. It was wrong to keep it when it wasn't being used. After throwing another dirty look at the lanterns, she glanced at Ryn. "Let's go see," she said quietly, nodding at the corridor that led to the Apothecarium and the catacombs.

"Now? I think Lord Raiden was going to show me later with some of the other mages."

"Well, I know where it is, and I want to get another look at it," Kira said, and then she had an idea and lowered her voice even more. "And maybe with your aura reading skills you can see something I can't."

"Don't you have dinner with Micah?"

"Oh!" she said, blinking and then glancing at the large gold-faceted clock at the end of the foyer. "I can't believe I almost forgot. I should go change and get the food! I made us a little picnic; we're meeting by the meditation pavilion."

He straightened and smiled, light in his eyes dancing, "Aren't you sweet."

Kira rolled her eyes. "We have to eat, don't we?" she said gruffly. "And you know perfectly well I'm not supposed to have guests in the Gray Wing anymore."

"Yes, that is quite annoying," he agreed. "You and Jun have that whole place to yourselves—did they even put any of those lanterns in there?"

"Not yet," she said, shaking her head. "I better go."

He bowed, at the same time waving with a grand gesture. She chuckled and skipped off to the Gray Wing, thoughts of warm clothes and delicious food quickening her pace.

She had just finished tying a knot in the maroon fabric she had used to bundle up the little picnic when she heard the heavy *boom* of the wing doors shutting. Hoping to catch Jun before she left, she headed out of the tiny kitchen with her picnic bundle. Jun was striding in the direction of his quarters.

"Hey," she called.

He whirled around. His face was blotchy and streaked with tears. Taken aback, Kira reached out with one hand. "Jun, what's wrong?"

Blinking, he mustered his thoughts and dashed the backs of his hands over his cheeks. "I—I—" He huffed, looking up at the ceiling as if to find words there.

She dropped her bundle and took a few steps toward him. "What's wrong?" she repeated quieter.

"It's—" he stopped, gulped, and said, "It's about my father and the other Gray Knights. I've had a letter."

It was as if a cold stone slipped heavy into Kira's stomach. "Did they set another trial date?"

"It's not a trial. It's an execution."

CHAPTER 10

COMMONERS AND MAGIC FOLK

With the sun fully down, the early spring night was brisk as she and Jun walked down the covered open-air walkway that led to the meditation pavilion beside the lake. Now swathed in several layers of clothing, with a real knit wrap around her shoulders, Kira clutched her bundle tightly as she walked beside Jun.

She couldn't leave him alone in the Gray Wing after his news, but she couldn't very well abandon Micah and her plans for dinner. Since Jun hadn't eaten yet, he had acquiesced to her awkward invitation, and they packed an extra cup and bowl. She was sure Micah wouldn't mind.

"Have you noticed it?" Jun asked after they had walked in silence for several minutes. There were a few other trainees about on the temple lawns, having their evening meal in the gardens, or laying in the grass with their noses in books, or simply enjoying the clear evening. It was still cold, but after a winter spent indoors, everyone was ready to be outside again. Kira glanced up at the sky, and as always was struck by the incredible number of glittering stars there. An ever-present reminder that she was not in the land she had grown up in.

"Noticed what?" she said.

He nodded at the lantern at the edge of the pavilion they approached. "Less ambient magic."

"Honestly I've been trying to avoid them," she said.

"Getting hard to do," he muttered.

They entered the pavilion and went about halfway down and sat on the edge, facing the lake.

"Micah will probably be a few more minutes," Kira said with a quick glance at the sky. Night was falling, and though she wasn't adept at telling time from such things yet, she was much better at it than when she had first come to the realm. "He never gets out early. If anything, he might be late."

"How come he still works there?" Jun asked. "They barely get any time off."

"Well, Spectra loves it, the herbal recipes, the cleaning, helping people... And Micah's told me he'd rather work somewhere he can watch out for her."

She opened the food bundle and positioned herself to watch for Micah. The smell of steamed vegetables and rice wafted up and Kira inhaled appreciatively, almost tasting the tangy brown sauce she had slathered over the vegetables before packing them up.

"The lanterns…" she said, circling their conversation back, "they feel… funny. Like you're being pulled at, you know?"

Jun made a noise of agreement.

She pulled out the ceramic cups and set them on the top step. Then she took out an object she had made from Light magic, which Jun was always quite impressed with. It was an insulated thermos—a word no one in the Realm of Camellia had heard before—that she made of Light. There wasn't any insulation between the double walls of the canister, but it kept tea warmer than if she had made a single-walled canister.

Jun unpacked the cheese-stuffed rolls she had bought. With a glance at the empty walkway, and a raise of his eyebrows at Kira, who nodded, he took a bite of one. "I notice the lanterns' effect mostly inside the Spire," he said between bites. "When I was in my study session with Master Koji, earlier. There's two lanterns on that floor now. I was trying to use illusionwork on a practice ball far away from me, right? But I needed to pull more Shadow and… I feel like I had to give it a much harder pull than usual, you know?"

Kira nodded slowly, picturing it in her head the way she pictured herself drawing magic from her surroundings. It often felt like she was reaching out and pulling, and the strength of the pull depended on how much she needed. Normally, everything she needed was right beside her. "Well, Tigran's trying to limit us doing 'unnecessary' magic."

An ugly sigh escaped Jun at Tigran's name. Kira's heart constricted.

She handed Jun the tea canister, knowing he would enjoy unscrewing the lid and pouring it out. He caught her eye as he took it from her and poured two cups. Kira lifted hers and gazed out at the lake, thinking. "We have to do something. I'm getting tired of waiting."

Jun didn't say anything, but they both looked up at the sound of footsteps on the walkway from the castle.

A smile pulled up the corners of Kira's mouth as she looked over, but the figure approaching had armor on, their shoulders bulky, and they carried a helmet under their arm. In the dim glow of Light magic, Kira could also see they had a white sash around their waist. The helmet under their arm dispersed a second later, confirming Kira's suspicion, and finally they came close enough for Kira to recognize Anzu's face. Relief flooded Kira's body.

"Oh, I forgot to tell you, Anzu's back," Jun said. "She's the one who brought the letters, but I didn't see her."

"Thank goodness, I've been so worried!"

She stood up and rushed to meet Anzu, calling, "You're here!"

They met halfway down the walkway, and Kira flung her arms around the taciturn knight. She hadn't realized how truly worried she had been about Anzu. Suddenly all of the thoughts she had been repressing surged forward—*I was worried about you, I thought Tigran caught you, that you might have been killed...*

Kira said, "What happened? Did the soldiers catch you following them?"

Anzu shifted her shoulders and glanced over at the darkening skies over the lake. "It was—nothing. Well, it could have been worse, anyway. We followed the soldiers at a great distance, and they never spotted us."

"Oh," Kira said, breathing a sigh of relief. "But what took so long?"

"Where did they bring the prisoners?" Jun interjected.

"To their barracks in Meridian. We didn't stay long enough to see them move anywhere else after that—we were already risking being seen by Tigran or the commander." Anzu glanced at Kira and added, "We ran into some aggressive soldiers on our way out of the city. They stopped us at the gates; we had gotten in just fine, maybe they weren't watching too closely then, but for some reason on our way out they took issue with our weapons and armor."

Kira's mouth popped open as she understood. "Because of Light magic?"

Anzu nodded slowly as if it pained her, but not physically. "They had the audacity to say we were holding magic and hoarding it; that it should be available to all. And yet they were siphoning it out of the very air, trapping it to be sold to the highest bidder!" She huffed and turned her face away from them. Kira had rarely seen her show such emotion.

"Sold?" Jun said quietly.

Her fists clenched, Kira said, "So that's his aim then? He's selling the magic. How did he explain this to the Empress? They said this was to balance the realm, so everyone could be on equal footing!"

Anzu grunted then shook her head. "Well, the soldiers who harassed us made us banish our weapons, and were attempting to have us taken in for resisting them—which we did not do," she said through gritted teeth. "I followed Master Starwind's orders, unlike Nari did. But we were able to get away, and had to hide out at some strange inn

Zowan had told me about, until we could risk leaving the gate again."

A rush of something hot and sickly swept through Kira's insides. She opened her mouth to speak, but Jun beat her to it.

"Wait, what? But Nari was right." He exhaled angrily. "The soldiers are out of control. They're stealing magic yet keeping us from using it? We've let Tigran do whatever he wanted for too long, and look what's happened!" Voice raised, he gestured toward a lantern beside the lake, a distinct darkness surrounding it where it had drawn in magic.

Kira watched Jun in trepidation. He had been Anzu's squire this past year, working closely with her whenever he trained at Gekkō-ji, or traveling around the realm on quests with her. Kira had never seen him talk to Anzu like this.

"Jun," Anzu began heavily, "I know you think we must act, but—"

"We have to," he said with some finality. "And soon. You know those letters you brought from Gekkō-ji? Well, one was from the palace, with my father's *execution date!* It's in three days! And we've been sitting around doing nothing!"

Anzu drew a visible breath at this news. "I'm so sorry, Jun."

"Jun, we haven't been doing nothing," Kira added quietly, wondering how in the world she could diffuse this situation—or if it was even possible.

Anzu said, "I understand you're upset, Jun. But what *could* we have done in all this time? Attacked the Imperial Palace? Killed Tigran right in front of the Empress? Even though the Commonality and the palace guards don't have magic, they are not helpless. And what would the common people think when we start assaulting the palace and her soldiers?

"There *is* inequity between commoners and magic folk," she said. "I'm not saying what they're doing is right—stealing magic to sell—but I can see how the commoners would see it as a solution, a way to balance the realm.

"We've been through a feud before. No one wants that again. We need to do what's best for the realm, to find a way to solve this."

Flinging his arms up, Jun turned around, away from them. "But the Gray Knights *exist* to serve the realm! And Tigran is going to execute them all! He's the one who should pay. We have to do something now. We can't wait any longer. *We don't have time for this!*"

Kira secretly agreed, but she wasn't about to rage at Anzu about it. In the back of her mind, thoughts had begun to percolate and solidify into something of an idea. She bit the inside of her lip as she glanced guiltily at Anzu.

Then her stomach gurgled, the awkward sound evident in the ever-darkening pavilion. Anzu took a look at the half-assembled picnic. "Eat your dinner," she said, without ire. "We can talk about this later."

Jun merely nodded, still facing away from them, his shoulders drawn up tight by his ears.

Kira gave Anzu a sad smile, and watched her walk away down the walkway and back into the Spire.

As she and Jun silently tucked in to the picnic—Jun dashing his hands across his eyes without comment—Kira finally realized: Micah never arrived.

CHAPTER 11

ELECTRIC BLUE

Kira lowered the bun she was about to take a bite of. The temple grounds were fairly quiet, though she could hear a few people in one of the gardens nearby, probably either practicing magic or having their own dinner in the fresh air. Anzu was gone, and the walkway into the castle was deserted.

Jun noted her worried gaze. "Do you think Micah got tied up at the Apothecarium?" he asked quietly.

"I guess so. I know there've been a lot of people there lately, and he and Spectra have been going crazy making remedies. I guess I'll check in on him before we go back to the wing, if he's not busy." She continued to stare at the walkway, frowning.

She hadn't even seen Micah for more than a minute since she'd been back. It wasn't unusual, but she had secretly been hoping he would have wanted to hear all about her knight ceremony.

He's just busy, I'm sure, she thought, refusing to admit that his interest in her might be waning. They were both busy, and she knew he cared for her. The last letter he had sent to her at Gekkō-ji had made her clutch her heart and fill to the brim with longing to see him again—which was perhaps why it was more of a blow when he hadn't made time for her now that she was here.

She idly took a bite of the bun she still held. As soon as the bread and cheese hit her tastebuds, she tore into it, finally realizing how hungry she was. It was gone in seconds. She washed it down with some tea, still warm thanks to her thermos, and reached for the covered bowl with the rice and veggies.

"Hey Jun," she said tentatively after they had both eaten their fill. "I've been thinking, after what Anzu said..." He glanced at her sharply, and she took a swift inhale before saying, "I don't agree with her either, first of all. And you're right, we *do* need to do something. We're knights now. The only ones with Gray magic free to do anything at the moment. And I hate to go against Ichiro's wishes, but..." She sighed, then drew her knees up to her chest, hugging them to herself. "Wait, did he say anything else in his letter to you? About us going to the palace, anything?" she asked him.

"Well, yes, we're expected to... *attend*. And just that the Empress had issued a decree for their execution, and the date. There's an invitation for each of us."

"Well, he probably didn't want to put much more in his letter, I guess," Kira reasoned. "But still. It's—I've been thinking. We'll have to go, obviously, but we can't stand idly by anymore."

He continued to gaze at a spot on his knee for a few seconds until her words sunk in, and he looked up, meeting her eyes. "Are you saying..."

"Yes. We need to—" She held up a hand, her heart racing as she spotted something bright next to the lakeshore. "Did you see that?" she almost shouted, stumbling to her feet.

"What? What?" Jun grabbed at her arm, following her down the steps and onto the lawn.

"I thought I saw—there was a woman—remember that wisp I told you about?"

She raced down the grassy lawn until she reached a white pea-stone path, which led through one of the gardens toward a small shrine. It was a beautiful building, with pristine roof tiles and an elaborate water-themed carving above the lintel. Three stone steps led inside, and on either side of them, identical statues of water spouts came up to Kira's waist. She had never gone inside before.

Her steps slowed, and she glanced back at Jun, who looked at her, wide-eyed. The lake was quiet, the stars reflected serenely in the still water. Everything she saw was bathed in the pearly glow of Light, and yet Kira was hesitant to look inside the shrine.

It always gave off an abandoned feeling, though some of the masters and trainees still came here to leave offerings or say brief prayers. The lake spirit Kagami was no more. She was yet another casualty of Tigran's obsessions with dark magic and destruction.

"You saw a spirit?" Jun leaned in and whispered close to her ear.

She shivered, but told herself it was because of Jun's quiet words so close to her. "I think she went inside."

Despite the creeping sensation at the back of her spine, and the sense of fear likely brought on by the occasional scary movie she had seen as a kid back in the Starless Realm, Kira took a step forward. She reached inside her consciousness to assure herself that she had a core of both Light and Shadow at the ready, though she didn't draw any weapons. Jun followed, inches from her.

She stepped inside; everything gave off a soft glow, though there was a stronger glow from a candle at the other end of the room. There was no one inside. She and Jun entered slowly, drawn toward the candlelight.

"It had to be her," Kira said. "It looked just like the wispy woman I saw back at Gekkō-ji. But what was she doing here? Don't most spirits stay in one place?"

Jun lifted a palm in a gesture that said he mostly agreed with her. "Well, you know there are some, like Kamellia, who serve all people in the realm."

Kira stared at the candle, wondering if it was always lit, in remembrance of Kagami, or whether the wisp spirit was somehow responsible. "Do you know of any other spirit she might be, one connected to the whole realm?"

He shook his head slowly, gazing up at the painting hanging on the wall above the candle. Kira looked at it too, and drew in a pained breath. It was of the beautiful lake spirit Kagami, her long black hair unbound, and painted in swirls all around her head as if she were underwater. Her serpentine tail, the scales glittering in the flickering candlelight, twisted in a coil. Above her stretched a dragon, the coils of its length looping over Kagami's floating hair, its scales glittering blue like so many gems and jewels.

"Who is that?" Kira asked quietly, though she thought she might know the answer.

Jun leaned closer, his hands clasped behind his back as though he wished not to disturb anything. "*The Dragon in the Camellias,*" he whispered, reaching out to point at the bright red flowers painted between some of the coils.

She came closer too, glanced down to make sure she wasn't going to bump into the table that held the candle, and gasped. There lay a dark scroll, the paper a deep blue color. It hadn't been there a moment ago when she had looked at the candle—or had it? On top of the scroll was a small white blossom. It was just like the one the wisp had left her back at Gekkō-ji, which had disappeared from her bedside when dawn broke the next day.

"She was here," Kira said with certainty, picking up the scroll in one hand, the blossom in the other. Would the scroll contain answers? Or only create more questions? The spirits were tricky, and they almost always wanted something in return. What would Kira have to exchange?

Gazing around at the rest of the shrine, she couldn't help but wonder if the spirit was still here, invisible perhaps. The wood floors and walls were pristine, a small shelf with incense sticks stocked and ready, though none were lit. The shrine was clearly still being maintained, in Kagami's memory.

Jun was staring at the painting. "The spirit of the mountain said she wanted to speak with you, right? This wisp spirit? Maybe she knows something that will help us defeat Tigran, or stop the tears or something."

Nodding, Kira turned back to the painting, rolling the scroll idly in her hand. After a quick glance at the departed spirit, she studied the dragon, the same dragon whose likeness was portrayed in a mural in the bathhouse at Gekkō-ji. The dragon who, it was said, created the Realm of Camellia, with portals from the Starless Realm. Then he disappeared, having spent all his magic.

Just as Kira was about to unfurl the scroll, a scream erupted outside.

Without even looking at each other, Kira and Jun bolted from the shrine, both summoning their armor. Kira roughly jammed the scroll in her deep pocket. Once outside, they summoned weapons. Kira's choice of weapon was a tall *naginata*, a polearm with a curved blade on the end. Jun always favored a sword, and he held his katana across his body as he jogged in search of the source of the scream.

Kira planted herself on the gravel path, the pole of her weapon dug into the stones beside her as she inspected the grounds. "There!" she called, and raced toward the meditation pavilion where they had left their picnic in their haste to follow the wisp.

A figure was visible on the boards of the walkway that led into the castle, and the source of their dismay was evident at once: a jagged and sickly glowing rent in the air—another tear.

Kira got there first. She ignored the cold fear rising in her chest as she bounded up onto the walkway, tossing her polearm aside, banishing the Light from it without even a thought. Sinking down to the still figure, but careful to avoid the tear, she sought their face and neck to look for any sign of life.

Her fingers froze as they reached the neck and she spied the familiar face. "Spectra?" she gasped, frantically prodding her throat for a pulse. Faintly, a weak throbbing met her fingertips, and Kira's head slumped down in relief. She looked up sharply at Jun. "Go get Micah—go get a healer!"

With a glance at the tear—the stationary electric blue gash at about chest height—Jun started running. He called back, "Stay away from that thing! And maybe move her away from it?"

His footsteps quickly receded down the walkway and into the castle. Her hands still on Spectra, Kira set her jaw, and gently positioned her hands under Spectra's armpits, then slowly dragged her across the wooden floor. When they were safely a few feet away, Kira checked Spectra's pulse and breathing again, and squatted back onto her heels, waiting.

At least she was alive.

What had happened? And why were the healers taking so long? Kira had no expertise in Shadow healing magic, and neither did Jun. It was a rare and powerful gift, which also required plenty of training.

After watching the rise and fall of Spectra's chest for a few breaths, Kira rocked forward off her heels and stood. Slowly she edged over to the tear, which was much like the one Zowan had found in the catacombs, but perhaps a different shape. It was a tear after all.

In the very fabric of the realm.

As she studied the strange electric blue glow which exuded that horrible feeling of wrongness in her very skin, her thoughts drifted back to Kagami's shrine, and the painting of the Camellian Dragon. Were these tears like the first portals into the Realm of Camellia? And—Kira's heartbeat sped up at the idea—did these tears *lead* to the Starless Realm?

She shook the thought aside. Even if it were a portal, she had given up long ago thinking she would ever return to the Starless Realm. She had been given an opportunity once—when those magical doors kept appearing across the realm. And she had turned her back on it.

She squinted at the tear, staring into its depths. She couldn't see anything besides the electric blue glow; no other world peered through the jagged cracks. No, this didn't seem like a portal of any kind.

So if it wasn't a portal, what did it mean?

She went back over to Spectra and brushed a lock of hair from the girl's forehead, watching her breathing again. Finally, footsteps rang out on the walkway, and four people came running toward her.

At the lead was Micah, and Kira's stomach did a flip at the sight of him. The strings of his worn apron flapped behind him as he sprinted toward Spectra and sunk to the ground beside his sister. "What happened to her?" he demanded.

"Well—we didn't—" Kira started.

"Make way." A tall matronly woman pressed through and began to examine Spectra. Kira backed away and let her work.

Coming up alongside Jun, for some reason, was Ryn. He gave Kira a look that seemed to portray his mutual surprise at the situation, then he, too, focused his attention on Spectra.

The healer ran her hands over Spectra, finally bringing them to hover an inch above her heart and head.

Micah kneeled beside his sister, one of her hands in both of his. Kira touched his shoulder, the only thing she could think of doing to help. He gave her a furtive look of thanks, eyes glistening, and returned his attention to his sister.

Kira went over to the others. Jun was staring at the tear, but Ryn was studying Spectra. "Can you read her aura?" Kira whispered to him.

Lips pressed tight, Ryn nodded. "I'm looking now," he said in a hushed voice.

Clutching her arms about herself, Kira waited. Her heart rate seemed to calm down, and she finally noticed how cold she was. The temperature had dropped with the sun, but with all of the surprise and shock of the past hour, she hadn't even noticed. She rubbed her hands up and down her arms to try to warm them.

After an interminable ten minutes or so, the healer finally spoke. "She is alive, though I can't say what is wrong with her just yet." After the briefest of glances at the tear, she added, "We will move her to the Apothecarium, and summon Lord Raiden."

Kira jolted forward, crouching beside Spectra. She placed her palms down on the floor on either side of her head and pulled on some Light magic. With an exhale, she sent the Light magic through her hands and back out into the world in the shape she wanted.

A tingly warmth in her hands became the wood-like poles of the stretcher she had conjured under Spectra. Without a word, Micah reached down to grab the poles after Kira had let go. The healer bent down to grasp the other side, but Ryn stepped up and put a hand on her arm.

"Mistress Nyoko, I think I should go with you," Ryn said. "I think I see something about her aura, but I need more time to study it." He met Kira's eyes, and she wondered if it was anything like the soul damage she had experienced last year.

Nyoko gave Ryn a brief searching look, then spoke to Micah, "Well, in that case, Micah, you go summon Lord Raiden. Master Kimura here can help me bring her," she added softly.

His jaw clenched, Micah allowed Ryn to take the stretcher poles from him, and he, Kira, and Jun watched the two of them carry Spectra down the walkway into the castle.

Kira instantly went over to Micah and put a hand on his arm, unsure. He didn't shrug her off, but instead turned toward her. She wrapped her arms around him, and he nestled his head into the crook of her neck. She didn't say *It's going to be all right*, because she didn't know, and she had no right to give him that hope, though she desperately wanted to. So, she gave him what comfort she could.

After a little while, Micah pulled away. He blinked a few times, though his eyes were dry. "I better go get Lord Raiden."

Kira nodded and began walking with him. "I'll come with you."

She glanced back at Jun, who said, "I'll stay here," with a purposeful nod at the tear.

"Do you know what happened?" Micah asked hollowly as they headed toward the castle.

"No. I'm sorry, Micah. We were in Kagami's shrine when we heard a—a scream."

He nodded, gazing down at his feet as he walked. Her chest filled with warmth as she snuck glances at him out of the corner of her eye. She wanted to reach out and hold his hand, but now surely wasn't the time. But she hadn't seen him in so long. She couldn't help it. She slipped her hand into his, and he looked up at her with a smile that erased some of the worry from his strained muscles.

The halls of the Spire were deserted, and they quickly made it to Raiden's study, but when she knocked and peered inside, she saw that he wasn't alone.

Commander Hagane stood in front of Raiden's desk, his straight-backed posture and disdain on his face enough to tell Kira they hadn't exactly been having a friendly conversation.

"Ah, Kira," Raiden said, beckoning the three of them in. "To what do I owe this late visit?"

She bowed low, partially to show respect she didn't have for the commander, but also to buy herself time to revise what she had been about to say.

"There's been an accident."

CHAPTER 12

SOMETHING ELSE ENTIRELY

To everyone's immense displeasure, the commander insisted on accompanying them to the Apothecarium. Kira hung back with Micah as they strode down the halls.

"This is all my fault," Micah was saying as they passed through the Jade Foyer. "I asked Spectra to go meet you; I got stuck running remedies all over the city today and I was going to miss dinner. I should have just gone to tell you myself, instead of delivering that last one. It wasn't that far."

Kira shuddered, wondering if she would be having this conversation with Spectra right now if that had been the case, and it would have been Micah unconscious in the Apothecarium in her place.

"It's not your fault," she said with certainty. "We don't really know what happened; it could have been anyone."

Now she noticed Micah's exhaustion, his heavy foot-falls, his expressionless face. She reached over and grabbed his hand again. He squeezed her fingers in response, and they slowed a little further from the other two.

"Ryn's there with her, I'm sure he'll be able to see something about her aura, if that's the case."

"Mmm," he said, then groaned. "I'm going to have to go home and tell our parents she was hurt. I'm supposed to watch out for her. I'm the only reason they let her come work here."

"Do you... Do you want me to go?" she offered as they came up to the doors of the Apothecarium. "And you can stay with Spectra?"

He sighed, following Raiden and Hagane inside. The lights were dimmed in the immense circular room, though Kira could see the twinkling glow of Light all around her, and the myriad of stars above shone through the glass-paneled ceiling. It was late, but healers and their apprentices still bustled about, with the gentle shush of a water fountain going in one of the rooms off of this one. They circled around counterclockwise, and headed through an arched doorway. Kira had never been farther than the main room before, luckily not requiring any healing during her time here, and never wanting to intrude too much while Micah and Spectra were working.

Down a short hallway and into one of many rooms off it, they spotted Spectra laying on one of two futons on the floor meant for patients. She was the only patient, and Ryn stood by her side, seemingly in a daze. Mistress Nyoko wasn't there, but a mortar and pestle sat on the wooden counter that ran along the back wall of the room, beside a single candle.

Commander Hagane waited outside.

Kira found herself standing next to Raiden at the back of the room after everyone else had filtered in. Micah lurched over to Spectra.

"What is Hagane still doing here?" Kira whispered to Raiden.

"Still installing those damned lanterns," he all but growled. "And informing me of their plans to distribute the collected magic among the people. Gloating, I think."

Her insides hardened as she remembered Anzu's story about the soldiers back in Meridian, and how they planned to sell the magic. "How can they?" she couldn't help but ask, albeit so quietly that Raiden had to bend down to hear her.

He shook his head, nostrils flaring.

As outraged as she was about Tigran's disgusting use of magic and might, Kira was more taken aback by Raiden's attitude. Normally, he would be crackling with lightning and rage, thunderclouds boiling above him. Perhaps his display of Shadow magic at the gates of Heliodor and the subsequent placement of the lanterns had dulled his temper. Kira just didn't know how long it would remain bottled.

Mistress Nyoko entered at that moment, bustling in with a small jar in her hands. She bowed to Raiden and at once dumped some beige powder into the mortar, and began grinding it with the other ingredients already there. As she ground, she spoke, "Her heart beats, her mind pulses, and her organs function, but she does not wake. It appears the strange blue tear by the pavilion struck her somehow, rendering her in this state."

"What?" Raiden demanded, then clenched his jaw as Commander Hagane glanced into the room. "Kira, you didn't mention—" he rumbled.

Kira froze. They hadn't even told the Commonality about the tears yet. "I'm sorry, I—"

Nyoko went on, clearly not knowing about the possible political ramifications, "There was some abnormal magic out by the meditation pavilion, some kind of blue light, hovering about this height." She gestured, then pointed at Spectra. "It is my theory that it struck Spectra in the heart."

Micah lifted his head at Nyoko's last words. "Struck her in the heart?"

He looked as though he had been struck in the heart himself. Kira longed to reach out and take his hand again, but she remained still. She could feel the narrow gaze of Commander Hagane, and thought he might be looking at her.

"Blue light?" Hagane said, angling himself to face everyone, but remaining outside the room. "She was struck by *Light?*"

Kira stiffened, hearing the inflection in his voice. She opened her mouth to say something, but it had become uncommonly dry.

"It's not *Light*, Commander," Raiden said. "It's something else entirely."

Hagane surveyed Raiden with obvious displeasure. "You knew of this—this—abnormality?" he said in a deadly calm.

"There has been one other."

Kira felt herself breathing so shallowly it was almost like not breathing at all—the tension in the small room was so thick she wished she could melt into the back wall. Out of everyone, Micah seemed to be oblivious to it all, with his entire being focused on his sister. Ryn stiffened, and his gaze at Spectra seemed blank. Nyoko had her back carefully turned, while she lit some incense with a spark of Shadow flame between two fingers. The scent of something citrusy began to waft throughout the room.

Hagane cocked his head, beckoning Raiden out into the hallway. But Raiden ignored this, remaining beside Kira and Ryn at the back of the room. Hagane narrowed his eyes. "And why did you not alert me at once?"

Kira had to give Raiden credit, she had never seen him display so much restraint before. She glanced down at his hands to look for the hints of lightning that often danced there—something he seemed unable to hide when he was in a rage—but to her surprise, they weren't dancing with lightning, they were shaking.

His tone was as glib as ever, though. "We hadn't gotten that far in our conversations. Here, I'll show you. We can leave Mistress Nyoko to treat Miss Jade. Kira?"

Kira followed Raiden out of the room, bustling past Hagane and leaving him to follow.

To Kira's immense relief, Raiden headed toward the meditation pavilion. She had no desire to be in such close quarters as the catacombs with Hagane. Raiden probably wanted to see the new tear, at any rate.

Outside, the crisp night air awakened Kira's senses, and she scanned the lawns and gardens beside them, searching for anything else out of the ordinary. It was truly night now, but everything was outlined for her in a subtle pearly glow. Raiden summoned a ball of flame and sent it upwards, where it divided itself and settled into the overhead lamps lining the walkway. Kira heard a soft grunt from behind her and wondered whether Hagane thought using Shadow magic to see was frivolous or not.

The tear was obvious as soon as they stepped outside. Jun still guarded it, though no one else was likely to be out here now that it was getting so late. Most acolytes were safely in their quarters by now, considering everyone had to wake before dawn for morning meditation.

Raiden halted before reaching the tear, bowing briefly at Jun, who offered Raiden a much lower bow. It looked much the same as when they had first spotted it: A jagged glowing blue streak giving off a sickly energy.

"Well?" Hagane demanded, still walking, his hands in fists as he came closer and closer. "Where is this abnormality that struck the girl?"

"Woah!" Kira cried, flinging her arms in front of Hagane to stop him from walking right into the thing.

He pushed back at her, both hands shoving her. She stumbled, at the last second redirecting herself away from the tear. She steadied herself, and looked up at Hagane, blinking.

And then he slapped her across the face.

She reeled backward, and her stomach flew through the bottom of her feet as she lost track of where the tear was. When she caught sight of it out of her popping vision, she hastily lunged to the side. Hagane stood straight as an arrow, glowering at her.

Suddenly Raiden stood between Hagane and Kira. "What is the meaning of this?" Raiden demanded, with some of his usual thunder.

Hagane's eyes bulged. "How dare you question me? I might ask the same of Lady Starwind."

"I—I was stopping you," Kira said, "you almost walked right into it."

"*What* are you talking about?"

"The tear," she said, pointing. At his irritated blank look, she went on, "It's right there. Can't—can't you see it?"

His eyes narrowed, and he turned to look where she was pointing, his body still angled towards hers, one wiry hand at the decanter on his belt. Kira's cheek stung painfully, particularly because he had slapped the cheek that was still healing from her knight ceremony. But inside her chest, a swelling of rage brought fire to her core.

"I see nothing," Hagane said with a sneer, now ignoring Kira and addressing Raiden. "What is this, Raiden; some feeble attempt to lure me out here to threaten me with your fledgling Gray Knights?" He spat on the walkway at their feet. "Need I remind you—"

Glaring at the desecrated walkway, Kira burst, "Look, I just saved you from walking into that thing. You saw Spectra back in the Apothecarium—she walked right into it and now she's comatose. You'd be flat on your back if I hadn't stopped you."

"I see *nothing* there," he seethed, getting right in her face.

Kira inhaled sharply through her nostrils. "You know what? Never mind, go ahead and get near it."

Hagane held her gaze for three incredibly long seconds until pulling back. And though her cheek still stung, and adrenaline coursed through her veins, it was the look in his eyes that made a wave of fear swirl in her gut.

No one spoke as he cocked his head and looked at the tear—or appeared to look at it. If he really couldn't see it, he was studying empty air.

Was he lying? Why would he? It didn't make any sense that he would have *wanted* to walk right into it.

Finally, he glanced down at his decanter, which glowed with more than just ambient Light magic. Who knew how long it had been collecting magic? Its contents glowed like a lightbulb, yet they seemed to shift as he moved a little, almost sloshing inside. As if attracted to the tear, the Light inside shifted toward it like a magnet. Hagane narrowed his eyes.

"If this is as you say—" He met each of their eyes, as if hoping to catch one of them lying—"And this thing took out that girl, then this is certain danger. It could be... that she didn't see it either," he added, almost reluctantly.

Kira let out a muted gasp. "It—perhaps you can't see it because you don't have magic."

He raised an eyebrow at that and glanced almost imperceptibly down at his decanter. "Perhaps. The girl?"

"She doesn't either," Kira said, not exactly pleased that she was conversing with Hagane, but glad that he was at least listening to her now.

"But what about Micah?" Jun cut in.

Her eyes rolling up in thought, Kira said, "I don't know—did he say he saw it? I thought he was just focused on Spectra—"

"Enough of this," Hagane interrupted. "I must report to the palace at once." He turned to Raiden, "You said there was another?"

"Yes, in the catacombs."

Hagane's mouth twisted in displeasure. "And if these things are appearing at random, and commoners can't see them, then we're all in great danger."

CHAPTER 13

THE DRAGON IN THE CAMELLIAS

K ira jerked her head up, disoriented. It took a minute to realize she had fallen asleep. She sat on the floor beside Micah, leaning against the wall of Spectra's recovery room. She had no idea what time it was, though she could tell the sun wasn't up yet, since Light still glimmered around her. Micah was asleep, having refused to walk back home, or even crash on the floor of the Gray Wing, as Kira had offered, rules be damned. So, she sat with him all night, watching over Spectra as she lay on her pallet as if sleeping.

Spectra was much the same as last night. Nyoko had come and gone several times throughout the night, checking on her, but she made no change for ill or good. Micah had put off sending a message by courier to his parents, in the hopes that she would be better by morning, but from the looks of it, he would have to go home after he woke up and break the news. She turned to look at him, his head lolling to his chest as he slept against the wall, legs crossed in front of him. She watched his slow breathing, and his soft eyelashes fluttering every so often with subtle restive eye movements. Her heart constricted as she put a gentle hand on his knee, his work apron still in his lap.

Kira drew up her legs to her chest, stretching out her joints as she did so, and heard a soft crinkle from her pocket.

She gasped, remembering the scroll she had hastily stuffed in there after leaving Kagami's shrine last night. Cursing under her breath, she drew out the rumpled scroll and cringed at the sight of it. The paper was an unusual dark blue color, and it now bore several creases. As she unfurled it, she tried to flatten them out, careful of the ornate writing done in silver ink. She blinked, not having seen anything like it before. After a quick glance at Micah, she read the title:

The Dragon in the Camellias

She cocked her head to the side, of course having read the story of how the realm formed on more than one occasion throughout her training. But after seeing the likeness of the dragon in Kagami's shrine, and the wisp seemingly leading her there, she was curious.

Long ago, on a fine sunny day, a man walked by a small river and met a dragon, though he didn't realize it.

The man was on his way to a nearby market town, and had never walked this path before.

After he had walked a long time, he came upon the most beautiful cluster of camellia bushes, flourishing with reddish-pink blooms. The flowering bushes lined both sides of the river, and their blossoms were reflected in the surface of the slow-moving river, making it look as if the flowers crossed over the river, too.

The man, tired from his walk and in awe of the beauty, decided to rest by the camellias before carrying on. As he sat resting, he thought of how his wife would so much enjoy this place, but it was very far from their home. It was so beautiful, that he decided to take a cutting from the bushes, and bring it to his wife to plant, so she could enjoy the beauty of the flowers every day.

As he approached the twining vines, a dragon rose from the water. The man had taken out a knife from his belt and was readying to cut the bush nearest.

"Stop!" the dragon cried, coiling out of the water. Its great blue scales glinted in the sunny water like a cascade of sapphires.

But the man did not hear him. In fact, the man did not see the dragon at all.

The man began cutting away at the bush. The dragon, desperate, roared, "No, please, don't take them!"

Try as he might, the dragon could not get the man to see or hear him. He yelled, he pleaded, he slithered close and begged. The dragon was not surprised, merely saddened. Many a man he had met in his long years, and few were able to see dragons, or for that matter, see magic at all.

Satisfied, the man removed his cutting and went off to the nearby market to complete his errands.

Before sinking back into his watery home, the dragon reached out with his magic into the camellia plant which had been cut. He soothed the plant, and healed the cut as best he could. He had nurtured these particular bushes for a very, very long time.

A little while later, when the dragon was curled back up in his watery home, the man returned, and he was not alone. A group of men and women from the market town followed with greedy eyes, armed with knives of their own.

"It's beautiful," they murmured, as they began cutting. "How did we not see this before?"

Though the dragon shouted, and pleaded, and yelled, and cried, they did not stop cutting. Each wanted their own cutting to bring beauty to their home.

Tears streaming down his scaly face, the dragon watched a young man approach, drawn by the crowd. His gaze immediately went to the water, where the dragon lay coiled, mourning the loss of the plants he had worked so hard to cultivate.

The young man rushed to the water's edge, bowling through those in his way. "Dragon," the young man cried. "Is this your home?"

The dragon nodded and smiled a watery smile, but the people dragging away cuttings paused, for they couldn't see who the young man was talking to.

The young man stared around and cried in dismay, "Stop—all of you! Can't you see the dragon? You're destroying his home! The beauty of these flowers is only here because of him!"

All of those holding cuttings stared wildly around the riverbank, seeing nothing but the scattered leaves left from their destruction, and the stumpy bushes, barren twigs sticking up like dull spikes.

"It'll grow back," one of them muttered.

"Dragon? What nonsense is this?"

"I see no dragon."

The young man, who had a habit of getting himself in far over his head, drew his weapon and brandished it at the crowd.

"You must replant those cuttings! It's the least you can do to make it up to the poor dragon."

"Or what?" the man who had taken the first cutting growled. He had cut a few more since returning with the others, for his neighbors and relatives.

The people began to advance upon the young man, who was, by all appearances, defending an empty patch of water.

The young man backed away until his feet reached mud at the rivers' edge. Knives began to turn in hand from the bushes to the direction of the young man.

The dragon, furious at the destruction of his beautiful flowers, and fearful for the kind young man, thought desperately of a way to help him.

So, the dragon called upon his magic, and reached out to his beautiful camellia branches. The branches, scattered on the ground, held in people's hands, or tied to sacks, began to twist and snake around legs and arms. The villagers stopped advancing upon the dragon's defender at once, and began to shout in dismay, until the branches covered their mouths.

The dragon told the branches to dive into the ground, finding soil again, but now they held their would-be captors in place. Knives were forced from hands, and angry fists pinned to men's sides.

The young man, stunned, bowed deeply to the dragon. "T-thank you," he said shakily.

"It is I who should thank you for defending me," the dragon said. "Not all people can see magic. Only those with the potential for magic."

After a moment, the young man asked, "Are there many more of you?"

The dragon nodded.

"I wish there was a place where everyone could see dragons," the young man said sadly. "Then they wouldn't ruin your home like that."

"Wish?" The dragon grinned. "I can do that."

The dragon reached out his magic as far as he could, gathering up as much as he could hold, and he let it out in a breath of blue fire.

The fire seared through the space between worlds. It molded a place out of nothing, crisp and newly forged, modeled after the only world he knew, with mountains and fields, rivers and forests, and above all: Magic.

When it was finished, a searing blue portal stood at the riverbank, with no sign of the dragon.

Confident that he would find the dragon on the other side, the young man glanced back at the greedy people still trapped by the branches, then stepped through the portal.

The people suddenly found themselves freed, but much like with the dragon, they couldn't see the portal. They only saw the young man disappear, never to be seen again.

The young man was only the first to pass through the portal.

It stayed open for many years, visible only to people who had the potential for magic. Many of them went through, though some who saw it chose not to.

Slowly, they came to realize, in this new place, some of them could wield shadows to do their bidding, or forge tools with solid light, something they had never done before in their old realm.

The young man, whom, as it turned out, could wield both light and shadow, never saw the dragon again, but told anyone who would listen his tale, about how they all came to be in the Realm of Camellias.

Kira sat still for several moments, blinking down at the blue paper. It varied only slightly from the one she had studied; it was less flowery and poetic, more genuine. The other versions had never embellished so much on the man who came through the portal, though.

It still sounded much like a parable—the part about taking too many flowers strongly reminded her of the teachings of the temples; how you shouldn't take too much magic from the realm.

That made her think even harder. Is this why the wisp had left the scroll for her? She now had no doubt that was what had happened. The small flower was an obvious clue.

But how could this help fix the tears? Or did it somehow have to do with defeating Tigran?

She sighed, shaking her head. Perhaps she could talk it over with Jun later, or Zowan. She glanced at Micah with a start; what time was it?

Stuffing the scroll back in her pocket, she reached over to poke Micah awake, at his request from the night before—the waking at dawn part, not the poking part—but just then she heard a soft step outside the door.

She looked around the corner and spotted Ryn. Carefully she removed her hand from Micah's knee and inched away to stand up. He could sleep for another minute. He looked like he needed it; at least in sleep the worried creases in his face were softened.

Outside in the hallway, she hissed to Ryn, "Where were you last night? You were gone when we got back from looking at the tear with Hagane."

He nodded, indicating they walk further from the patient room, and she acquiesced. Not caring about her rumpled clothes, stiff neck, and stale breath, she followed him into the large main room of the Apothecarium. Healers and trainees were already busy with their work.

"I had to go and check something," Ryn said, circumnavigating the room and leading them out into the castle.

"What did you need to check? And where are we going? I still have to wake up Micah." She glanced back, already feeling guilty for leaving his side.

"I'm sure someone else will wake him," he said as they reached the Jade Foyer. "And we're going to the stables."

"What? *Why?*" She blinked the sleep from her eyes, fully awake now with curiosity.

"Because your friend Jun just packed up and left the Spire, that's why," he hissed.

"What?" she shouted, forgetting where she was. The exclamation echoed all the way up through the chambers above. Admonitions rained softly down from the higher levels, shushing her. She and Ryn hastily left the foyer.

"What?" she repeated, now rushing down the Hall of Spirits with him. "Do you know where he's going? Did something happen?"

"Yes," Ryn said. "I mean, I don't know where he's going, but something quite horrible has happened."

Kira felt like she had missed a step as her stomach flipped. "Well?" she demanded.

"A messenger came, from the palace—"

"But Hagane only left here around midnight, how could they get back here so quickly?"

Ryn sighed. "It seems Tigran and the rest discovered the tears themselves, *and* the fact that commoners can't see them—I heard one of the advisors was struck. It appeared on the palace grounds. Empress Mei has completely outlawed magic."

"Completely—outlawed—*what!*" she hissed, her whole body vibrating with shock as she stopped in her tracks. They had reached the narrow tunnel leading out of the castle's foundation, and they were quite alone. "How—how does she think that using magic is the problem? It's bottling it up that's doing it!"

"I know. They're not going to sell it anymore, at least. The messenger just said the palace would be confiscating all the magic they could, since it had caused so much damage already."

Suddenly feeling trapped inside the damp dark corridor, Kira began racing for the exit, a bright rectangle of sunlight at the end.

No magic. Why in the world would Tigran do that?

And where the hell was Jun going?

They reached the stables, but Jun was nowhere in sight. Kira searched up and down the aisles, looking for his horse, but he wasn't where she had last seen him, which was two stalls down from Naga.

At last, she heaved a great sigh, throwing herself against Naga's door. The mare nosed Kira's hair, and Kira turned to pat her cheek.

"Where might he have gone?" Ryn asked, leaning against the stall across the way.

"I don't know," she said. "He could have gone back to Gekkō-ji, or back to his estate—" She gasped. "His father. At the palace. His—well, execution is in two days. We were both expected to be there. Do you think he might try and do something—"

"Stupid?" Ryn interjected.

"I was going to say crazy," Kira said in a low voice. "And yes. Either way. But why leave now? Why wouldn't he tell me?"

Ryn shrugged, then straightened up at the sound of footsteps coming down the aisle. Half-hoping it was Jun returning, Kira pushed herself off the door and started walking toward them, but halted in her tracks as she recognized the green-clad soldiers. Two of them, and they were carrying swords, likely steel, if magic was truly outlawed.

"What is your business here?" the tall dark one demanded.

Kira drew herself up to her full height, still reeling in confusion from Jun's departure, but almost certainly ready to pick a fight with these two. But before she could say anything, Ryn stepped up to her side and said, "Grooming our horses. They need to be brushed down."

The curvy woman with him narrowed her eyes at Kira, who nodded, her jaw clenched. Then the woman said, "Very well, get on with it then. But you won't be taking those horses out anytime soon."

"What do you mean?" Kira blurted, her fingers inadvertently reaching for the hidden dagger she kept at the small of her back.

The woman didn't miss the gesture, and put her hand on her own sword, then slid her feet into a wider stance. Ryn elbowed Kira, not-so-subtly.

"The Empress has issued a decree, as of this morning," the woman said. "There will be no more practice of Light or Shadow magic until the anomaly of the tears across the realm has been solved, except for official purposes."

"What does that have to do with us going anywhere?" Kira said, unable to help herself.

"And *second*," the woman continued, "Everyone, possessing magic or not, is to remain where they are—no travel, no quests, and no leaving the temple. It is for the safety of everyone."

It felt as if the breath got knocked out of Kira's chest. She couldn't speak, couldn't come up with any kind of retort. *What?*

The other soldier elaborated, "These tears they found across the realm, they're dangerous, and commoners can't see them. We're all to stay in place, you see."

Kira met his eyes as she spoke, "I see. Well. We'll get back to brushing then." She turned her back on them, blood roaring in her ears.

No wonder Jun left, she thought, refusing to turn around and watch the soldiers leave, despite the creeping feeling scurrying up her back. *Ryn must have only heard the first part of the decree.*

Though she didn't fear the soldiers checking up on her, she and Ryn brought out the grooming brushes anyway, and began to work on Naga. All the while as she brushed down Naga's coat, untangled the knots in her tail, and picked her hooves, though they were still quite clean from yesterday, Kira's mind raced. Ryn worked in equal silence, and she was glad for the brief calm, and the task at hand.

Finally, when they could do nothing else, they closed Naga's stall, having mucked it out and given her fresh hay. "Let's go to the Gray Wing," was all Kira said.

Ryn raised his eyebrows at her, but followed.

"I don't care if Kusari comes to yell at us. I don't want to be accosted by any more soldiers."

"I couldn't agree more. Besides, I'm sure you need to pack."

Kira exhaled, frowning at him, but didn't say anything. She knew he could read auras, but he couldn't read her thoughts. *No, only Yuki can do that, and she's probably in lessons right now.* She chuckled aloud, and said, "Come on."

They cloistered themselves in the training room inside the Gray Wing, the room deepest inside the wing, giving them the sense they couldn't be overheard or interrupted. Kira had snagged a few floor cushions from the common room, and they set them down in the middle of the polished wood floor. "Normally I could have made some from Light, but…" she trailed off, "Well, I was going to say it was scarce, but now it's just illegal." She shuddered.

Frowning, Ryn sat, folding his long legs underneath him. "It's all looking rather dire, yes. So what's your plan? I didn't need to read your aura to see your brain churning."

A chuckle escaped her, and she flung herself down on her stomach on a pillow, facing the doors. "I don't know," she said with a sigh. "I need to get to the palace. That's where Jun's headed, I'm sure of it. Whether he's going to try and stop the execution, or just be there to give witness, I don't know."

"I figured as much myself," Ryn replied, leaning back on his hands. "Now, surely the Commonality will have blocked off the gate to Heliodor, as well as the temple gates, so leaving on foot is out."

"I don't exactly have the skill to fly on the wind, and I'm no good at illusionwork like Jun is. I bet that's how he got through the gates." It had been strange, the few times Jun had tried to show her how to use Shadow magic to look invisible—or blend in by using illusions, as he specified, but it wasn't one of her proficiencies.

"Ah yes," Ryn said, "A shame. It's rather too bad he didn't just take you with him."

Kira huffed. "Maybe he didn't think I would want to go? I don't know."

"Or perhaps he didn't think he had enough time?"

"Yeah," Kira agreed half-heartedly, "I just don't know how I can leave now. And I *have* to go after him. It's just—I have a bad feeling about this."

"Hmm. It's not as if you can ask Raiden or Zowan for help," Ryn said.

"Right. There's no way they'll want me to leave, especially if we're on some kind of lockdown. Then there's the fact that I can't do any magic, well, *shouldn't...*"

She didn't want to think about what would happen when she showed up at the palace when she wasn't supposed to be traveling. But at this rate, she wouldn't have that problem if she couldn't figure out a way out of the Spire.

"So a thoroughly non-magical escape," Ryn agreed.

"If only we could pick the Spirekeeper's brain, I'm sure she knows every single way in and out of the temple grounds."

"Pick her brain?" Ryn said, forehead wrinkled at the strange term.

"Get inside her head, I mean, or ask what she knows," Kira clarified with an eye roll.

A slight smirk perked up the corner of his mouth. "You mean read her thoughts, perhaps?"

Kira gasped. "Yuki! I bet she would know. I mean, I know she can't help but hear things people think, and she does a lot of her chores working with Kusari."

"I bet we can catch her after Meditation," Ryn said, his gaze flickering toward the training room door.

Nodding quickly, Kira pushed herself up off her stomach and rose, feeling slightly guilty for skipping Meditation herself, but what with Spectra's accident, Jun's disappearance, and the new decrees, she had quite enough to think about. And since she often moved between the two temples, her instructors knew not to expect her at every single lesson.

As soon as they reached the walkway leading out to the pavilion, Kira's stomach clenched. There was a newly-built wooden structure around the tear—which she had nearly forgotten about—and it was being guarded by a Commonality soldier.

Meditation was just wrapping up, and they hovered by the entrance to the foyer as the bleary-eyed trainees bowed to Mistress Korinna from where they sat on their mats and began to get to their feet. Trainees from other parts of the temple had already begun to move through the foyer, on their way to midday meals or other lessons, so Kira hadn't particularly been paying attention to the people around her until someone clapped her on the shoulder.

"Kira," Zowan said, "Just get out of Meditation?" He glanced down the walkway with its new obstruction, gaze lingering on the soldier standing there.

"Um, no actually," she said truthfully, "I was up all night in the Apothecarium—did you hear about Spectra and everything?" She clenched her stomach, watching as the trainees left Meditation. She hadn't seen Yuki, yet, but she would need to talk to her now if she were to have any chance of leaving in haste.

Zowan nodded. "Yes, *everything*. Which is why I wanted to talk to you."

Ryn tactfully stepped aside, meandering further down the walkway.

"What do you mean?" Kira said, licking her lips.

"This decree from the palace," he said in a low voice, "It's obviously Tigran's doing. The Empress has never done this kind of thing before. Outlawing magic? She didn't even try that during the feud." He shook his head. "I know it's going to be difficult, but we need to follow the decrees—the penalty is death. Raiden and I are working on figuring out what these tears are; we just need some time to convince the Empress. If we can, then she'll know that Tigran was leading her falsely this whole time. But we'll need to be patient."

A swirl of irritation and surprise writhed in her stomach. Of course Zowan wanted her to be a good little knight and follow the decrees. *All this is happening, and we're still sitting around doing nothing!*

But she was more than a little surprised to hear that Zowan was working together with Raiden on *anything*. "I—right," she said lamely.

"Have you seen Jun?"

His tone seemed benign, so she said, "Uh, not yet."

"Well perhaps we can all have dinner together later, like we used to. I'm sure he's going through hell right now knowing he can't go to the palace, to say—to say goodbye."

Unexpected shock reverberated up through her chest, and she nodded stiffly. "I can't even imagine. Though, I'm not sure if being there would be more difficult..."

Zowan shook his head. "I've known the Kosumosos for quite some time. And I think Jun would want to say goodbye to his father. I'm sure this is going to be difficult for him. Unless Raiden and I can figure out a connection between the tears and the lanterns before tomorrow, then no one's going."

Kira pressed her lips together and nodded slowly. Out of the corner of her eye she saw a short figure speaking with Ryn. "I think I should probably get going," she said, tamping down the overwhelming guilt surging through her.

"Of course." A brief smile illuminated his face, and he clapped both hands on her shoulders. "I knew you would handle this well. You're going to make a fantastic Gray Knight. We'll get magic back eventually."

Kira felt as if she had been struck in the chest. All she could say was "Thanks," before he turned and headed toward the stairs leading up into the Spire.

Blinking, Kira dragged her feet over to Ryn and Yuki, trying to regain her composure. Zowan couldn't know she was trying to leave, and he didn't seem to know Jun was gone. So why had every word hammered in a nail of guilt?

She forced herself to smile at Yuki, who had started to grow out her hair; it now just barely brushed the shoulders of her yolk-yellow robes.

"Ryn says you're looking for some way out of the temple?" Yuki asked quietly. There were a handful of people left in the foyer; a group of girls lingered by the fountain, and a pair of acolytes were heading casually down the Hall of Spirits.

"Yes," Kira said. "Do you know of any?"

"Ah, well, yes," Yuki admitted. "I might have heard of something. Not on purpose—"

"I know," Kira said, holding up her palms. "I'm not judging you."

Yuki ducked her head, then said, "It's down in the catacombs."

CHAPTER 14

BETWEEN WORLDS

A small bag hanging from one shoulder, Kira went to the Apothecarium at lunchtime. She couldn't leave without seeing Micah—and she had to get out of the Spire before it was too late, and Zowan came to check up on her and Jun.

Spectra wasn't on the pallet where she had lain last night, and Kira began to panic slightly. Micah was nowhere in sight, so Kira walked down the corridor looking for another patient room, or someone who could tell her where to look, unease growing. At last, she ran into Mistress Nyoko, who was backing out of a large room full of various dried plants hanging from the ceiling, with more heaped on the counters, and stored on the shelves. Nyoko carried a tray filled with jars of herbs and remedies, her dark gray hair braided neatly down her back.

"Oh, here, let me show you," Nyoko replied when Kira asked where Spectra was. She led her further down the hall, around a corner, and into a smaller room with a single pallet on the floor. A brazier hung from a corner of the ceiling, some kind of citrus incense wafting over the room. Kira's nostrils flared at the familiar scent—one which had permeated her quarters for quite some time last year, after she kept fainting due to her soul damage.

"What is that for?" she asked, pointing at the brazier.

"Ah, a combination of medicinals for awakening, brightening, and bringing consciousness forward. It is used in healing or sometimes meditation."

"Oh. How's Spectra?" Kira could clearly see she hadn't changed much, though someone had brushed her hair. With a tender thought, she wondered if it had been Micah, and then a pang of jealousy flitted through her.

So shocked at the odd emotion, she didn't hear what Nyoko said next, but it didn't seem important, since the healer was now heading out of the room with her tray of medicines. Kira stepped into the room carefully, as if movement would set off the jealous thoughts again.

She had never cared before how much time and attention Micah spent on his sister. And Spectra was in a coma for goodness' sake! What was wrong with her? She had always found it heartwarming that Micah cared so much for his sister, who sometimes had a hard time. But Micah was always there for her. *And he's there for me, too, even when we're apart, I just don't need him as much as Spectra does.*

Somewhat mollified, she approached Spectra and crouched down beside her, whispering, "Sorry. I don't know what I was thinking."

As she expected, Spectra said nothing and continued to lay peacefully on the pallet. A few minutes later, Nyoko came back in, and Kira perked up at the sound of another set of footsteps accompanying her.

"I believe Micah went home to let his parents know what happened to her," Nyoko said, ushering Ryn in the room. "Now, Master Kimura, what is it that you wanted to tell me?"

He bowed at both of them, then gestured to Spectra. "I've spent enough time around Spectra with Kira, so I've gotten used to the nuances in her coloring. Something seemed different last night—still seems different. I couldn't quite figure it out, but I went through my journals and I figured it out."

Something about his tone made Kira cock her head to the side. Ryn continued to speak while studying Spectra, "And it occurred to me, I had only seen it before in two other peoples' auras—ever, in my entire life. Yours, Kira, and, well, the Lord of Between."

Kira choked, "The—wait, what?"

What did she have in common with Tigran, first of all? And what did it have to do with Spectra now?

She opened her mouth, but couldn't form any words.

Mistress Nyoko seemed speechless for a moment herself, but asked, "And do you have any idea what it means? How we can treat her?"

At that moment, another mage walked in the door, and Kira caught her breath. Raiden took up the entire doorway in his dark robes decorated in silver raindrops. She adjusted her bag further behind her body.

"I have a theory," Raiden said boldly, "But it's not something to be treated."

Kira bristled, "What do you mean? What's wrong with us—with her?"

To her surprise, Raiden smiled, looking startlingly like Zowan in that moment, with his wavy black hair sweeping his shoulders, yet his face looked more lined than ever before. "There's nothing wrong—the layer Ryn sees on your auras is merely an effect from touching the space between worlds. Something that *you* have done as you crossed from the Starless Realm, and something the Lord of Between has done, as we know. With Spectra, now we know what these tears are made of. Or, I should say, what the tears are revealing."

The breath that flowed out of Kira's chest almost hurt. "Oh. I guess that makes sense then." It was merely a mark of touching the space between. Then he was right, this information was nothing they could use to help treat Spectra. And these tears... really *were* tears in the universe.

"Kira, may I speak with you?" Raiden asked, and her gut clenched. She nodded, gathering herself up and following him out of the room.

Her thoughts raced. Did he already know Jun had left? Did he know of her plan? She followed him out into the hallway, palms sweaty. A wave of relief flooded her when he stopped there. Surely, if she was in trouble, he would have taken her somewhere else to thunder at her.

"Zowan told me he would be having dinner with you and Jun tonight."

She pressed her dry lips together and nodded. She needed to leave, and soon.

"I..." Raiden trailed off, startling her. "I have a favor to ask of you."

"Um, what is it?"

He bowed his head. "My nephew has grown more cordial with me this past year, which I should be lucky for, considering. I am also thankful that he chose you as his squire, as I believe you training here has made his transition back home a more pleasant one. But things are still—not as I wish them to be.

"I know what I did after the Fall of Azurite was—incredibly wrong. To keep them here. His girls. But I thought—" He shook his head. "It doesn't matter what I thought. It was wrong. I want to make it right, or as right as I can. He's the only family I have left. His mother—my sister—passed away long before he even came to train at the Spire. I am the only family he has left."

"Not the *only* family," Kira said, trying to keep the harshness out of her voice. "He has me, and Jun, and Anzu."

Head still bowed, he said, "You're right. You're right. It's selfish of me to demand his forgiveness. But I wonder if you could—If you could find out if there's anything I could do to begin to repair our relationship."

She opened her mouth, but he held his hands up as if in surrender. "I know. I know. There's probably nothing. But I have to try. I can't go—I can't continue without trying."

A small battle was raging inside her chest. Seeing Raiden's insecurity—the man was near tears, for goodness' sake—and so desperately wanting to repair things with Zowan, Kira was torn between staying the night just to try. But the longer she stayed, the higher the chances of someone finding out that Jun was gone, and then she would have no chance to go and get him. With the way he had raced off without a word, she knew he was up to something rash and dangerous. She couldn't lose Jun, of all people.

Nodding, feeling like a traitor, she said, "Of course, I'll try and ask."

Raiden sighed as if a great weight had been lifted from his shoulders. "Thank you, Lady Gray." He straightened, lifting his chin to his normal posture, and said, "It is all this nonsense with the lanterns, the tears, and the commander—he deigns to threaten me with—" A cough exploded out of him as he caught sight of two soldiers coming down the hallway.

"What is your business here?" Raiden demanded. "This is a place of healing."

Kira recognized the somewhat kind man she had met in the stables. It was he who spoke first, saying, "We are to investigate the girl who was attacked."

"Attacked?" Raiden said. "It was no attack. But you must speak with Mistress Nyoko."

In all the confusion between the soldiers following Raiden into Spectra's room, Nyoko chivvying them all out and leading them to her study, Kira slipped away.

Heaving a sigh of relief as the doors to the Apothecarium shut behind her, she shut her eyes for a moment.

Raiden and Zowan. There was no way she could stay, though. And she hadn't found Micah, either, the whole reason she returned to the Apothecarium.

Brushing her shoulder where her armor normally would be, she headed for the Gray Wing for one last thing. The trousers she had worn last night were crumpled in the trunk in her closet, a dark blue scroll somewhat flattened in the pocket.

***

The stairway was cold and dark, just like the last time she was down here. Wanting to conserve the small amount of magic she kept stored at all times, she lit a torch at the top of the stairs with a brief spark of magic.

She knew it was selfish to retain some magic—was she as bad as Tigran for trapping it?—but she couldn't help it. She would go without Light weapons and would have to make due with the steel dagger she always carried, but she had no idea how to spark a fire without a match or a lighter, and those didn't exist in this realm.

This realm. It was easy to forget sometimes that she had ever lived in another place, unless, of course, she thought of her mother. Her mother, who had moved from place to place, always looking for a way back home, back to Camellia. Kira swallowed past a lump in her throat, nodding to herself. "Well, I found it," she whispered. "I made it."

Whether she was assuring herself, or the departed spirit of her mom, she didn't know. But the words leaving her lips made brief clouds of white in the increasingly cold air as she descended below ground.

When she reached the first level down, a dark shape moved toward her, and she nearly leapt out of her skin.

"It's just me," someone chuckled loftily.

"Ryn!" She put a hand to her heart. "You almost gave me a heart attack! What are you doing here?"

"Oh, please, you thought I'd let you run off on an adventure to find Jun all alone?" A small knapsack hung from his shoulder. She pushed forward, resigned and secretly relieved.

"Let's go then."

"Well, that was easy," he said, catching up to her with his long strides.

"You're a grown adult. I can't tell you what to do."

"That's right," he said, nodding. "Though, I *am* a teaching master at this temple, perhaps I should tell *you* what to do."

They reached the next set of stairs and Kira looked at him pointedly.

He shrugged. "But I don't really feel like it."

Kira scoffed, and they continued on. "Good. Because you're the one who enabled me to go, anyway. But seriously Ryn, are you sure? I—I don't think I'll be able to come back. Not unless the Empress drops the decree."

"I'm sure," he said, all hints of joking gone. "And besides, if we're not allowed to do magic, what's the point of staying?"

"There's no one else down here that's going to tag along on our quest, is there?"

"I doubt it," he said. "Though I only just slipped out of the Apothecarium before you."

She shook her head, snorting through her nostrils.

It was only a few minutes later that they reached the level where the great electric blue crack in the air menaced at them. Kira sucked in a sharp breath, wondering if it had changed, if it looked bigger than before.

They both veered over to it, without saying a word to each other. "Maybe they should block this one off," Ryn said.

"I'm sure the soldiers will get to that, once they're done interrogating Nyoko." She inched forward, trying to study the tear. "So if the tear left a mark on Spectra's aura, just like mine... Are we sure it's not a portal? I can't see anything through it though, it's all just—"

"Bright. Yes. Perhaps it doesn't lead anywhere?"

"Maybe."

As they continued down the next set of stairs, a jolt rent through her core when she envisioned more tears appearing across Camellia—but what if some of them led somewhere? What if they became portals back to the Starless Realm?

CHAPTER 15

RISKY

"They probably know by now," Kira said, studying the faraway horizon as Light magic blinked into existence all around her. The sun had set, and they were on the other side of Heliodor's wall, somewhere in the mountains behind the Spire.

"Well, you really shouldn't have invited everyone to dinner if you weren't going to show," Ryn said, tossing his head and leading the way across a small stream. As soon as they had come out of the tunnel that led from the catacombs, Kira had noticed Ryn was wearing double katanas. It reassured her to a degree, knowing him to be a skilled swordsman due to his ability to read auras, but she knew it was a skill that troubled him, ever since the feud and all of the fighting he had done. She didn't want him putting himself through the anguish it took to wield those swords again.

"Ha ha," she said. "What was I supposed to do, tell them Jun was taking a bath? Come back later?"

Ryn snorted. "I'm sure you could have come up with something."

"Too late now," she said, throwing back her shoulders and readjusting her bag. She heaved a sigh, looking up at the mountainous terrain ahead. "Wish we could have taken our horses. But we'll definitely get there in time. I just worry about what Jun might do *before* the execution."

"Well, we can't stop and hire a horse in Arishi either, if the Commonality is enforcing the travel ban."

"I know." She spared a guilty thought for leaving Naga, but surely Zowan would take care of her once he realized Kira was gone. She didn't even want to think about how long it would be until she returned. It was likely she was on the run now, just like Mistress Nari.

Kira looked back only once to get a glimpse of the tall Spire dominating the sky, and a pang of fear and sadness struck her as she thought of all the people she loved inside of it. Micah, whom she had last seen asleep this morning, though spending all night with him in vigil watching Spectra had been intimate in its own way, and waking with her head on his shoulder was something she had certainly never done before.

Zowan, who was probably sick with worry over the fact that neither she nor Jun were anywhere to be found. And the pathetic note she had left him, tucked under a tin of tea in the Gray Wing's kitchen, with only the words *I'm sorry,* written on it. At least he would have Anzu to console him—and she would probably keep him from rushing off to find the two of them, anyway. Even Lord Raiden, who had so tenderly bared his soul to her this morning about his fear of Zowan never forgiving him.

She gnawed at the inside of her lip and took a step forward, turning her back on Heliodor.

The descent of night brought a sense of calm for her, as the pearlescent glow of Light twinkled to life all around.

No longer wondering if the Commonality had somehow followed her—she was one of the only people who could see in the dark in these parts—they stole through the night like phantoms.

Ryn followed close behind her, and at one point put a hand on her sleeve. It made her smile, almost as if they were holding hands. But she had never thought of Ryn that way—would never—he was older than her, for one, and he never seemed interested in girls.

They had agreed that they shouldn't summon any flame, and the sky was blanketed in clouds, blotting out the stars and moon.

"It's a good thing you can see in the dark," he muttered as they crossed through a dark wood somewhere around Arishi. "We wouldn't have gotten very far otherwise."

"Good, yes," she replied quietly, "But at least you can't see all the creepy things darting about. Just squirrels or bats and whatnot, but creepy."

He gave a hollow laugh. "No, but I can hear them, and that's even worse."

"What I wouldn't give to see Thistle right now," Kira said. "He can be a pain sometimes, but he's useful."

"I can imagine," Ryn said.

"You know…" Kira started as they came out of the woods near the Kaidō road. "If we hurried, we could make it to Mount Gekkō by the morning. I'm sure Thistle would find us."

"And then what? Stay for breakfast and borrow some horses?"

Kira almost laughed, but the idea pained her heart. What she wouldn't give to go back home to Gekkō-ji and sleep in the dormhouse, wake up, and have all her problems be someone else's.

"No," she said heavily, "But there's something I'd like to talk to Gekkō about—something to do with stopping the tears. There's this scroll… Well, I'll show you in the morning." She was glad she remembered to grab it.

"And I bet there's someone inside Gekkō-ji who can get us some horses. We might need to leave the palace hastily."

***

"This is too risky," Ryn admonished for the twentieth time sometime around dawn as they lurked in the woods at the bottom of Mount Gekkō.

From their vantage point in a thick copse of black pine trees they could see the soldiers guarding the lower gate. Kira had hoped Thistle would find them the closer they got to the mountain, but it was growing lighter and lighter out, and so far they hadn't seen the flying squirrel or the spirit of the mountain.

"Plan B, I guess," Kira said in a falsely cheerful voice as she turned to Ryn, who gave her an exasperated look.

"Fine," he said, waving his hand for her to get on with it. In his other hand, he held the dark blue scroll he'd been studying. "And when they execute us, be sure to go last so you can say a few words over me."

Kira blew out a breath that was part laugh, part scoff. "I'll start composing our epitaphs right away."

He nodded gravely, then turned back to reread the scroll.

Kira ripped a scrap of paper from a journal in her bag and wrote a short note in charcoal to the one person inside she knew would almost certainly help them: Nesma.

Hoping her words conveyed just enough information for help, but not enough to indict Nesma should she get caught with it, Kira pulled as much Shadow wind as she could from her surroundings. It was quite enough. Once outside of Heliodor and the dense net the lanterns cast there, the magic felt like it usually did. But she was sure if she went inside Gekkō-ji, it would be scarce again.

With the outright ban on magic, Kira said a prayer to Gekkō as she sent the note flying on the wind that no one would see the note besides Nesma.

And then they had to wait.

She knew it was risky. She knew it would be near impossible for Nesma to get through the gate, especially with two horses in tow. But as they had drawn further and further away from the Spire, Kira realized the situation she had put herself—and Ryn—into. They were outlaws now, just like Nari. Kira hadn't acted as dramatically, though she wished she had, but disobeying the Empress' decrees was on equal footing—and carried a sentence of death. They would most certainly need a fast escape from Meridian once she found Jun.

A small part of her worried that Nesma might not want to help her, even if she got the message. Kira still had mixed feelings about turning down Nesma's offer of squireship, and even now guilt assailed her for asking for help.

"You sure you don't want to just steal a couple of horses from the village?" Ryn asked half an hour later.

She grit her teeth. "Not unless we have to."

"This execution is supposed to be—what?—tonight?"

"Yes. At sundown. Let's give it another hour. And this isn't just about the horses; I need to talk to Gekkō. I want to know what he knows about the wisp, and what the story of the Camellian Dragon could mean. Maybe it can help us plead our case with the Empress—or help with the tears, *something*."

Ryn rubbed his hands together, trying to warm them. "Well can we move about a little? I'm freezing. Maybe we'll find that spirit of yours somewhere else."

Nodding, Kira adjusted her bag and looked to the east where they could meander in the woods between the mountain and the village, but would still be able to easily return to get a view of the gate.

They walked slowly, the woods thick with damp leaves. Spring was taking its time, and winter seemed to be refusing to relax its grip. There weren't buds yet on any of the trees or bushes. It was just one more unusual and unsettling thing piled on the rest.

A girl screamed from above, high at the top of the mountain.

Kira's heart took off like a frightened rabbit, thumping wildly in her chest. A fraction of a second later, Ryn grabbed her arms as she started to run.

He pulled her down to the ground, and they crouched there among the crushed leaves, listening.

Listening.

A group of boulders blocked their view of the gate, but the next second they spotted two soldiers rushing up one of the dirt paths that wound up the mountain. Kira squeezed Ryn's hands gratefully, but didn't let go. All she could hear was her fast breathing, which clouded in front of her face, blowing fog over the leaves.

Was that Nesma? Please be okay. Please don't let this be my fault.

But how could it not be? She had risked Nesma all over some stupid horses and a fairytale about a dragon and some flowers.

They waited in silence, straining their ears for any further sounds from the temple. But there was nothing else.

Ryn nudged her, and she opened her eyes—not even realizing she had closed them in her stressed and tired stupor—to look where he pointed.

On the outskirts of the village, a girl led three horses down an empty lane.

Kira gasped. "*Nesma!*" With a glance at Ryn, they stole from their hiding place as quietly as they could, and came to the edge of the woods, Kira's heart nearly dancing out of her ribcage.

"Nesma!" she hissed, beckoning the girl to the trees.

A smile lit up Nesma's narrow face, and she quickly urged the horses over to the woods. The brown mare at the front eagerly nosed Kira's hand as she came over. "Hi, Meluca," Kira said in surprise. And then she turned to Nesma and threw her arms around her. "What happened? Who screamed? Is everyone okay?"

As she disentangled herself from Nesma, Kira heard a lofty musical voice respond, from somewhere above her. "Everyone's fine, thank you very much," Thistle said from atop a black mare's head.

"Thistle!" Kira clapped her hands over her mouth at the loud outburst.

"Here," Ryn said, taking one of the horses' reins and pulling them deeper into the trees. "Why don't we start moving and they can regale us with their tale while we get away from here."

"Good idea," Kira muttered. She kept sneaking glances at Nesma as they walked, skirting around the village in case there were any Commonality stationed there. With the tears appearing at random, the soldiers could be anywhere, if they were truly trying to protect the commoners. And besides, Commander Hagane was supposed to be on a trek across the realm to install more of those lanterns. The army could be anywhere.

As they crossed a small stream, Kira met Nesma's eyes, and they both spoke at once.

"I'm sorry—" they both said.

"What? What for?" Kira demanded.

Nesma looked down, "For putting you on the spot when I asked to be your squire?" she said in a small voice, turning it into a question.

Kira closed her eyes briefly. "Don't be sorry," she said, reaching out and squeezing Nesma's hand. "I'm the one who's sorry for turning you down. And I'm here to make it up to you. I accept."

"What?" Nesma stumbled. Kira caught her arm, and they stopped walking.

The horses took the opportunity to take a drink in the stream, and they let them.

"I want you to be my squire," Kira clarified. "If you're up for it. But I don't know how good my standing is anymore now that I left the Spire against the Empress' decrees, so I would understand if you don't want to. You can go back to Gekkō-ji and stay safe there, that is if you can—"

"I can't," Nesma said, throwing out her chin. "And I don't want to. I made the decision when Thistle brought me your note."

Kira cocked her head to the side and looked at the flying squirrel, who made a strange motion as if shrugging. "I found it lying in the woods. You know, there isn't enough magic to send a message very far."

"What? Really? I thought I gave it plenty."

A lilting giggle escaped him. "Aren't you studying advanced Shadow magic, young mage? What are they teaching you at that temple? Wind isn't a finite substance you can *give*. It gathers more as it goes, to continue on."

"Oh." Kira cut her gaze to Ryn, who gave her a look that indicated he hadn't known this either. "Well, this is why I don't send messages long distance," she muttered.

"And I could tell it was your magic," Thistle said, "So I found the only person I thought you might be sending an illegal note to."

Kira's face warmed. "I'm sorry, Nesma, I really shouldn't have put you at risk."

"It's fine," Nesma said. "Really. I'm glad you came. After we heard about the decrees, I was worried about you and Jun, stuck at the Spire. So what's going on? Why did you come here?"

"It's Jun," Kira told her, and then went on to explain where she thought he had gone.

"For an execution of all the prisoners?" Nesma said, looking down and picking at her nails. Jun's father wasn't the only prisoner. Kira hadn't heard any news about Nesma's sisters "escaping", so perhaps Tigran was letting them take the fall.

"Yes, I think so. I'll understand if you don't want—"

"I want to go," Nesma said quickly.

"To Meridian then?"

Nesma nodded. "To Meridian."

CHAPTER 16

THE NATURE OF PEOPLE

A t dusk, the city of Meridian came alive. The glow of Light magic twinkled everywhere, which was heartening, but they had also lit plenty of lamps along the docks along the river, which was where Kira, Ryn, and Nesma had decided to enter the city.

"Are you done yet?" Kira asked Ryn quietly from their place in the shadows just outside the wall. Her horse stomped her foot, and Kira felt just as impatient.

He tugged on the thread he was sewing into place and broke it with his teeth. "Done. Here." He handed the needle back to Kira, who banished the Light magic.

The thread they had ripped from the hems of their robes, not wanting to risk using Light for thread, or for anything they would carry on their persons, for that matter. They had checked and double checked their clothes and belongings, should they be searched, but Kira had already dispensed with her armor back at the Spire, and

Nesma didn't wear any. *We should buy some if we can*, Kira thought, feeling strangely naked, then shook her head. *Focus. Not important right now.*

But it *was* important—considering they were walking unarmored and barely armed into the den of vipers that was the Imperial Palace.

Kira and Ryn had ripped up their mage's robes, keeping the tight section for the torso and using the longer fabric at the bottom to fashion rough hoods. It hadn't been a long ride from Gekkō-ji. They wanted to keep their identities a secret—for now—and the robes were a dead giveaway. Nesma's plain trousers and wraparound jacket didn't identify her as a non-commoner, and now that Ryn had finished his hood, they were ready to go in.

They were just waiting on Thistle now.

Kira ran her hands over her shoulder bag nervously. "Everyone ready?"

"Yes, Kira," Ryn droned, settling his hood over his face with neat precision.

"You're sure you want to come?" she asked, looking at Nesma now.

"Yes," Nesma said, quietly but with some force. She had a silk scarf wrapped around her head covering her hair. It was pink with flowers embroidered on it. Kira had given it a second glance when Nesma had pulled it out from around her neck where it had been hidden by her shirt—but on second thought, Kira figured it would actually blend in by standing out. It wasn't exactly a scarf a knight would wear.

Kira forced a smile at her, not willing to voice her worry for the slightly younger girl. She had clearly made up her mind.

Something small dropped on Kira's shoulder, and she had to repress a shriek. The resultant squeal under clenched fingers made the others look at her, and Thistle, who was now perched on her shoulder.

"Why must you do that?" she demanded, craning her neck to look him in the eye.

"Sorry," he admitted. "I thought I had more time to get over the wall, but one of the soldiers turned around to pick his nose."

Kira paused, wondering if he was joking, then said, "So, should we wait? Or are they moving?"

"They're moving. You should enter in about one minute, then you'll be able to follow behind them all the way up to the palace, with enough distance that they won't see you."

"Wait, what?" Kira said. "I thought we were going to go to the Wicked Wharf to lay low until an hour before sundown?"

Thistle shook his tiny head. "The patrol patterns are too tight over there. Unless you want to risk it?"

Kira drew in a sharp breath through her nose and held it for a second, thinking. "No. We'll follow them to the palace and wait there—somehow."

"The prospect of hiding at the tavern was much more enticing," Ryn said, adjusting his hood again. "But if we get pinned down there, we're no help at all."

"I don't want to hide near the palace either," Kira said. "But we'll be closer. And maybe we can find Jun quicker."

Nesma said nothing, only took a deep breath and inched away from the wall.

"It's almost time." Thistle's whiskers twitched once—twice, then, "Now."

Working to unclench her jaw, Kira led the way. Thistle burrowed his way mostly behind her neck, hidden by her hood. "I wish you would perch somewhere else," Kira whispered as they approached the gate. Meluca trailed behind her on her reins.

"No one wishes that more than I," the lilting chuckle came. "Your hair reeks of lavender."

Kira almost snorted, feeling his whiskers twitching on the sensitive skin of her neck, but the gate was in sight.

"But Gekkō wants me to remain with you, since he let me leave the mountain," Thistle hissed. Just as they fell in line behind a lone wagon laden with sacks of rice, and the soldiers came out to demand identification of its driver, Kira felt a strange sensation drip down her body, and at once knew herself to be illusioned.

Thistle was able to tap into Gekkō's magic, but it made her nervous when he was so far away from the mountain. It had failed once before—he had run out. It made sense to Kira, what with the way Light magic worked. So they had agreed to use it only if necessary, and there was no other way to get through the gate undetected.

On the other side of the gate, a warm tingle ran up from the soles of her feet to the top of her head. Beside her, she saw Ryn reappear, and behind him was Nesma. The soldiers were still questioning the rice farmer, and though their pushing was making Kira itch to go back and knock some sense into the soldiers, they had to continue on.

Now came the tricky part.

The streets were surprisingly busy, considering the decrees forbidding travel. Kira was glad to see the rice farmer finally be admitted to the city far behind them—at least Tigran and the Commonality weren't stupid enough to stop food from going in and out. But she had expected people to be shut up in their homes, to keep them safe from the threat of the tears. She had read enough books and learned enough history back in the Starless Realm to know what martial law and evil dictators looked like.

But she had forgotten the nature of people.

They were curious; they were scared. They wanted to be with other people and share their fears, but more importantly, to experience community. They gathered in small groups at street corners, in the eateries, by the boats unloading at the docks. They glanced at the soldiers with more curiosity, though not enough distrust in Kira's opinion. The soldiers hadn't yet shown their true colors to the commoners—yet—disguising everything they were doing as something to better the realm.

It was easy to walk through the streets with the cover of so many people out and about. Thistle kept an eye on the soldiers' patrol far ahead, peering out from behind Kira's neck to watch the distance they kept between them. Of course, thanks to Thistle scouting the streets earlier, Kira also knew that at an equal distance behind them, the next patrol would be coming. The feeling of being trapped would follow her until she left this city, she thought.

As long as we find Jun, that's fine.

Her heart jolted when the Imperial Palace came into view. Up until recently, her visits here had been somewhat tedious. But at this very moment, she knew the Commonality were preparing for an execution behind those walls.

The Gray Knights were shackled, their final moments laid out before them. Though the loss of any of them would be terrible, the fact that one of them was Jun's father made it so much worse. And all of them had fought alongside her father.

She glanced over her shoulder at the sun in the cold sky. There were still a few hours yet until sunset. There was still time to find Jun—unless he had already gotten himself into irrevocable trouble.

Whether there was time to do anything to stop the executions, well...

We'll cross that bridge when we get to it, Kira thought, eyeing the moat around the castle walls and the wooden bridge they were about to cross.

"Everyone ready? Everyone good?" she said out of the corner of her mouth.

Ryn made a grunt of agreement, and Nesma mumbled something that sounded positive. Thistle's whiskers twitched on her neck. Kira turned to look both her friends in the eye, to reassure herself. Nesma looked as if she had rid herself of all emotion. Ryn's handsome face was arranged into a carefully crafted bored expression she knew he used to hide his true emotions. As a wave of apprehension flooded her, she threw back her shoulders and strode forward.

Their footsteps rang out on the wooden bridge, and the soldiers posted on either side turned at attention. Kira flung back her hood, and she felt Thistle burrow down inside the bunched fabric.

"I'm here to see the Empress," she called.

CHAPTER 17

SOMETHING BIG AND STUPID AND HEROIC

"Just who do you think—" the soldier cried, raising his hand in a swift motion. As he brought it down, Kira's fist went up, catching his hand before he could strike her. She held his wrist, quivering from the impact, as he tried to pull out of her grasp. She looked him straight in the eye. "I am Lady Kira Savage Starwind, and I have an invitation."

With her other hand she pulled the scroll from her bag, holding it out of his reach but bringing the Empress' obvious seal into view. The other soldier still stood several feet away, poised as if ready to spring at anyone's movement, but eyes wide with fear.

She felt the hand release its tension, and she let go, turning her body one step away from him, and unfurling the scroll. His eyes skimmed it reluctantly as he grimaced.

"Aye, well, be that as it may," he conceded, "There's a decree against travel, also signed by Her Majesty. Punishable by death. How did you come to be in Meridian, then?" he demanded, jutting his chin out at her.

She frowned, "What? I've been here for days," she lied. "I'm allowed to travel within Meridian, aren't I? Her Majesty requested my presence today," she insisted.

He glanced at her companions and then narrowed his eyes at Kira. "Been here for days?"

"Of course," she said easily, "We've had lodgings down at the Wicked Wharf, that's when we found out about the decrees—"

"Well, fine!" he snapped. "Go on. And I expect I don't need to remind you that magic is now strictly forbidden inside the Palace, as it is across the realm. You will be executed immediately if you attempt to use magic in Her Majesty's presence."

"We understand," Kira said, taking a shaky breath and hoping the soldier didn't see her pulse beating like crazy at her throat.

He jerked his head toward the half open door, saying, "Go."

Kira swallowed the lump in her throat and pulled on Meluca's rein. But her foot caught on something, and as she reached to pull some Shadow magic to catch herself, she saw the soldier's foot pull back.

Oh no. I can't! She wrenched the magic back in before it could get out. The action swept through her body like a hot knife, and she fell to the ground, Meluca's reins slipping through her fingers. Gravel ground into her palms, and she caught herself before her torso hit.

"Kira," Nesma gasped, rushing over.

"Watch your step, Lady Starwind," the soldier said, with the audacity to hold out a helping hand in front of her face.

She ignored it, pushing herself up on her scraped palms and drawing herself back up. She was just about the same height as the soldier; she looked deep into his eyes and said, "I will."

With a forced smile at him, she turned away and led Meluca inside the gate, focusing all of her attention on the sounds of Ryn and Nesma following behind her, watching her back.

She kept it together all the way down the white gravel path that swept in front of the palace, but when they reached the stables and drew in the brief shadow behind the inner wall, she gasped, catching Meluca's reins up and burying her face in the mare's neck, shaking.

She allowed herself five seconds. As the fury and fear fought to steal the breath from her lungs. Then she patted Meluca, and swallowed. The others were leading their mounts inside, and the sounds of footsteps were coming at them from two different directions.

From behind Kira, a pair of stablehands scurried forward, young boys with their hands outstretched, ready to care for the horses. Kira gave Meluca's cheek another pat, and handed her over. Thistle let out a light chirp, and Kira nodded carefully. "Please find Jun," she whispered, feeling him slide from her shoulder and leap away—now invisible.

As soon as Kira and the others exited the stables, they were greeted with a most unwelcome sight.

Approaching from the white stone slab walkway that led into the palace, strode a small delegation of soldiers, and at their center, Tigran Tashjian.

Oh, great.

Rolling her neck slightly, she grit her jaw and went out to meet him, a cordial smile plastered to her face.

His expression seemed a similar farce, and so was the bow he gave her when they came face to face. "Lady Starwind, we weren't expecting you today; Empress Mei had thought you to be training at the Spire."

She bowed back, only lowering as far as was required. Ryn and Nesma had drawn up by her sides.

"I was, but I had decided to come to Meridian early. We had already left by the time word of the decrees was spreading—or so I hear."

"I am sure," he said snidely. "Then I suppose you'll be staying with us in Meridian, then, until further notice." He held out his arm, inviting her down the path.

Kira tossed a glance over her shoulder to check that Meluca was being taken care of, but the mare seemed like she was in good hands. Ryn gave her shoulder a quick squeeze.

"Yes," Kira said to Tigran, heading down the stone pavers toward the ornate side door to the palace. To her relief, Tigran walked by her side, and not behind her. She had hoped she would have more time to look around for any sign of Jun with little to no supervision, but they had accepted Tigran's interfering as a possibility.

"Of course, Her Majesty didn't foresee this crisis before the trial was set," Tigran was saying, "And it was quite a difficult decision to make on her part to issue these decrees."

"I am sure," Kira said, keeping her voice as respectful as possible. *Trial*, she scoffed in her head. *Why not just call it what it is? An execution.*

She was keenly aware of the four soldiers walking on all sides of their small party, and the weapons they carried. But she couldn't resist asking, "The tears are a great danger. Do you know what's causing them?"

His step didn't falter one bit, but she saw his shoulders tighten under his gemstone encrusted coat. "Some type of insidious magic, no doubt, which is why Her Majesty has put a stop to its use. It's a shame, of course, for someone like you."

"Like me, yes," she said. "But my main concern is for the good of the realm, *of course*. And I grew up not needing magic for anything, so I think I'll survive."

"I certainly hope so."

His words zinged through her, jolting her nerves. She longed to reach for the dagger tucked into the back of her cloak, just for some feeling of security, but she knew such an action wouldn't be wise. Not after the incident at the gate, surely. She settled by reaching her consciousness inside her core and putting a mental finger on the ball of Light she kept stored there.

As Tigran held open the large wooden door for her, she caught a strange glimmer in his eye. Excitement? Envy? Her gut clenched. Disdain, she would have expected. Anger, or annoyance at the very least. But the curious look in his gaze chilled her to the very soul.

What did he want from her now?

She wasn't about to stick around long to find out. *Find Jun. Find a way out. And if we can bear witness to the "trial" and execution, so be it.*

She didn't kid herself that they might be able to do anything to stop it—she, Ryn, and Nesma had discussed it at length on the ride here. It would be far too dangerous. As much as she was ready to publicly turn against Tigran, she knew it would be smartest to remain as innocent-looking as possible until they were out of his clutches and out of Meridian.

When they entered the foyer, Kira was disgusted to see at least five lanterns from where she stood. The decorative stone pillars glowed menacingly, collecting magic—stealing it. They were lucky there wasn't a huge tear across this very foyer. Kira resisted the urge to reach out and feel how much Light essence permeated their surroundings, not wanting to risk it.

When they were all inside, Kira cleared her throat and said, "I would like to speak with the Empress. These tears, and the decrees for that matter, concern the safety of the realm."

Forcing herself to breathe slowly, she clenched her fists, glad the words she had practiced on the way here had come out in some semblance of what she intended. She just didn't know how much longer she could keep up this act with Tigran.

"I'm afraid the Empress isn't..." His eyes left Kira's, and he turned to watch two soldiers run toward a lantern in the corner of the foyer. It was glowing bright red.

"Stay here," he ordered Kira and the others, giving them a brief searching look before heading over to the lantern. After a brief inspection, Tigran and the soldiers strode down a corridor adjacent to the lantern.

"What—" Kira stepped forward, and one of the remaining soldiers barred her way, forcing up a polearm between them. Kira took a glance at the sharp end of the polearm and froze, but didn't back down.

"What's going on?" she demanded. "Why is that lantern red? What's wrong?"

The soldier raised an eyebrow at her. "It means someone's doing magic."

Kira quit breathing. *No. Jun. Please don't be Jun.* Was he sneaking around using illusionwork, trying to find his father and the Gray Knights? Why, oh, why couldn't he have waited for her so they could have come together?

She glanced at Ryn, whose polite mask had faltered for a brief second as he cut his gaze at her. She took a long, steady breath that almost hurt her lungs, and backed down from the soldier.

"I see," she said to the woman—who was a girl, really, maybe a year or two older than she, though Kira herself was almost eighteen. "So the lanterns detect magic as well?" she said, changing tack.

The girl nodded, pulling her polearm away but not relaxing her stance. Her face softened a little though, and her eyes brightened as she pointed at the red lantern. "The Commonality only just developed it. After what happened with Advisor Goten, we were all sca—concerned about the tears. But since they're magic, the lanterns will be able to detect those too. But they glow yellow for that. Red means magic is being drawn on nearby."

"Ah," Kira said, slipping her hands into her pockets in forced casualness. "That is impressive. But did you say Advisor Goten? What happened to—"

At that moment the doors burst open from the corridor where Tigran and the soldiers had disappeared. They were accompanied by another person, who lurched after them, their wrists bound with thin silver chains.

"Oh no," Nesma gasped.

Kira's fists clenched, and her wrenching heart now sped up. *"Nari?"*

Kira and the others stood frozen. The two soldiers guarding them seemed to think their duty was over, and went to join in escorting Nari.

Mistress Nari's long black coat and wide-legged pants were coated with dust, and her hair was tucked back in her customary long braid. Her gray-streaked hair now had a bright white strand running from the temple, thicker than ever before. How long had it been? Only a week or so, surely? She moved gingerly, and Kira remembered the multiple wounds she had suffered at the hands of the soldiers back at Gekkō-ji. But she held her head up as straight as ever.

Guilt flooded Kira as she realized the relief she had experienced upon seeing that it wasn't Jun. But still, someone had done magic, inside the palace no less. And that was now a death sentence.

Nari looked up as she was hauled away, meeting Kira's eyes with shock. She mouthed something, but Kira couldn't tell if it was *no* or *go*.

Well, it's too late to go, Kira thought to herself.

The great doors leading outside boomed shut behind Nari and the soldiers, leaving them alone with an irate Tigran, whose nostrils flared as he stared at the closed doors.

Kira's gaze flitted from side to side as she realized they were alone with him, but just as quickly spotted a palace servant entering timidly from the same corridor, carrying a small tray.

"And so ends the legacy of Nari Hyacinth," Tigran said finally, his expression settling back into his normal calm. "Not only did she violate the decree against magic, but she was caught in Empress Mei's quarters."

Kira's mouth popped open, but she couldn't think of anything to say. The servant approached them, her footsteps quiet in silken slippers, the tray she carried filled with empty jars and tins of what looked like medicinals.

"The Empress is quite ill," Tigran told Kira, at the same time gesturing the servant to join them. "Miss Emiko here has been treating her for years, but nothing any of our healers does seems to work. It has been quite mysterious. But now I think we have an idea of what the ailment could be."

"What do you mean?" Kira said, a heavy feeling settling in her stomach.

He jerked his head toward the closed doors where Nari had disappeared. "Mistress Nari was caught using magic inside the Empress' quarters. Her Majesty has been plagued by this mysterious ailment for years, which would come and go. Now I wonder if we could track the instances of her falling ill to visits by Mistress Nari, since it is clearly a magical illness."

The servant perked her head up, which was covered by a navy blue silk cloth. "It doesn't respond to anything," she said, eagerly joining in on the conversation as Tigran motioned her over. "All of the palace healers have been perplexed by it for so long. A wasting illness of some kind.

But if it was magic..." she trailed off, glancing at Tigran with hopeful eyes.

"Then we might have just found the cure," he said with sickening victory.

Still dumbstruck, Kira stared at the servant, wishing she had something to say. Now that she thought of it, the Empress had been ill several times over the years, on occasions when Kira visited the palace. She particularly remembered the time when the Storm King had come for his first visit since the end of the feud, and everyone had wondered whether the Empress was really ill, or just using it as an excuse to avoid the confrontation.

But Nari? Kira blinked. Why would she hurt the Empress in any way? No, this was just more of Tigran's deception, surely. And an illness that no one could cure? That sounded quite convenient. Nari was the perfect scapegoat.

Now what were they to do? She couldn't demand to see the Empress anymore. But would Tigran go forth with the executions?

Of course he would. That was surely his plan all along.

And if the Empress was ill—

She gasped. The Empress was *ill*. Tigran. It must be Tigran! It wasn't some illness, it was Shadow magic. Shadow magic that could make a person sick, instead of healing them. She was sure of it. A sickness that couldn't be cured by either magic or herbs.

A sickness which had spread before, through the Spire after the Fall of Azurite.

As her mind whirled at the revelation, she glanced at Ryn. He caught the overwhelmed look in her eyes, and said, "Perhaps we could be escorted somewhere to wait until the trial."

Kira nodded, revived a little by Ryn's intervention. "Yes. Please." She didn't look at Tigran, who was giving instructions to Emiko.

Emiko nodded, a hopeful smile at her lips. "Right away," she said, giving a slight bow to Kira and the others before trotting back toward the Empress' quarters, tray rattling.

"I will escort you to the Gyokuro Room to wait. We have some adjustments to make before sundown."

Kira grimaced as she followed Tigran out of the foyer, knowing quite well what those adjustments would entail now that they had captured Mistress Nari.

This rescue mission was looking grimmer and grimmer by the second. What were they supposed to do about Nari? Kira couldn't come to her defense, surely, without looking like she was taking a side.

But what did it matter, now?

She grit her teeth, glancing out of the corner of her eye at Tigran. It mattered because Ichiro had wanted them to remain neutral. She should trust her grandfather on this. Tigran was too dangerous to take down on their own—and the fear of being arrested herself brought waves of apprehension flooding through her.

It wasn't *death* at Tigran's hands she feared.

Keeping at least three feet of distance between her and Tigran, they strode down the halls of the palace as he led them to a room she had never been in before. It was an open sort of foyer that looked out onto a square in the center of the grounds. The sliding doors were open slightly, bringing in a brisk chill.

But the chill that struck Kira's back had nothing to do with the weather. It was the immense wooden platform that had been erected in the square, with enough kindling underneath to set the whole thing ablaze in seconds.

Tigran watched her as he gestured politely to the hard benches set in a circle in the small open room. She did her best to keep the fear out of her eyes, and only nodded curtly in thanks before sitting down, perching at the front of a bench. Tigran gave them a slight bow before retreating out of one of the open doorways.

Nesma looked like she had seen a ghost, and indeed, was staring out at the pyre as if it had already been lit. Soon, her sisters would perhaps stand there—and if they didn't, it meant they had been freed.

"I don't like this," Kira said, easing forward to peer down the palace hallway. "He wants to keep an eye on us, no doubt," she muttered. From here, she could clearly see four soldiers at their posts down two different corridors.

"I can't believe they captured Mistress Nari," Nesma whispered, and they leaned in close to hear her. "You don't think she was really making the Empress ill, do you?"

"Of course not," Kira said. "I bet it's more of Tigran's propaganda to cover up his own ill deeds. And actually, I think the illness—"

The sound of a quiet footstep outside their room made Kira stop talking, and she sat up even straighter than before. She hadn't seen anyone come down the corridors.

She looked at the others, shaking her head. "I could have sworn..." she muttered.

"How much longer until sundown, do you think?" Ryn asked.

"I don't know," Kira said, her gaze flickering toward the pyre outside the open sliding doors. "Wish I could tell time with Shadow magic," she muttered.

Ryn made a strange face, but it seemed like he was looking at something just behind Kira.

"It's pretty handy," a voice said in her ear, and she nearly leapt out of her skin.

A hand gripped her shoulder, and she fought the scream that climbed up her throat. Instead, she drew her dagger, at the same time grabbing the hand on her shoulder.

Ryn and Nesma were halfway out of their chairs when the voice said, "Relax, it's me."

"Jun?" Kira demanded through her teeth. An exasperated "Oh" came from Ryn.

"Yes, it's me," Jun hissed. "Will you let go?"

She released his still-invisible hand, and peered out into the hallway. One of the soldiers was looking in their direction, but he didn't seem ready to come investigate the outburst.

"What do you think you're doing, sneaking up on us like that?" she said, looking around for some sign of him.

"Sorry," he said, suddenly coming into view somewhere else—behind a small partition where the soldiers in the hallway wouldn't see him.

Kira's insides burned in fear, but one look at the nearest lantern told her that it hadn't registered Jun's release of Shadow magic. Perhaps it only glowed when someone pulled magic instead of releasing it? She shook her head.

Jun wore all black, the non-descript trousers and jacket something he would have worn back at Gekkō-ji for training. He also had a mis-matched collection of leather armor that he must have picked up on his way here.

Relief at seeing him was quickly eclipsed by something else.

"How could you leave without telling me? I would have come with you! And now—"

She looked around at the small antechamber and huffed. "Now we need to get you out of here without Tigran seeing you. You can't do illusionwork again without setting off the lanterns. You're lucky releasing it didn't set them off." The mischievous smile Jun wore sank a little, but he stuck out his chin defiantly.

Nesma stood up and began to pace.

Putting away her dagger, Kira said, "Look, we already lied to him saying we were in the city when the decree went into effect. And I doubt he believed us. But there's *no way* he would even pretend if we said you—"

"I have a plan," Jun said, holding up a palm to interrupt her.

"I certainly hope so, Kosumoso," Ryn remarked.

Jun shot him an annoyed look, and swept some strands of hair out of his eyes. "Look, I had a lot of time to think on my way here—and I'm sorry I left without telling you, but I didn't think I had enough time to get out. Now that I've had a chance to look around, I actually—"

A loud boom sounded, and they heard what sounded like dozens of footsteps. Kira met Jun's eyes in a panic.

If he used magic, the lantern would go off, and either Jun would be captured and killed, or one of them would be blamed.

Kira's nails dug into her thigh where her hand rested.

"I—" Jun glanced at the corridor.

They couldn't see anyone yet, but from the sounds of it, a large group of people was headed their way, and would likely turn the corner in a few seconds.

Ryn strode over to Jun, and grabbed him by the shoulders. "Go—out this way." He guided him over to the sliding doors. "There aren't any soldiers out there yet, at least not nearby."

"How do you know?"

"Auras," Ryn said simply. "I saw yours right before you appeared."

"Go," Kira repeated, standing up to join them. "We'll find you again later—or maybe you'll have to find us."

Jun nodded and ran a hand over his chest plate before slipping out the opening.

"Don't use magic until you're a good distance from us," Kira hissed after his retreating back.

He held up a hand and kept jogging in the shadow of the building and out of sight.

Kira closed her eyes for a brief moment, hoping—praying—that no one would spot Jun. She turned to look back at the others, but didn't have time to say anything. The oncoming footsteps rounded the corner, revealing the entire court of palace advisors. Or, nearly all of them. She didn't see Tigran or Goten among them.

Coming up behind the advisors were a group of soldiers escorting three women.

Kira easily identified Nari by her height, but she couldn't see the others. Was it Nia Mari and Nikoletta? Kira glanced at Nesma, who had pressed herself up against the back wall of the antechamber. Joining her, Kira grabbed Nesma's wrist and gave it a squeeze.

Quietly, Ryn came over to stand beside them, since it was clear that the advisors were heading this way to get to the square. The sunlight outside was dwindling, and the idea of what sunset would bring twisted in Kira's gut and burned there. What could they do? Jun had said something about a plan, but that worried her more than anything. She just hoped it wasn't something big and stupid and heroic.

CHAPTER 18

FALLEN

C aught up in the procession, Kira made sure to keep hold of Nesma's sleeve as they followed alongside several dour-faced advisors. Amid their greetings and muted exclamations of surprise at the fact that Kira had made it, a nervous energy permeated the group of advisors, several of which Kira had gotten to know fairly well during her visits to the palace.

"Where is Advisor Goten?" Kira asked Jai Takasan, whom she had never liked, but was nearest.

To her surprise, he stiffened, and replied curtly, "He has been stricken, by one of those... things."

"Really?" Kira said, but Takasan drifted away from her, whether intentionally or not, she couldn't tell. He took up a hushed conversation with Advisor Kando.

"But he has Light magic," Kira muttered in confusion to Nesma, who was walking straight-backed beside her now that they were outside. Nesma shrugged, her eyes on the pyre platform.

Kira flinched as a warm weight landed on her shoulder, which then scurried into the fabric of her hood.

"I haven't seen Jun yet," Thistle said quietly, as Kira repressed a shudder at his sudden, invisible appearance.

"Hopefully no one will *see* him," she muttered. "We did, briefly. Stick with me."

A squeak of assent sounded from within her hood, and she focused on following the crowd.

The advisors seemed to know where to go, now lining up in front of the pyre, leaving an aisle down the center of the crowd. The soldiers and their captives stood at the back of the crowd, though Kira could only see the top of Mistress Nari's head over everyone else's.

Nari stood tall, and though they had seen her perhaps half an hour ago, one of her eyes was now swollen, and blood dripped from both nostrils. Anger surged in Kira's chest. She couldn't see Nia Mari or Nikoletta, but she was shocked Tigran was going through with executing them. Perhaps with so many soldiers now, it would have been hard to cover up. She just hoped they were bound with whatever magic-sapping chains the Commonality liked to use, not that there was much magic in the area.

Two soldiers peeled away from the group and headed toward the main gate. Kira stiffened, gaze darting to the lanterns placed all around the square, but none of them were glowing red. She just hoped Jun had moved far enough away to use his illusionwork again.

I wish I had Yuki's mind-reading proficiency, she thought suddenly. *Or some way to talk to Jun and tell him the most important thing right now is the four of us getting out of here alive.*

She hated to leave Nari to her own fate, and the Gray Knights of course, but she couldn't think of anything she could do to stop this, short of treason. The Empress had made her decision, had made her decrees. If Kira went against the Empress' word now, she would get put right up on that platform too. Or worse, become Tigran's experiment once more.

Kira was still shocked at Nari's capture. She had escaped Gekkō-ji and been on the run for—how many days now? But she had infiltrated the palace and gotten herself into the Empress' quarters. For what?

The sun dipped below the walls surrounding the palace grounds, and Kira's stomach did a little flip as sunset drew near. Tigran had arrived silently, and now stood by the platform, adjusting his bejeweled collar.

A palace door slid open. Empress Mei, surrounded by attendants, stepped out gingerly, walking as though she were a cracked teacup that might fall apart at any moment. Whispers slid through the crowd, gasps, and then applause. The Empress held her regal head high, giving them all a slight nod as she slowly made her way toward where Tigran stood at the head of the crowd. Everyone assembled bowed deeply.

When Kira rose, she could see there were bags under the Empress' eyes, and the attendant closest to her was holding her arm, as though helping keep her upright. It was the healer they had seen earlier, and her face was shining with admiration and delight.

When the Empress came to a halt in front of the center of the platform, the advisors ceased their polite applause, and a grim shade of seriousness descended on the crowd. Empress Mei held up a hand, and the sound of clinking chains caused everyone to turn and look toward the gate.

Kira felt as if she were watching a particularly depressing movie which she couldn't pause. The soldiers who had run off before now marched at the head of the procession, and Kira knew exactly whom they were escorting down the wide stone path.

Their faces gaunt, Kira almost didn't recognize Jun's father; his hair was completely gray, and his normally impeccable posture had sunken him to a hunch. He looked like an old man, even older than Ichiro. Kira glanced around the square, wondering where Jun could possibly be at this moment, and whether he had seen his father yet. It was then that she finally caught sight of the two women standing next to Nari.

It wasn't Nia Mari and Nikoletta.

Kira glanced at Ryn, a question on her lips, then back at the women. "Is that... Ayana?" Kira muttered incredulously. Ryn glanced sharply toward the captives.

"And Tokusei," he confirmed quietly. Kira vaguely recognized Tokusei, a member of the Third Shadow Guard, just like Ayana.

The Gray Knights and their escort were now drawing even with the other prisoners, and they were all ushered forth down the aisle. Silent, the advisors watched the procession, many with their faces carefully blank. Kira was strangely comforted to see a few of the advisors watching the procession with regret in their eyes. *So not all of them are Tigran's puppets*, Kira thought.

The soldiers led the prisoners up onto the platform, where they were placed a few feet apart. Nari at one end, beside the two Shadow mages, Sir Jovan in the middle with the rest of the Gray Knights beside him. Kira's stomach began to ache at the sight of them, and she couldn't help but stare at the kindling underneath as she pictured it lighting. How long until that happened? She took several panicked breaths.

Could she really just watch them die like this?

She flexed her fingers over and over, open and closed. What could she do? Threaten twenty soldiers with a single dagger?

"Today we right a wrong which has been done to the realm," Tigran announced. "Several wrongs in fact. Just this morning, the Commonality caught Nari Hyacinth in the egregious crime of poisoning the Empress with her magic, a malady that has afflicted the Empress for years on end. For this most despicable crime, and under Her Majesty's recent decree halting the use of magic, there will be no imprisonment. Her Majesty witnessed the crime herself, and wishes to mete out swift punishment. Along with Nari's two Shadow mage accomplices."

Empress Mei bowed her head, her long eyelashes fluttering.

Gasps and mutters broke through the crowd as the advisors focused their attention on Nari. The Empress lifted her chin high, and gave a small nod to Tigran. Sickened, Kira glanced between the Empress and Tigran. She felt almost feverish in her anger. *Tigran* was the one who had poisoned the Empress with his magic. She just knew it.

"And for their crimes against the realm," Tigran went on, "and particularly the deeds of Jovan Kosumoso, a man who broke his oath to serve and protect this realm. All here today will answer to justice. Her Majesty's period of contemplation is over, and she has deemed them all guilty. There will be no trial."

Keenly aware of the breath surging into her lungs, Kira watched as the assembled soldiers moved closer to the platform. At that moment, the sun dipped below the horizon.

Kira only knew because the decanters hanging from the soldiers' belts began to glow. Her nostrils flared as she looked around, momentarily distracted from the spectacle of the soldiers lighting torches.

There was no ambient Light magic in the whole square. She locked eyes with Nesma, who had come to the same conclusion. The distinct lack of Light was almost as disturbing as the impending executions. The absurd amount of lanterns constantly drawing magic from their surroundings had worked. There was nothing here besides what the soldiers carried.

Nesma opened her mouth as if to say something, but a whistling sound flew over them. Kira looked up in time to see a bright white dagger flying straight towards Tigran and the Empress.

The healer holding the Empress' arm yanked the woman aside. Tigran stepped back and raised his arms in front of himself, though he had no armor, no shield. In the millisecond that it happened, Kira was impressed at his ability to not use his Shadow magic in this moment of peril.

Miraculously, the flying dagger missed him, landing right where he had been a second ago, clanging to the ground. Kira vaguely noticed that the lanterns surrounding the stage had gone red, right before hands seized her from behind.

"Wait, what?" she yelped, trying to yank free. Thistle struggled, scratching her neck and shoulder as he fought for balance.

Sheer terror flooded through her as she panted, pulling on the grips as they tightened around her biceps. She caught sight of a green uniform behind her. The faces of the soldiers became blurry as she was whisked forward and thrown onto her knees.

Pain like she had never felt jolted up from her kneecaps as they struck the hard stone. Before she knew it, her hands were wrenched behind her back and clasped tightly with a thin chain. Every erg of magic stored in her core leaked out of her—and a different kind of pain rang through her pores as it was taken.

Shouts rang out, and from the corner of her eye she saw Nesma charge forward, but Ryn held out an arm to stop her. The relief she experienced seeing them safe was brief, for she was being dragged up to stand in front of Tigran.

Up close he was handsome as ever, but the slight sneer that probably no one but her could see was all the ugliness she knew. "Finally," he breathed into her face. "'Tis a pity, though, that you fought against me."

Louder, he said, "It is a dark day indeed. I never would have wanted to believe it, but you all saw it for yourselves. A direct attack on the Empress—and though I am of no importance, myself—with Gray magic no less. She has condemned herself. No one else in the palace can use Gray magic, which is what this clearly was."

"No! I would never," she gasped. "And that wasn't me!"

A jolt of rage surged through her. *Jun!*

How could he *do* this to her?

"I'm sorry, Starless Girl," Tigran whispered in her ear as he turned her away from the crowd, motioning to two soldiers. "But I have no use for you anymore, not now... Ah yes, Sorin, put her with the others."

Panting, Kira somehow lost all sense of her body as her legs traitorously followed the urgings of the two soldiers who had gotten hold of her. Thistle's weight suddenly lifted from her neck, though she couldn't see him anywhere

249

since he was still illusioned with spirit magic. She didn't see Ryn and Nesma in the crowd anymore—had they somehow escaped in the commotion? They were better for it, she knew, but an overwhelming sense of abandonment assailed her as her feet numbly shuffled across the platform and she found herself standing next to Nari, her heart beating so fast it felt as if she were having a heart attack.

Tigran began to speak, but Kira couldn't understand his words anymore, it was as if time moved in jerks and spurts. Slowly the Empress raised her right hand, finding the strength to utter a few words, words of condemnation no doubt.

Far too quickly the soldiers were nearing the kindling with their torches. Sparks crackled. As the torch flames licked up the dry kindling in one, two, three places, something happened that no one had been expecting, least of all Kira.

An enormous bright tear rent the air inches from her feet.

A scream ripped from her throat and she stumbled backwards as the electric blue light tore through the fabric of the realm. Thistle's warm weight suddenly lifted from her neck as he lurched away from her—away from the tear.

The tear made no sound, though Kira couldn't hear *anything* despite the open mouths of the obviously-screaming advisors and soldiers drawing weapons.

The silent flames grew, feeding their hungry mouths on the dry sticks below the platform. Heat surged upward, along with bitter smoke. The soldiers advanced on the condemned, unleashing their steel, some even daring to form crude Light weapons. An arrow struck the platform at Kira's feet, almost hitting the tear.

Mesmerized, Kira's gaze landed on the tear, crackling as it continued to rip, tear—

"Kira!" someone screamed from beside her. Nari lurched forward, wrenching her arm nearly out of its socket as she pulled her away. Another volley of arrows from the soldiers, and Kira staggered, suddenly losing her balance as a heavy thud hit the platform.

Mistress Nari had fallen.

Just as invisible hands seized her from behind, Kira spotted a familiar narrow face peering out a window of the palace, and she blacked out.

CHAPTER 19

BEST BET

She became aware of herself again as those same hands slapped her across the face. She blinked heavily. It felt like only seconds had passed, but she was no longer on the pyre.

"Kira!" a voice shouted. "We have to get across the moat!"

"W-we?" she stuttered, looking around and seeing no one. No... not no one. A rustling corner of a cloak, devoid of an owner. A dragging chain, hanging from nothing. Was it illusionwork? Not only could she not see anyone, but they were somehow across the square by the gate, the burning pyre a hundred yards away.

"What happen—"

"Nevermind, just go! I have to help the others!" Finally, she placed the voice. It was Jun.

A push from unseen hands toward the open gate propelled her forward, and she finally registered what was going on. The tear. The pyre burning.

The others?

The others. Not Nari though. The fall, the reverberation of a weight on the platform had woven its way up through the soles of Kira's feet and rattled her heart.

Who else had been left behind? She couldn't bear to look back at the square, where the shouting was growing even more panicked. A sudden wave of calm swept over her as she finally focused her thoughts and stumbled forward, gaining momentum as she ran across the wooden bridge.

There were no guards. They had all left their posts for the execution or the chaos that ensued instead. Instinctively, Kira reached out and drew her steel dagger. Though there was a slight glow of Light this far from the conglomeration of the palace lanterns, she wouldn't risk pulling any magic. Not after that tear.

She would have to do without.

She followed the sound of footsteps onto the main street, her grip on the dagger becoming sweaty in the cool spring air. She had no way of knowing who else the footsteps around her belonged to—she just had to keep staggering forward. Away from the palace, away from Tigran, away from the burning pyre she had almost fallen on. All she knew was that she was alive, and so was Jun.

Suddenly all the other footsteps stopped, and Kira halted, drawing into the darkness beside a shop that overlooked a canal.

Kira looked up at the sky, streaked with a swirl of pink clouds, and she spotted the dark plume of smoke issuing from the palace grounds.

A warm feeling trickled up her spine. She looked down and saw her feet misting back into view, along with the rest of her. Shaking, she looked up to see who else crouched in the shadows of the shop.

Jun appeared right by her side. "Sorry," he panted, "It was rough, but that was all the Shadow I had."

Kira nodded numbly at him, then spotted Nesma. She strode over to throw her arms around the girl, who was shaking. Ryn came over and put a hand on Kira's back. Tears stung her eyes and silently rolled down her cheeks as she took them all in. Her friends, along with Jovan and what looked like most of the Gray Knights. They had made it.

"We should move," Sir Jovan said quietly, his head bowed a little. "I don't have—" he choked, gesturing vaguely at his own hands.

"It's all right," Jun said, grabbing both his father's hands and giving them a squeeze. "I'm all out too. And I don't think we want to cause another tear, anyway."

"Cause?" Kira repeated, eyes squinting.

Jun waved his hands. "We should get going. Come on, help me with Lord Dorado."

Kira and Ryn walked on either side of Dorado, who had evidently twisted his ankle when they had fled from the blazing platform. And though part of Kira wanted to go back and fight, to wring a confession out of Tigran, the fact that they had escaped the palace at all was a miracle. But they weren't free of the Commonality's grip yet. They still needed to get out of Meridian.

They hustled down a side street and over to the canal, descending the ramp-like side and splashing into the cold calf-height water. In front of Kira and Ryn trudged Nesma and Sir Jovan, the other Gray Knights, and the mage from the Shadow Guard, Tokusei. Jun followed from behind, watching their backs.

"Wait, where's Ayana?" Kira asked.

Tokusei turned around, her eyes dark, her short hair ruffled. "She didn't make it." She bowed her head, then faced forward again.

It felt as if Kira's heart was creeping up her throat, and she swallowed, the pain receding down her chest. Both Nari and Ayana. Gone.

From beside her, Dorado muttered quietly, "The Shadow mage? I think she was the one who got me off the platform; the soldiers had me cornered between the flames and their blades." He bowed his head too. "I will honor her sacrifice the rest of my days," he said grimly. "As soon as we get out of here, I will say a prayer at the shrine of Kamellia for her soul."

The remaining sunlight fading, they followed the direction of the flowing water toward the river. The water was freezing this time of year, and the fact that the sun had gone down didn't help much with the chill. Kira tightened her grip on Dorado's arm before pulling her hood closer around her neck. She would have liked to actually put her hood *up*, but couldn't risk not being able to see out of her periphery. Though they were out of view from anyone at street level, Kira felt like a fish in a barrel down here. She sloshed through the water, her feet going numb from the cold, trudging further on, just hoping they were almost at the river. Almost there.

Almost.

"There you are!" a voice called, and a small weight dropped on her shoulder.

"Thistle!" she cried, her free hand going up to pat him, which he allowed, nuzzling into the side of her neck.

"I'm sorry I left you—" he squeaked.

"It's quite all right," she said, still stroking his fur.

After she was sure Thistle was secure in her hood, she continued to slog through the freezing canal, supporting Dorado with the help of Ryn.

They could barely see—only the lights by the docks ahead guided them, since there wasn't much Light essence to see by. It unnerved Kira to no end.

She had been able to see in the dark every night since her mother died, when her Light magic manifested.

But now, all was dark. Tigran had been busy. And now, so was Hagane, on his quest across the realm to install the lanterns. She wondered where they were now, with their wagons creaking along, powered by Shadow, placing even more lanterns.

Where will we go? She swept the thought aside as she looked up and down the river. They needed to get out of Meridian first.

Dorado hobbled over to the edge of the canal and sat down on the stone slope. He nodded gratefully at Kira and Ryn before sinking his head down into his hands. Kira bit her lip at the defeated sight of him. In fact, all the Gray Knights looked defeated, but she didn't blame them, after their year-long imprisonment under the Commonality. She couldn't even imagine what they had been through.

Tentatively she reached out and squeezed Dorado's shoulder before coming over to where Jun stood at the mouth of the canal. Her breathing was shaky as she tried to wrangle all of her thoughts—where to go, what to do next—it felt as if all the air around them pressed heavily upon her. It didn't help that they were still down below street level, facing a somewhat busy wharf.

Before she could decide on which question to ask Jun, Thistle perked up and said, "I can go check the docks for soldiers. I can illusion myself still."

Kira nodded gratefully, and they all hunkered down into the shadows of the canal, their feet soaked, and their clothes getting wetter and wetter. She had long since lost the feeling in her toes, and would have given almost anything to summon fire at that moment. She settled for rubbing her hands together and breathing on them.

"I can't believe Nari's gone," Nesma was saying behind her.

Kira turned around to face Nesma and Ryn.

Ryn's head was bowed, "And Ayana. I trained with her at the Spire. She fought in the Shadow Guard longer than I did—it was her only calling, she always said."

Tokusei sat in silence on the canal bank, head in hands, elbows on her knees, staring at the dark water.

Kira looked up at the sky as if searching for answers. Clouds obscured the blanket of stars normally visible, but patches of the bright orbs peeked out from cracks between the clouds here and there. She tried to focus on a small patch of stars, the multitude of them always a fascinating sight.

Finally, she let out a sigh and turned back to Jun, who was sitting with his father.

"We need a boat," she said. "I'm sure the gate will be closed, if the soldiers have reached them by this time."

"Yes, but what about the river gate?" Ryn asked, over-hearing.

"Ugh, I didn't think of that," she said, rubbing her hands together again.

"Actually, we have a bigger problem," Jun said in a low voice, standing up and turning his back on his father to speak to Kira.

"What?" Kira asked, her stomach dropping.

"My father's lost his magic."

"I know," Kira said, "We all did when the—"

"No," Jun insisted, grabbing her by the wrist. He looked her square in the eyes. "It's gone. They *took* it while he was in prison. All of them—" He swept a hand to indicate the other Gray Knights sitting downtrodden on the banks of the canal.

She put her hand over her mouth. "Gone?" she said behind her fingers. "But how? They're here, they're—" Flashes of her kneeling inside a metal circle hit her, wrists chained as Tigran tried to siphon away her soul's magic...

Jun nodded as if in a trance. "They survived it. But they can't do magic anymore, even if there was any to be found. I'm just glad he's alive—that they're all alive."

"I—me too," Kira said. "Maybe Tigran got better at... whatever he was doing."

Covertly, she glanced around, wondering where Thistle was. If they could just get out of the city, then they could deal with this, with everything. She looked around at them all. There were eleven of them, huddled under the bridge, waiting for a solution to swoop down on them. And it was then that Kira realized: she and Jun were now the only two in the whole realm who could wield Gray magic.

Her stomach lurched. *It's just us, then*.

Looking at the thoroughly defeated Gray Knights, she thought of her father. These were his men and women, all six of whom served under him when he was their leader. They had all fought together, trained together. All under Rokuro. The man she had never met, but could only strive to understand now. Something in her core seemed to warm at the idea.

"All right, here's what we need to do," she said, and Jun, Ryn, Nesma, and the others all perked up. "Once Thistle gets back, I'm sure he'll have scouted a safe way for us to get to the gate. Then we're going to need a way to get through—either without magic, or very little. Ryn, Nesma: do you have any magic stored?"

Nesma shook her head, but Ryn nodded.

"Okay, so we have some Shadow magic. And unless we can bust into those lanterns and steal some, that's probably all we've got to work with."

One such lantern sat right in their line of sight on the docks, glowing faintly. "I doubt we could do that without notice, even if it is possible," she said, almost to herself. The others murmured agreement.

"I could bind the soldiers at the gate?" Tokusei said, lifting her head up out of her hands. "But I don't have any magic."

Distant memories of invisible Shadow barriers blocking her vision like a blindfold, and tying up her hands made her rub her wrists together. "I never liked those binds myself," Kira said wryly. "But I think that might be our best bet. Ryn? Want to try giving her some of your Shadow magic?"

CHAPTER 20

FAR FROM HERE

In the end, they decided not to take a boat.

Half an hour later, they all crouched behind a smelly warehouse which seemed to contain one thing only: cabbage. Having crept through the warehouse district beside the docks with Thistle as their guide, they trekked—sopping wet from the knees down—through the dark streets. At first Kira had worried about the water tracks they would leave, but the alley behind the warehouse was damp with rotting cabbage juice from the crates of spoiled goods stacked up nearby, and she doubted anyone would follow them here.

Wrinkling her nose, Kira poked her head up behind Tokusei, who stood at the corner of the building, watching the soldiers at the gate. Thistle had perched on Tokusei's shoulder, eager to watch from the front of the alley.

"Well?" Tokusei asked Ryn beside her.

"There, there, and there," he said, pointing out the soldiers. "And way up there."

"Ah," Tokusei said, following his finger. "I didn't see that one. All right, then. I'm ready for it."

Ryn nodded, and the two of them clasped hands timidly. "I hope we don't lose any," Ryn said, glancing at the lantern near the soldiers.

"Hopefully not," Kira replied. "It shouldn't go too far if you're releasing it right into her hand."

They grew quiet, and Kira wondered what it might feel like for Ryn and Tokusei, the transfer of magic directly from palm to palm. Maybe when they got out into the countryside she could give it a try, she thought, still wondering where they were headed once they got through the gate. *Far from here.*

It seemed to work, when Tokusei's face brightened and she turned her attention back to the gate.

Kira knew Tokusei was at work when the two guards right next to the gate froze, reaching for their eyes with scrabbling hands—then, their hands clapped together, bound at the wrists.

When they fell to the ground from ankle binds, the soldier patrolling up top paused to look down, and then he too fell victim to the binds.

Hope surged in Kira's chest. But a guard in the gate-house ran outside to see the commotion, and Tokusei gasped.

"I—I don't have any more—"

Kira lurched into motion. Without even thinking, Kira pushed her way forward, lunging out of the alley.

The soldier's eyes were covered, but not his mouth. "To the gate!" he called. "To the gate! Sound an alarm!"

She sprinted toward him, dagger in hand. He heard her footsteps and turned. Her heart slammed against her chest as she drew her dagger back, ready to throw it at the un-suspecting soldier.

She nearly dropped it instead. The thought of killing him, a probably innocent eighteen-year-old recruited to protect his fellow commoners, made her stop in her tracks.

"Soldiers fallen! To the gate!" he shouted. She cursed and kept running. With all her strength, she threw herself on top of him and tackled him to the ground.

In the tumble, she wrestled with his flailing limbs in order to cover his mouth. But she couldn't hold both his hands and keep him quiet—he reached for her throat, all the while trying to scream under her palm.

Having tossed her dagger aside while trying to sub-due him, she glanced at it in the dim starlight and won-dered: Could she really kill him? He lurched underneath her, fighting her. He was just trying to warn his comrades—friends, most likely.

Was she savage enough to kill this man in cold blood?

But in the next second, her own friends surrounded her, saving her from having to answer that question. She had been fighting with the soldier for only few seconds, time enough for Ryn, Jun, and Nesma to come up and help. Ryn ripped his makeshift hood off and wadded up the fabric, stuffing it in the soldiers' mouth.

Jun produced a thin chain, one of the manacles the others had worn, and made quick work of securing the man's wrists. In a daze, Kira stood up as the others worked together, dragging the man back into the shadow of the gate, back inside the gatehouse, along with the other two guards. Blindly, Kira followed them inside—the least she could do was help open the gate. She couldn't believe she had frozen up like that.

"Are we just going to leave it open?" Ryn asked as he and Kira pushed on the enormous wheel a few minutes later. The gate mechanisms creaked and clanged as they raised the heavy wooden door.

"If we leave it open, they'll know we went out this way," she said, grunting with the effort. "But if we raise it, run out, and let it drop, I'm sure someone will hear. I guess they'll know either way."

"Let's drop it," Jun said. "It'll slow them down at least. Do you think anyone heard that guard?"

Kira's face warmed. If only she had silenced him in time. She could have easily thrown the dagger as she had advanced on him.

"Doesn't matter," Ryn grunted. "Nesma, can you signal to the others?"

Nodding, Nesma inched out of the gatehouse and gave a short whistle. Kira and Ryn had nearly gotten the gate up—it was becoming harder and harder to push. Jun tried to join in, but there was really only enough room for two people.

"Make sure the others get through first," Kira told Jun, jerking her head toward the gate. Out of the corner of her eye, she saw Tokusei leading the injured Gray Knights, Thistle on her shoulder. As they stole through the gate, Kira counted them. Seven. Plus Ryn, Nesma, and Jun.

Her hesitation with the soldier was ten times as embarrassing when she realized all the Gray Knights had probably seen her falter. Would they think her weak? Unable to protect the realm?

And if she couldn't kill the soldier to keep them all safe, what was she going to do about Tigran?

"Kira, let's go," Ryn said, jerking her out of her anxious trance. The wheel had gone as far as it would go. Everyone else was gone, through the open gate.

"Right," she said, and gave a sharp nod. She and Ryn let go at once, gunning for the open gate as it began to fall. The rush of adrenaline surged through her system, wonderfully flushing all the negative thoughts and leaving her panting outside the gate, clutching her thighs. A muffled boom sounded as the gate met the ground. They made it.

"Come on," she said to the others, leading the way to the woods. Her stomach sank as she remembered leaving Meluca and their other horses at the palace. She glanced around the woods, at a loss. How would they flee now? Some of the Gray Knights could barely walk.

It was Tokusei who came to her aid. "Our mounts are hidden not far from here. Mine... Ayana's and Nari's."

Kira swallowed and nodded, following Tokusei through the trees. "How long have you been working with Nari?" Kira blurted.

"Oh, ever since the Gray Knights were imprisoned," Tokusei explained. "But I hadn't actually met her until a few days ago. We just corresponded over reconnaissance missions until then."

"Oh," Kira said, feeling guilty for thinking Nari and Ichiro hadn't done anything about Tigran all year.

"You're lucky they were light on soldiers," Thistle remarked as he swooped over to her shoulder.

Kira nodded, taking a deep breath of the night air and finally shedding the feeling of being trapped. Now they just had to find their way through the woods in the dark. And then there was the problem that they only had three mounts...

Another thing raising her spirits was the subtle glow of Light around them as they walked through the trees. It grew more and more the further they got from the gate.

"The city must be saturated with those lanterns," she said to Thistle. "And I think that's where the rest of the soldiers are—installing more across the realm." He chittered in agreement before swooping off into the trees, silently leaping from branch to branch.

The clouds had begun to disperse a little, shedding more starlight for everyone who didn't have Light magic to see by.

With a start, Kira peeked at Sir Jovan, wondering if he could still see it. She had a sinking feeling that he couldn't.

As if to verify her depressing theory, one of the Gray Knights tripped on a tree root, cursed, then shared a few words with Jovan who walked beside him.

Jun came up to her then, and she muttered, "I feel guilty taking any Light magic." She gestured around them, "There's already enough captive. And those tears..."

"I know," he said heavily. "I really wouldn't want to cause another one."

She halted in her tracks. "Do you mean... What?"

"Oh," he hesitated, looking guilty. "Back at the palace—Mistress Nari and I thought—"

"*You* did that?"

The blankness on his face said it all.

"Wait... Mistress Nari? When did you talk to her?" she demanded.

"In the palace—"

"Before or after she got caught?"

He licked his lips. "Before. I ran into her in the Empress' corridor. It was her idea, actually, to make the tear for a distrac—"

Fire burned through her chest. She pulled back her arm and hit him right in the face.

He reeled back, clutching his cheek.

Kira fumed, "Don't you dare say you did that for a distraction, Jun! Those tears are serious, and it almost got me!"

"Well, the distraction worked, didn't it?" he shot back.

Kira's gaze slid to the rescued knights, but her temper flared once again. "It was you who threw the dagger at Tigran, wasn't it? It wasn't you up on that platform, it was me about to be burned to death!"

"Well, I didn't plan on you being there!"

"I—how—Why didn't you tell us when you met us inside the palace?" she demanded, well aware that everyone was probably watching them.

He had the nerve to shrug, saying, "I'm sorry, I wasn't thinking—"

"No kidding," she scoffed, crossing her arms. Her knuckles hurt where she'd hit him, but she didn't want to rub them. She lowered her voice, "You put me and Ryn and *Nesma* all at risk. And now we're—we're—we can't go back there, anywhere." She gestured wildly, encompassing Meridian, Gekkō-ji, and the Spire. "This isn't what Ichiro wanted us to do."

Jun set his jaw. "Well, it's what Mistress Nari wanted!" he shot at her. "She disagreed with him—she was working to overthrow Tigran, actually doing something!"

"And look what happened to her." The quiet words slipped from her mouth unbidden.

"She knew the risk," he said, equally quiet. "She told me. She said she would rather die to help the cause than live with what Tigran had set into motion."

Arms still crossed, Kira dug her fingernails into her palms. "Fine," she said, and turned her back on him. "Let's just get as far from here as we can."

They found the horses nosing through the damp leaves for grass. Thistle was perched on a branch above them. Kira let Jun divvy the mounts up, too incensed to confer with him about anything at the moment.

In the end, Dorado with his sprained ankle, and two Gray Knights got the horses. Lady Sasha looked like she would fall asleep at any moment, with dark circles like bruises under her eyes.

Tokusei had refused her own horse, insisting someone else ride. "Ayana and I were caught just before Mistress Nari," she explained to Kira as they walked behind the rest. "Tigran works quickly—none of us realized he had a way to detect magic; we thought Ayana could hide us."

Kira nodded, knowing Ayana had been the one to teach Jun illusionwork back at the Spire. "So, you're in the Third Shadow Guard, right?"

Tokusei nodded. "Sagano is going to have a fit when he finds out we left Heliodor—probably already did. And, well, I'll have to give him the news about Ayana."

"I'm not sure we should return anywhere near there," Kira said as they followed the horses. They had begun walking with no destination in mind, only *away* from Meridian.

"The Commonality is traveling across the realm installing those lanterns," Kira said. "And Tigran is bound to alert them that we're..." She couldn't think of the word. *Outlaws* seemed too comical, too dramatic. "...on the run."

They trudged on for another hour before they deemed it safe to stop and light a fire. The trees were growing sparse, but they found a dense copse of trees to settle in. Her teeth rattling with the chill, Kira helped Nesma quickly gather some kindling and dry leaves. With the smallest amount of magic, they set it ablaze. It took a little more coaxing, and a few more modest sparks, but soon everyone was gathered around a crackling fire, holding up their hands or fanning out their wet clothes. Kira looked around the circle, suddenly feeling a tiredness that surely didn't belong to her years.

Ryn stood at the edge of the circle, facing the direction of Meridian. After Kira had warmed up somewhat, she came over to join him.

"Thistle?" she said quietly, and the small ball of fluff dropped out of the nearest tree and onto her shoulder.

"Yes?" he said, looking between her and Ryn.

"Do you know what this is?" She pulled out the dark blue scroll, which she had tucked into her bag. She had stopped worrying about the wrinkles, and it was now a little flattened, but she had managed to keep it dry at least.

He tilted his head from side to side. "No, should I?"

"The wisp left it for me. You know, that spirit Gekkō said wanted to talk to me? It's about how Camellia came to be."

"Oh, the Camellian Dragon." He glanced up at the starry sky, thinking. "I wonder why the wisp gave you that."

"Well, that's what I was hoping you could tell me," Kira said, her hopes falling. Regret flooded through her—they had detoured to Gekkō-ji to find Thistle, and now they had taken Nesma on the run too, and he didn't even know what this was about? *If we had gotten to the palace sooner, maybe we could have saved Nari...*

She swayed on the spot, and Ryn reached out a hand to steady her. "You look like you need something to eat and drink," he said. "I'll go take Jun or Nesma and have a look around. We all need something, by the looks of it." Kira glanced over the defeated-looking crew and nodded. She wasn't sure how much was hunger or grief that made her suddenly weak, but she found a rock nearby and sat down as Ryn sauntered off. Thistle swooped over to perch on a stump beside her.

Kira unfurled the scroll, half-consciously running her fingers along a crease to flatten it. The silver writing glowed even brighter with the delicate glow of Light magic. The sight of so much Light had given her almost as much relief as escaping Meridian—at least the whole realm hadn't had its magic stolen just yet.

"The wisp left this for me in Kagami's shrine," she told Thistle. "It just talks about how Camellia formed—the dragon, the camellia flowers, and how the people went through the portal into this realm. What does that have to do with Tigran, or the tears or anything? And who is this wisp spirit? Why won't she talk to me?"

Thistle's whiskers twitched, and he looked down at the ground. "Well, I—er—think Gekkō was hoping you would tell us that."

"What?" she demanded, briefly getting her feet under her, but she was too tired to stand. "You don't know who she is either?"

He shook his head. "She appeared on the mountain a few weeks ago, and it was clear she was searching for someone. Gekkō did manage to speak with her once, but she only said she wanted to help you."

Kira huffed and closed her eyes. A dead end after all.

She let her gaze wander to the fire where Tokusei and the Gray Knights sat, no one talking, just staring at the fire. A few were asleep, curled up with nothing to rest their heads on besides clumps of fallen leaves. Jun and Nesma must have both gone with Ryn to look for food.

"I'll just have to figure out who she is next time she appears, then," she said into the quiet night, the only sounds the crackling of the fire and the quiet chorus of some peeping frogs. "But the story. Is there anything about the creation of the realm that could tell us about the tears?" she insisted. She couldn't give up now.

He gazed at the fire too, the blaze reflected in his large black eyes. "I wasn't there," he said simply. "Nor was Gekkō. Not when the realm first came to be. Lord Gekkō was once a man who lived on the mountain long, long ago, before the mountain even had a name, before there was even a temple there. He cared for the mountain, the people there, and all the plants and animals. After he died, the villagers created a shrine in his honor, as he was sometimes seen walking the paths of the mountain with his walking stick."

Kira thought about that for a long time. She knew more about the spirits than she did when she first came to this realm, but much was still a mystery about their magic, certainly. "So, do you think the wisp is a new spirit or something?"

"That seems likely. Now, the dragon..."

"Was he real? Do you know what happened to him?"

Thistle glanced away from the fire and met Kira's eyes for a second, then, said, "Real, yes. He still watches over this realm, but he can no longer help."

Kira furrowed her brows at his vagueness. "Do you know where—"

Just then, Ryn, Nesma, and Jun came back into their camp, each carrying a sack. Kira stood up at once. "I thought you were going to do some hunting or something," she said, eyeing the sacks. "You stole those?"

Ryn let go of his burlap sack and it settled on the ground like it contained some sort of grain. "Barley, from an estate nearby," he explained. "And beans, and apples," he gestured at Jun and Nesma, who looked slightly guilty.

"Won't someone notice?" Kira asked, her annoyance warring with the saliva gathering in her mouth at the mere mention of food.

Jun said nothing, only pulled some magic from the air and formed a cauldron on a tripod hanging over the fire. Ryn explained patiently, "It would take forever to forage and hunt enough for this many people."

Kira's face warmed. "You're right. I'll go find some water."

Thistle followed her wordlessly, swooping from branch to branch alongside as she looked for the stream they had passed before making camp.

"Do you think I should look for the Camellian Dragon?" she asked Thistle quietly when they were out of earshot from the others. "Is that why the wisp left the scroll?"

"I don't know," Thistle said from somewhere to her right. "Many have tried. And how do you propose he will help? He used all his magic to create the realm."

"Oh, well, I don't know, I guess. Do you have a better explanation for the scroll then?"

"Well, no, not really."

"Some help you are," she muttered, though she knew he would hear. "Well, what about the spirits, then? Could they help us fix the tears? If we can, maybe the Empress would be forced to listen to us about Tigran's lies."

Thistle twitched his whiskers thoughtfully. "Perhaps. I know Gekkō has long been conversing with the other spirits to fight back against the atrocities of this one man. It may be that Gekkō has worn them down to a point where they will take instruction from a human, though it would be difficult."

Kira grunted, knowing just how difficult the spirits could be. She would never forget how Gekkō tricked her into confronting the Storm King to stop the feud in the first place.

On her way back, with a thin Light bucket in hand, she had another thought. "Who was the young man in the story?" she asked Thistle. "The one who defended the dragon, and the first in the realm?"

"According to their genealogy, the royal line descended from that young man, which is where Empress Mei's lineage comes from. Didn't they teach you that at the temple?"

CHAPTER 21

WITH A LITTLE HELP FROM OUR FRIENDS

After everyone had eaten, their bellies warming and giving life to some of the Gray Knight's faces, Kira turned to Ryn and Nesma—still ignoring Jun—and said, "We should move again, get further from the palace before it starts to get light out. Find somewhere to hunker down until we figure out where to go."

Nesma nodded, her gaze on the woods around them. She had taken up a post just at the edge of the firelight, a long bow in her hand, and a quiver of Light arrows slung on her back. Kira's stomach flipped as she suddenly remembered something.

"Nia Mari," Kira blurted. "I saw her at the palace. In a window just above the square."

Without turning, Nesma said in a hollow voice, "Yes, I did too."

Kira flicked her gaze toward Jun and he frowned in concern.

Nesma went on. "I mean, I knew Tigran wasn't going to execute them."

"I'm sorry," Kira said, going over to her. What else could she say? *It would have been great if they executed your sisters?*

"At least they didn't try to manipulate me," Nesma said, gesturing toward her head. "I'm sure Nikoletta was nearby too. He will have freed both of them. I'm surprised he let them sit in those cells so long," she added bitterly.

Jun sidled over to their little group just outside the firelight. "I'm sorry, Nesma," Jun said. "They don't deserve their freedom. None of those monsters do."

Kira nodded in agreement. "You're right," she said. "And as much as I'd like to go to Gekkō-ji to ask Ichiro to assemble all of the knights to advance on the palace, we can't. Even if they didn't fight with magic now, the Commonality is too powerful, and Tigran must be controlling the Empress or something, with that illness…"

"I can't believe he blamed that on Nari!" Nesma burst out in sudden fury. "And now…"

"And now," Kira said sadly, glancing up at the sea of stars above, saying a brief prayer in her head for Nari's spirit.

"Do we really think the Empress will get better?" Ryn asked skeptically. "You think Tigran is somehow—"

"I know it," Kira said. "Or, I think so. I'm fairly certain he's been making her sick this whole time—just like another mysterious illness no one could find a cure for, back at the Spire after the Fall of Azurite. When—"

"When Zowan's wife and daughter died?" Jun asked, brows furrowed. "Do you really think so?"

She crossed her arms, wishing they could be having this conversation closer to the fire, but she didn't want to disturb the others; they looked like they needed the rest. "I do. Tigran—or Kage as he was known during his training days, was kicked out of the Spire. And he framed Raiden for the Fall of Azurite. Who's to say he didn't infiltrate Heliodor afterward in a disguise and create that illness with Shadow for more revenge? Or maybe it's spirit magic, which could be why no one could figure out what was wrong, now that I think of it."

"And you're saying he's been using it to control the Empress?" Jun said, "Making her sick, and now that he's got Nia Mari and Nikoletta back... Plus the stored magic..." He drew a breath and puffed up his cheeks.

"Yeah," Kira said, nodding. "I don't like it either. Which is why we shouldn't waste our time raising an army against him, not right now. We'll be crushed." She leveled a look at him in the dim light.

"I never suggested that," Jun said, holding up his palms. "What are you looking at me for?"

"Because you ran out of Heliodor without telling me, to bust into the palace to do what exactly?"

"I was trying to see if I could find any evidence on Tigran to show the Empress to stop the execution, all right?" he said.

"And did you?" Nesma asked.

He shook his head. "No, but Nari found me—well, we found each other, in the Empress' wing. I was illusioned, and Nari didn't think anyone was in the Empress' study. Tigran's quarters were clean, and I was out of ideas."

They all gazed at him openmouthed. Finally, it was Ryn who said, "You trespassed into the Empress' study?"

Jun pressed his lips together, tight. "I know. I—" He huffed. "But I thought maybe if I found something that proved Tigran was a liar, I could maybe... I could maybe change her mind about the execution."

Kira bit the inside of her lip, not blaming Jun one bit. Of course, she hadn't grown up respecting and admiring the Empress, who was apparently descended from the very first person to enter the Realm, but still...

"I knew you were off to do something stupid," she joked lightly, trying to signal she was done being mad at him. It had been a huge risk to do what he did, even with Nari's blessing. It was just too bad Kira hadn't known about it first. "That's why I came to find you. Well? Where do we go now?"

"We can't go back to Gekkō-ji," said Nesma, who was staring forlornly out into the semi-darkness, one hand on her longbow.

"Nor the Spire," said Ryn, "But we knew that when we left."

"And I think we need to get as far away from Meridian and the—"

"I think we should go to Azurite," Jun said, his voice low but insistent.

"What?" Nesma said, "What for?"

Kira kept quiet, getting a hint of an idea behind Jun's intentions.

"The Tiger's Eye Crystal," Jun said, confirming it. "My father and the others were robbed of their magic. I want to help them get it back."

"Jun," Kira began, then lost her nerve. What could she say?

She was saved having to crush Jun's dreams by none other than Sir Jovan, who must have overheard them and was now walking their way, a silhouette against the dancing flames.

"There is no use, Jun," Jovan said. "I'm sorry to say it myself."

"But—"

"It is gone. We were lucky to survive his hedonistic experiment with our lives."

"But it worked on Kira!" Jun burst.

Kira swallowed a lump in her throat, resisting the urge to rub the back of her neck where she always felt the ghost of the damage Tigran had done to her, almost taking *her* magic. And her life.

"The crystal only worked on Kira," Jovan said, "Because her aura and her spirit remained intact—it was only superficial damage."

"Wait," Jun said, a crack in his voice, "Your spirit, you don't—"

"We no doubt still possess them, if that's what you're worried about," Jovan said, putting a hand on Jun's shoulder and giving it a tight squeeze. "Otherwise we'd be dead. But the magic was severed. Kira's connection between magic and soul was merely injured."

Jun nodded tightly. "Well then. I guess we don't need to go to Azurite."

"Tigran might expect us to go there anyway," Ryn said. "After last time."

"Mmm," Kira agreed, distinctly remembering the confrontation behind the waterfall.

"Where do you think we should go?" Jun asked his father.

Jovan rubbed his stubbled chin, and Kira thought he looked strangely vulnerable without his usual armor.

"We need armor," she blurted, "And real weapons. And more food."

"Yes," Jovan said, "And a place to heal." From the way he said it, she didn't think he was only referring to Dorado's sprained ankle and the cut on Sasha's arm.

"So we're just going to hide?"

If Kira hadn't been looking at her as she said it, she never would have believed the words had come from Nesma's lips. Kira's own mouth popped open in surprise, then she closed it.

"No," Kira said thoughtfully. "I have an idea how we might be able to kill two birds with one stone."

She almost laughed at everyone's expression at her metaphor, though Jovan was nodding thoughtfully as if she had said something deeply profound.

"If we can fix the tears," Kira continued, "the Empress will have to listen to us. Or her advisors, or the people of the realm, if we can't get the palace to listen."

"And how do you propose we do that?" Ryn asked, raising one eyebrow.

"With a little help from our friends," she said, glancing at Thistle on her shoulder.

CHAPTER 22

EVEN IF WE'RE APART

"We can't drag them all across Camellia," Jun hissed at her half an hour later as they regretfully banked the fire, attempting to erase all evidence they had been here. Kira could feel sunrise approaching, and they didn't have much darkness left.

Kira pursed her lips, watching Tokusei help Dorado stand. "I know," she said quietly. Before she could offer any half-hearted suggestions for alternative ideas, Jun took her hand. "Look, I'm sorry about what happened at the palace."

She stiffened, gently pulling her hand away and focusing on the water she had brought over, which she dumped on the fire, producing a cloud of hissing smoke. She pulled a slip of Shadow magic into her and reached out to the ashen water that had sunk into the earth, then pulled it back up to further dowse the firebed.

"I shouldn't have thrown the dagger, and I shouldn't have caused the tear—"

"Then why did you?" she demanded, heat rushing to her words unexpectedly. She let the water sink into the earth with finality.

"I—Well it was Nari's idea for the disruption to begin with," he said, ducking his head. "She had gone to the palace to free the Gray Knights with Ayana and Tokusei. Ayana dropped the illusion when they realized I was in the study, but when she went to put it back on, well those lanterns—"

"Right."

"And she must not have had enough magic for Mistress Nari," he said. "But Nari told me about their plan to rescue my father and the others. And," he sighed, "you were right, that was why I went."

Kira played with the buckle on her bag for a few minutes, struggling to find the right words to say. She watched the others brushing leaves back into place, and picking up their meager belongings. Nesma had magicked straps so they could carry the sacks of food—now considerably lighter after feeding eleven people—and Ryn and Tokusei had slung them across their backs.

"I..." Kira began, "I understand, Jun. And it's all right. Just promise me you'll tell me about these kinds of things *before* you go running off next time."

"I'll try?" he said with a shrug.

She rolled her eyes. "I guess you didn't have time. And look where we are now," she said, forcing a smile to her face. "We rescued your father and the others." The fate of Nari hung between her words like a ghost.

He looked around. "Right where we planned to be, I'm sure."

"Well, I could do with a real blanket and a bath," Kira said, trying to change the subject.

"Yeah, you could," he said, pretending to sniff in her direction. "But seriously, I don't think the Gray Knights are up for a trek across the realm to find spirits who will help us."

"You're right," she said with a sigh. "But where can they go? Surely not your estate, nor the Starwind estate. And I'd feel guilty if a village took them in and got caught by the Commonality. Hagane's roaming about, you know. This really isn't a great time for almost a dozen people to be traveling across Camellia."

"I wouldn't want to run into that commander," Jun agreed. "He's got a look about him—"

Kira gasped. "*Commander*. Aita! They can go to the Stone Mountains, that's where Aita's been in hiding! Do you think Lady Madora would give them shelter too?"

"It's an idea," Jun said warily.

"I know she places a lot of value on magic, but surely the fact that your father and the others are the Gray Knights means something, right?"

"It had better," Jovan said, coming up behind them. "Did I hear you say Lady Madora? What does she have to do with this?"

"Nothing, yet," Kira said. "We were just wondering whether you and the rest of the Gray Knights might go there, to the Stone Mountains, to recuperate."

Jovan stroked his stubbled chin. "Madora has managed to stay out of the conflicts of Camellia for some time. I'm not so sure she'll want to harbor six fugitives. I would be shocked if Tigran could penetrate her defenses, so it would be safe, but that's if she accepts us."

"Aita is there," Kira said, "And she defected from the Commonality. Madora let her in."

"I only met Aita twice, but she seemed like a skilled fighter. I'm sure Madora saw her value there."

"Well, you're all skilled fighters," Jun said.

"Yes, but Madora's view of magic is different than most. It is more coveted down in the Stone Mountains, because fewer people have it. For all I know, she would look down on us for... having it taken from us. Or she would want something in exchange for our safety, since we would be of no use to her."

Kira pressed her lips together. She could already feel the draw of her new quest—what answers might the spirits have, now that these tears were ripping up the realm? She didn't have time to go to the Stone Mountains to make an alliance with Lady Madora, even if she wanted to. They had to start on the spirits.

"I'll go," Jun said. "I'll go with you, and speak with her."

"Jun—" Kira began.

"Look, she wanted you on her side because you had Gray magic, right? At the time you were the only new trainee with it. Well, I have it too. I'm just as valuable."

Jovan pursed his lips, thinking. Finally, he sighed, flicking his gaze to the south. "If you're willing, son. But this could mean a diversion of your path in life; you might be bound to stay in that region, not serving the rest of the realm. I'm not sure our safety in this one moment in time is worth that."

"I think it is," Jun said. "And besides, our paths are already—obstructed." He flung out an arm, indicating the chaos their lives had become. "We can't go back to the temples; who knows if we'll ever finish our training or be able to return home? I think we should go. And I'll do whatever it takes to see you safe, Father. If Madora lets me, I can find Kira again and help keep the realm from tearing up anymore."

A sudden scratchiness clawed at Kira's throat as she said, "Are you sure, Jun?"

What if something happened and she never saw him again?

He nodded, seemingly out of words. She lunged forward and put her arms around him tightly, her eyes stinging. "You take care of them, then," she said into his ear. "And you be safe, especially with Lady Madora. She could rival a trickster spirit with her guile, you know."

Pulling away, he nodded. Jovan discussed the plan with the other Gray Knights, while Ryn, Nesma, and Tokusei finished the final touches on cleaning up the camp. Kira dashed her damp eyes with the backs of her hands.

"Well, we better get going," Kira said a little while later. With a watery smile, she told Jun, "At least you'll be as far as possible from Tigran down in the Stone Mountains."

A slight smile came over him and he ducked his head, now fiddling with his knapsack. He pulled out something small and black, and pressed it into her hand. "Here, I want you to have this."

She opened her fingers to reveal the small black fabric charm with the Kosumoso crest embroidered on it, which he normally hung from his doorknob back at the Gray Wing to signify that he was in residence. She grinned up at him.

"It's just us now," he said to her quietly. "We're the only ones in the realm with Gray magic. We have to stick together, even if we're apart."

"I wish I had something to give you," she said, then she gasped, digging into her bag. "Here," she said with a chuckle.

His eyebrows rose. "Are you sure?"

"Absolutely." She had placed into his hand a thin slip of plastic with the words *North Noxbury Public Library* written on it, among other things. Her only remnant of her life in the Starless Realm. He had seen it before, since she always carried it with her, wherever she went. "Just don't let Lady Madora take it."

After Jun said a hasty goodbye to everyone else, he joined the Gray Knights, who all looked eager to leave this place and find somewhere more permanent to rest. Kira remembered quite well the depression which had enveloped her when she only had a small amount of soul damage; she couldn't even imagine how they felt, after having all the magic completely severed from their spirits. Not to mention a year in prison...

Someone cleared their throat behind Kira, and she whirled around to face Tokusei. "Oh," Kira said.

Tokusei smirked. "Oh, indeed," she said, running a hand over her cropped hair. "Do you mind if I come with you and your friends? I don't very much want to go hide in the Stone Mountains," she said quietly enough so the others wouldn't hear. "Not that there's anything wrong with that, but, I want to help."

Nodding, Kira said, "Of course. I'm sure we could use the help. You're sure?"

"I'm sure. I can't go back to Heliodor, though I know Tai will be worried sick..."

"Tai?" Kira asked. "From the Guard?"

"That's the one," Tokusei said. "Sagano hated it when we got married. He didn't want a couple in the Guard, but our posts are permanent until we finish our rotation."

Kira allowed herself a smile. "Well, I'm hoping we'll both get back to Heliodor someday. We don't want Tai and Sagano to be worried, that's for sure."

Tokusei gave her a smile, but Kira could see the pain behind it. She vowed to fulfill that promise.

Finally, Jun and the Gray Knights turned south and began their trek into the early dawn. Kira turned to Ryn and

Nesma, who both stood there looking at her expectantly. "Let's get away from here—Thistle?"

Leaves shook overhead, and he chirped down at her in response.

"Any suggestions for spirits we should seek out first?"

"Nearby? There's Takanashi over near Nanoka; Gekkō has spoken to him before."

"Perfect," Kira said. "That's plenty far from Meridian."

"But sometimes he wanders into the Seven Days Forest," Thistle said.

Kira hummed. "Well, if we run into any Ga'Miri raiders, so much the worse for them."

CHAPTER 23

THE TRICK

Though Kira would miss him, they sent Thistle back to Mount Gekkō, to carry the news to the spirit of the mountain and Ichiro. He would find them again after.

Between their exhaustion and paranoia at being spotted by the Commonality during the day, they decided to make camp after only traveling a few hours. They found a stream at the bottom of a gulley, where a dark cave welcomed them into its damp depths. It wasn't large, but the four of them fit, and they felt secure.

"Hopefully Ichiro can alert Raiden," Kira said, biting the inside of her lip as they settled into the cave. Sudden emotion welled up inside her chest at the thought of what her grandfather would think. They had gone against his wishes. The idea that Ichiro would be disappointed in her made her eyes prickle with tears. She gulped, then tried to take a deep breath. *I'm sorry it happened this way*, she thought, shoving down the emotions with the words she longed to speak to her grandfather. *But it's better this way. We saved the Gray Knights, and now we can get to work on fixing the tears and taking down Tigran.*

She was glad, really.

It had been exhausting pretending everything was okay, and leaving Tigran to grow too powerful. Part of her thought Nari and Ichiro had made a mistake in waiting so long to take action, but she knew they must be afraid—of starting another feud, or risking all the trainees under their care. But still, maybe Tigran wouldn't have gotten so out of control with the decanters and lanterns if they had acted sooner, and the realm wouldn't be tearing itself apart. She brushed aside the fear of Ichiro's disappointment, shaking her head. But according to Tokusei, Nari had been working behind the scenes with the Shadow mages...

"I hope Thistle isn't gone too long," she said to the others. "He's going to be our best bet in talking to the spirits and getting them to help. But if Gekkō and Ichiro send him to the Spire, who knows how long he'll be, sharing the news with Raiden and everyone at the Spire."

Ryn gave her a sad smile, likely knowing Kira really meant all of the people at the Spire she had left behind.

"I wonder if Spectra's any better," she said quietly.

"What happened to Spectra?" Nesma asked.

"Oh, right, I never told you," Kira said, then they spent most of the morning discussing Kira's short trip to the Spire and everything that had happened between the wisp, Spectra's accident, and everything else.

They rationed the food, but had plenty of water to drink, and each took turns keeping a lookout at the mouth of the cave so the others could get some sleep. It was quiet, and Kira was relieved not to hear an army marching by.

She whiled away the hours of her shift fiddling with the water in the stream, moving it about with a tiny amount of Shadow magic. It kept her nerves calm, since she had to be in complete control of her emotions.

When it grew dark, they regretfully packed up and left the cave, heading for Nanoka.

"At least I'm not the *only* one who can't see in the dark now," Ryn muttered to Tokusei as the darkness grew thicker and thicker and Kira and Nesma led the way.

Tokusei snorted. "Honestly, doesn't that get annoying?" she asked the girls with Light. "Never just enjoying the darkness? How do you even sleep?"

Kira chuckled as she walked, keeping a close eye on the thinning woods. They were coming up on the Kaidō Road, and would follow alongside it as long as they could, staying out of sight. She had no doubt the Commonality would use the imperial road, and it would be best to see them coming.

"It's dark behind our eyelids," Kira said.

"Really," Tokusei mused. "Well, that's good. I'd go insane otherwise."

"The benefits outweigh the cons, I think," Kira said. "I've never been afraid of the dark, but now there's no complete dark; nothing's ever going to sneak up on me out of the darkness, I'll always be able to see where I'm going. And I wish you could see what the stars look like," she added, glancing upward briefly. She never got tired of looking at the gorgeous celestial display.

They made it just outside Nanoka before daybreak.

"No Commonality lanterns," Ryn said.

"Which is good and bad," Kira said, wondering how long they might be in Nanoka, and how high up on Hagane's list the town was.

Since Thistle hadn't caught up with them yet, they circled around the southeast side of the town, searching for somewhere they could wait out the day. They were all dead on their feet, despite having each taken sporadic naps during the previous day in the cave. Staying up all night had a way of filling you with fatigue. Finally, they found a small animal barn which leaned to one side, on the edge of a dilapidated property. The weeds were up to the door latch of the old barn.

"I think it's safe to say this place is abandoned," Kira said quietly, opening the latch and peering inside, her other hand on her dagger. She peered inside, but then shook her head.

"I don't like this. We'd have a roof over our heads, but there's only one exit."

They nodded and went around the other side of the barn, back toward the woods. Kira looked back at the abandoned property as she stepped over a fallen post in the fence.

"Probably abandoned it, tired of getting hassled by the Ga'Mir," Tokusei said, following her gaze. "This is about as far east as you can get."

After all her History and Strategy lessons back at Gekkō-ji, and everything Zowan had taught her, Kira still didn't actually know much about Ga'Mir or its people—or why they would cross the Seven Days Forest just to pillage Camellia. But their raiders were fierce, and still wreaked havoc on Camellia from time to time.

Eventually they found a small rock formation that Kira hoped might contain another cave, but there wasn't one to be found. Merely a thick crack running up one side, with vines snaking their way up to get sunlight atop the rocks. "Hmm," she said, looking around. "What do you guys think?"

"Here?" Ryn asked, skeptical.

"Well, with a bit—" Kira reached out her Shadow magic into the soil and found the vines. She also reached out to the bushes growing a few feet away, and poured a tiny amount of Shadow magic into each of them. With an exhale, she watched the bushes grow higher, as if watching a fast-motion replay, while the vines doubled and tripled themselves, reaching their twisty fingers to ensnare the branches of the bushes.

"There," Kira said. Tokusei whistled in approval.

"That should do it," Ryn said, admiring the wall of greenery that formed a shelter against the rock formation. "Nice job, too."

She chuckled and ducked inside, kicking away some of the leaves as she found a place to sit. "Well, squiring under Zowan had me out doing a lot of quests last year. And he's not really one for staying in taverns."

"Huh," Nesma said thoughtfully, admiring the trailing vines that hid them from view. "Wish I could do this with Light."

Kira hummed. "Well, I've thought about that myself. You could make vines and leaves out of Light too, but the detail involved might take a long time, if you want it to look real..."

They busied themselves settling in, and Kira and Nesma summoned some blankets to spread out, making it quite cozy. Kira's stomach grumbled as Nesma rustled in the food bags. They only had three apples for the four of them. Nesma tried to hand Kira one but she waved her off.

"You take it," Kira said.

Nesma rolled her eyes and summoned a knife in her hand quick as a flash, and cut one of the apples in half, splitting it with Kira.

She grinned. "Thanks. I'll take first shift; you guys rest."

There were no complaints, especially after Kira and Nesma used Light to supply even more blankets to ward off the chill. They agreed not to light a fire. Even though they were farther from Meridian, they still felt vulnerable.

Kira stood by an opening in the foliage, peering out. She was trying not to worry about Thistle. She didn't think the spirit of the mountain would make him stay behind now; the crisis affected everyone, and Kira desperately needed him to help fix it. If anything, Ichiro might have asked Thistle to go to the Spire to spread the news. They had no good ways of communicating now that Nari—

Her chest turned to ice at the thought of Mistress Nari.

She had saved Kira, in that last moment. It could very well have been Kira fallen dead on that platform, but no, Mistress Nari had saved Kira at risk to herself.

But of course she had, Kira thought in awe. Nari had always served Gekkō-ji, and the realm, sending its knights to make the region safer, even if she was sometimes surly.

When this is all over, I wonder if I can help make a shrine dedicated to Nari back at Gekkō-ji. I'm sure Ichiro would approve.

Thoughts of Nari made her think back to her mountaintop duel, and the sentinel she'd created as a distraction. She wished she knew how to make them carry messages like Nari's had. There were plenty of people she would love to talk to right now. Jun, to make sure he got to the Stone Mountains safely. Micah, to see if he and Spectra were okay, and Zowan, to ask his forgiveness for leaving, and to tell him that she was all right.

As she fiddled with a slip of Shadow wind, making a patch of spiky-looking plants sway in her own little breeze, she wondered if she would ever get to complete her Shadow training. There was so much left to learn; she had barely scratched the surface on the proficiencies she might be good at. The only interesting one was the fact that she could listen to things that were far off, but it hadn't really served her much since she discovered it. She wished she had a cool proficiency like the illusionwork Jun could do, or healing or something. Her masters had stressed that not everyone needed a unique talent; merely being able to wield Shadow at all was the true gift.

She let go of the wind by the weeds and pulled some new Shadow magic to her, still relieved at the availability of magic around her. She sent it back out to listen for her, all around. She heard a few birds flitting about on the ground, displacing leaves as they searched for scarce bits of food. A distant rooster crowed.

Then her heart slammed against her chest as she heard the distinct sound of light footsteps. She drew her dagger, but remained in place. Taking a frustratingly calm breath, she tried to soothe her panic in order to focus on her Shadow hearing. It sounded like just one set of steps, which was better than many. But where were they coming from? A strange sensation made her ears prick, and somehow she could tell the sound was coming from the east.

Could it be a scout from Ga'Mir?

There it is again. Kira froze, but then another sound made her loosen her grip on her dagger.

"Whoops!" said a child's voice, then the sound of something falling to the ground. A ball perhaps, because a rolling sound followed it.

She let out a relieved breath and stood, inching out from the vine enclosure. *Village kid, playing in the woods, I guess*, she thought. Not Hagane's soldiers come to take more magic. No, not yet.

They could still be discovered though, if the kid found them and told anyone about them. She quietly circled around the rock structure and tried to pinpoint where they were coming from. She froze, hearing the child's footsteps again. Fingers clutched on the massive rock beside her, she peered out to look.

A little boy of perhaps seven or eight was tossing a ball up and down to himself as he strolled through the woods, stopping occasionally to admire an interesting tree, or a fallen leaf. He had a mop of dark hair, and his clothes were ripped in a few places, quite noticeably at his knees. He looked right at the rock structure, and started heading toward it. Kira clenched her dagger, wondering what she was supposed to do. She couldn't harm the boy, that was for sure.

At that moment, he looked right where she stood and smiled.

"Come on," he said, waving her out. A shock went straight from her chest to her stomach. It wasn't his sudden appearance, but the fact that the ball he held was glowing with some strange purple magic.

Spirit magic.

She had seen Gekkō wield some oddly-colored magic before, and was pretty sure it was only something the spirits had. Was this the spirit Thistle had wanted them to meet?

"Takanashi?" she whispered.

His face lit up, and he nodded eagerly. He tossed his ball in the air one handed. "Come on," he said again, waving back toward the edge of the wood he had come from.

She hesitated, looking back at where the others slept, hidden from sight behind branches and vines.

"Do you know something about the tears? How to fix them?" she hissed, coming closer to him but studying their surroundings in case anyone else was wandering these woods.

He gave her a knowing look, nodding again. "Yes. I'll show you."

She took a step, then paused. Pressing her lips together, she glanced back at the others. "I can't—hold on." She went over to where she had left the opening in the vines and pulled them back a little. Nesma was closest, her hair fallen over her face. Kira shook her shoulder.

"Huh?"

"Hey, can you take over? I'll be right back."

"All right," Nesma muttered, rubbing her eyes and slowly pushing herself up.

Kira nodded and turned around to look for the boy. The ball had disappeared, but he still stood there with an eager smile on his face. "Okay," Kira said.

He laughed and turned around, an excited spring in his step. Kira didn't mind the walk in the morning light, though her legs *were* a little stiff.

Kira opened her mouth and stopped herself from starting to say *um*. She swallowed, then said, "I believe you know Lord Gekkō? He's the spirit of the mountain at Gekkō-ji where I train."

"Yeah," he said, shrugging. Now the ball was back, but a smaller one, and he was tossing it from hand to hand as he walked.

She had to fight from chuckling. She hadn't dealt with little kids in a while, and a spirit who was the embodiment of a little kid might be a little much.

"Well, you probably know there's something wrong, right? With the tears in the realm? I'm trying to find spirits who might be able to help us fix them, or stop Tigran. Do you know who that is?"

Takanashi turned back to her and gave her a patronizing look. "Here, catch," he said.

He tossed her the ball, which felt like it was made of fabric and stuffed with sand or something, and Kira smiled.

They walked in silence for a few minutes, Kira idly tossing the ball to herself (Takanashi had made another one and was doing the same), not wanting to keep pestering him with questions. It seemed like he wanted to show her something, and she knew spirits all worked in their own ways. She wondered if it was another tear—maybe he could show her how to fix one?

They came to a brook and Takanashi hopped onto one of the stones that led a haphazard path across. Kira cocked her head to the side, wondering if she should follow. She felt bad waking up Nesma, and wanted to get back to their campsite, but if Takanashi had something to show her, well, that was why they were here in the first place.

She followed, making sure each rock was steady before moving on. She did *not* want to fall in. She wasn't able to dry her clothes with Shadow wind as easily as Jun could; she would just end up windblown and still damp. *Although I could probably use a wash*, she thought as she watched Takanashi hop onto the bank on the other side.

As soon as Kira got to the other side, Takanashi started walking again. Kira looked back at the sun's position in the sky. "Um—can you tell me what it is you're showing me? Is it something to do with the tear?"

She turned back to look at him, and he was gone.

Openmouthed, she looked around furiously. "What—where?"

Sudden panic lurched through her as she worried whether it was some kind of trap. She was glad she had woken Nesma before leaving the others. What kind of spirit would lure her—

Plenty of them, she realized. Plenty of them were dangerous, or at the very least, difficult. Her heart racing, she turned and surveyed her surroundings. Takanashi could still be here. But what had he lured her here for?

Trying not to panic, she went back to the stones crossing the brook. She should get back to the others, above all else. She cursed herself for following the spirit without telling them what was going on. What if something happened to her? What if it was a trick to lure her away from the others?

Or, another unpleasant thought struck her as she placed her foot on the first stone, what if she had just blown their opportunity with Takanashi? Was he testing her?

Gathering her courage, she took a deep breath, resisting the urge to hoist her dagger in front of her, and said, "Takanashi? Are you there? Please, we really need your help. Would you speak with us?"

A delicate wind blew over the brook, almost pushing her off balance, and the ghost of a giggle wove through the clearing.

Then another breeze rattled the barren tree limbs above her, and Kira almost fell off the rock at what she saw next.

Takanashi had returned, and behind him, holding his hand—nearly translucent in the morning sun—was the wisp.

CHAPTER 24

LISTENING

"Um," Kira said.

The wisp pushed Takanashi forward, and he came to a halt before Kira, staring at his feet with a mutinous look on his face.

Kira didn't know what to say. She looked at the wisp, but the spirit was even more difficult to make out during the day. The soft feminine face seemed like it was looking at Takanashi from under her cloak hood.

"Takanashi," Kira said, still confused but wanting to take advantage of the return of the little boy. "What do you know of the tears? Do you know how to help fix them?"

He seemed to look everywhere but at Kira for a minute—his shoes, the tree beside her, and finally, he looked at her and said, "They're hurting. I can feel them. And it hurts."

She finally stepped back onto the bank and automatically sunk to a crouch to be closer to his eyeline. "I'm sorry," she said. "I'm just trying to help."

He shifted his feet, and the wisp seemed to put her hands on his shoulders—milky white light enveloped his shoulders anyway.

"You should talk to the dragon," he said. "He'll know what to do."

Kira's jaw dropped, but she quickly picked it up. "The dragon? The Camellian Dragon?"

"Yeah, sure."

"Do you know where to find him?"

He looked at her incredulously, then his eyes rolled up and he collapsed into a fit of giggles. Then, without warning, he disappeared on the spot.

A fabric ball fell, as if he'd thrown it at the last second, and landed right in Kira's hand.

Kira was left facing the wisp. She drew a deep breath in through her nose. "Thank you, for getting him to come back... He's a trickster spirit, isn't he? I think I've seen his statue in the Hall of Spirits."

The wisp nodded.

Kira shook her head ruefully. "I really shouldn't have followed him. I should know better."

It was hard to tell, but Kira thought the wisp was giving her some kind of admonishing look.

Now that she was face-to-face with the wisp, she felt an immense pressure in her chest. Could she finally get some answers? Terrified that the wisp would disappear without imparting some knowledge, Kira squeezed the little fabric ball thoughtfully.

"Takanashi mentioned the dragon," Kira said carefully. "But Thistle said we should be asking the spirits for help. The dragon... No one knows what happened to him, right? And you left me that scroll," she added, hoping it didn't sound accusatory.

The wisp tilted her head from side to side, and Kira realized maybe she couldn't speak. *Well, this is going to be difficult*, she thought.

"Do you think we should look for the dragon?" she asked.

Without hesitation, the wisp nodded.

Kira bit her lip. "Do you know where to find him?"

The wisp spread her hands out.

A child's laughter rang out, far away, and Kira turned to look, narrowing her eyes as she wondered if Takanashi was making more mischief again. And then she thought of Nesma and the others unsuspecting in their hideout.

"You know, I should probably—" she turned back, and the wisp was gone.

Kira let out an explosive sigh. "But we were getting somewhere!"

***

Around sunset, when Kira woke from an uneasy sleep, she was disappointed to find that Thistle still hadn't arrived.

"I don't think we need him to help us talk to Takahashi anymore," Kira told Nesma as the two of them sat in the shelter. "I'm just worried about him." Nesma was practicing making leaves with Light magic. Ryn and Tokusei had gone to scour the edge of the village for any food they could easily acquire.

"Mmm," Nesma agreed, "and it doesn't sound like he is the helpful type, either." She put her hands together and then drew them apart slowly, her fingers drawn together as a bright Light appeared, forming in the shape of a small vine, with two leaves on it. Then, Nesma focused her will, and the bright vine faded to a realistic green color.

"Nice." Kira grinned. "And, no, he was the opposite of helpful. But he did tell me about the Camellian Dragon. And the wisp said so too..." she rambled, having already told them all about her adventure this morning.

Nesma continued to slowly draw her hands apart, and as she did so, the vine got longer, and another leaf would appear. Finally, when it was as long as Nesma's arms could reach apart, she stopped, and let it drop into her lap with a soft *fwump*. She picked up one end and gave it a little wiggle. "A little stiffer than I meant," Nesma said.

Kira picked up the other end, admiring Nesma's—her squire, for goodness sake—handiwork. She tried to channel her inner Zowan, and after a year following him around Camellia, she could do it quite well. "Nice work," she said. "It's not something we learned at Gekkō-ji, with our textbooks of all the things we needed to learn to make. You learn a lot more when necessity calls for it."

She smiled at that last bit, almost a direct quote from Zowan.

"And besides, it looks perfect, if you were making it for cover or something. It wouldn't really matter if it *felt* like a real vine or not."

Nesma held it up to the real vines Kira had encouraged to grow into their shelter. "Actually, it would be kind of interesting if I made them to be really stiff, like metal or wood."

"Hey, now you're thinking like a Shadow mage, outside the box."

"Outside the...? Nevermind," Nesma said with a chuckle. "Well, if we needed a trap or defense even, we could make vines where the leaves had sharp edges."

Kira whistled. "There's an idea."

They went on discussing uses for magically-made vines, just as if they were back at Gekkō-ji considering the current piece of magic they were trying to learn, until Ryn and Tokusei returned a little while later. As they spread out a rudimentary meal of barley cakes and dried fruit, a pang of longing went through Kira. She already missed her days training at Gekkō-ji, now that she had ascended to knight. And now she was cut off from the Spire, too. She shook off the sadness that threatened to overwhelm her and laughed at Ryn's short prayer he directed to Takanashi over the trickery that went into acquiring the food.

As it began to grow dark, the absence of Thistle's presence grew stronger and stronger. "I think we might as well stay tonight," Kira said as they brushed off the blankets covering the ground. "I'm sure Thistle could find us anywhere if we decided to leave, but to be perfectly honest, I think we could all use the rest. I mean, I definitely could."

No one disagreed. Tokusei offered to take first watch, and Kira only half-heartedly argued with her. Kira and Nesma summoned more blankets with Light, glad there was an abundance of essence out here in the countryside, because the nights were still cold. And though Kira had long gotten used to living without modern heating, normally if she camped out anywhere, she had the benefit of a fire.

As she snuggled into her particularly fluffy blanket, she noticed something lumpy in her pocket.

"Oh," she said, withdrawing the small fabric ball Takanashi had left her. She set it on the blanket beside her and looked up at the stars, which were particularly beautiful tonight. It sometimes reminded her of that famous Van Gogh painting, with the swirls and brightly glowing stars.

She tried to close her eyes and go to sleep, but she couldn't help but wonder what they were supposed to do next. She had told Jun and Thistle they would look for spirits to help fix the tears, but Takanashi and the wisp both told her to find the Camellian Dragon. And for some reason, she trusted the wisp, even if she didn't trust Takanashi.

She wished she could talk to Zowan, or Ichiro, or Raiden and ask them what to do. She turned over, listening to Ryn's quiet breathing beside her. She listened to the light breeze, for the sound of a flying squirrel that wasn't here…. *listening*. She gasped quietly.

If I can listen at a distance with Shadow, she thought, *can I do the opposite?*

CHAPTER 25

THE SEVEN DAYS FOREST

U nsure of their path, or indeed which spirit to approach next, they decided to stay one more day outside of Nanoka. They had enough food for a day or two, and without anything else to do, everyone became very interested in Kira's new project.

After spending perhaps an hour doing some meditation, she was ready to begin.

Nesma volunteered to walk over to the brook, and Tokusei went with her, curious about the experiment, but also, Kira thought, to protect her.

In addition to the threat of the Ga'Mir and the Commonality, Kira was a little nervous about Takanashi. He had played a harmless trick on her, but the next one might not be so harmless.

"I can hear them talking," Kira told Ryn as they sat on some blankets. "They're by the brook now."

"You told them you were going to do that, right? The eavesdropping?"

"Yes!" she snorted, punching him lightly on the arm. "How else am I supposed to know if it works or not?"

"Mmhmm. Well, go ahead, don't mind me." He lounged on the blanket covered ground, long legs in front of him.

She sat up straight, floating her eyelids shut. Gently resting her palms on her knees, she sent out her awareness.

There was Shadow essence all around her; in the air, bumping into her skin, in the ground and the roots of plants and trees beneath her. She reached out to the Shadow in the air and drew it in, envisioning it going into her lungs. A sudden panic gripped her as she wondered if what she was doing was right, or safe even. But she tamped down the rise of emotion and breathed out a word, imagining herself as amplifying it on the exhale with the Shadow magic.

"Nesma," she breathed. "Can you hear me?"

She pictured the Shadow magic carrying her words like smoke rolling through the air, on their way to reach Nesma by the brook.

Would it take a while to reach Nesma as the words slowly traveled to her?

Would it even work?

Just as she was dragging in another breath to try again, she heard, distantly, "Uh, Kira? Try again, but a little louder. I wasn't sure I heard you at first, but I'm pretty sure I did!"

Kira gasped and looked at Ryn, who had a pleased smirk on his face.

"Your aura just lit up all pink. It worked, I take it?"

She bobbed her head. "I'm going to try again." Quickly she shut her eyes and gathered the Shadow about herself. She drew in a breath and said in a more normal volume, "How does this sound?"

She made sure she was listening, and the first thing she heard was leaves shifting and then a gasp. "Kira, you did it! It works!"

Then her ears were assaulted by a terrible repetitive sound—clapping, she realized—so she dropped the listening as quickly as she could.

"Oof," she said, bringing her hands to her ears.

"Something wrong?" Ryn asked.

Kira shook her head, grinning. "Just learning the downside of super hearing."

They experimented all day. Ryn wanted a turn next, so he strode away with a grin before disappearing into the trees. Nesma came rushing back with Tokusei at her heels.

"That was amazing, Kira!" Nesma said. "Is all Shadow training like this? This was actually fun."

Kira chuckled, settling back down on the blanket as Nesma and Tokusei joined her. "Not often," she admitted. "But the lessons where we explore our proficiencies are a lot of experimenting like this."

"Nice job," Tokusei said. "I knew I'd get to see something interesting if I stuck around with your team."

Kira snorted, but a pleased flush warmed her cheeks. "I'm sure you get to see lots of interesting talents being in the Shadow Guard."

"Sometimes. But it's also about imagination, you know? We're not all weather mages using the wind."

"Don't I know it," Kira said. "My wind skills are terrible. And I haven't started studying any other weather magic."

Nodding, Tokusei said, "Well, stick to your strengths, Kira. Ryn's probably at the brook by now."

"Right."

While Kira tested out her newfound skill, she couldn't help but feel like something was wrong, something she couldn't remember. By the time they broke for dinner right around sunset, and Kira had tested her Shadow speaking even farther, she realized what was bothering her.

"Thistle's still not back," she said, after they finished eating. They were sitting in the enclosure again, watching the last of the sun's rays dissipate in the hazy orange sky. "But I think we should move on."

Nesma didn't say anything, but started picking at her fingernails. Ryn folded his arms over his chest and said, "I think you're right. We shouldn't stay here too long; we already did what we came for."

"Right," Kira said. "Takanashi wasn't much help. But where do we go next? I—I think we should look for the Camellian Dragon."

Ryn furrowed his brow. "Kira, I'm not sure that's a... feasible option."

Sudden heat flooded to her cheeks at his tone. "I know it sounds farfetched; I know the stories say he disappeared after the realm was formed, but Takanashi told me I should. And so did the wisp."

His pitying expression made her grow even warmer. "A trickster spirit, and one you don't even know, though? Why should we believe what they say?"

"I—" she paused to gather her thoughts. "The wisp was helping me. She made Takanashi come back after he played his trick on me. And besides, Gekkō told me about her. It's not as if she's just some random—"

"But didn't Thistle say they didn't know who this spirit is?" he reasoned.

"Well, yes—"

"Then I think we should be looking for more spirits who can agree to help us fix the tears. Like we told the others, and like we told Thistle."

Kira opened her mouth. She sighed and turned to Nesma. "What do you think?"

"I—um—I..." her wide eyes flitted between Ryn and Kira. "I think we should probably look for more spirits. I mean, we've only just started. And besides, *no one* knows what happened to the Camellian Dragon. No one."

She looked at Tokusei, who held up her hands as if in surrender.

"I'm just along for the adventure," she said. "It's your call."

Without looking directly at Ryn, Kira said, "Fine. We'll keep looking for spirits. We'll leave when it's dark and head south. I'm sure Thistle will find us when he can."

***

After Kira sent some Shadow magic into the vines and bushes of their shelter, encouraging them to become even more overgrown so as to completely hide any sign of the enclosure, they set out into the darkness. Their bellies were as full of barley soup and plums as they could manage, and they filled several Light-made canisters of water at the brook. They followed the edge of the Seven Days Forest, in the hopes that it would keep them safe from the Commonality.

Clouds shrouded the stars. Kira led the way, with Nesma watching their backs since they were the only ones who could actually see. Kira didn't go particularly fast, still hoping Thistle would catch up to them soon, and not really even sure where she was heading. "Where's a spirit when you need one?" she muttered, and Ryn chuckled beside her.

"If only Lord Raiden were here," Ryn replied. "He knows everything about all of them. Well, maybe not *everything*," he conceded. "But quite enough about their lore."

"I wonder who's the oldest spirit in Camellia," she said, casually sending her Shadow hearing out in all directions to alert her of any coming danger. It was a strange balance she was working on, listening to things nearby but also far away, without getting distracted by one or the other.

"I'm not sure," Ryn said. "My first guess would be the spirit of souls, but you never really know."

"I met Kamellia once," Kira said.

Ryn stumbled to a halt. "Really? Were you d—did you—" His eyes bulged.

"I wasn't dying or anything," she said. "It was atop the Spire, actually."

"It's quite a spiritual place," he said, clearing his throat and resuming his normal aloofness. Kira was surprised at his outburst, but then again, she hadn't grown up with spirits existing in her everyday life—especially one who shepherded souls on after departing.

When the first hint of dawn appeared on the horizon, they stopped where they were and turned deeper into the forest to find somewhere to make a camp. Just as Tokusei was about to cross a small ridge that seemed to hold a promising dip in the land for a shelter, Kira heard something that made her fling her arms out to halt Nesma and Ryn who were on either side of her.

Tokusei saw the motion and immediately sunk to a crouch, her eyes wide.

Kira looked around the forest wildly, and when she saw no evidence of the twenty or so footsteps she heard, she experienced the slightest amount of relief. "I'm hearing it farther away," she explained to the others, and she hustled Ryn and Nesma over to the ridge. The four of them hastened behind it.

Ryn had drawn both his swords and stood well behind Kira, so as to mask his height with the ridge. Kira slinked up to the edge and closed her eyes to concentrate better, sending out a wave of Shadow that sailed gently through the air toward where she had first heard the footsteps and now wagon wheels. A panicked thought hit her—Tigran's lanterns at the palace could sense magic. What if the soldiers and their decanters could do the same?

She dropped the magic like dropping a hot pan grabbed with a bare hand. The searing sensation that rattled through her was enough of a punishment.

"What is it?" Nesma whispered.

"I—" Kira choked, the pain settling in her chest like an immense weight on her torso. "I dropped it. The magic. I think it's the army—about twenty people—but I got worried they could sense the magic."

Tokusei stiffened. "They might. They could at the palace."

"We'll just have to wait it out," Ryn said, and Kira felt a flood of relief at his words, suddenly feeling incredibly grateful for his presence, guarding her against whatever might come at them.

She snuck a quick look of thanks at him, and he nodded, a slight twinkling in his eyes. She wondered if he sensed something in her aura, but didn't care. "Wait a minute," she said, "you'll be able to see their auras coming, right?"

"At a certain distance, yes. If they get too close, for example."

"But isn't that Shadow magic you use to see auras?" Nesma asked, an edge of fear in her voice.

"It is," he qualified, "but it's passive. I don't have to do anything to see them, so I doubt it's something they could detect..."

Kira dug her fingers into the chill earth at her feet as they sat and waited. The sparkling morning light that washed through the woods clashed with their current predicament.

The seconds ticked by and Kira's heartbeat thumped too fast. She wondered whether the Commonality was just placing lanterns, or if they were on the hunt for Kira and the others. She wondered if Tigran would be with them, or just his lackey Hagane.

"Hey, Ryn?"

"Yes, Kira," he said sardonically.

"You can't see them, yet, right?"

"I hope you're not doubting my faculty of thought enough that I wouldn't have told you they were nearby, are you?"

She snorted. "Come on, I want to get closer." She glanced at Nesma, and held her gaze for a second, assuring herself she would be all right. Belatedly she realized they needed to secure more non-magical weapons, because

Nesma was still unarmed, and obviously afraid to summon anything.

Kira handed Nesma her steel dagger. "Here, you take this."

"What? No, you need it."

"I'll have Ryn."

Nesma's face crumpled slightly, and she accepted it with a nod of thanks.

"Let's go," she said to Ryn. "You two stay here."

Tokusei and Nesma nodded, hunkered down at the crest of the ridge. Kira followed Ryn slowly through the trees. He made a zig-zag path from tree to tree, which Kira would have found almost funny if she weren't unarmed and approaching a contingent of the army.

The trees were thinning, and Kira found it harder to go to each tree. The sun was completely up by now, but she just had to trust that Ryn could see the auras. Finally, he motioned to her, and tugged on her sleeve to pull her close. They were pressed up against a big oak tree, and Kira thought she could hear the footsteps now with her own ears. She could certainly hear the wagons creaking.

The surprise that she had heard them from such a distance was outweighed by the slip of fear pumping adrenaline into her veins. She grabbed Ryn's forearm, and he hissed, "Wait, you'll see them in a moment."

Furrowing her brow, she scanned the edge of the tree-line. "This is the Kaidō Road?" she said, noticing a swath of brown on the landscape just outside the trees.

He nodded. "I think so; we must have walked further than I thought last night. I didn't think the road was this close to the forest. We must be near Sayuri."

A soldier came into view then, preceded by the sound of the men, and the creak of wagon wheels. Dread rolled over Kira at that sound, and then she saw them. The seemingly-normal wagons pulled by captive Shadow magic. She could now see decanters hanging above the wheels, positioned with a very narrow opening pointed down toward each wheel, perhaps dripping Shadow magic onto them.

So Tigran is still allowed to use magic, for official purposes, is he? she seethed. Of course, it would be a lot more difficult to put these blasted lanterns all over the realm; a wagonload full of them wouldn't be an easy burden for a horse or a mule.

Sparing a sad thought for her own Naga, and a twin flicker of disappointment for abandoning Meluca at the palace, Kira watched the contingent proceed down the road, counting heads and trying to discern anything else she could.

Her gut tightened, and she dug her fingers into Ryn's wrist. "That's Nia Mari," she hissed, shrinking fully behind the tree now, her heart leaping into her throat.

"Do you think she can sense us or something?" she said under her breath, her body pressed hard against the tree bark.

"I don't know," Ryn said, equally as quiet. "I know Yuki can sense thoughts without trying, but she's more like me that way. Mind manipulation on the other hand..." he trailed off as Kira started to feel slightly sick.

The Commonality was one thing, but Nesma's sisters were another.

As much as Kira wanted to run back to the safety of the ridge, she waited, each breath cutting in and out of her lungs like fire. Instead of continuing to count soldiers, she counted her breath, her chest rising and falling, her fingers of one hand pressing into the bark, the other wrapped around Ryn's wrist.

And she waited. Waited for the loss of control to come. Or a shout to ring out. Or the footsteps to come their way.

But finally, finally, the creak of the wagons and the marching steps faded, until it was completely silent save for the few birds chirping in the trees. Kira let out an explosive sigh that turned into a nervous laugh.

Ryn took his hand back and rubbed his wrist idly. "Well, then," he said.

Kira closed her eyes for a second, and said bitterly, "I guess Nia Mari must have gotten a pardon from the Empress after all."

CHAPTER 26

THE REALM'S MAGIC

K ira took first watch, secretly hoping if she was alone, the wisp would come again and she could find out more about the Camellian Dragon.

The wisp certainly seemed to want to tell her something. Why else did she keep coming back?

They stayed on the ridge; they knew where the army was, and had no desire to follow them. *Not like we have anywhere to be*, Kira thought to herself as she took a sip of water from her canteen before standing up to stretch. Thinking she could stroll around their campsite under the guise of checking for danger, she drew some Light magic and summoned a dagger, since Nesma still had her steel one.

As she was walking away, a quiet voice called, "Can I ask you something?"

It was Nesma, wrapped in a blanket made of Light, curled up on the ground a few feet from the others. Ryn and Tokusei didn't stir, and Nesma quickly pulled the blanket off and joined Kira so as not to disturb them.

"Sure, I was just about to go on a walk around."

An abundance of pine needles softened their footsteps, the burnt orange forest floor a soft reprieve from the loud crunchy leaves of their last encampment. They walked in silence for some time, Kira trying not to feel resentful that she might have gotten to see the wisp again. She clutched her jacket tighter, wishing she had a nice mug of tea to take the chill off the brisk morning air. Perhaps she could use a Shadow flame to warm some water without creating smoke.

Finally, Nesma cleared her throat. "Is it—back when you fought with—with Nia Mari and Nikoletta," she began. "They tried to control you, right?"

Kira pressed her lips together, slowing her pace and thinking back. "I think so. But somehow they didn't get much of a chance. I remember they were trying to control Raiden, and Ichiro, but they couldn't hold both at the same time. And back when we fought them in the garden at Gekkō-ji..." She wrinkled her brow. "No, I don't think they ever did."

Nesma took a deep breath. "That's kind of what I thought. But I... I never asked. Well. I thought maybe they were taken care of for good, but that was stupid," she said, choking on her words as her eyes brimmed with unshed tears.

Turning to her, Kira grabbed both of Nesma's arms and looked her right in the eyes. "It wasn't your fault," she said. "It was never your fault. They were—excuse me for saying this—they were terrible people for doing that to you. For *ever* controlling you. And I'll be damned if I can't help make it right. They should be locked up. They will be again, when this is all over."

The creases around Nesma's mouth deepened. "I had hoped they would be. But even the Empress has been fooled. Unless we take down Tigran... I don't think... I don't think..."

She cut herself off and scrunched up her face, forcibly holding back tears.

"Oh, Nesma." Kira flung her arms around her, but Nesma remained frozen.

"I just wondered," Nesma said hollowly, "whether there might have been something you did to keep them out. Was there?"

Kira pulled away a little to look at her. Her face was emotionless, her eyes dark with unshed tears. Kira shook her head. "I didn't. I don't know how they didn't get in, because I didn't do anything special. And I don't think there was anything you could have done either."

Nesma's throat bobbed as she swallowed, and a streak of tears slipped out of each eye. Kira hugged her again, speaking into Nesma's hair, "I wonder if it's something passive, like what Ryn said about his aura magic. A passive way of blocking them? I don't know."

This time Nesma pulled back, her mouth open in thought, "Didn't you say Ryn saw something different about your aura, and something about Spectra's—"

A sudden whistling sound flew by Kira's ear, and her arms were wrenched together by something, her Light dagger fallen to the ground. Next thing she knew, her legs clamped together, another cord tight around them, and she was on the ground. Another whistle sounded, and Nesma's body hit the ground too.

"Nesma!" Kira gasped, working desperately to free her hands. In the time it took her to inhale a breath, she had pulled some Light magic in, and then formed another blade in her hands, ready to undo the rope that was coiled around her wrists.

Someone kicked the knife out of her hands, causing it to cut across her knuckles. She cried out at the pain, which was surprisingly intense for such a small wound, but a hand clamped down on her mouth.

A surge of fire rushed through her at the feel of hands on her. She couldn't make out her captor, only a dark cloak with braided blonde hair peaking out from under the hood. They grabbed the bolo around her wrists and hauled her up by that, still covering her mouth.

"I bet you ten silver coins they're essence users," her captor sneered. Another person scoffed, and through Kira's thumping heartbeats she tried to listen to see if Nesma was okay.

"You don't have ten silver coins. But that would explain it," the other attacker said. Kira heard a squeal come from Nesma, so at least she was conscious and alive.

Something told Kira this wasn't the Commonality. That made her pause for a second. Then it must be—

Suddenly her captor flipped her around and she was facing the sky, hanging from her wrists, with her heels on the ground. They began to drag her.

"Hey!" she called, now that her mouth was free. "Let me go!" She kicked her bound legs uselessly.

Then she was on the ground, and the face of a sharply featured blonde woman was directly in front of her own. "One more word, and I gut you," the woman said in a guttural accent, and Kira felt the sharp tip of a knife just under her bottom rib on her left side. Her chest heaving, she nodded.

When they began dragging her again, Kira caught sight of Nesma, who had been tossed over the other captor's shoulder, and they walked as if she weighed nothing. Nesma's long unbound hair hid her face from view as she hung upside down.

Ga'Mir, Kira thought. *It has to be. We should have known we weren't safe in here.*

Terror seized her as she remembered Ryn and Tokusei back at the campsite. Were there more Ga'Mir? Would they be captured too? And for that matter, where were they even taking them?

Kira found that out too quickly for her liking, when the destination became clear. The forest had grown dark, despite the early hour. The trees above formed a thick canopy, making the morning chill even more harsh. And when Kira was shoved to a stop, she spotted an enormous electric blue tear on the edge of a rocky outcrop.

Part of the tear seemed to hover right on top of a broken tree—and Kira realized, the fallen tree beside it was quite fresh. The tear had broken the tree right in two.

Her mouth hanging open as she examined the tear, she didn't see the others at first. Or, perhaps they hadn't wanted to be seen, because it was as if six people materialized from behind trees or beside bushes and rocks. Their dusky orange cloaks lined in fur camouflaged with the fallen leaves and pine needles of the forest.

The woman dragging her stopped and hauled Kira to her feet, roughly turning her to face the tear. One of the other Ga'Mir women stepped forward—because it seemed they were all women, from the way they wore their simple armor and vests, and a few even wore skirts over animal skin leggings.

"Look at it," the woman hissed at Kira. Nesma was hauled to her side, but fell to her knees at the force of the push from her captor. Shakily, she got back to her feet.

Ignoring her racing heart, and squashing down the first sarcastic remark that came to her tongue, Kira said, "I see it. And I'm trying to fix them."

"A likely story," an older woman called, coming up to stand directly in front of Kira, who had to work hard not to flinch away at the sight of the woman's sword, un-sheathed, coming right up to her. The woman's hair was long and light colored, with a few small braids woven in. She pulled back her hood revealing a gently lined face with a straight nose and eyes darkened with kohl.

"Why did you do it?" the older woman demanded, her sword coming closer with the question.

"Do w—" She glanced at the tear. "I didn't do that! I just told you; I'm trying to fix them."

LIZ DELTON

The woman shook her head slowly. "Savages. Your people do whatever you want with the realm's magic, and you ruin it."

"I—what? It wasn't us!"

"Let's just get rid of them, Hilda," urged the girl who had dragged Kira. "And we can move on. These two are worthless."

Hilda held up a hand. "Quiet, Senga." Then she shook her head. "Who are you children and what are you doing here?"

Kira stuck out her chin. "I am Kira Starwind, soon to be Gray Knight of the realm. This is Nesma, my squire. And who are you?"

Eyes narrowed, Hilda turned her back on them, lowering her sword but not sheathing it. Kira was studying the interwoven geometric pattern down the back of the woman's cloak when she whirled back around. "You use the realm's magic, then."

It sounded like an accusation. "Yes," Kira said defiantly.

Hilda spat on the ground. "No wonder this is happening," she said, gesturing to the tear. "If you only used your own magic instead of tearing apart the realm…"

"But this wasn't us!" Kira insisted. "And it's not from using Light or Shadow magic," she added, eyebrows fur-

340

rowed. She had never heard the Ga'Mir had a distaste for magic.

But the woman kept quiet, so Kira went on, "The tears are because the Commonality is storing all the magic in these decanters and lanterns—they're bottling it up, ruining the balance. *That's* why this started, that's where all these are coming from."

"All of them?" Hilda said in a deadly whisper. "Just how many are there, child?"

Kira bit down on her lip at the word *child*, but answered, "I don't know, a handful, as far as I know."

"How do we know she's not lying?" one of the others demanded. "They were the only ones nearby this *thing*. This is the only one we've seen, and we've been in here for—"

Hilda cut her off with a hiss. "If what the girl says is true, we are all in grave danger," she said, her gaze flitting between Kira and the tear by the rocky outcrop.

The girl beside Nesma shifted, facing Kira now, too. "Who is this Commonality you're talking of, hm?"

"Um, the Empress' new non-magical army," Kira said. "But the man leading them is the one responsible for all of this imbalance—the tears."

"Non-magical army?" Hilda said. "It sounds like your Empress finally did one thing right."

"Well, no, like I was trying to say, they're run by this man—"

"Maybe we should give you to the army," Senga said, elbowing Kira sharply in the side.

Kira heard Nesma take in a sharp breath. "No," Nesma said.

"Ah, she speaks," Nesma's captor said. "And why shouldn't we, little mouse?"

Nesma opened her mouth, but said nothing.

"Manners, Astrid," the older woman said. "We're not savages."

Rage was building in Kira's chest, swelling like a balloon. Finally, she burst, "Look! This wasn't us." She pointed at the tear. "They're happening randomly all over because Tigran and the Commonality are stealing and hoarding magic! I'm trying to fix them before the realm gets torn apart, but they've outlawed magic entirely."

"Well, it's for the better," one girl said. "The way they use their magic…"

"Let's dump them and leave them for the army," Astrid jeered. "If their magic is illegal now, they'll take care of these two. We've better things to be doing."

Kira could see Nesma shaking. And then everything started moving too fast to follow.

Astrid reached a hand out for Nesma's shoulder, but Nesma dropped to the ground. Hilda lunged toward the two of them, perhaps trying to diffuse the situation, but Nesma, with wide eyes, darted away—toward the tear. She managed to kick off the cords around her feet and lunged right for it.

"Nesma, no!" Kira shouted, trying to kick off her own cords and lurching forward.

Nesma looked back at her just before reaching it, and Kira saw the look in her eyes.

She reached out and struck her palm against the electric blue light, and dropped like a stone.

CHAPTER 27

HEART

"Nesma!" Kira shrieked, slipping on the pine needles as she tried to sprint toward her fallen friend.

But she forgot her ankles were still bound. A terrible pain shot through her right ankle as the cord wouldn't let go, and her ankle twisted as she fell. She hit the ground, with her hands still bound before her, getting a mouth full of pine needles.

"Nesma," she panted, pushing up on her elbows and hauling herself to her knees, trying to ignore the screaming pain in her ankle. She scooted closer and her hands searched for Nesma's face. Flashbacks of what happened to Spectra shot through her as Nesma's dark hair slipped through her fingers. Her eyes were closed, but she was still breathing.

Kira was distantly aware of a conversation going on between the Ga'Miri women behind her. She couldn't take note of anything besides Nesma's pulse, throbbing gently at her neck. Crushing dread clamped down on Kira as she wondered whether Spectra had woken up yet, whether the Spire healers had figured out a cure by now.

Nesma lay at an awkward angle, and Kira gently arranged her arms beside her torso through blurry eyes. Finally, she became aware of a presence behind her.

Hilda cleared her throat and asked brusquely, "She did that on purpose. Why?"

Kira shook her head. "I don't know. My other friend Spectra was struck by one—she was common and couldn't see it—but I *told* Nesma about it. She knew they were dangerous. She knew—" She gasped.

"What?"

"She knew something about them changed Spectra's aura. To look like mine. And Tigran's. A change that... might be part of what keeps people from manipulating your mind."

"What nonsense is this?" Astrid asked from a few steps away.

Kira turned around, one hand holding Nesma's. She locked eyes with Astrid. "You kept saying to give us to the army. Well, Nesma's sisters have Shadow magic that they use to manipulate minds, and they've done it plenty of times on her. They're part of the army.

"Just before you captured us, Nesma was asking me how I was able to fend them off," Kira said, abruptly wiping away a rogue tear that slipped out of one eye. She didn't know why she was telling them all of this, except nothing seemed to matter anymore. She gave Nesma's hand a squeeze. "I think Nesma thought that maybe touching the tear would alter her aura, make it so her sisters couldn't manipulate her. Because apparently there's something unique about my aura, and Spectra's changed to look like that after she touched the tear..." she rambled off as she connected the dots.

The women were silent. Then—

"Astrid, leave us," Hilda said. "Go back to camp and get Signe."

"What? Why?"

"Do not question me." It was said with as much steel as the woman's sword possessed, and just as sharp. Astrid turned away and strode further into the forest. When her footsteps had faded into the shadowy trees, Hilda said, "Here," and held out her sword.

Kira looked at her for a second, then held up her bound wrists. With a satisfyingly sharp slice, the cord was cut, and the bolo dropped to the ground. Kira sunk back onto her bottom and tried to move her throbbing ankle in front of her to undo the cords. She hissed between her teeth as she got the foot in place.

Hilda studied her for a second, then said, "May I move her?" Kira looked back at Nesma and nodded.

The woman gently put her hands under Nesma's armpits and pulled her a few feet away from the tear. Kira scooted closer to her friend. She smoothed the hairs surrounding Nesma's face, a hollow feeling growing inside her.

How could she have let this happen? She was supposed to be responsible for Nesma. She closed her eyes, not caring that the Ga'Mir might see the hot tears leaking from them. She dashed them away with the backs of her hands and clenched her stomach around the ache that had formed.

It was a few minutes before Kira noticed that the other women had faded away too, leaving just Hilda and the other girl Senga. The older woman had sheathed her sword, but Senga still had her dagger free.

"She is your friend," Hilda said, not quite a question.

Kira nodded nonetheless. "She wanted to come with me to help. I shouldn't have let her. I shouldn't have accepted her as my squire. This is all my fault."

Hilda didn't answer. Kira started wondering how she could get away with summoning a stretcher to drag Nesma back to the others, when these women seemed to despise Light magic, but then realized she might still be their prisoner too.

"Look," Kira said, turning to face Hilda. "I think you know we didn't cause that." She pointed at the tear. "Can I take her and go? I need to get her somewhere safe."

The woman made a gesture to Senga, who walked a few feet away and turned her back on them, apparently busying herself with something Kira couldn't see. Hilda came closer and crouched down beside Kira, surprisingly agile.

"Yes, but you don't look like you're in any shape to do that. I will see the two of you safely away. Senga will draw up something to carry her. But you must wait until Signe arrives." With that, Hilda glanced over at Senga, and Kira followed her gaze, then did a double take.

A strange bed of leaves at Senga's feet were melding together under the tips of her fingers, meanwhile the tree Senga had her hand on seemed to surrender strips of bark at her very touch. She picked up the pieces of bark and laid the leaf bed over them, somehow molding them together. When she got up and walked around to find two sticks, Kira turned openmouthed toward Hilda. "How is that not Shadow magic?"

Hilda gave her a knowing look, though she could see the distaste in her eyes. "What *you* use as magic is what makes up our world. You take it, and make it do what you want. It is not good for the realm. And you have never listened.

"What *we* use is part of us. And the world around us responds to our desires." She put a hand on her heart.

"What—soul magic?" Kira recoiled, thinking of Tigran.

"Mmm, perhaps. It could be called that, I suppose."

Kira inched away without even realizing it, her heart beginning to thump uncontrollably. *Oh no.*

"It is nothing to fear," Hilda said, affronted, concern deepening the wrinkles of her face. "It is *your* magic that is eroding the realm," she added haughtily.

"Well—no, it's the *absence* of the Light and Shadow, really. But, are you sure?" She looked into Hilda's frank face, and her no-nonsense green eyes, and believed her. "I thought soul magic was... bad. It's what Tigran does, when he takes other people's soul magic—"

"Now *that* is despicable. No, no, no no. We Ka'Mir do not practice in that way." Kira was surprised to take note of the soft way she pronounced the word. "I have always despised your people's way of using Light and Shadow, but at least you returned it when you were done. These things you say this man has been doing... Well, I can see now that you are right. You are good to fight against him.

"But what *we* do is inside of us." She placed a hand on her heart. "It is as strong as our hearts. So perhaps you would call it heart magic. It is not like drawing essence from a soul. That is *abhorrent*. It is drawing essence from your will, your fire, your spark."

"Do all Ka'Mir have this kind of magic?"

Hilda made a snorting chuckle. "It is not a Ka'Mir sort of magic. It is all of us. When the Great Dragon opened the doors, only those of us with magic could see them. Your Light and Shadow are what make up the realm, the Ka'Mir have never used this magic, it is savage to use the place where you live in a such a way." The disgust was evident in her tone, but Kira ignored it. It sounded like an age-old distrust that she didn't have the energy to dissuade.

And there was that mention of the dragon again...

"Wait—oh—" Kira shook her head; a particularly strong twinge of pain shot up her ankle as she did so. Though she wanted to ask about the Ka'Mir's take on the dragon, she was too curious. "So anyone can use magic like that? Without using Light or Shadow? *Anyone?*"

Senga finished the makeshift stretcher, with several branches for support. Kira stared as she brought it over, silent as the two Ka'Mir lifted Nesma onto it. Kira put her hand to her throbbing ankle, wondering just how she was supposed to get back to Ryn and Tokusei like this.

The thought of making some crutches out of Light magic made Kira uneasy in more ways than one—the Ka'Mir certainly wouldn't allow it, and Kira wasn't sure it was safe to use that much Light magic with so many tears appearing.

The idea of being helpless on crutches was almost as painful to her as the twisted ankle.

"Yes, anyone," Hilda continued when Nesma was settled. Senga retreated again, and quietly took out her own sword to polish it while sitting on a stump. "But not everyone has such strength of heart for great feats."

A thousand questions swirled in Kira's head about heart magic, and the Ka'Mir, but the one she blurted out was, "Why are you here?"

Hilda raised a blonde eyebrow, then said, "Ah, there's Signe." Another woman was coming from the direction Astrid had disappeared into; she was rather skinny and unarmed, a willowy brown skirt whispering over the leaves as she went. She was almost identical to Senga, and given their names, Kira assumed they were related, or possibly even twins.

The newcomer put a hand on her heart in some sort of greeting. Hilda stood and murmured a few words, pointing at Kira and Nesma. Signe's eyes darted toward the electric blue tear a few times.

"Wait a minute," Kira said, glancing at it herself. "How can you all see the tear if you don't have Light or Shadow?"

Hilda pursed her lips. "We can sense it. And we saw the tree snap in half when we felt the disruption. This is why we stopped here, to inspect the anomaly."

"Oh," Kira said.

"You say it's invisible?" Hilda asked.

Kira nodded and opened her mouth to explain—

"—Your ankle?" Signe cut in, pointing at where she clutched her leg.

Kira nodded. Signe sunk down, her skirt pooling around her. She put a hand on Kira's ankle, and closed her eyes briefly. A pleasant sensation began to seep into Kira's ankle, but it was so faint she thought it might just be the warmth from the woman's hand.

"And what has happened to the girl?" Signe asked, her hand still on Kira.

"She touched the tear," Kira said in a hollow voice.

Signe's eyes widened, and she made some kind of movement bringing her fingers to her forehead. She shared a look with Hilda, who nodded, then Signe lifted her hand away from Kira's ankle, and Kira knew she wasn't just imagining it: her ankle did feel better.

"Wh—" Kira started, but realized she didn't need to ask. She stretched the ankle, waiting for a twinge of pain, but it was perfectly normal. "Thank you."

It reminded Kira of Shadow healing, but it must be magic as Hilda described it: from the heart. For a second, Kira's hand drifted toward her own heart, wondering.

Then she saw Signe reach for Nesma. Would this strange magic be able to heal Nesma? Kira's breath caught in her chest. She scooted closer as Signe placed her palms on Nesma's forehead and heart. The woman's button nose wrinkled when she closed her eyes, concentrating. Hilda hovered a few feet away, frank curiosity on her face mingled with concern.

As Kira watched Signe breathing rhythmically for a few minutes, she marveled at how little she knew about the Ka'Mir. Even the fact that everyone called them *Ga'Mir* made Kira cringe a little. And how had she never heard of their kind of magic before? Maybe it was part of why they were always raiding here, west of the Seven Days Forest. But most of the women she had seen had a gaunt look about them, a hungry look, and their clothes and armor were in good repair but well-worn with age.

Sweat beaded on Signe's temples, but still there was no change in Nesma, no fluttering of her eyelids, no change in her breath. Nothing.

"Ahh!" Signe shouted in agitation, flinging her hands away. "I am so close! I can feel her in there. What is this magic?" she demanded of no one in particular.

"You try," Hilda said, and it took Kira a second before she realized she was talking to *her*. "You know her better, she is closer to your heart."

"Me? What, with your magic?"

"No, *your* magic. From your heart."

"But I..."

Hilda tucked her chin and said, "With all that training you said you had? Aren't you some kind of warrior or knight? I'm sure you can manage."

"Light knight," Kira muttered, then she looked into Nesma's face and took a steadying breath. "All right. Just tell me what to do."

CHAPTER 28

HEART MAGIC

P alms pressed to hearts—her own, and Nesma's—Kira looked for the space between breaths. She looked for the space between heartbeats, like Signe and Hilda told her. She thought she caught it once, felt a brief thrill of excitement, but it was gone quicker than it had come.

The fact that searching for the spark of heart magic was much like meditation back at the Spire was not lost on her. The fact that she was learning a wild new magic out in the Seven Days Forest with women from Ka'Mir was another distraction from her finding that space between.

The space between.

Hatred rushed up in her chest, and she had to take several moments to get her breathing back on track. Her thoughts had drifted to Tigran, and his so-called lording over the space between worlds. Of course, he claimed to be the master of traveling between realms—and Kira had

LIZ DELTON

always wanted to know what he possibly did in the Starless Realm, or whether he just used it to travel through—but she wondered if he knew anything about this kind of magic.

She hoped not. She had no doubt he wouldn't stoop to use a gentler magic like this kind, which was more about shaping the world around you with a spark of desire from your heart, or so Hilda had told her.

No, Tigran liked power. He craved the raw power of soul magic, and when he couldn't get enough of that, he went for other people's soul magic. And even that wasn't enough for him. Now he was taking all the magic of the realm. Didn't he know what he was doing? Didn't he know he was ripping Camellia apart?

It took all her energy to divert her thoughts back to the task at hand. She cracked her eyelids and looked at Nesma to remind herself of the importance of connecting with her heart. A brief smile, and then she closed her eyes again, searching.

She grew almost dizzy riding the wave of her breath, seeking the crest, where *in* met *out*. Where one heartbeat stopped and another started. And all the while, she focused on thoughts of healing. Thoughts of Nesma waking up. Making her desires clear, should she finally find the

356

right spark. She couldn't tell how much time passed, and a dull ache began in her torso after a while.

Right about when she realized it was late afternoon, and that the dull ache was hunger, she felt a strange flutter under her fingertips. Then suddenly, a hand grabbed hers.

She looked around, but it wasn't Signe who had grabbed her hand. It was Nesma.

Her eyes were still closed, but she clenched Kira's wrist with a strong grip. Kira gasped in shock.

"Keep going," Signe urged softly by her ear, and Kira closed down again, searching for what she had briefly held in her mind's eye. Where was it? The joy that it seemed to be working gave her hope as she watched the next crest in her breathing, hoping to line it up with the same lull in her heartbeats. She focused her thoughts on Nesma opening her eyes, of her waking up. The girl was like a sister to her.

The hand twitched, and Kira opened her eyes again.

Nesma looked up at her, her face clammy and her eyes wide. "Kira?" she asked, then her face went slack, and her eyes shut again.

"What? No!" Kira scrambled for Nesma's hand, which had dropped. "What happened? I did it!"

Signe put a hand on her shoulder, and said gently, "She's just asleep now, actually asleep."

"Oh," Kira said. "Oh. Well, um, wow. I can't believe I didn't know you could do this kind of magic."

"I'm sure there's a lot you don't know about us," Hilda said. "But for now, why don't you introduce us to your friends?"

"Fr—" Kira looked up and spotted Ryn and Tokusei standing ground twenty paces away, each wielding one of Ryn's swords, with looks of vengeance upon their faces. And—to Kira's shock and absolute happiness—Thistle upon Ryn's shoulder.

She gasped and lurched to her feet, but stopped herself from running toward them when Hilda and Senga both took defensive stances with their broadswords. Senga was now holding a round wooden shield she had gotten from somewhere.

"I—" Kira said, "Yes, these are my friends," she told Hilda. "Ryn! It's all right, it's all right! Lower your swords!"

Ryn looked at Thistle, whose whiskers twitched as he said something Kira couldn't hear from this distance. Then they warily came closer to the small camp, giving a wide berth around the tear by the rocky outcrop.

"What happened to Nesma?" was the first thing Ryn said as he got close.

Kira stood, testing out her ankle for a second before putting any actual weight on it. *Good as new*, she thought. "She, um, she touched the tear."

"*What?*" Ryn said, livid. "How? Why?"

"We can talk about it later," she said. "I want you to meet the Ka'Mir women, Hilda, Senga, and Signe."

"Ka'Mir?" Ryn echoed quietly, his face turning to stone. His gaze darted about, and Kira could tell he was analyzing escape plans, and the auras of the women in order to judge the likelihood of their attack. Tokusei edged away, setting her feet more firmly in a subtle defensive stance, though she kept her sword down.

"Thistle," Kira said, hoping to diffuse the situation. "Have you met anyone from Ka'Mir before? Did you know about their kind of magic? Heart magic?"

Thistle shrugged—or what passed for a shrug with a six inch high ball of fur—and said, "Sure."

"What?" Kira asked. "Why wouldn't you tell anyone about this?"

Another shrug, "No one asked." Kira refrained from rolling her eyes. Then Thistle swooped over to Kira's shoulder and perched there, his tiny paws clinging to her hair for a second as he situated himself. The fluffy weight on her shoulder was far more reassuring than it should have been, she thought. It was nice to have him back.

She gave Nesma's shoulder a quick squeeze before standing and going over to Hilda. "These are my other friends traveling with me," she told the woman. "I need to figure out a way to stop Tigran, before he destroys the whole realm. Do you know of any spirits nearby? We were looking for spirits to recruit to help us fix the tears and stop Tigran, though one of them told me to find the Camellian Dragon."

"What makes you think the spirits will help?" Hilda said, she crossed her arms, making her leather armor creak.

A dull heat crept into her cheeks, but Kira said, "Well, Lord Gekkō of the mountain I live on has been helping me—this is Thistle, his companion. And there was another spirit, the one who told me to find the dragon."

Wondering when she would see the wisp next, and whether she could get any more information out of her, Kira winced, though when she looked at Ryn, he didn't look upset at her mentioning her alternate plan of finding the dragon.

"Ah, the dragon," Hilda mused.

"Do you know where he is, or what happened to him?"

"I do not," she said. "I had always assumed he passed when he created the realm, from such a large feat of magic."

Kira looked down at the pine needles on the ground. "I hope not. That's who the wisp said I should find."

"That is the other spirit you mentioned?"

She nodded, but Ryn interjected, "How do we know the wisp isn't another trickster? We can't waste time on a dragon we'll never find. Just look—what is this tear doing out here anyway, where there's no lanterns sucking up magic? This is bad. We should be finding the spirits—Thistle will help, right?"

Thistle shifted from foot to foot, his soft fur rubbing against Kira's ear and neck as he did so. "I—I agree with Kira," he said in an uncustomarily small voice.

"What?" both Kira and Ryn said.

"Really? Why?" Kira added.

He settled down, but his still-twitching whiskers rubbed against Kira's neck. "Well, um..."

Kira could see his big black eyes darting toward and away from the Ka'Mir women, who were staring with frank interest at the spirit.

"It's all right," Kira said quietly, "I trust them. They healed Nesma, well, they showed me how, actually."

Ryn's mouth popped open audibly, "You could have told us that!" he exclaimed. "Here I thought she was comatose like Spectra!"

Gasping, Kira said, "Spectra! I could heal her now!" But then she groaned. "If only we could get into the Spire. But anyway—Thistle, what do you..." she coaxed, now noticing the hint of fear in his eyes.

"I don't think the spirits are going to be much help," he said quietly. "Our... our magic is fading now, too."

***

They allowed the Ka'Mir to lead them back to their larger camp, which consisted of fourteen women, a smattering of tents made of woolen fibers, and the most enticing campfire Kira had ever seen. She beelined right for it, and as soon as she felt the waves of warmth coming off it, she felt her jaw unclench. Her stomach growled loud enough for Hilda to hear.

"Food," the woman said, nodding at a younger girl who was tending a spit roasting over the fire. Kira's mouth watered at the sight of the meat, and she lost herself for some time in the food and the warmth. In the back of her mind, she kept an eye on her surroundings, on the women moving around her, and the location of each of her friends, but for several blissful minutes, all she did was eat.

Nesma needed the stretcher after all, still sleeping when they decided to retreat further into the forest. Kira was a little worried that her heart magic hadn't worked, but Signe had assured her that her brain and heart patterns were that of someone merely asleep. Kira was eager to try the heart magic again, but after Thistle's pronouncement, she had a lot more on her mind.

Finally, when they had eaten their fill, and drank all the water they could hold, a hush settled over the campfire. Many of the other Ka'Mir went off to tend to other things, and only Hilda and Senga remained, though Kira could see Astrid on the outskirts of the firelight, clearly visible to Kira with her Light. Thistle perched himself on the log Kira sat on, his huge black eyes gazing eerily at the fire.

Kira tentatively reached toward him and stroked his back. "Thistle?"

He jerked out of a reverie and looked up at her. "Oh? Oh. Yes." He glanced around at all those assembled. "Well, when I went back to Gekkō-ji to deliver your message, I of course met with Gekkō first. And he told me. He's not sure if it's the lanterns and their way of pulling in magic, or whether it's a result of the cracks in the realm, but either way. It's fading. I... I can't borrow his magic anymore, either. It's too weak. He almost didn't let me leave the mountain. But after I spoke with Ichiro, he wanted me to go to the Spire too, and I was able to convince Gekkō to let me go, so I could help you."

Kira groped in her pocket, and realized the fabric ball Takanashi had given her had disappeared. Was it a coincidence, or was his magic fading too? She glanced at the others around the fire. Hilda looked entranced at Thistle's presence, and Kira could tell she was hesitant to speak to the spirit.

"Is it happening to all the spirits?" Kira asked.

Thistle gave a small nod. "It's possible. It's likely. Which is why Gekkō thinks you should find the Camellian Dragon."

A chill ran down Kira's spine, despite the warmth from the fire. She ran her fingers along her arms. "Does he have any idea where to find him?"

Thistle shook his head. "He wasn't old enough, remember? Though if you ask me, he's quite old enough to be getting along with," he joked lightly.

Senga choked on her canteen, clearly unsure whether to laugh or not.

"This is going in circles," Kira said. "I want to find the Camellian Dragon, but if it's a wild goose chase then we're just wasting time."

She shot her gaze to Ryn, who looked amused at her Starless expression, but he frowned in support of his agreement.

"And no one had any more ideas about the cracks?" Kira asked Thistle. "Ichiro, Zowan, anyone? Because if they're appearing in the middle of nowhere out here, where no one's taking magic, this can't be any good."

Thistle's whiskers twitched. "No, it's not. Raiden had me do a quick check over the Spire, and I found two more inside the temple grounds, and one in the city."

Blinking, Kira stared unseeing at the fire, icy fear coming up from her stomach. That many tears had appeared at the Spire since she had left—how long had it been? "Three in three days? Four days? That's—that's bad."

"Well, there were a lot of lanterns," Ryn said. "The palace has never treated the Shadow region fairly since the feud, you know. So I'm sure the Commonality is getting their payback now. Probably put extra in Heliodor."

"Oh, and I had two other messages for you," Thistle said to Kira somewhat ominously. She bunched up her fists, then nodded for him to go on. "Zowan was furious with you for leaving, though he said to say: *You can do this Starless Girl.*"

She nodded, tears immediately pricking in the corners of her eyes.

"And your grandfather said to tell you that everything he said before is now worthless, and to do what needs to be done, and fast."

"What was worthless? His advice?" she said, brow furrowed.

"Something like that," Thistle conceded, "I'm paraphrasing. He wants you to do whatever it takes to stop the tears and stop Tigran. And I agree. We shouldn't hold back—the commoners especially are in the most danger right now with all these tears popping up, but pretty soon all of us will feel the effects of this magical drain."

It was like a massive weight settled on her heart. It was all up to her now. Or, at least, it felt that way. Jun was gone with the now magicless Gray Knights to the Stone Mountains, and both temples were on lockdown with no magic.

She would do what had to be done. They needed to stop these tears from forming, and fast.

Trying hard not to think about Micah and the possibility that he might encounter a tear, and fall into a coma like Spectra...

Kira glanced down at Nesma sleeping peacefully beside her and relaxed a little.

She could heal it; she could fix it.

Shadow healers were rare, so she had never even dreamed she could heal someone. It was notoriously difficult, and healers had to train for a long time, learning everything there was to know about the body. But something about the heart magic was simpler yet more powerful.

"I—I don't know where to start," Kira finally admitted, then turned toward Hilda and Senga. "I don't suppose you know who the oldest spirit in Camellia is? They might know about the dragon, or been around when the realm was formed, when they were living."

Hilda frowned and shook her head.

"What about the young man..." Kira mused. Do you know the same story about how the realm formed—" Kira pulled out the heavily battered blue scroll from her bag and handed it over. After Hilda and Senga scanned the scroll in the firelight, they discussed the legend at length.

"Of course, the tale I was told is slightly different," Senga said. "The World Dragon is said to have blessed all the people who came through the portals—it wasn't only that they could see magic to come through, but that we were all given a gift." She put a hand over her heart for a second, and Kira smiled briefly.

"That's interesting," Kira said. "So maybe he didn't disappear after forming the realm."

"And he could be anywhere," Ryn said.

Kira pursed her lips. "Yes, but if the realm is breaking, he should be the one who knows how to fix it. Right?"

The others all nodded; Kira could even see Astrid nodding from outside the firelight. As Tokusei did another pass around the perimeter behind Kira, she began to feel the lure of sleep calling to her. She shook her head. "I want to figure out where to go," she said, partially to herself. "We've already, um, wasted some time today—who knows how many more cracks are forming everywhere else? I don't suppose you have any horses we could borrow?" she added, looking at Hilda.

The older woman scoffed. "Hardly. Horses mean money, and food, both of which are the reason we're—" she drew herself up— "the reason we're here. We need it. And we can't get it in Ka'Mir."

Kira stared into the flames. "I'm sorry," she said, at a loss for anything else to say.

"We don't have any horses," Senga said, "But we could get you some. We just can't keep them."

"Oh?" Kira said, perking up again. "That would make this a whole lot easier. Once we figure out where to go, anyway."

"I'll ask Astrid to look for some," Hilda said, craning her neck to signal to Astrid, who nodded. She slipped away into the darkness, and Kira couldn't tell whether said horses were going to be acquired by magic or by stealth or both. "Now, if only you knew where to look."

Nodding slowly, Kira gazed at the flames, idly wondering if there were any more of the mildly sweet cake-like things Signe had handed out earlier. But then a thought struck her like an oncoming bus.

Maybe not *where* to look, but *when*.

She sat up so straight it was like a sword made up her spine. "I know where to look."

CHAPTER 29

THE STONE MOUNTAINS

Walls of rock rose like skyscrapers on either side of Kira, as she led her pilfered bay mare at a walk down the narrow track that wove through the Arashi Pass. Nesma sat behind her, her thin frame easily able to fit onto the mare's wide back. Ryn and Tokusei flanked them, and from the rear, Senga, riding a grayish white mare of massive proportions.

After finding out Astrid had acquired the horses with a bit of heart magic influence—coaxing the horses to want to leave their cozy barn on a farm outside of the Seven Days Forest—Kira and the others decided to depart immediately for the Stone Mountains as soon as possible. The Commonality could be anywhere now, and the missing horses would certainly be cause for suspicion.

Hilda had filled their bags with provisions, and their bellies with breakfast before they departed. And when Senga begged to go with them, Hilda had agreed.

Kira was immensely glad for Senga's presence, and, she had to admit to herself, incredibly curious. Though it might have been preferable to let the healer Signe come, Senga could at least teach Kira more about heart magic, if she agreed. They hadn't spoken much since departing the Seven Days Forest, galloping through the deserted countryside with a few stops to give the horses a break.

They spotted three more cracks along the way.

"How are you doing?" Kira asked Nesma for the millionth time. They were passing under a natural rock bridge, and the hairs on Kira's neck tingled. There could very well be Stone Mountain guards hidden up there, or anywhere on the rocks above them, but Kira had to trust that Lady Madora would be happy to see her. Or, at the very least, not hostile.

"Fine," Nesma answered quietly, her hands slung loosely around Kira's waist. That was about as much as she had gotten out of her since she had woken up back at the camp.

"Let me know if you want to stop."

"Kira, I'm fine."

Kira turned around to look at her with a frustrated sigh. "Well, sorry for worrying about you, but you ran right at that thing not knowing you would wake up!" The irritation bubbled up unexpectedly.

Nesma clamped her mouth shut, staring straight ahead.

Turning back to face front, Kira tried to squash down the unexpected emotion. Nesma had no idea how worried Kira had been. What if they hadn't healed her? What would they have done then? She thought she knew Nesma's reasoning, but that was a bridge of conversation she had yet to cross.

Kira caught sight of Thistle, who was perched on Ryn's horse. The flying squirrel looked unusually forlorn. The worry on his face was clear.

She knew how he felt. They all did. But at least she had the glimmer of hope from the magic the Ka'Mir had shown her; probably the only thing helping Kira sit up straight in her saddle at the moment, her eyes clear to the task ahead of her. It wasn't enough to heal the realm, or stop Tigran. They needed a much bigger force than that. It wasn't like she could put her hand on a tear and try to heal it with her heart. She would drop in an instant.

The dragon was the key. Even Gekkō said so.

They would need to convince Lady Madora to look back in history with her Shadow magic, to find evidence of what happened to the Camellian Dragon. Kira's theory, which she had discussed more in depth with Ryn on one of their pitstops, was they would need to try to look back for the young man the legends talked about, the one who was the first to enter the Realm. But from Kira's experience with

Lady Madora, she wasn't sure it would be possible. When they had looked back to find out about Kira's parents, Madora had needed to use some of Kira's blood. And the only person in the realm they knew to be descended from the young man, according to legend, was the imperial family. There was no way they could get to the Empress now. And certainly not to acquire blood.

Maybe there's another way, Kira thought. The serene tinkling of water reached their ears, and she spotted a small rivulet of water cascading down a mossy rock face, several flowering air plants perched on the sides, reaching their long thin fingers out for sprays of water and passing nutrients.

An hour later they reached Lady Madora's fortress.

Sandy-cloaked guards appeared out of nowhere. They dismounted in the open space in front of the stone edifice which protruded from the side of an enormous rocky plateau. Thistle swooped over and landed on her shoulder, and his fluffy presence was a comforting weight. A mixture of excitement and dread filled her, but the fact that Jun and the Gray Knights were inside—they should be, anyway—helped propel her through the door. The guards at the double wooden doors lowered their spears and let them pass, so they could enter the darkened vestibule. A layer of dust hung in the air all around them.

The vestibule gave way to a narrow corridor overlooking an indoor fountain. Lush greenery framed the entire right side of the hallway, and Kira thought she spotted a frog lingering on the side of the walkway.

"This is not what I expected," she muttered to Ryn, who walked at her side. Thistle chittered.

"Can't say I did either," he said, surveying the tropical flowers growing from the walls in what must be vertical planters of some kind.

When they reached the end of the hallway, a guard approached them, saying brusquely, "This way. Lady Madora is waiting."

They stepped up their pace, Tokusei and Senga behind her, and Nesma trailing at the rear. They followed the guard, and turned down a long stone corridor. Kira lowered her voice and asked Ryn, "Have you taken a look at Nesma's aura lately?"

"Yes," he said darkly. "I've been meaning to say something. Why do you think she did it?"

"Before the Ka'Mir captured us, she was asking me how I resisted her sisters' manipulation," she said quietly, not wanting anyone else to hear. "And I think she thought whatever was special about my aura might have been it. Whatever kept them from controlling me. And when she learned the tear changed Spectra's aura too..."

He hummed in thought. "I truly don't know."

The guard abruptly halted, and when they came level with him, he gestured them inside a room with beautiful red double doors.

Kira's gut clenched at the sight of Lady Madora, who sat on a throne-like chair at the other end of the admittedly small room. It reminded her of the lady's caravan, with shelves all over packed with various artifacts and baubles. *She's a collector*, she thought. *Of memories, and people*.

Lady Madora had dispensed with her hooded cloak as well as the fabric she had worn across her blind eyes when Kira first met her. Her mostly gray hair was pulled back into a severe bun at the nape of her neck, and Kira could see the subtle black tattoos at the woman's wrists, peeking out from under the red sleeves. This room was warm, much like the rest of the fortress, yet Kira still hadn't seen any fires or braziers.

Madora beckoned them forward with an impatient hand. "Come," she said, a slight smile curling up the sides of her mouth.

Though they knew she couldn't see, they all gave Lady Madora a bow. Stopping a few feet away from the woman, Kira straightened and said, "Lady Madora, I hope you are well. It is Kira Savage—Starwind, and I've come with my friends Nesma and Ryn, Tokusei of the Third Shadow

Guard, Senga of the Ka'Mir, and Thistle, companion to the spirit Gekkō."

"Well," Madora said. "I am well enough. But I hope you bring better news than my last visitors."

"Are they here? Did they make it?" Kira asked.

Madora nodded. "Sir Jovan and his people are guests of mine; they should be along shortly. Now, what is it you need? Or are you, too, merely hoping to take advantage of my hospitality?"

Kira bowed her head, glad Madora was getting straight down to business, though Kira didn't quite like her tone. "I do need a favor," she admitted. "And we are willing to work out a deal. But I hope you know that what we seek will help everyone—the realm—"

"And what will be left of the realm by the time you're done? The interfering from the Commonality has created chaos—even here in the Stone Mountains. Though they have not yet attempted to place any of those lanterns I've been told about, we were delivered an imperial decree forbidding magic." She scoffed. "As if our meager use of magic is to blame for the rips that now scar our territory," she spat. "I am told that magic is dying, that our realm will be torn to shreds. What is it you need so badly that you have come seeking help from me now?"

The force at which Kira had to hold herself still and not betray any emotion was almost physically painful. Was it worth it, aligning herself with Madora?

Her bold statements about the realm made her insides grow cold.

"There are two things I want to ask you, the first, I was hoping you would tell us for free."

"Oh?"

"Tigran Tashjian. I believe Lord Raiden has spoken to you about his true identity. His name was Kage, and he was from the Stone Mountains."

"That is not a question." The woman's fingers clenched on the hard wooden armrests of her throne.

"Who was he? Do you remember him?"

Madora bowed her head slightly. "I have spoken with Aita and Raiden about this at length already, so I will tell you. I remember him only because of his absence. He was one of the few who had Shadow magic, so of course when he went to train at the Spire, we watched him go, never sure if he would return or not, like many others. But we do not stop anyone from pursuing proper training.

"He returned several times to visit his ailing mother. She grew worse and worse until one of his visits when she began to show improvement. Then, each time he visited, she seemed better. I began to wonder if he was learning healing at the Spire, which would have been quite advanced for his age, but when I asked him, he said no."

"Soul magic," Kira said. "Is that when he started using it?"

"Perhaps," Madora said. "I am no expert, but I have heard once you start taking magic from your soul, you damage it. It is no wonder he has no restraint in his actions anymore. I only wonder now what he intends to do with all of this captive Light and Shadow magic."

"They were going to sell it to commoners," someone said, and Kira turned to see Jun and Sir Jovan enter the room.

Kira had to fight from running at Jun and squeezing him into a tight hug. She settled for a bright smile, relieved to see they had made it all right.

She turned back to Lady Madora. "Right," Kira agreed. "Under the guise of making things even and balanced throughout the realm. I just don't know what was in it for him. Money seems too insignificant for him."

"He has always disdained traditional training ever since he was expelled from the Spire," Jovan said. "Whenever I talked to Tigran, he had a clear distaste for the temples. I always thought it was because of the feud, and the damage it caused, but once I learned he was actually Kage, it made more sense."

"But the cracks," Kira said, "Do you think he meant to cause them?"

Madora shook her head, and Jovan said, "No. After all, he is a part of this realm too, why would he want to destroy it?"

"But he can travel between realms. The Lord of Between, right? What if he's trying to destroy this one, so all that's left is the Starless Realm?"

They were all silent for a moment, until Lady Madora spoke up, "But there isn't any magic in the Starless Realm; why would he want to go there?"

Jun gasped. "What if he was planning on bringing all that captive magic?"

Kira raised an eyebrow. "That's possible. But I'm pretty sure there is magic in the Starless Realm. I saw Light magic before I even came here."

Senga stared at Kira, her mouth open. *Oh, right, I forgot to tell them that part*, Kira thought with a thrill of amusement.

She continued. "Anyway, that's the main reason I'm here: the cracks. We tried to engage the spirits to help, but—" she flicked her gaze toward Thistle, and he nodded, "But the spirits can no longer help. Their magic is fading. Whether it's from the lanterns or the cracks, we don't know. That's why we need you. We need to find the Camellian Dragon."

The wrinkles in Lady Madora's forehead deepened. "What ever for?" she asked, genuinely curious.

"Several of the spirits told us to seek him," Kira said. "And, well, since he formed the realm, we thought he might be the best being to help us fix it. If we can find him."

"And just what is it you're willing to bargain with in order to find this information?"

Kira opened her mouth, but Jovan said, "Me. My most hated memory, my most shameful, whatever you like. I will show you." He shot a quick glance at Kira, who stood frozen in place. Secrets and bad memories, that's what Madora traded in.

Madora considered it for a moment, then said, "No. That is not enough. And besides, how do you propose I look for him? What thread could I possibly follow that far back? It's not as if you have a vial of the Empress' blood, with her heritage going all the way back."

"I will tell you how to do heart magic," Kira said, clasping her hands behind her back, her heart racing at the front of her chest. She spoke carefully, enunciating every word. "I have learned from the Ka'Mir, a way to do magic without Light or Shadow—and that's not even the best part."

"Interesting," Madora said after only a moment's hesitation. "I accept. But that still doesn't solve the problem of a thread to follow. I can't just peer into time, child."

"Use mine," Jovan said, and Kira had to hand it to him, though he still looked gaunt and tired, he was still trying to help the situation—magic or no. "My family has a clear line centuries back, perhaps even farther."

Fingers tapping the armrest of her throne-like chair, Madora said, "We can try."

CHAPTER 30

ALL THE WAY BACK

"Now tell me, what is the best part of this magic?" Madora inquired several minutes later as they waited for a guard to bring Madora's supplies for the seeing session.

It was just Kira, Madora, Jun, and Jovan at the front of the room, with Thistle perched on Kira's shoulder. Nesma, Ryn, Tokusei, Senga and the other Gray Knights lingered at the back of the room doing their best to stay out of the way, but their curiosity was obvious.

"The best part," said Kira, "Is that *anyone* can do heart magic." She said it while looking at Sir Jovan, and she got to see his darkened eyes light up at this news.

Jun's face changed drastically too. "Really?" He glanced between Kira and his father.

Kira nodded. "Really. They showed me how to use it—and that's what we used to heal Nesma when she touched the tear."

"She—" Jun cut himself off, evidently not wanting to launch into a whole conversation about that in front of Lady Madora. Kira gave him a look trying to say, *I'll tell you about it later.*

"That is valuable indeed," Madora said, and turned to Jun's father abruptly. "Jovan, I don't need your payment. Only your contribution so that I might find a connection to follow back."

She must have heard the guard coming, for she reached up her hand, and the guard dropped a bodkin into it, mostly made of some kind of bone. One end was wickedly sharp. With a shudder, Kira remembered using the same bodkin to prick her own thumb years ago when she found out who her father was. Madora now handed it to Jovan, who took it without hesitation and jabbed it into the flesh of his thumb.

The simple bowl the guard had placed on the table was a mirror of water, the surface of which quickly became stained red. Kira watched in fascination as Madora took Jovan's other hand, and the two of them began to gaze into the past.

Of course, only Madora and Jovan could see anything different. Kira and Jun sat in silence, watching the two of them sitting there as if in deep meditation. Kira nodded to a corner of the room, and Jun followed her there.

They found a stone bench tucked in an alcove under some bookshelves. Thistle swooped away, back toward Madora, evidently to watch. He settled himself on a small table beside a pot of ink.

"This will probably take a while," Kira whispered to Jun. "I just hope someone in your family line knew something, or saw something about what happened to the dragon."

He nodded, still gazing at his father. "Was that true?" he said quietly. "What you said about the magic?"

She grabbed his hand and squeezed it. "Yes. I did it. I used their magic, and I could tell it didn't touch Light or Shadow, or my soul, even. I never knew the Ka'Mir hated our magic so much—oh, and everyone had it wrong all this time, it's not even called Ga'Mir—"

They spent the next twenty minutes catching up on what had happened to Kira and the others after they had parted ways.

"Well after all this is over, you'll have to show us how to use that kind of magic, or do you think—"

"Senga volunteered to come with us; I'm sure she'd do it. Well, I think Hilda wanted one of her people involved—the cracks and the spirit magic fading affect them, too."

"Yeah," Jun said, rubbing his chin. "That worries me. A lot. Without spirit magic, even worse things are going to happen. Some of the crops rely on the blessings from the spirits. And what about Kamellia? What will happen if she can't lead departed souls on?"

"I hadn't thought about that," Kira said in a haunted whisper. "Have you noticed... Shouldn't spring be here by now?"

Jun's eyes bulged. "I mean... Let's just hope that's not because of the tears..."

After a few minutes of stewing over this latest mystery, Jun asked, "What's wrong with Nesma, do you think? She didn't even come over and say hello to me."

Kira shook her head a little, then explained what happened and her theory.

"She's terrified about her sisters. But she seemed almost mad at *me*. Because I told her it was irresponsible to go after that tear. We don't even know if it worked, or if the space between worlds is really what gives that protection."

"Ah, I see," he said.

Ryn loped over and leaned against the corner of the alcove. "How long do you think this is going to take? I'm starving."

Kira shrugged, though her stomach felt as if it were gnawing itself apart with hunger.

"We can get some of the guards to bring something," Jun said, and before Kira could say anything, Jun motioned one over. The man had grizzled brown hair and a matching beard, and he wore the usual sandy-colored cloaks of Madora's guard. He was armed with a short, curved sword, and only responded with a nod and an unintelligible mutter when Jun made a request for food.

"That's almost friendly of him," Jun said when the man departed, his sandy cape swishing around the doorframe with a whisper. "That's Rolian. I've gotten to know most of the guards inside the fortress, but I still haven't gotten a clear picture of how many patrol the mountains outside."

Kira made a thoughtful sound, impressed at Jun's ability to survey Madora's holdings. In no time, a pair of kitchen hands came with trays of sweetbread stuffed with nuts, and pitchers of fruit juice. It was heavenly. As they ate, Kira asked Jun, "So what else have you been up to since you got here?"

He glanced at Jovan, then back at Kira. "Mostly spending time with my father and the other Gray Knights. I haven't liked to leave them alone. But Madora's people have been helping get them back to physical health, at least. The rest of the time I've been trying to come up with a strategy to take down Tigran."

A thrill ran through Kira. "Good, because I don't really know if this whole dragon thing is going to work out. Even if it was my idea first. "

"I guess we'll see. I thought if we lure the Commonality into—"

"Jun."

They turned to see Madora and Jovan both standing, a dark stain spreading on the floor.

The bowl had spilled, the bloody water dripping from the table.

It was Jovan who spoke. He beckoned his son forth, and Jun hastily wiped his sticky fingers on his trousers and came over, Kira at his heels.

"Did you find the dragon?" Jun asked, a note of confusion in his voice.

Madora shook her head. Kira's heart sank to the bottom of her feet.

"But we went all the way back. Back to the young man who helped the dragon," Jovan said, dazed.

"And?" Jun said. Kira felt a strange, excited turmoil in her stomach.

"Well," Jovan said shakily. "Our family line went all the way back. *All* the way back to the young man who came here first."

CHAPTER 31

LINEAGE

"So *you're* the descendants?" Kira asked.

The entire room had gone silent; only the tinkling of a small fountain outside the room could be heard.

"But—" Jun started, "I don't—Isn't the imperial family the direct descendants? Isn't that..." He stopped, his mouth opening and closing without making any sound.

Jovan sunk back into his chair, disregarding the liquid still dripping from the table.

"Well this is..." Jun said, "I don't—It's not the dragon, but it's something, right?" He turned to Kira, hope kindling in his eyes mixed with the excited confusion of the revelation. "We could go to the palace, and demand that Tigran step down, if we're really—"

"But how will we prove it?" Kira said. "Only Lady Madora and the other person," she gestured at Jovan, "can see the vision; do you think they would really believe us?"

"Well, what proof do you think the Empress has about her lineage?" he quipped.

"Jun, I know you want to—"

"And there's the fact that we learned this using illegal magic," Ryn added. "How are we supposed to explain that?"

Jun deflated visibly, hanging his head. "I just thought..."

Kira came over and put a hand on his shoulder. "I know. But did you learn anything about the dragon?" She didn't know what to think about the revelation of Jun's heritage—they would have to unpack that later.

Madora pursed her lips, but she let Jovan speak. "Nothing. Though we were able to see part of the world outside of the portal before Joyato came through—that's his name, Joyato—the men at the riverbank called out for him. We didn't see the dragon. He must have disappeared after the portal formed. Joyato looked for him for a long time after arriving here."

Every erg of emotion melted from Kira as quickly as if burned away. Nothing. They had found nothing.

Well, not nothing. They now knew the Kosumosos were really descendants of Joyato, and, Kira supposed, had the realm claim to the imperial throne. She glanced at Jun, wonder in her eyes, but she couldn't read Jun's expression.

"We still have no proof," she muttered, and Ryn brushed her arm in reassurance.

"We'll figure something out," he said.

She closed her eyes for a second, searching her brain for any indication of what she should do next. It was clear they didn't have much time, what with the cracks getting worse, the spirit magic fading, and even the late spring, which even Lady Madora had commented on in passing.

What am I supposed to do?

Just as she thought about going somewhere to be alone—maybe the wisp would come find her and give her another clue—she glanced over to look for Thistle, who she had last seen on a table beside an inkwell. He was still there, but had curled up in a little ball, his eyes closed.

"Thistle!" she yelped, lurching over to him.

He stretched a little and muttered something, but didn't wake up.

"Thistle?" She reached out and picked him up, sure he wouldn't mind. Panicked, she looked around at the others, who were all staring at her.

Something about the warm, furry helpless creature in her hands radiated purpose through her very bones. It wasn't normal for him to just fall asleep in the middle of the day, in the midst of a world-changing revelation. This was something bad.

They needed to fix this. Now.

"You know what?" she said, focusing on Thistle curled in her hands to keep from shaking. "We don't need any proof. I say we go to Meridian. The magic's failing—there's too much contained. And, well... I think we're going to have to release it."

Something woke her late that night, but it might have just been Nesma turning over in her sleep. That was all Kira could tell had happened, anyway. They were sharing a room with Senga and Tokusei. Though Lady Madora had offered them separate quarters, Kira didn't feel comfortable being split up. She closed her eyes again and turned onto her other side. *It took long enough to fall asleep the first time*, she thought bitterly, punching her small pillow into shape. Thoughts of riding to Meridian tomorrow kept creeping up on her, and the checklists of everything they needed to do.

She had been up late with Lady Madora, teaching her heart magic. Senga had come too, and Kira had fulfilled her payment to Madora, and then some. She even explained how they had woken Nesma from the coma the tear had put her in. "You should know," Kira said. "In case one of your people gets hurt."

Madora had been able to access the barest hint of the magic, and then she had Kira instruct one of her guards on how to do it too.

The man had no Light or Shadow magic. After he had leaped from his chair, staring in wonder at his own hands at the feeling of heart magic, Lady Madora had offered a rare smile, and Kira grinned back. So it really could work for everyone.

Though Kira had longed to stay up catching up with Jun, she crawled into bed instead, hoping they would have more time to talk later. *When* that would be, she had no idea, if they really were going to attack Meridian tomorrow.

In the windowless stone room, an unpleasant jolt ran through her stomach, and she turned back onto her other side again, restless. Just as she was finally able to calm her thoughts, and began to drift off again, an enormous boom shook the whole room.

She lurched upright, wrenching the blankets off and jamming her feet into her shoes. She was standing before she even knew what happened. Dust rained down from the ceiling, and she ran to the door. Behind her she heard the others rousing too, and Tokusei joined her at the door, one of Ryn's swords in her hand.

Kira poked her head into the hallway, and saw one of Madora's guards running, shouting something to another guard further down the hallway.

She grabbed her bag, scooped up a sleeping Thistle from her blankets, and followed.

She quickly found the source of the crash.

People began to converge upon the fortress' main foyer. There were plants and dirt strewn about, and water leaking across the floor.

An enormous bright crack ran through one corner of the room and into the ceiling. The stone had broken apart, causing half the walls nearby to shift, and from the shouted orders Kira heard, the upper floors were in danger of collapse too. The guards pushed everyone out of the foyer, and tried to shepherd them away.

"Ryn! Jun!" Kira called as soon as she saw them. They were splotchy with the stone dust that was floating everywhere, but seemed fine.

"You all right?" Jun asked her. "Our room was one of the ones—"

"You were upstairs?" she demanded.

He nodded. "I should go find my father, him and most of his men had lower-level rooms, but..."

"Go ahead. Be quick," she said, and a sudden jolt ran through her as she glanced up at the tear. "I want to leave for Meridian—now, I mean."

"Right," he said, and skipped off. She had noticed a change in him since Lady Madora's reading, but it could just be excitement that they were finally taking action.

"Let's get the others," Kira told Ryn. "Are you ready?"

"Of course," he said, brushing dirt off his shoulders. "Though maybe we can get Tokusei her own sword. She keeps stealing mine."

Kira snorted and went in search of the armory.

***

Whether it was because Lady Madora finally understood the true gravity of the situation and that even her secluded region was at risk, or whether Kira teaching her how to do heart magic was more of a payment than she had estimated, they were outfitted with as much armor and weapons as they could carry.

The guard Rolian met them there, already outfitted and ready to go. "Lady Madora wishes me to accompany you," was all he said. Kira nodded, and Jun gave the guard some kind of salute that made Rolian crack a reluctant smile.

Kira quickly found enough armor that fit her, glad for something protective, though she missed her Light armor she could shed at will. *It's better this way*, she thought. *We won't technically be breaking the no magic decree until we have to, and we won't be in danger of having any magic taken from us.*

Two Gray Knights remained behind, Dorado and Sasha, perhaps because of Dorado's broken ankle, but perhaps because their eyes were so heavy with terror they barely lifted them to say goodbye to the others. Kira thought she understood. They had been imprisoned in Meridian for a whole year under the Commonality. Going back now was either grave stupidity or immense bravery.

Maybe it was a little bit of both.

When they were leaving the armory, a short woman with stocky muscles stepped in front of Kira. "I'm going with you," Aita said.

"Oh!" Kira said, taking in the former commander. "Aita, of course." Aita looked well, and she had a surprisingly earthy scent to her, though Kira supposed that just happened when you lived in a fortress of stone. But the dirt under the woman's fingernails and the scent of flowers when she turned made Kira wonder who was behind the skilled gardening in the foyer.

"Did you see the tear?" Kira asked her as they all but marched along the corridor, Jun leading them to the rear exit now that the main doors were blocked. Kira was trying not to think of the size of the rip that had torn up the foyer.

"I did," Aita said woodenly. "And I've seen a few more. I go on patrols with the guard. It's getting out of hand."

Kira nodded. "That's an understatement." She reached down to gently pat Thistle, who was nestled in her bag. He still hadn't woken up, but he muttered in his sleep occasionally. Was he running out of magic to live? What would happen when there was no spirit magic left anywhere? She did her best not to think about it.

Without taking formal leave of Madora—Kira thought the urgency was obvious—they quickly found their horses in the stables and were mounted and on their way out of the Stone Mountains in no time.

Kira took advantage of Madora's hospitality even further, and sent one of her guards with a message straight to Gekkō-ji to alert Ichiro. He could send reinforcements if possible, and if not, at least he would know what Kira had gotten herself into.

When they crossed into the Shadow region, and skirted close to Heliodor, a sudden idea struck Kira.

She slowed her horse, and cocked her head at Jun and Nesma, who were closest. They slowed too, and pulled up beside her. "What is it?" Jun asked.

"We're going to need all the help we can get," Kira said. "Finding and releasing the magic. I want to see if we can get Zowan, or Raiden, or anyone to come with us."

Ryn came up behind her and chuckled.

"You want to just stroll past the soldiers and ask them?" Jun asked.

A slow grin appeared on Kira's face. "No, I'm just going to call them."

He wrinkled his face in confusion, but Kira was already threading a slip of Shadow magic through her consciousness and reaching out to listen. It was early, but there was a distinct chance Raiden would be in his study.

The only real problem was she hadn't done this at such a distance yet.

She drew in a deep breath, focusing on the small ball of Shadow at her core. When she let the breath out, she envisioned traveling from where she sat on her horse, down the valley, through the city of Heliodor, and into the temple to find Raiden's study. She did it over and over, listening. She traced the path down the corridors, reaching out, eager for the slightest sound, when finally she heard a door slam. She cringed, but didn't pull back her hearing.

"—Don't know what we're supposed to do, Uncle."

"Zowan," Kira gasped. Her heart wrenched at the sound of his voice, making her think of the smell of moss and clean leather. Without wasting time, she focused even harder on *where* she heard his voice, and brought the magic to her lips.

"Zowan," she said again, but this time—hopefully—the sound would cross much further.

She waited, still vaguely aware of her own body, but picturing the scene inside Raiden's study.

"Zowan?" she called again, projecting.

Silence. Then, "Starless Girl?" his voice asked. "Why in the name of Kamellia do I hear your voice right now?"

"She *can't be here*," Raiden said, causing Kira to smile.

"I learned something new," she said, and could have sworn she heard Raiden bark out an incredulous laugh.

"But listen," Kira said, "we're outside Heliodor right now, on our way—"

"Don't you dare enter the city, Kira," Zowan said.

"We weren't planning on it," she said, "I actually—"

"Get as far from here as you can, then. The Commonality is here—a massive force. And so is Tigran. They've got the Spire surrounded."

CHAPTER 32

STRONGER WILL

K ira wrenched her eyes open and stared around, first finding Jun. "They're there; the Commonality and Tigran. At the Spire."

She could almost see the fire light in Jun's eyes at her words.

"Then we're going in, right?" he said.

She bit her lip. "But if they stockpiled the magic in Meridian, then it might not be heavily guarded..." She bobbed up and down on her feet a few times, thinking.

Zowan and Raiden were besieged. All the acolytes and mages trapped, without their magic. Yuki, Spectra... And Micah.

"The fight is here," she said. "Zowan said they had the Spire surrounded. If they're trying to arrest everyone or something it's going to turn into an all-out battle."

Nesma nodded. "And the army should have their wagons with them, right? We can release that magic."

"Right," Kira agreed. "Maybe we can get in through the catacombs."

Ryn shook his head. "Actually, it doesn't have to be that hard."

It was surprisingly easy getting into the city through the gate. Ryn could tell from a distance that the gatehouse had been abandoned. That alone sent a chill down Kira's spine. This was all wrong.

"They must have all the soldiers up at the Spire," Kira said quietly as they passed through the empty gate.

Not only was the gatehouse deserted, but so were the streets. Tokusei whistled low. "What happened here?" she asked. Normally at this hour, the streets would be filled with merchants and their customers, trading coins for breakfasts and wares. But they encountered no one.

Kira focused on keeping her head up, and not throwing up out of nerves.

Tigran was up there, with what might be all his soldiers. "What do you think they're doing here?" she asked Jun and Nesma, closest to her. "Do you think I should try and talk to Zowan again?"

"Maybe they've finally stopped pretending this is all for people's safety and came to round up all the mages," Jun said. "But I don't know, you could—"

A crack like lightning shot through the air, and they all dropped to a crouch; Kira flung a hand over her head, but whatever it was, hadn't happened too close.

"Was that the Storm King?" Aita said.

"No, look," Rolian said, pointing around the corner of the next street.

A crack had torn through a building, the roof of which had toppled half into the street.

Kira reached into her bag to pat Thistle's fur and reassure herself that he was still breathing. Doubt that they should be in Meridian muddled her thoughts. Should they have gone there to find Tigran's stockpile?

"Let's hurry," she said. "I don't think we're going to get a better chance at Tigran—and we can only hope he's got at least some of the trapped magic with the army. Releasing something ought to help with this." She gestured at the crack and the desolation all around them. "But if we can defeat him here, then we can do whatever we need to in Meridian."

No one argued. Her words almost reassured herself that she was doing the right thing. Almost.

They pressed on, eyes and ears alert. Kira counted mentally in her head: *Me, Jun, Ryn, Nesma, Tokusei, Rolian, Aita, and Senga—though I'm not sure how much of a fighter she is, but she was pretty good to capture us—and then there's*

401

Jovan and the other two Gray Knights, except they don't have their magic...

Well, none of us will.

Their forces against an army. An army that had sucked up all the magic in the city.

As they approached, Kira could feel an odd staticky feeling in the air. There was no more Light or Shadow essence left. None.

They were one street over from the temple entrance when they heard another crack. It was so close Kira felt as if it had jolted up her own spine. They paused for a second, then advanced up to the bridge.

Shouts from inside the temple grounds made Kira freeze for a moment. She motioned to Ryn to go forward and look for aura signatures nearby. He nodded and swept ahead, both swords drawn and held back so he could run. He stopped at the corner of the wall and looked inside, gaze intent, then gave Kira a *go ahead* gesture.

She held up a hand to the others to wait, spotting the two lanterns on either side of the bridge.

"I've been wanting to do this for a long time," she said, and stepped up beside one. It was stone, like the others, with a glass orb inside. In the orb, though it was invisible in the daylight, must be the trapped Light and Shadow magic. She could feel it when she reached out to it with her thoughts.

The polearm she had taken from Madora's armory was long and sharp, the blade sturdy. She jammed it inside the lantern, aiming for the glass' center, but the glass that held the magic captive didn't break. "Come on!" she shouted, jamming the blade in again, and again, and again. It glanced off, scraping against the side, but not shattering it. She knew she shouldn't be surprised.

She let out something that was a mix between a sigh and a scream. Someone caught her arm. It was Jun. "Maybe let's just go—"

"Hold on," she said, panting. "If we go in and can't even free the magic he has, then what's the point?" *I wish Zowan were here*, she thought suddenly. *What would he do?*

She searched her brain, and the memories from her last year training with him flooded her. The quests they had gone on, the meditations on magic. But it was one of her very first lessons with him that gave her an idea.

She thrust her hand into the lantern, grasping the glass and quickly reaching her consciousness out to touch the magic inside, just like the many times in her training she had tried to break another's will. To break a sword, a weapon, you just needed to have a stronger will than the person who had created it.

Well, this is just glass, and my will is stronger, she thought, giving it a burst of strength as she pictured Tigran's face bursting like broken glass beneath her hand.

Suddenly her hand was wrapped like a claw around empty air, and the tinkling of glass told her she had done it. She let out a yip of excitement just as the wind picked up. Looking up at the Spire towering over them, she spotted storm clouds and wondered whether this was Raiden's doing, but it seemed unlikely unless he had massive amounts of magic stored up.

As quickly as she could, she explained to the others who had magic what she had done. "Any lantern you see!" she shouted over the worsening wind. "Any little bit should help! Let's move!"

They slowed when they reached the crest of the lawn that revealed the castle. Kira, Ryn, and Jun dropped to the ground and crept up to the lip of the rise. Kira gasped.

What looked like all the trainees were assembled—it was morning, meditation time, how could she have forgotten!—under the meditation pavilion, surrounded by soldiers. More soldiers were stationed at the main entrance of the castle—the single narrow corridor through the enormous stone foundation—and behind the pavilion beside the lake.

"Maybe we should have gone through the catacombs," Kira said under her breath.

"Look!" Jun said. "The wagons by the lake. That must be where they've got the magic they've been collecting!"

"But even if we go around by the stables," Kira said, "they'll see us, unless we can come up with a distraction."

The wind buffeted the lake, and blew through the pavilion. Kira could see the wooden structure around the original tear they had found, but from their vantage point, she could see another two: one in the small woods by the stream where they practiced elemental magic, and another near the stables. She gripped the grass in front of her face, trying to ignore the fact that it still looked somewhat gray, still not having come back to life after winter. *This isn't right.*

"They're rounding up the mages," Ryn said. The soldiers were beginning to shove the acolytes into a tight group under the pavilion, and another set of soldiers was coming through and touching their wrists.

"Wait, is that—" Jun said.

"The manacles," Jovan said, coming up from behind them, also on his stomach. "They are going to imprison all the mages, then?"

Kira's throat constricted, cutting off her breathing. "No, no. We have to get in there—do something, they've probably got Zowan too, and Raiden—"

A gust of wind blew through the pavilion, knocking one of the younger trainees to the side, who bumped into a soldier.

The soldier pushed back—*no, that's not just any soldier, that's Commander Hagane*. Fear tightened her lungs as she watched Hagane pull his arm back and strike the young boy with the full force of a backhanded slap. The boy nearly fell to the ground, but caught himself at the last second.

All chaos broke loose. Master Korinna who taught meditation was the first to intervene. She struck her wrist up, palm open, straight into Hagane's nose, throwing his head back. As he reeled, blood spurting from his nose, she twisted and kicked him in the gut. He bent in two, clutching his torso, while she grabbed his hair and brought a knee to his face.

Meanwhile, the rest of the soldiers had begun their retaliation, but the trainees were not as defenseless without magic as the Commonality expected. Kira watched with her mouth hanging open as Yuki engaged in hand-to-hand combat with one of the soldiers, able to read his intentions before he did anything. Before the soldier took out a decanter of Light and threw the contents at her, she darted away, narrowly avoiding the Light shards that formed.

"Well, this is distraction enough," Kira said weakly.

"Hurry," Jun said, waving the others around. "We're going around by the stables."

Wishing they had enough magic to illusion themselves, Kira sprinted for the stables, the others following swiftly behind. Cradling her bag in front of her to keep Thistle safe, she hoped to all the spirits in the realm that the soldiers wouldn't spot them. And where was Tigran?

Don't worry about him right now, she told herself. *Let's just get to the wagons and release the magic—stop the realm from breaking apart.*

By the time they reached the stables, panting, the fight at the meditation pavilion had moved to the courtyard by the lake where the wagons stood.

Kira cursed and turned to Jun.

"Looks like we're going to have to join the fight," he said, grinning.

The two of them started for the courtyard, Kira gripping her polearm so hard she dug her fingernails into her palms.

A deafening crack rent the air.

"Kira look out!"

Someone dove at her, yanking her to the side, and suddenly she was on the ground in a tangle of limbs. She looked around wildly, wrenched some hair out of her face, and spotted Nesma, who had pushed her aside from a falling piece of timber.

She stared at the timber for a second, then slowly looked up.

At the Spire.

Her chest swelled painfully at what she saw. An enormous crack, through the very tower itself.

She looked back down around her—the top floor of the Spire had sheared straight off, and was coming crashing down on the courtyard in front of them.

She watched as the top fell as if in slow motion. She had stood up there countless times, where she had even once flown off it with Raiden. Then suddenly it met the ground, breaking into matchsticks at the force, shaking the stones beneath their feet.

"Jun?" she shouted, her heart hammering.

"Here," he said, picking up his katana from where he had dropped it.

"Change of plans," Kira said. "I'm going inside to find Tigran—he's bound to be with Raiden, and Raiden might need all the help he can get. You go to the wagons with everyone else—"

"I'm coming with you," Nesma said.

"No—"

"*No*, I'm coming."

"Fine! Let's just go! Jun—handle the wagons, will you? Get that magic out!"

He was leading the assault before she had even turned away, with Rolian right beside him, followed by Ryn and all the others.

Kira bolted through the door to the stables, Nesma following fast behind. Wishing she could banish the polearm so she didn't have to run with it, Kira rounded the corner leading into the castle and skidded to a halt, checking first.

"Want to give it a try?" she asked Nesma, pointing at the lantern positioned there.

Nesma's face was almost unrecognizable; there was a deep hatred there, and her eyes looked more closed off than ever. But she nodded and reached inside the lantern while Kira peered around the corner.

It was clear. In her head, she plotted out the quickest route to Raiden's study, thinking that might be a good place to start, when she heard the soft clink of broken glass.

"I did it!" Nesma cried, a little joy breaking through the emotionless mask.

When Kira smiled, her own face muscles felt good. "A little more magic back in the realm," Kira said. "Good job. All right, let's go!"

She tried to ignore the bangs from outside, the shouts, the clash of metal. She hoped any second now the wind outside would die down—would she know when the magic was released back into the world?

A tiny, terrible thought came to her as they approached the Jade Foyer. What if it didn't work? What if the cracks kept coming?

But as they stumbled to a halt in the Foyer, all thoughts were driven from her head as the whipping wind drew her attention upward.

She had already forgotten about the Spire.

The break was high up, but Kira could see the bare sky above, a pinprick of roiling clouds, instead of the comforting wooden tower that normally looked down on her. And the tip of the tear that had caused it shone like a frozen bolt of lightning coming from one side.

The sight of the crack made her knees tremble, and she grabbed Nesma's arm. Nesma met her eyes and clutched Kira with both hands, leading her over to the side of the foyer, underneath the galley and out of the wind.

"What's wrong?" Nesma said. "What is it?"

"I—what if we can't do it?" Kira said, looking up to where she knew the tear to be. "The realm's falling apart." She put a hand in her bag, feeling the comforting softness of Thistle's fur. "And I think the spirits are dying."

Nesma's grip on Kira's arms tightened.

Suddenly, Kira's eyes filled with tears. She focused all of her energy on not letting them spill over, holding her breath and staring at a spot on Nesma's leather armguards. What she wouldn't give for everything to be all right, and to go rest in her quarters in the Gray Wing right now...

"We didn't find the Camellian Dragon, and—and I don't know if I can defeat Tigran," she said, the words hurting as she forced them out.

"Kira," Nesma said, "You're not doing this alone. I'm right here with you. And Jun will get to the wagons."

"But I don't know if that will even work," she said, finally reaching up to brush the tears away before they spilled over.

Suddenly Nesma's arms were around her, and Kira dropped her face onto her shoulder, tension easing in the back of her neck.

"Let's find the Storm King, like you said, and if he's with Tigran, so be it."

Kira drew away, seeing the knowledge in Nesma's eyes that her sisters were likely with Tigran, and that she was ready to face them.

"Are you sure?"

"Why do you think I came with you? I'm sure. Even if touching the space between did nothing. I have to face them."

"Well, squire, I'm glad I'm not alone," Kira said, and turned toward the stairs leading up. Then something bright white out of the corner of her eye made her turn, and she repeated, "*Alone...* The wisp! Nesma, this way!"

Turning away from the stairs, Kira bolted after the bright light, which had winked away toward the Apothecarium. "The wisp knows something!" Kira said, her polearm scraping against the wall as she went. "She usually finds me alone, but if we can talk to her..."

Kira tried to wrench open the doors to the Apothecarium, but they were bolted shut. She banged on them with her fist, then rested her forehead on the smooth wood. "They must have secured the door." But then she lifted her head and looked to the left, where a door was slightly ajar. "The catacombs," she said, "she went this way!"

They didn't dare summon any fire, not wanting to risk yet another tear. Kira didn't want to know how many countless cracks now spread across the realm. How many was too many? How many before the realm was crushed, consumed, broken into pieces and spiraling into the space between?

It was almost worse than running through the battle outside, creeping through the darkness, running their hands along the walls, the walls in which numbers and names were carved, then finding the next set of stairs down.

"Too bad it's not night," Kira whispered on the fourth floor down. "Then we'd have Light to see by."

"Maybe not," Nesma said darkly.

"You're right."

She wasn't at all surprised to find the wisp on the fifth floor down, hovering beside the tear in the center of the room.

CHAPTER 33

THE SKY

Kira didn't dare breathe as they hurried forward, finally able to see by the sickening blue glow from the tear, worried the wisp would run away, disappear, leaving them with nothing.

"Please," Kira said when they got closer, bowing as deep as she could. "Help us. What can we do to stop the realm from breaking? Do you know where to find the Camellian Dragon? Will he help us?"

The wisp looked up, as if gazing at the Spire above them, her soft face somewhat visible with her hood away from her face.

"Up there?" Kira said, "What's up there? The Spire's broken, there's a massive tear—"

The wisp brought up a hand, pointing up. Then she looked back down, and gestured as if cutting her own arm.

"It's a cut?" Kira said.

The wisp nodded eagerly. Her mouth moved, as if she longed to form words. But Kira thought she could read some of what passed through her ghostly lips.

"Dragon?" she said, frustration seeping into her, "Where is he?"

The wisp pointed at the sky.

Kira let out a heavy sigh and glanced at Nesma, who looked just as confused. "Flying in the sky?" Nesma suggested.

The wisp shook her head, and looked at the tear again. She pressed her lips together, then went up close to it. She reached out a hand, and a scream met their ears as the wisp touched the tear.

The spirit's face contorted as if in great pain, but they could hear her. "Ahhh!" She grit her teeth. "The sky!" the wisp gasped in a ragged voice. "He *is* the sky! He's wrapped all around Camellia, he's what keeps the realm together, he's the stars—and he's *hurt!*"

"The sky?" Kira and Nesma gasped, and in Kira's mind, she pictured the sky—a blanket of diamonds. So many stars that the other realm was considered starless in comparison.

The dragon. Made of starlight.

"But—" Kira started.

"You have to call to him!" the wisp ground out. "Kira, I know you can do it! You have your father's strength!"

Kira fell to her knees at the sound of her name.

From her mother's lips.

She didn't even feel the pain of the stone hitting her kneecaps and reverberating through her body, or feel the polearm as it slipped from her fingers. Her mother?

She didn't feel the pain in the next moment, either, when someone hit her in the back of the head with her own polearm.

"Nesma?" she mumbled, coming to a moment later, wondering why Nesma of all people would hit her in the back of the head. And then she wrenched into consciousness.

The wisp was gone, but the tear shone just as terribly electric blue. A cut, on the Dragon himself.

The dragon that was wrapped around the realm. It was no wonder no one had seen him since the realm had formed.

The other revelation she had made would have to wait. She wasn't even sure she had heard correctly. Because it was impossible.

She looked around for Nesma and quickly spotted her, but she was bound with rope and standing beside one of the last people Kira expected: Kusari, the Spirekeeper.

"Come with me," Kusari said, gesturing with Kira's polearm.

Kira's eyebrows drew down, and she nodded in confusion, going ahead of Kusari and getting close to Nesma. Her first wild thought—that Nesma had hit her, and been controlled by Nia Mari or Nikoletta—now seemed more feasible than the Spirekeeper attacking her.

Unless of course Nesma's sisters had gotten to her first.

Kusari poked Kira in the back with the butt of the polearm to push her out of the stairwell and into less stale air. Kira was relieved to be aboveground at least. She knew where Kusari would lead her, and was therefore unsurprised to see Tigran standing in the center of the Jade Foyer when they got there, surrounded by rows of soldiers.

His uncustomary short hair was combed back, and he had dispensed with his normal gem-encrusted coat in favor of plain black robes befitting a mage. Unlike the soldiers that surrounded the foyer, he didn't have any decanters at his belt.

"So you're admitting it then?" Kira said, her nerves making her speak, "That you're a Shadow mage."

He bristled. "Of course not," he said. "I never completed my training due to some overzealous mages who were threatened by my power."

417

Kira glanced suspiciously at the soldiers, who showed no reaction to this news. "I see. So I guess the Empress and everyone know who you really are now? They didn't find it suspicious that you'd hidden it all these years?"

Tigran smiled, opening his arms wide. "Her Majesty has always been grateful for my counsel, and when I revealed a past for which I was persecuted, my actions discriminated against, she pardoned me for any misleading I might have done. She is, in her words, indebted to me for discovering the treason of Mistress Nari, who had been poisoning her with magic all these years."

"That was you!" Kira yelled, and Kusari poked her in the back, with the sharp end of the polearm this time. Kira inched forward, her back stinging, but didn't want to get any closer to Tigran. She still hadn't spotted Nesma's sisters, but there were shadows on the galleys above...

"You made the Empress sick," Kira jeered, "whenever it was convenient for you to take her out, just like you caused the mysterious sickness here at the Spire all those years ago after the Fall of Azurite, weakening the Spire!"

Someone burst through the soldiers, though he didn't make it far, held down by a pair of arms on either side. "You!" Zowan shouted, his teeth bared. "It was you!"

Kira spotted Raiden a few feet behind him, looking about twenty years older since she last saw him; his face crumpled as he looked at his nephew.

"Now that is a lie," Tigran said, turning to face Zowan and Raiden nonetheless. "How *ever* would I get into the Spire when I had been kicked out?" he said snarkily.

"You can shapeshift," Kira said, still hoping the soldiers would hear something they didn't like. "With your soul magic."

He barked out a laugh, the sound eaten up by the wind echoing through the Spire. "Ludicrous. Soul magic? I think someone would have noticed if I had used up my soul's magic," he said, turning back to Kira.

Her heart was racing, but she had gotten this far. And she didn't see Jun or the others anywhere—she could only hope to distract Tigran and these men while Jun released the magic.

"Well that's why you stooped to stealing other people's soul magic. Like you almost got mine. But you didn't, and I fixed it." She stuck out her chest, wishing she still had her polearm. She belatedly remembered her dagger tucked at her waist, not that it would do much against all of these soldiers, and with Kusari pointing a weapon at her back.

"Clever," he said, still not admitting to anything. He gestured to people behind her, and someone pushed her forward. One of the soldiers was holding Nesma's re-strained hands, and it seemed like Kusari was the one pushing Kira toward the center of the foyer.

A loud noise from outside rattled the windows, and Kira didn't know whether it was another tear, or something else. *Please be Jun freeing the magic*. The wind howled, and the darkened clouds above made Kira wonder whether there was a lightning storm coming too, or whether the realm was really truly falling apart.

"Why are you doing this?" she demanded, her heart thudding painfully. "You know the realm's breaking, right? You've killed all the magic, and the spirits are dying! Haven't you seen the plants? We're all going to die!"

This got a reaction out of the soldiers, who shifted a little, and traded a few glances and words, though the wind was so loud Kira couldn't hear anything, not even the water tinkling through the fountain beside Tigran, who was now three feet away from her.

She still shouted, for the benefit of the soldiers. "You're the one who made the tears by bottling up all the magic! Why are you killing the realm?"

"It is the mages who are breaking the realm!" he called. "They have broken the law and continued to practice magic wildly. Which is why we're here."

He reached out and grabbed her arm, drawing her closer. "Because it shouldn't exist," he said close to her ear, his breath hot on her neck. "Because the Starless Realm is the *real world*—and ours is just a parasite. We stole their magic. And we fall behind, clinging to the scraps we get from the mother realm. I'm just returning the magic to where it belongs."

Kira felt as if she'd been struck in the heart.

But at the word *mother*, she looked up at the sky. To the dragon.

I need to get closer.

She caught Zowan's eye, and realized that Anzu was standing beside him, bound with manacles. Her heart melted at the sight of them. At least they were both here, alive. Kira jerked her head, trying to tell Zowan she needed to get away.

After a year of constant training with him, he understood. He nodded and whispered something to Anzu.

Almost as one, they struck the soldiers on either side of them, Anzu whipping her manacles over the head of the soldier next to her and pulling tight.

Zowan rushed forward as Anzu backed up, the soldier she held suffocating. She dropped him in her path of retreat, unconscious. Tigran turned at the commotion and raised his arm.

A massive ball of lightning formed there, quicker than anything Kira had ever seen. Tigran pulled his arm back and threw the lightning, right at Zowan. The shock of Tigran finally doing magic in public didn't even register.

"No!" Kira shrieked, lurching forward.

Zowan darted to the side, but the lightning followed him like he was made of metal.

Suddenly the lightning arced backwards. Two hands purposefully reached up, the bound lightning streaking from each finger, and a man's blood-curdling scream scoured the air.

Raiden dropped to his knees, eyes empty, and fell forward, his mage's robes whipping around him in the last wind they would ever command.

CHAPTER 34

ALL THE MAGIC

Each painful heartbeat went on for an eternity as Kira stared down at the floor. *Raiden.*

No.

Her hand moved seemingly of its own accord and reached for the dagger at her belt, and next she was looking up into Tigran's face. The handsome face of the man who had deceived them all since the beginning. The man who *wanted* the realm to die. To bottle up the essence that made this realm exist and bring it to the Starless Realm.

The man who had taken everything from her. And now he had taken Raiden. She couldn't even process the idea. Raiden had always been an immovable force, the most powerful Shadow mage she had ever known.

It seemed like everything had slowed down, because Tigran turned his head just too slowly to see Zowan rip a sword out of a soldier's hand, and run it straight through him with a howl of rage. Tears fell from Zowan's eyes.

Tigran gripped Zowan's shoulder, hard, and Kira felt more than saw the magic shift in the air.

Instinctively she reached out and slashed Tigran's arm, the shock making him turn toward her, halting whatever insidious magic he had planned for Zowan. She couldn't lose Zowan too. Not now, not this way.

She shoved her hand in Tigran's face and blasted him with the last of her Light magic, blinding him momentarily.

He pushed away from her and Zowan, the sword grotesquely sticking out of him, his arm bleeding, and clutching his face with his other hand.

For a second, Kira thought they had defeated him, and relief shot through her that she didn't have to deliver the final blow. But then, blinking rapidly, Tigran wrenched the sword from his middle with both hands and tossed it aside with a clatter, staggering to remain standing. Zowan looked like he wanted to retrieve it, but edged to the side as Tigran's hands began to shimmer with magic.

The haze of magic surrounded him, and then Kira was looking at the man who she had once seen in Lady Madora's vision, what he really looked like, back when his name was Kage.

There were murmurs among the soldiers, loud enough that they could hear them over the wind, but they still stood their ground.

Kage ran a hand over his middle and Kira was terrified to see that it had healed. The cut on his arm was gone too.

In his original form, Kira noticed two fingers missing on one hand, which he had lost a long time ago when summoning the doors that brought her to the realm. So his healing capabilities must have improved recently. Perhaps with the addition of the Gray Knights' magic.

The idea made her stomach roil.

At that moment, there was a commotion from the Hall of Spirits, when two sets of people Kira had never expected rushed into the foyer: Hilda and her Ka'Mir warriors, and Lady Madora's guards, their sandy-colored cloaks flapping in the high wind.

The Commonality turned as one to meet their new challengers, and Kira lurched forward, dagger outstretched. It was now or never. Kage had to go down, then they could release what was left of the magic.

He moved like a much younger man—one who hadn't just been stabbed through the gut—as he held his palms out to her and deflected her swipe with just air. She didn't know whether he was using soul magic or Shadow magic, but Kira couldn't feel enough Shadow essence around them to actually use it herself. Whatever Kage had used for the lightning had been absorbed back into the soldiers' decanters and the remaining lanterns.

Kira fought from looking where she knew Raiden lay; she couldn't think about that right now. She swiped and stabbed, only to be tossed aside by Tigran's increasingly agitated bursts of magic. Zowan darted in to retrieve the bloodied sword, and joined in the fight, the two of them dancing what felt like a well-choreographed rhythm, after so much time spent training and fighting together.

All around them, the people from Ka'Mir and the Stone Mountains fought to keep the Commonality at bay. Kira spotted a bright white sash in the crowd, Anzu wielding an enormous sword at a group of soldiers who were fighting tooth and nail to get to Tigran to protect him.

Tigran was fast, and Kira suspected he was using soul magic when he darted from one place to another with such speed that he blurred. She wished she had some kind of secret weapon, or anything better than just a plain steel dagger.

"Even the people from the Stone Mountains and Ka'Mir want you taken down," Kira said as Tigran blasted her a few yards back. He didn't seem to want to kill her—not yet anyway—and was merely defending himself.

Was he stalling? Waiting for his men to do his dirty work, or waiting for the realm to rip itself apart?

"The...?"

"*Ga'Mir*," she said, "They think soul magic is abhorrent too. You know, like how you stole the magic right from the Gray Knights' souls," she shouted.

Zowan lunged forward, but Tigran knocked him to the ground, and he smacked his head on the stone floor. Dazed, he tried to get up quickly, but stumbled. Kira side-stepped to get closer to him, to get between him and Tigran.

Tigran's eyes twinkled with devious intent. "If only your father were still alive, I could have taken his, too; the magic of their souls is quite strong." For a second, he hovered off the ground, a devilish smile on his lips, then he pushed her to the ground with a blast of magic.

Her dagger clattered out of her hands, and it was swept into the tangle of feet that was the clash of Stone Mountain guards and the Commonality.

She sucked in a breath and held it, trying to calm her thunderous heartbeat. She scrambled to her feet, but Tigran was advancing on her. She had nothing left. No magic, no dagger. Zowan had gotten to his feet but was now fighting off two soldiers.

Nothing left.

But she did have something. Something they all had.

With a glance up at the sky, she took a quick breath in, and found the place between breaths, between heartbeats. With one hand on her heart, she slammed her other fist into Tigran's chest with as much force as she could manage.

He flew back, clutching his chest, eyes wide as he slammed into the floor.

Blinking, he shook his head, and as Kira tried to find the space between again, she watched as one of the Commonality soldiers stepped out of the scrum toward them.

The soldiers' sword came down upon Tigran's neck with swift finality.

Kira gaped at him, but just then, the room shifted. It shifted as electric blue light burst forth and the realm was torn, right through the side of the foyer where the stairs led up to the Spire.

The castle shook, small beams and bricks falling from high up in the tower. Screams rent the air as people dodged the falling debris, and Kira grabbed hold of the soldier who had killed Tigran for support as the shaking subsided. He was wide-eyed, younger than even she was. His mouth kept opening and closing, and he finally said, "I heard him. He took their magic. The Gray Knights—I thought he—I—they…"

She squeezed his arm, and said, "It's all right," even though it wasn't. She felt he deserved some sort of kindness in this moment.

Out of nowhere, an intense pain slammed onto her shoulder, and as she fell to the side she spotted another brick falling from above and managed to roll out of the way. But with her attention focused on the falling bricks, she almost didn't see the sword coming right for her face until—*wham!*—she got her arm up just in time, and the force of the blow hit her armor so hard her arm went numb. She kicked, managing to sweep her attacker's legs out from under him. Kira scrabbled away from her attacker, grabbing the hand of the soldier who had killed Tigran, who still stood there in a daze.

"Here, come with me, I need to find Zowan, and Nesma for that matter." She ran her hands along her numb arm, and her fingers came away sticky with blood. The sword had managed to slip into one of the cracks between pieces of armor; she couldn't tell how bad it was since she couldn't feel anything. And her shoulder hurt enough from the falling brick that something might be broken.

Oh, what I wouldn't give for healing magic right now.

As she wondered whether she might be able to use heart magic and teach herself how to heal in the middle of all of this, she dragged the dazed soldier with her, searching for her friends. He went with her easily. She dodged through the fighting, but saw no sign of Nesma or even Anzu. Finally, she spotted Zowan, fighting alongside Hilda.

"Hilda!" Kira cried. "What are you doing here?"

"You were taking too long. The tears weren't getting any better," the old woman said, slashing at a soldier with her broadsword. "I figured you needed some help. And the gates to the city were wide open as we passed Heliodor."

Kira snorted. Zowan pushed away his foe, who took the opportunity to draw back to safety among his fellows.

"I need to talk to the Camellian Dragon," she shouted in Zowan's ear, her mission now crystalizing into clarity. "Even if they released the magic in the wagons, it's probably not enough to keep the realm from ripping apart!"

"How in the world are you going to do that?" he asked. "And what happened to your arm?"

"It's fine." She looked up and pointed. "I need to get up there, but the stairs—" She looked over at the sinister tear that had ripped a chunk out of the wall and looked like a serious concern for the Spire's foundation. It was then that she noticed Nesma near the stairs, keeping people away from the tear with Yuki of all people by her side. The soldiers, guards, and Ka'Mir couldn't see it.

Now that she looked around, Kira saw the Commonality being overwhelmed with acolytes, though they still didn't have any magic to wield, and were doing their best to steal as many weapons as they could. Kira didn't see Jun, but if the trainees had gotten away from the soldiers outside, then the fight was probably over out there, right?

She shook her head, and looked back at Zowan. "I don't think we have time for the stairs, anyway," he said, and wrapped a strong arm under her shoulders, his sword still in his other hand. She hissed, some of the feeling now returning to her arm.

"Do you have enough magic for this?" Kira demanded.

He nodded. "Can't you feel it?"

She reached out and was shocked to find a somewhat normal feeling of magic around her. "Jun must have gotten to the wagons!" They lifted off the ground in a whirl of wind.

But as another crack sounded somewhere they couldn't see, the achievement didn't seem that important.

They pushed up through the Spire, the space around them growing narrower and narrower the higher they went. Kira didn't want to look up, but had to eventually.

The top level had been sheared off, and the corner of the tear protruded about halfway into the empty space. With a push of Shadow energy, Zowan deposited them onto one of the galleys opposite the tear. The wind howled above, and the clouds had turned a sickly green. Even though it was now probably approaching midday, a darkness had spread over everything. Kira shuddered and drew in a deep breath, pulling in as much Shadow magic as she could comfortably hold. It sailed through her synapses like putting on a comfortable pair of pants after being uncomfortable all day.

Though she didn't know where the dragon was, she reached out her thoughts and sent them up as high as she could.

"Help us, please!" she said in her magically distant voice, and sent her magic to hear for her, too.

"Are you sure about this, Kira?" Zowan said, still clutching her around the shoulders.

She nodded and continued speaking to the dragon—she hoped. "We're trying to return what they took—the magic! But what can we do to stop the tears?"

Still she heard nothing. Panic struck her as her gaze drifted down over the railing at all those fighting below, and the bottom dropped out of her stomach. What if she was wrong? Had the wisp led her astray? Another trickster spirit?

But how had the wisp still come to her, if all the spirits were losing their magic?

She thought she knew the answer to that, but she wasn't ready to admit it to herself yet. What she did know was that she trusted the wisp, with her life.

I need to go further, she thought, and pushed the boundary of her magic, higher, higher toward where she envisioned the stars.

"Hello?" she called. "Please!"

Maybe I don't have enough Shadow magic for this, she worried, so she looked into herself and tried to find the space between. Between breaths, she felt the flicker of magic, so strongly she wondered how she didn't realize she had this power before.

Harnessing the strength of the power she had found in her heart, she pushed her consciousness high above, toward the stars.

Suddenly the wind stopped roaring.

She opened her eyes, but everything was a sea of glittering blue. And though she could see the vast expanse of stars, she felt like she was in some kind of dream—floating away from her body which was no doubt down below in the Spire.

"Hello?" she said, though she wasn't certain she had a mouth with which to say it.

Did I do this? she wondered. *Did I project* myself *instead of just my voice? Was heart magic really that powerful?*

"There you are," a voice said, and though she didn't seem to have a body to turn, suddenly an immense sphere came into view.

It was black rimmed in white, and it blinked at her.

"I—you are—" she stuttered.

"I am," the voice said, and the blue background for the stars glimmered, and she realized it was blue scales. Glittering blue scales that made up the stars.

"I..." This was all too much. How would she even get back to her body?

"I'm trying to stop the tears—is there any way, can you heal them, or tell us what to do to stop the realm from ripping apart?"

The dragon heaved a cosmic sigh, the enormous eye in front of her blinking once. "I cannot," he said, the voice sending a strange feeling over her—though it was likely because she didn't have a body to *feel* anything. "But if you can restore the balance..."

"How?" she demanded. "I don't want the realm to collapse. Kage was wrong, this realm is wonderful, and not just because of the magic."

Though she couldn't see the dragon's mouth, she thought she felt him smile somehow. "I'm glad you think so, young one. But I am growing weak, I won't be able to hold it together much longer. I am the only barrier surrounding this realm. I thought I could do everything. It was foolish of me, but at the time, I thought..."

"Just tell me what to do!" Kira shouted into the glittering void.

"The essence needs to balance, to flow freely, otherwise the realm will continue to topple, breaking the foundation even more. Release it all—please—I can't—I'm already using everything I have to enclose the realm from the void. The essence, it needs..."

"But I don't know where it all is," she said, panicked, "And it might take time to get to it—"

Distant echoes of crashes and shouts reached her, and she couldn't tell whether she was actually hearing them with her ears, or whether from her projection she could somehow hear them down below.

Then there was the sound of a soft breeze, and Kira realized it was the dragon sighing again. The eye closed, a sapphire against diamonds.

"Are you... Are you still there?" she asked quietly.

He didn't answer. Had he gotten so injured that it was too late? Then the eye opened again, and he said, "I cannot... I cannot draw the magic from the realm and still protect it. You will have to gather it for me, all of it, Light and Shadow, every last erg."

"But how? A lot of it's still trapped—I think maybe Tigran was going to bring it to the Starless Realm, and was destroying this one on purpose... But he was wrong. There *is* magic there."

"That is good to hear, young one. But this world will not last much longer if we do not do something. Since creating this place for Joyato, I realized I couldn't create something out of nothing. So when I poured all the magic I could find into a pocket in the spaces between, I realized it needed protection, something to keep it from fading away into the ether. And I was happy to provide that protection for the ones who needed it. But I cannot collect the magic once more. My energy is nearly expended holding back the eternal space."

"What do I need to do?"

The enormous eye squinted as if in pain, then he said, "Return to your body, where you can touch the magic, and gather it up."

Then she felt a sudden pressure on her forehead.

She lifted a hand, then realized she had a hand to lift. She rubbed the skin of her forehead, blinking as she looked around the destroyed tower, at Zowan, who had both hands on her shoulders and was shouting, "Kira!" right into her face.

"I'm here, I'm okay!" she told him, grabbing his arms to steady herself against sudden vertigo. He pulled away slightly.

"I was just—We need to... He told me to gather it all up," she said dazedly. "I think he meant all the magic. How am I supposed to do that?"

She looked up, wishing she had asked for more instruction. All the magic in all the realm? She had only ever pulled magic from perhaps ten feet away. And that was when it was freely flowing. She knew there was still captive magic somewhere, wherever the lanterns stood, and wherever Tigran had been stockpiling it, probably in Meridian.

But there was no way...

Just then, her shoulder went ice cold, and she turned to face the wisp.

Zowan stepped back and bowed at the spirit, and Kira lowered her head too.

"Can you help?" Kira asked. "Am I really supposed to gather up all the magic?"

The wisp nodded, and Kira tried peering under her hood, trying to see her face. Had she imagined it? Because it couldn't be... her mother was gone.

Suddenly the wisp grabbed her wrist, the grip cold but surprisingly solid. "You'll need all of your strength, and some of mine," the words echoed through her head.

Kira almost pulled away at the intrusion of words, but at their familiarity, she froze.

"It really is you. Is it? I mean... *is it?*"

Her mother nodded, still holding her wrist. "The Camellian Dragon guided me to you when my soul crossed back into the realm through the first small crack. And I somehow became... aware again. I discovered I could make myself visible somehow. So I came to you."

Kira's knees trembled, and she grabbed her mother's wrist with both hands. "I can't believe—all of this—"

"We'll have time enough later," her mother said, "But right now you need to gather all the magic—

A hot tear leaked from Kira's eye and she let it run down her cheek, gazing into her mother's face. "You're right. I have to try and fix it," Kira said. "*We* have to fix it." She looked at Zowan, who was studying the wisp, and Kira didn't blame him. Was she a ghost? A spirit? Was she back for good or just passing on?

The tower lurched under her feet, and Kira choked, grabbing the railing with a flung-out hand. Zowan steadied her and himself. Her mother looked over the railing, and said, "Maybe you should get down from here."

Kira almost laughed at the motherly advice she had never thought she would hear again, but said, "No, the Spire is the highest thing in Camellia. I think from here we can..."

she trailed off, again realizing the enormity of what the dragon had told her to do.

She shook her head. "But I can't. I can't pull it all in, and I can't hold it. Not even Raiden or Nari could have done something like that. It's impossible."

"All the magic in the realm?" Zowan said, his face showing the exact emotions Kira felt.

"I think it'll heal him, once he gets it all back."

"Kira," her mother said urgently, "You share a connection with the dragon—you've been touched by the space between worlds, it's made a mark on your aura. I think that's why you were able to project your consciousness to him—and if you can use that same magic, you can channel your magic through him—to gather up the magic and give it to him."

"I... Okay—Well, I can try."

She grabbed Zowan's hand with her other hand, and said, "You can help too, but just with the Shadow, give it to me through my hand. Let me just try to reach out to the dragon first..."

The cold grip of her mother's hand squeezed harder, and Kira began to reach out to her surroundings, pulling. At the same time, she drew in air, found the space between breaths, and reached out to the dragon above. She thought about his signature on her aura, that she'd acquired on her way between worlds.

She tried to forge a connection with him, a bridge between her spirit and his—and a peculiar ebbing feeling that washed over her made her think she had done it. It was something glittering, something vast and peculiar, right alongside her own self.

Everything around them was filled with the essence. But now that she was connected with the dragon, she could feel *everything*. It felt like her brain spanned the entire realm—and now all the magic was spread before her. The entire realm, pools of magic, streams and glittering trails of it, with knots of it gathered here and there. A massive heart at the center of the realm, what must be the Commonality's stockpile in Meridian. It all looked the same to her, Light and Shadow, but that made sense to her, since they were just two sides of a coin, the same essence that made up the realm, just light and dark, tangible and intangible.

It came down to a matter of breathing. As she breathed in, she used the dragon's realm-encompassing spirit to pull magic from the realm—from all over. She first focused on the deep pockets of magic in Meridian, the worst tie-up of the essence. And as she breathed out, slowly, with her heartbeat as a steady background, she pushed the magic through the connection she shared, high above the clouds to the dragon that encircled them. Encircled the realm.

She didn't know how long she stood there, holding Zowan and her mother's hands. Holding onto, and being held by, the dragon's spirit. It was too much to keep focusing on the magic in Meridian, so she swept over the realm, picking it up wherever she could, making it feel like she was making more progress.

Zowan gripped her hand so hard as if she were in danger of falling off the Spire. She let out an involuntary giggle, since well, they *were* in danger of falling off the Spire. She drew a breath, and kept on siphoning any kept magic she could see in her vast mind's eye.

Suddenly they were thrown to the side of the railing, and Kira was grateful for Zowan's vice grip as she slipped partially under the rails.

"Kira!" he shouted, gripping her arm with both of his hands.

Her legs had slid over the side, and she scrabbled to get hold of the railing with her elbows. "No! The magic, we were getting it!"

"I think it's working, Kira," Zowan said in a terrifying voice. "I think it's working a little too well. That wasn't a crack. That was the magic coming out from the tower."

CHAPTER 35

HEART'S DESIRE

The floor lurched again like they were on a ship at sea.

"But I need to be close to the dragon to connect," she said, panicked eyes darting about as she clutched the railing. Her mother hovered worried beside her, and Zowan had hooked one arm through the railing, and was clutching her around the shoulders with his other arm.

"How much is left?" he demanded. "How much longer?"

She shook her head, "I don't know, but just hold on, okay? Hold onto me until we can get it all! We're so close!"

Without waiting for a reply, she quickly found the space between heartbeats and slammed her consciousness high above. The ebb and flow with her breath seemed stronger; and she might have been imagining it, but the wind buffeting her body seemed weaker. *I think it's working*, she thought.

It is, an ethereal thought came back to her.

She paused in her magic-gathering. *Was that—is that you?*

Yes. The connection you have forged is strong; you're pulling magic from all over the realm. But you have to get all of it—everything I used to form the realm. Otherwise the cracks will never heal, and they'll just keep reforming—breaking the realm all over again. We need it all. I'll hold the realm together in the meantime.

Kira focused on her breathing, pulling, pulling, picking away at the cache at Meridian. She did everything she could to get the magic across the realm, avoiding the place where she stood at all costs.

She set aside her fear, knowing that Zowan had her back—literally—at the top of the broken Spire. And she swept her consciousness over the realm, through the dragon's connection, pulling, always pulling. Light and Shadow. All of it. Finally, it seemed like Meridian was just a mundane city, no massive caches of magic. No twinkling pulses anywhere else. She tried not to think about the magic she had undone. The bridge she had once helped fix near a farm using Light. The cherry tree at Gekkō-ji, with blossoms made by all the Light Knights through the centuries.

The only thing left now was the Spire.

She pulled back her consciousness a little and spoke, her eyes still closed, her connection with the dragon buzzing between them. "We have to do it now," she said, her voice shaking. "We have to get it all."

Both of Zowan's arms clamped tight around her, and she buried her face in his shoulder for a second. He shouted into her ear, "Do it now!"

She didn't know whether she was using her connection to the dragon's spirit to pull the remaining magic out of the Spire, or whether it was of her own power, but she felt a surge of Shadow from beneath her feet.

And that wasn't the only surge. Her gut turned over as the tower began to swiftly tilt to one side. Suddenly Kira could see the horizon through the opening that had been pointing at the sky. They slammed into the railing as the tower lurched. Her heart banged in her chest as her feet left the floor, but it was a gentle lift, and not the violent ejection she had expected.

Zowan raised them up using Shadow wind, the air a perfect cushion as he lifted them out of the broken Spire. Kira's mother hovered beside them, a translucent mark on the unnaturally dark afternoon sky.

They all looked down as the many levels of the tower lurched dangerously side to side, and finally, collapsed inward, each floor crashing in, one after the other. Kira had always known the Spire was held up with magic, she just never thought it would come down—or that she would be the one to do it.

Raiden would have been furious.

Even though she knew the others below must have seen it coming, the thought that her friends could be down there under that rubble sent waves of nausea over her. She needed to get back down on the ground.

But first, she needed to finish what she had set out to do.

Reassuring herself her connection to the dragon was strong, she made one last pull as Zowan held them aloft. There was only the smallest amount of magic left, and the dragon had said she needed to get all of it. She gave a yank, and sent it buzzing along the connection, the final piece. She had done it.

From her connection, she felt an elated sigh reverberate through her, somehow like the sound of a gong ringing.

She had done it. Somehow.

But unfortunately, what she *had done* was pull the Shadow magic from the wind keeping them up.

They began to plummet in slow motion at first. Kira's stomach was somewhere in her throat, and a scream in her chest unable to get out. She clung desperately to Zowan, suddenly feeling like an idiot cartoon character who had run off a cliff, legs pumping in empty air.

"Zowan I'm so sorry!" she shrieked.

"Kira! You *didn't!*"

"I had to! That was the last of the magic!"

But as she looked down at the broken debris of the tower surging up toward them, the wind whipping all around them as they fell, she caught her breath.

It wasn't the *only* magic.

Without looking down to see how close they were to the ground, she quickly tried to focus on the space between breaths, but she was still breathing panicky and her breaths all seemed to meld into one another. *Slow down*, she told herself.

And she found it. The spark that was her own strength, that she could use for her heart's desires.

What she really desired more than anything was to *slow down*.

The spark came to life, flashing out from her heart. Her will. Her spark. And the wind died down in her ears.

She wrenched her eyes open, never realizing she had shut them. Clutching Zowan even tighter, she finally looked down.

They were floating, still falling, but it had worked.

That was when the rain started. A soft spring rain, warm almost. She and Zowan landed softly on a broken piece of roof. The rain felt good on her face, and she looked up to see a peek of sunlight coming through the clouds. A tiny slip of a rainbow reflected back at her.

It was easy to make the connection to the dragon now. *Can you hear me down here?* she asked above.

I can now, the dragon said. *It is done. The magics are balanced. Your people can use them again—that is what I brought it here for.*

A smile bloomed on her face as she looked up at the clouds, not seeing a single crack or tear. *Thank you*, she said.

It is I who must thank you, young one. All these years I have been content in protecting the realm, I didn't notice the one who abused the magic, abused the portals. And there was no one who could hear me—until your mother's soul slipped through that first crack.

Kira perked her head up, looking around for the wisp, her mother's spirit. But she had gone, or Kira couldn't see her in the sunlight that was now peeking out through the rainclouds. A shard of broken glass in the rubble drew her eye. *Wait*, she said to the dragon above. *There's one more thing we need to do. Can I—*

Of course.

It was getting easier, finding the spark inside her. She brought her consciousness to the dragon again, now swimming in the heady flow of magic that radiated off his presence.

She swept over the realm again, feeling for those tiny pieces of glass, the decanters, the lanterns.

If we don't do anything, they'll just start sucking up magic all over again, she said to the dragon as she reached out, using his all-seeing consciousness again as if she really knew what she were doing. And it was easy, once she found the spark, to make her will known. Her heart's desire that these glass prisons never hold magic again.

Though her mind was far away, with her ears she could hear the faint tinkling of breaking glass. She could feel the strange magic embedded in silver rings in the glass that Tigran had fashioned to imprison the magic.

You are very wise, the dragon said as she pulled away again.

And you are very generous, she told him. *Making this realm and giving us this magic. Are you sure it's all right to use Light and Shadow?*

It is why I created this place, for anyone to have magic who might. It is a gift.

I promise I'll make sure no one abuses it like Kage did ever again.

She felt him smile.

Tell your Gray friend he reminds me of Joyato. It is a comfort.

Can I ask—do you have a name?

An internal sigh came over her, and he said, *It has been generations and generations since I have been called by a name. But in the time before Camellia, I was called Sora.*

Thank you.

She closed the connection, though she knew Sora was still there, wrapped around the realm, protecting them, holding the realm in place. A gift.

All around her, she noticed the lawns of the temple growing greener, as if someone had removed a black and white filter on a photo. The magic essence was returning to the realm. Buds pushed themselves from the tips of tree branches, and birds darted about, chirping. Kira could feel the essence of Light and Shadow all around her, but didn't take any. It was abundant, flowing through the earth and everything around her. As it should be.

Zowan was already finding his way down from the roof where they had landed, and Kira shook herself, focusing on where she stood, and not up past the clouds. "We need to find the others," she said. "Jun and Nesma, I don't know whether—"

It was then that Kira caught sight of her mother again, darting through the rubble. Kira followed her, hoping she would lead them to her friends, or at least to safety. Kira leapt from timber to stone, slipping on roof tiles, steadying herself on Zowan and he on her. "Jun!" they called, "Nesma! Ryn!"

The tower had fallen near the lake and meditation pavilion, and completely crushed Kagami's shrine, but most of the rubble was in the footprint of the Spire, where the Jade Foyer had been. They made their way around by the stables, which thankfully were untouched. Kira spared a thought for poor Naga and the other horses who must be terrified. "Jun!"

Just as she was about to use some magic to project her voice, or listen further across the grounds, she saw a group of people by the lake shore.

Hagane and Nia Mari stood in the center of a group of people, their backs to each other. They were surrounded by Shadow mages, the Ka'Mir, and the Stone Mountain guards, hideously outnumbered. Kira didn't see the Commonality soldiers anywhere. She wondered what had become of the boy who had killed Tigran, and whether he had survived the collapse of the tower. Had they all fled already?

They approached carefully, just as Nesma stepped forward out of a group of mages.

"Nesma," Kira whispered, pushing through the crowd, her gaze darting between Nesma and her sister. Had Nesma's theory been right? Was it the mark on her aura from the space between worlds that kept Nia Mari and Nikoletta from manipulating her?

At the sight of Nesma approaching, though, Hagane swiveled around and pulled his knife on Nia Mari, scraping it up against her throat. Nia Mari did not look impressed with this development.

"Stay back, all of you!" Hagane shouted. "And don't you dare try your evil magic on me," he hissed to Nesma, whose hair was loose, her face smudged with dirt. She had both hands on her katana.

"I'm not like them," Nesma said quietly. "Not at all."

By this time Kira had gotten to the edge of the crowd, Zowan somewhere behind her. Kira had lost sight of her mother's spirit, but was certain she would find her again. Kira had no weapons, though she still had her armor on. It was a little battered on her right shoulder where she had been hit with debris, and the cut on her same arm stung. Unsure of whether to intervene or not, she watched as Hagane slowly removed the knife from Nia Mari's throat, his eyes bulging in fear.

"No, Nesma's not like me," Nia Mari said to him, as he put the knife to his own throat and paused.

Kira glanced at Zowan, but he looked just as uncertain about interfering.

"No!" The shout came from Nesma as she sprinted forward, katana wound up by her shoulder, ready to strike. "You'll not harm anyone else!"

Hagane stumbled away from Nia Mari, his mind evidently released.

Kira was busy thinking of weapons to summon with Light magic as Nesma advanced on her sister. But she didn't falter, didn't stumble, didn't stop until she was right in front of Nia Mari, blade to her neck.

"You're done," Nesma said.

Panic flared Nia Mari's nostrils, her eyes wide. "Y-you."

At that moment, Nesma hesitated. Would she strike? To bestow the punishment for years of torment, of manipulation? The battle of emotions on Nesma's face waged furiously, until finally, her eyes shone with her decision.

Kira walked forward and placed a hand on Nesma's shoulder, beaming in pride at her friend and squire. "We don't have to be as savage as they are, or like they think we should be," she said quietly in Nesma's ear. "I think she would be comfortable again in those anti-magic cells beneath Gekkō-ji. But it's your choice."

Nesma stared at her sister for a moment, then nodded.

Kira glanced around, but she didn't know where they could get their hands on any of those anti-magic manacles the Commonality had used.

She cringed, knowing something had to be done. She raised a hand toward Nia Mari. Barely knowing what she was doing, she focused her will on the space between heartbeats.

Nia Mari's eyes rolled up as she dropped.

"How did you do that?" Nesma whispered in awe. "What did you do?"

"I just really wanted her unconscious for everyone's safety," Kira said, grinning sheepishly, pointing a finger at her heart.

Nesma cast a glance at the destruction all around them, then looked up at the brightening sky. Kira rushed forward and threw her arms around her.

"You did it," Nesma said.

"We all did it," Kira replied.

CHAPTER 36

THE COUNCIL OF CAMELLIA

As she entered the rubble, something drew her forward, no matter how difficult it was to scramble through, no matter how tired her muscles were. There was one last matter to attend to.

She heaved timber aside, shoved stones out of her path with her good arm. All the while, Jun and Zowan followed her, ensuring the way was safe, all the while looking for survivors.

What drew her forward, she was too tired to put her finger on. All she knew was she had to keep going.

It wasn't Raiden. The others had quietly informed her that he had been moved before the Spire collapsed. She couldn't bring herself to think on him any further, it was much too painful. It made the breath going in and out of her lungs turn to needles in her chest when her thoughts unwittingly flitted to him. So instead she focused on shoving aside timbers and stones.

It certainly wasn't the body of Tigran she was interested in, though she had heard the soldiers whispering something about whether he deserved a proper burial. She wasn't sure she cared. Not with what he put her own family and the entire realm through. She would leave that decision up to others.

She found out what it was when she got to the doors of the Apothecarium.

A steady banging resounded from the doors. Over and over. It echoed through the destruction like a canon.

She glanced at Jun and Zowan, and equally wide-eyed, they helped her shift the rubble blocking the doors.

Dust hung in the air all around them, and she was on the brink of collapse by the time the door shifted open a few inches. The banging stopped.

Indistinct shouts came from inside, and Kira hastily pulled on the last piece of timber blocking the door, Zowan shoulder-to-shoulder with her, Jun managing the far end.

On loudly complaining hinges, the massive door swung open.

She caught a glimpse of broken glass covering the floor, before she found the green eyes of the person standing behind the doors. Micah dropped a heavy wooden stool upon seeing her, and lunged forward. Her chest tight, she collapsed into his arms at once, inhaling his familiar scent. His strong arms held her upright, and all tension evaporated from her body. Her jaw unclenched, and warmth filled her chest. It had been Micah that had drawn her inside.

Zowan clapped Micah on the shoulder as he stepped past, to assess the damage inside, no doubt. Though from what Kira saw, it looked like the ceiling in this room had remained structurally sound—minus the shattered glass, anyway. Jun followed, leaving Kira and Micah standing in the doorway, between two different kinds of destruction.

"I was so worried," Micah mumbled into her hair.

"You're all right," Kira said, pulling back to look at him. There were cuts on his hands and face, but he looked otherwise unharmed. Her intense gaze was met with his equally scrutinizing one. Gingerly he took her hands in his.

Hope rose in her chest, making her cheeks flame. It was all over. Really. Tigran was defeated, the realm was saved. She was free to live her life however she wanted here in Camellia. Because Camellia was the only place she wanted to be.

"Have I got a story for you," she said, pulling him closer.

"I'm sure it's a fantastic one," he murmured.

As she crushed him to her, their lips met, and she knew in her heart they would have all the time in the world for stories.

***

The other set of green eyes fluttered open for the first time and looked around the room. "Kira!" Spectra said. "What are you... Why is everyone..." Spectra tried to get up from her pallet on the floor. Kira put a strong hand on the girl's chest.

"Stay down, trust me," Kira said.

"If you say so," Spectra said, surprisingly accepting.

Micah rushed forward to grab Spectra's hand. She smiled sleepily at her brother.

Mistress Nyoko busied herself checking Spectra's vital signs, nudging Micah out of the way with her efficiency. Nyoko had been reluctant to let Kira try a strange magic on Spectra—she hadn't yet mentioned who she had learned it from. But since nothing had worked so far, the head Healer had been willing to let her try.

The Apothecarium was miraculously intact, thanks in large part to the long-ago architects relying on metal and might to secure this section of the Spire, and not magic.

"I'm so glad you're okay," Kira said, when Spectra's curious gaze met hers again. She spotted someone walking by the open door, and stood up. "I'm sorry, Micah will have to fill you in on everything," she told them as she headed for the door. "I'm supposed to—"

But someone caught her hand, and she was suddenly pulled into a tight hug. Micah, arms enveloping her, whispered, "Thank you," his voice cracking. "You saved her."

"Of course," she replied, "I had to."

He pulled away and kissed her on the forehead. "I better let you go."

With a squeeze of his hand, she nodded and headed purposefully from the room, a warm pleasant feeling settling in her core. She glanced down at her bandaged right arm, courtesy of Mistress Nyoko. The cut had been healed and now looked several days old.

"Hey, Jun!" she called, catching up to him in the hallway. "How's it going?"

He wiped his forehead, which was marred with dirt and sweat. "Better now," Jun said. "Master Starwind just arrived with people from Gekkō-ji."

"Really?"

"They were in Meridian, at the palace. Master Starwind got your message."

Her jaw dropped. "I had forgotten about that. Are they okay?"

Nodding, he said, "They brought some people from the palace, though."

Wrinkling her forehead, she followed him into the large round room where all the ceiling glass had broken, revealing a pink-streaked sunset sky through the empty panes. Acolytes were still cleaning up broken and disturbed jars of ingredients among everything else.

After reuniting with Micah, her first priority had been searching for survivors. It hadn't been easy going back out into the rubble, but with Ryn's help identifying auras, they were able to work effectively. All the injured and fallen were brought into the Apothecarium. Micah had joined Kira as they searched, manually lifting fallen debris alongside her. They worked for hours. She talked and talked, until her voice was hoarse, telling him everything that had happened to her since leaving the Spire with Ryn. And when it came time to tell him about healing Nesma with heart magic, they decided to take a break from the search and see what Kira could do for Spectra.

But the search still continued. The Commonality had reluctantly reported several missing soldiers, and rumor had it some had refused to follow the mages when they told them to evacuate the collapsing tower. They had already found Nikoletta among the rubble.

There were pallets set up all throughout the Apothecarium, even here in the main atrium. Healers rushed about, furtively accessing their Shadow magic to do what they could for the injured.

Ichiro and Senior Advisor Jai Takasan stood by the large doors, looking shaken and tired. Her grandfather enveloped her in a tight hug, forgoing all normal courtesy.

"I'm so sorry," Kira said as she pulled away. "We were going to Meridian, but then we realized the army was here and—"

"It is quite all right. From what I hear, you did a marvelous job."

She looked at Jun and away. Her face warmed, and she stuffed her hands in her pockets. "Well, why don't you two come with us..."

Mistress Nyoko's study was the only place where they didn't have patients on every available surface. It was filled instead with books and a variety of plants and sculptures of black birds, which leered down on them from the bookshelves. Jun sank onto the couch by the window, his palms on his knees.

Ryn and Nesma were already there, sunk deep into the soft cushioned chairs Nyoko had furnished her study with. Upon seeing Ichiro and Takasan, they sat up and bowed from where they sat. Kira wished she could curl up on the couch by the window and sleep for days.

Before anyone could say anything, the door burst open and Zowan came striding in. "Ah, they told me you were here," he said to Ichiro, then gave a curt nod to Takasan, who nodded gravely. Before Zowan could shut the door, three other people came striding in: Hilda and Senga, followed by Rolian.

Rolian avoided eye contact with everyone, but made his way over toward Jun and sat next to him.

Hilda went straight for Kira in the center of the room, Senga at her heels.

"What is this?" Takasan demanded with some of his usual bluster, though it was tinged with exhaustion. "Who are all of you?"

Kira cracked a smile. "This is Hilda and Senga from Ka'Mir—and then there's one of Lady Madora's guards, Rolian. They led their people against the Commonality to save the realm."

"I... see," he said, eying Hilda with barely veiled distaste. "Well, I'm afraid I have some grave news from the palace."

Kira glanced at Jun, but he was watching Takasan.

"The Empress has finally succumbed to her illness and passed on," Takasan said.

The room was silent. A few people mouthed prayers to Kamellia for the safe passage of her spirit. Kira clasped her hands together and stared at the floor, in remembrance of the woman who had been tasked with ruling the realm.

"It was Tigran," Kira said finally, shaking her head. "It was all him. Her illness, lying to her all these years, and then when he got Nia Mari and Nikoletta out of prison, probably controlling her."

Kira had already tracked down the soldier who killed Tigran, who had heard every word of Tigran's nefarious confession. The soldier was recuperating quietly in a comfortable chair somewhere in the Apothecarium, more for mental injury than physical.

He had volunteered to give a written statement, which Kira was glad for. She hadn't wanted to press him in his current state, but the truth needed to be upheld. There was no time to waste anymore on falsehoods. Tigran would no longer hurt the people of this realm with his lies.

Takasan went on, "The lanterns started bursting. The soldiers said the magic had been let out. And that was when the Light knights arrived," he said with a nod to Ichiro. "But the healers found Empress Mei in her chambers," his voice cracked.

Ichiro, who was closest, put a hand on Takasan's arm. "We will all need time to heal from this. More than time, we will need unity and understanding."

Kira smiled at him. "That's right. And I learned a lot from the Camellian Dragon—Sora, he told me his name was. And as for the imperial—" her gaze roved over to Jun, but he was shaking his head rapidly at her.

Her mouth dropped open a little, then she changed the subject, "Anyway, I agree, we will all need to unify. And I promised Sora to make sure we maintain the balance, and respect his gift. We can't allow something like this to ever happen again."

There were nods all around the room, and Ryn muttered, "Too true." The awe in many of their faces at the mention of the dragon made her cheeks warm, and she looked down at the floor.

"But there is no Empress," Takasan said, "No heir, and not even a Grand Steward. Many of the advisors fled after what happened to Goten, but I hear you have a treatment for those who came into contact with the tears?"

Kira nodded, making a mental note to visit the palace to personally heal the one advisor she actually liked.

"I fear we are far off from unity," Takasan ended, clasping his hands behind his back.

"Actually, I might have an idea," Kira said. Jun shot her a look, but she shook her head minutely. "In the Starless Realm, we had all kinds of rulers. And lots of places had more than one, in different positions. Now, I know

Camellia has always been ruled by the Imperial family, but now that Empress Mei's reign has ended, and there is no one else of that lineage—" she paused, giving Jun one last opportunity to speak up.

"Well," she continued, a slight smile on her face, "I think we have the beginnings of a council right here. Stone Mountains," she said, gesturing at Rolian, "Ka'Mir. Light region, Shadow region," she nodded at Zowan, but then she froze, for a second having thought it was Raiden who sat there solemnly, dark wavy hair obscuring part of his face. "And of course, Senior Advisor," she nodded with finality toward Takasan, who stroked his chin in thought.

"Where is Sir Jovan?" Takasan said. "I am in desperate need to apologize to him and the other Gray Knights. They should weigh in on this council idea too."

Jun finally spoke up, "He and the others are helping find more survivors. And, well, they're not technically Gray anymore."

The uncomfortable silence that followed Jun's quick explanation of what happened to their magic forced Kira to speak once again. "But there's good news, another kind of magic we never knew possible, and we have the Ka'Mir to thank for enlightening us."

Hilda lifted her chin at her in acknowledgement. "We have lived beside one another in contention too long. The

Ka'Mir have always disapproved of the way you all use magic. If you will truly exercise more restraint utilizing Light and Shadow, I for one am happy to share the learnings of our magic. And perhaps some trade can be arranged for us, then there will be no need for our people to go hungr—to attack yours, anyway."

Takasan pressed his lips together tightly, but nodded and mumbled some kind of thanks. Kira knew it was a lot to ask that he accept peace with the Ka'Mir right away—it had taken quite some time to convince him and the other advisors that Shadow mages weren't the enemy, either.

"Well, then, the Council of Camellia?" Kira said, looking around at everyone.

Ryn grinned at her, "I don't think I need to be here for this—but I think you're forgetting, the council will need a Gray Knight or two."

Kira ducked her head, and she was pleased to see that Jun wasn't objecting.

Zowan cleared his throat. "I disagree, Ryn—I think you *do* need to be here."

Huh? Kira thought.

Zowan stood, pacing beside the bookshelves, two enormous raven statues peering down at him. "I never intended to remain at the Spire. Nor did I ever wish to lead it. But after today, and everything I witnessed." His voice cracked, and he cleared his throat again. "I will do it. But not alone."

"Why me?" Ryn said, his face frankly suspicious. "I only know aura magic."

"You know far more than that," Zowan said. "But I must admit my interest in your skill does lie in your aura reading skills. I don't know if any of you realize, but when the Spire fell, we lost something invaluable to our Shadow training: the Dragon Crystal. The only one of its kind. Without it, mages will fail to see the full possibilities of their own magic. But with you, Ryn…"

Ryn pursed his lips, then glanced at his double swords which he had discarded on the table beside him. "I'll do it."

Jun turned to Rolian. "And you, are you in?"

Rolian did a quick survey of the room then addressed Jun, "I must speak with Lady Madora, but since she sent such a large contingent to help, I don't see why she wouldn't want the Stone Mountains to have a seat on the council—though perhaps she herself will fill it," he said, ducking his head.

"I think that's settled then," Jun said, with a shadow of a wink at Kira.

***

"What was that about?" Kira asked Jun ten minutes later as they went to go fetch some more water for Spectra's room. Micah was back to helping carry the last of the injured inside, but he checked in on Spectra every time he brought someone in.

Spectra was sleeping again when she and Jun came back to her room.

"I—well..." Jun began. He huffed and looked around the room. Kira had already set up a sleeping pallet for herself, in hopes that she might at some point be able to catch some sleep. "I don't want to be Emperor," he said softly. "See? It even sounds ridiculous."

Kira shrugged. "I don't blame you. Did you talk to your father about it?"

"After we left the Stone Mountains. He was just as shocked as I was. But what does it matter, really? Besides, I've trained all my life to be a Gray Knight. I would never get to leave the palace, or go out and do anything. I'd rather just go on quests."

"You and me both, Kosumoso. But it looks like we've been sucked into this Council."

"Well, it was your idea, Starless Girl."

"Yeah," she said, shrugging. "But I want to keep my promise to Sora. And if we all band together, people from different regions and callings, I think that lessens the chance of anything like this happening again." She waved her hand vaguely around them.

Just then, Zowan poked his head in the room, and Kira could see Anzu hovering behind him. "Are you two all right in here?" he asked. "I'm going to try and work my way deeper through the debris and assess the structure of the rest of the castle."

Kira bit her lip and scrabbled to her feet. "Are you sure?" she asked.

"Well, yes, Anzu's coming with me, and I'll be able to use Shadow to—"

"No, I mean, *are you sure*? You want to lead the Spire?"

He leveled her with a look, and said, "I am."

"Okay, I just—"

"Look," he said quietly, "I could never forgive my uncle for the things he did. And he accepted that. Yet he continued to try. I thought it was because he couldn't stand to be wrong, to never be forgiven. But he was a brave man. And a caring man. And I know—" He paused, clearing his throat. He reached back without looking and grabbed Anzu's hand. "I know that he loved me."

"That is what I will do, to honor him. His sacrifice. To honor the magic we have been given, this gift."

Kira looked up at him with a watery smile, then flung her arms around him. "I love you Zowan. I'll be here to help you as much as I can. We'll get the Spire rebuilt."

Zowan glanced up in the direction of where the Spire used to stand. "Should we, though? All that magic held captive?" He ran a hand through his hair.

"Sora did say it was all right to use his gift," Kira said. "But maybe not in excess. I *do* have some other ideas," she said, tapping her heart.

CHAPTER 37

SAPLING

Kira held her bag close to her chest as Naga trotted up the road that wound up Mount Gekkō. She and the others had finally gotten some sleep over the last few days, but sleep was *all* Thistle would do still. She was just glad she he was still breathing.

It had been two full days since the fall of the Spire. Two days as they attempted to clear the unending debris, as they reacquainted themselves with magic again. As Zowan started to grow into his new role; it was clear he was a natural leader. As Kira spent all her waking moments with her friends, surrounding herself with love in the face of all that the destruction had wrought.

And two days as Kira waited for Thistle to wake up.

She knew the spirit of the mountain could travel to other places, had done it before. So why hadn't he come to check on Thistle? Perhaps he was far too weakened by the damage to the realm, and couldn't leave the mountain.

The ride from the Spire with only Jun, Nesma, and Micah had been like a balm on her nerves after everything that had happened. Ryn had surprisingly turned down Kira's offer to come on their quest, telling her the acolytes at the Spire needed him more than she did.

Anzu had offered to come with them, but Kira declined; she knew Zowan would need Anzu's steadfast presence as he navigated his new role.

The day after the Spire fell, they had held the funeral rites for Raiden at a small temple in Heliodor. Kira had seen sketches on Zowan's desk—formerly Raiden's—of plans to erect a small shrine in his uncle's honor.

"This place brings back memories," Micah said as they passed through the first set of gates into the grounds of Gekkō-ji.

Kira looked up. "Good memories?"

"Meeting you."

That brought a smile to her face, until Jun pulled his horse up behind them and said, "So, could be better then, eh?"

"Jun!" Nesma said, reaching over and smacking him on the shoulder.

Jun chuckled, a mischievous grin on his face. Micah merely rolled his eyes then gave Kira a knowing look, his green eyes sending a thrill of happiness straight to her core.

It was calming and surreal to go through the motions of unsaddling their horses in the stables and putting away the tack. All the while, Kira kept wondering why the spirit of the mountain hadn't found them yet. Would Thistle ever wake up?

They headed for the temple square when they finished, the smells from the kitchen house tempting them down the stairs that led from the stables. Though Kira's mouth watered at the familiar smells, she had another destination in mind.

"I'm going to go find Ari and make sure he's all right," Jun said, "I'll find you later."

Kira waved him off with a grin. "I'm sure he'll be glad to be relieved of his duties!"

Jun laughed and headed for the dormhouses. He and his father were planning a long retreat back at their estate once the Spire was in better working order.

Jovan and the others, though missing their Shadow and Light magic to aid in the cleanup, hadn't shied away from the manual labor, nor were they shy about learning everything they could about heart magic from the Ka'Mir.

And Kira knew it wasn't just so they could replace their lost magic. Jovan was already talking about setting up training for anyone else who wished to learn it. Hilda had gone back to Ka'Mir, to spread the word to the other settlements about what had happened and what would become of the council, but Senga had remained behind at the Spire, becoming fast friends with Anzu of all people.

Micah's hand slipped into hers as they crossed the temple square, and Kira was glad for the strength of it when they got to the place where the cherry tree once stood. Kira moved on. There had been no other choice.

Nesma mentioned checking on Hana and Michi, and made for the girl's dormhouse, leaving Kira and Micah alone to take the stairs up to the garden.

Under the newly budding trees, they walked the paths in silence. By the time they reached the statue of Gekkō, Kira wasn't surprised to see the bench there empty, just disappointed.

She sighed and sat down, gently pulling out Thistle and setting him in her lap. "I figured he would have come to us by now," she said quietly, gazing up at the statue of Gekkō.

"I'm sorry Kira," Micah said, putting a hand on her shoulder and squeezing.

"It's all right. It's just—Thistle..."

Kira caught movement out of the corner of her eye, and her breath caught in her throat. But she didn't have to chase the near-translucent wisp now gliding through the path in the trees.

She put a hand on Kira's shoulder, and Kira could hear her speak. "He's gone, Kira," her mother said. "I searched the whole mountain, and asked the nearby spirits too." She hadn't seen her mother since after the Fall of the Spire, but had perhaps been too busy even if she had been nearby.

Kira just stared at Thistle. Her mother reached down and put a hand on Thistle, stroking his fur. "He helped you, didn't he?"

Nodding, Kira tried to swallow past the lump in her throat. "From the beginning. It was hard, coming to Camellia at first."

"Oh, Kira."

Kira closed her eyes as her mother's fingers slid from Thistle's back to grasp her hand. They were cold, and not as solid as she would like, but they were there.

Both Kira and her mother unclasped their fingers, because the tiny little body of the flying squirrel between them was twitching. Specifically, the whiskers.

"Thistle?" Kira said, rubbing his back with her thumb.

"Yes, but why'd you have to go and wake me?" he complained.

A massive sigh of relief built in her chest, and she closed her eyes. "Well, you've been out for a while," she said, mostly to keep him awake instead of curling up and dozing off like he seemed to be attempting. "And, well, we can't find Gekkō," she added in a quieter voice.

He perked his head up at that. "Huh. Neither can I."

He sat up on his hind legs, pensive.

"Are you going to be okay?" Kira asked finally.

"I... think so," he admitted. "But..." He twitched his whiskers again and looked up at Kira's mother with a sleepy smile. "The... mountain might get lonely. We could use a new spirit."

***

It was almost sunset when Kira found Jun, just outside of the Moonstone. "Come on, we have to meet Ichiro," she said. "We need to catch up before we go to the palace tomorrow."

"All right, all right," Jun said. "I don't know why you need me there, anyway, when they've got you. I want to start working on excavating the Gray Wing so we can actually have somewhere proper to sleep when we get back to the Spire."

"Yeah, you and me both," she said. "But this is just the beginning. And we have a responsibility."

"And you have the ear of the dragon," he said with a grin.

She scoffed, "Don't say it like that! Descendent of Joyato," she muttered.

He laughed it off.

Just before they stepped inside the Moonstone, Ichiro came outside to meet them.

"We have many things to discuss, but first—" He gestured toward the square. Together they headed for the center of the courtyard, where a bare spot of earth lay before them.

Ichiro took Kira's hand and placed something small in it. It was a seed.

As the sun set and Light magic began to wink at them from everything, together they dug a small hole.

"I know things will change," Kira said. "And it's not going to be the same as it was. So why don't we start here?"

Jun raised an eyebrow at her, and Ichiro smiled.

Kira reached inside herself and found the spark. She held her hand over the planted seed for a moment, focusing her will, her strength, her hope.

And out of the soil, a tiny sapling sprouted, growing taller and taller until it was nearly as tall as she. As she took a step back, admiring her work, a small bud formed, then opened up to reveal a delicate white blossom.

About the Author

Liz Delton writes and lives in New England, with her husband and sons. She studied Theater Management at the University of the Arts in Philly, always having enjoyed the backstage life of storytelling.

World-building is her favorite part of writing, and she is always dreaming up new fantastic places.

She loves drinking tea and traveling. When she's not writing or reading, you can find her baking in the kitchen, out in the garden, or narrating books on her podcast, Fictional Bookshop.

Visit her website at **LizDelton.com**

Also by Liz Delton

REALM OF CAMELLIA
The Starless Girl
The Storm King
The Gray Mage
The Starlight Dragon
The Fall of Azurite

SEASONS OF SOLDARK
Spectacle of the Spring Queen
The Mechanical Masquerade
All Hallows Airship
The Clockwork Ice Dragon

EVERTURN CHRONICLES
The Alchemyst's Mirror

FOUR CITIES OF ARCERA
Meadowcity
The Fifth City

A Rift Between Cities
Sylvia in the Wilds

WRITER'S NOTEBOOKS
Writer's Notebook
Teen Writer's Notebook
Guided Writer's Notebook